This
One
Life

ALSO BY AMANDA PROWSE

Novels

Poppy Day

What Have I Done?

Clover's Child

A Little Love

Will You Remember Me?

Christmas for One

A Mother's Story

Perfect Daughter

The Second Chance Café

Three and a Half Heartbeats

Another Love

My Husband's Wife

I Won't be Home for Christmas

The Food of Love

The Idea of You

The Art of Hiding

Anna

Theo

This One Life

Amanda Prowse

LAKE UNION
PUBLISHING

Published by Lake Union Publishing, Seattle

www.apub.com

Amazon, the Amazon logo, and Lake Union Publishing are trademarks of Amazon.com, Inc., or its affiliates.

ISBN-13: 9781662515187
eISBN: 9781662515170

Cover design by Emma Rogers
Cover image: ©Viktoria Kazakova, VectorArtist7, Eganova Antonina, Bahruz Rzayev / Shutterstock; ©Malte Mueller / Getty Images

Printed in the United States of America

This book is dedicated to the memory of Sarah.
Between sisters, invisible threads are the strongest
ties.
She was the very best sister, so loving and wise, and
always with that brave smile.
We miss her every day but the memory of her
sunshine will forever warm our hearts . . .
From all who loved you, Sarah.

Prologue

'Where's your sock?'

Marnie looked down at the little girl who, as ever, had rushed out of the school gates, keen to be free of the building that held her prisoner between eight fifteen and three fifteen each weekday, with an hour off at lunchtime for good behaviour. Not that her behaviour was particularly good, if Marnie were to believe what was written in the end-of-term reports or the snippets of tight-lipped disapproval that were traded on parents' evening.

'Disruptive!' the teacher had called her.

'Enthusiastic,' Marnie had countered.

'Noisy!' was another one.

'Confident?' Marnie preferred.

'Always asking questions . . .' The woman had spoken with a sigh.

'And how very fortunate are you to have such an enquiring young mind among so many dumdums . . .' Marnie would never back down in defence of the child, who had experienced more than most. Marnie was her champion, her flag bearer, her support system and the one who would love her till her last breath on earth.

The teacher had stared at her with a look of resignation. As if she understood that there was no force more powerful than a besotted matriarch with a fearless mouth.

She smiled at the haphazard jumble that gambolled towards her; sweater in her hand, one frayed sleeve trailing on the floor, the book bag open with loose sheets of paper threatening to fly away at any moment. Shoulder-length dark, dark hair that was partly over her pretty face, and a healthy splatter of whatever red stuff she'd had for lunch on the front of her white polo shirt.

This was Edith-Madeleine, aged seven, named after both of her great-grandmas, but known simply as Edith. Edith was the child who would fall off the wall, tumble into a pond, spill her drink, drop her ice cream, get her clothing snagged in a bush, and drop or slop whatever she was carrying. She was also loud – a glorious bundle of infectious energy.

'I've still got one sock!' Edith beamed as if this was compensation enough, lifting her foot to show that, yes, there was one slightly grubby knee-high sock slouched down around her ankle.

'Fancy-pants houses!' she shouted, changing the topic entirely, and pointed at the restored Georgian splendour of a row of terraced properties that were close to her primary school.

It was another world, one of high-end opulence – neat topiary set in square slate planters, glossy front doors, polished brass steps and an abundance of ungraffitied red brick. Large sash windows allowed tempting glimpses of oversized lamps, occasional tables, wide squidgy sofas and daring art. A fancy-pants world indeed, and one that Edith liked to point out as they walked past. It was a part of their walking home ritual that never failed to amuse them both.

Beneath Marnie's laughter, however, was the tremble of recognition, aware as she was that this glimpse into a life beyond their means had the power to unsettle as well as amuse. It could place spikes among the soft acceptance of life. It could sow a seed of discontent that was hard to uproot. A bit like looking at what you might have won in a game show before it was whipped out of sight. If only they had been luckier . . . got the answer right, or – as was the case with the upmarket houses they peered into – been born into a family like that. Marnie understood that dissatisfaction with your lot in life could be the most destabilising thing of all. Far better, in her opinion, to live contentedly with all that was familiar.

She chuckled. 'Yes, now, back to your missing sock. I can see you've still got one, darling, but what I'm more concerned about is the foot without a sock – the sock that's missing.'

'Oh!' She watched the little girl's expression of surprise, as if genuinely not understanding which sock they were referring to. 'I had to use it for something.'

'Right.' Marnie opened her hand as she turned to walk away, knowing that the child would slip her hand into hers, just as she had since that very first day of school nearly two years ago now. The time had flown and yet not a day passed when she didn't thank her lucky stars and all of heaven and earth for the chance to mother this amazing tiny human who was sunshine itself. A second chance, almost, and one she had never expected. Marnie braced herself for what came next – usually a convoluted, unimaginable story to explain a situation.

Edith did not disappoint. Skipping now, she pulled Marnie's arm up and down as they made their way along the uneven grey pavement.

'I found a mouse.' Edith looked up and grinned, little animal lover that she was.

'How exciting.' Marnie did her best to hide the shiver of revulsion at the thought of the tail on such a creature. She'd never been too good with tails, or anything that scampered, preferring the lumbering gait of a big old dog like Frank, who had been her childhood love. He had been as stinky as he was ungainly, but how she had loved him.

'Well, I didn't find it, Travis found it.'

'And he told you where it was?' As was her habit, Marnie tried to jump ahead.

'Yes, but it was dead.'

It was a fascination how the child's face could go from triumphant to devastated in such a short time.

'Oh, well, that's very sad.' She squeezed Edith's sticky little hand.

'Anyway, I told Travis we should give it a fumeral.'

Marnie suppressed her laughter. It was close enough, and who knows how long the stinky little thing had been dead for. Maybe *fumeral* was actually very appropriate.

'That was a great idea.'

'We were going to tell Mr Lawal, but Travis said he might not let us bury her on school property.'

Her . . . ? All right, then.

'Travis is smart.' Smarter, Marnie hoped, than his dad, Travis Senior, who was currently serving an eight-year stretch for conspiracy to commit fraud. His mother lived three floors below them in the flats. A nice lady who looked far, far older than her years. Not that stories like hers, like theirs, were unusual in their little slice of East London – far from it.

'We named her Minty and found a place to bury her by the football posts. And then' – Edith swallowed, catching her breath; she did this sometimes, spoke so quickly that she ran out of steam – 'I said we couldn't just put Minty in the dirt! We needed something to wrap her in.'

'Ah!' Marnie could see where this was going.

'So I took my sock off and she fitted right into the foot bit like it was a little mouse pocket! And then we dug a hole and put her in it, and only Travis and I know where Minty is buried and I might visit her sometimes.'

'Well, you can't say you didn't do your best by her at the end.'

Edith nodded. 'We sang a little song.'

'Oh, you did? What did you sing?' She was curious.

'We were going to sing a hymn, but we didn't know any, so we sang that song . . . erm, I think it's The Beatles? The one about my troubles being far away. But it made me a bit sad because Minty's troubles weren't that far away, because she died . . .' Edith sang the lines, right there in the street – suddenly, loudly, tunelessly and with gusto.

It made Marnie's heart swell.

'Well, that was lovely.' She knew her husband, Doug, would be delighted that Edith had chosen a song from one of his favourite bands. 'I'm sure Minty would have loved her send-off.' She couldn't wait to tell him all about it when he got in from work.

'What's for tea?'

And just like that, the subject was changed and Edith was thinking about grub.

'Macaroni cheese.'

'Yes!' Edith did a little hop with pure delight and it warmed Marnie's heart. This was the child's nature: sweet, excited, and happy with whatever fell into her lap. The fact they'd had macaroni cheese for the previous two nights, as it was cheaper and easier to make a big old trayful and eat it till it had gone, was neither here nor there.

'Have you got any homework?'

'Nope. Just reading.'

It delighted Marnie how Edith so loved books that compulsory school reading didn't feel like homework at all but was simply one of her joys.

'I think it's Pop's turn to listen.'

'But he always falls asleep before I've finished!'

Marnie laughed at this truth. 'He works hard up the market, baby girl, and when he sits down at the end of the day, it's like his body switches off so he can get up early and go do it all again tomorrow.' She hated that this was his routine, wishing for him – wishing for them *both* – that things might get easier as they aged. Not that they were ancient, far from it, but she noticed them both slowing down a little, with a reluctance in her bones to rise on a cold day or to tackle steps at speed.

'Can I go to work with him at the weekend? I can help!'

'I'm sure he'd love that. Have you been practising your calls?'

'I have.' She watched as Edith took a deep breath. 'Get your pots and pans here! Your buckets, your bowls, your drainers, your tea towels, your pegs! Come on, lay-dees!'

Marnie doubled over with laughter, unable to contain herself as the child did her best to imitate the male voice that called this very patter to the crowds.

'Did I do it good?'

'You did it very good,' she had to admit. 'Reckon you'll do Dougie out of a job at this rate!'

'He could have a rest then.'

The sweet sincerity of her words was as touching as it was kind.

'Yes, he could, my lovely one. Yes, he could.'

'Afternoon, Marn!' Mrs Nelson, in her familiar wrap-around pinny, called from the doorway of her flat as she tottered along the path with a bulging bin bag in her hand. Marnie noticed how in recent years the elderly woman had grown a little unsteady on her feet.

'Afternoon, Mrs Nelson. Do you want me to take that out for you?' It wasn't far to the communal bin store, but if it saved the old lady a job . . .

'No, you're all right, love. It's the only exercise I get nowadays!'

Marnie Woods had lived on the Brenton Park estate since she was a child, taking over the lease from her mother when she died almost twenty years ago now. The casual observer might see the grime, the grotty communal walkways, the urine-scented lifts, the graffiti, the large dumpster from which garbage overspilled, the abandoned rusting cars and vans, the kids clustering in the foot of stairwells smoking pungent weed, and the loud, loud fights conducted in several languages that were the inevitable consequence of living in such close proximity, the uneven paving stones, and the clots of dog shit peppering the thin grass wherever it sprouted. But Marnie knew better than to be fooled by such aesthetics.

She more than understood that what the untrained eye did not see was what made the place remarkable: the kindness of neighbours, the strong bond of those who had grown up there and the sense of pride that, when the chips were down, they rallied together. All anyone had to do was ask that young woman on the fourteenth floor whose baby son was proper poorly, something to do with his liver, just how their community worked. The Residents' Committee had figured out that if each flat gave a couple of quid, the little one could have his mum on hand for gruelling treatments, and they could travel by cab. Nearly everyone had given and it had been perfect. The woman and her family, having only arrived on the estate eighteen months ago, had felt the arms of her neighbours around her. It didn't change the bowed stance of deep worry that aged her, nor the blank-eyed stare of impotence that she wore as she walked to the shops or took the older kids to school, but Marnie hoped, in time, it might act as a balm of sorts. To know that they were thinking of her. To know they had her back.

'Where's your sock, Edith?' the old lady hollered as she held the dripping bag at arm's length.

'Oh, me and Travis had to bury Minty, who died today. We put her in my sock and dug a hole by the goalpost on the playing field. But that's a secret, Mrs Nelson. We don't want anyone else to know in case they dig her up.'

'Sweet Jesus! Who'd dig her up?' Mrs Nelson shook her head at the horror of the idea. 'Anyway, I'm sorry for your loss and may she rest in peace. I'm assuming she was a creature small enough to fit in a sock?'

'She was a mouse, Mrs Nelson. At least, we think she was a mouse. She'd gone a bit flat and a bit . . . dusty.' Edith wrinkled her nose.

'Right! Well, that's enough detail for us all. Let's get you home!' Marnie pulled a face at her neighbour, who laughed.

'We're having macaroni cheese!' The child danced on the spot.

'Good for you! Reckon I'll be skipping supper tonight. I've a head full of images of Minty that are enough to put me off eating for life!'

'Sorry about that, Mrs Nelson.' Marnie was sincere.

'No, don't be sorry. I could do with losing a few pounds.' She patted her ample tum.

'Only on your body and your wobbly neck thing, Mrs Nelson.' Edith patted her own chin. 'Not on your legs! Your legs are like little sticks!' Edith offered the compliment that was anything but.

'Mrs Nelson, I . . .' Marnie felt her face turn puce as she searched for the right words.

'What is it they say, Marn? Out of the mouths of babes . . .' Mrs Nelson suppressed a laugh.

'Something like that.' She smiled at the old woman who trundled to the bins. Marnie couldn't wait for Doug to get home. He was going to howl at this.

'Do you think Minty is in heaven?' This was quite a standard conversation twist for Edith; the verbal darting left and right, up and down.

'Well . . .' Marnie always trod carefully, not wanting to destroy any hope that the little girl might carry, but also unable to lie outright. 'I think the truthful answer is that I don't know. And I think what counts is that you gave her a lovely funeral, which was a very kind way to say goodbye to her.'

'But do you think she's in heaven?'

'What do you mean by heaven? What do you think it is?' Marnie stalled.

'Mouse heaven! Where there's all the cheese they can eat and tiny mouse cafés and little mouse swimming pools and mouse sweetie shops and mouse hotels and mouse motorways where they drive tiny cars to go to mouse cinemas, and mouse chip shops and mouse pubs . . .'

She got the idea. This too was a familiar topic for Edith: what happened when people died. Where did they go? Where did they live if they didn't live with you anymore . . . ? All pieces of the puzzle the child was trying to figure out.

'I think you have a wonderful imagination! And how great to think of Minty in her tiny car, pootling up and down the motorway to visit swimming pools and cinemas.'

Edith wasn't done. 'I think cat heaven – where there are cat beauty parlours and cat shopping malls and cat beaches and cat sunglasses shops and cat restaurants – would be mouse hell, because if Minty turned up there by mistake, she'd just be a snack, wouldn't she?'

'I guess she would!' Marnie chuckled. 'You amaze me, Edith Woods. You're quite right, you know; one person's heaven could be another person's hell, and that's very smart.'

'Like Pop with prawns.'

Marnie laughed harder and squeezed her hand. Her beloved girl. It was a fact in their home that she and Edith loved a treat of a prawn cocktail or a prawn sandwich, but her husband found them to be slug-like and would heave at the sight of them.

'Yes, like Pop and prawns.'

The beep of a horn was loud and drew their attention.

Marnie smiled at the sight of the battered blue van pulling alongside them as Dougie wound down his window. She was always pleased to see the man she so loved, who now winked at her. And still, after all these years, his flirting fired a spark inside her.

Edith shook her hand free and ran to the van, poking her head through the window to give her pop a big kiss on the cheek.

He beamed. 'Hello, little sausage.'

'Are you coming up? Have you finished for the day?' She pointed up along the walkway overhead to their flat on the seventh floor, sounding quite adult, as was her way.

'I have, my love. I got off early – not much doing, I'm afraid.' A look of defeat flashed across his face that tore at Marnie's heart. 'I wondered if I'd see you on your way home.'

'And here I am!' Edith jumped up and down on the spot.

'What happened to your sock?' Dougie looked quizzically at her bare leg.

'It's a long story, my love. A *very* long story.' Marnie pulled a face and he nodded his understanding; long stories and the scrapes Edith got into were not strangers to him.

'We'll save it for when we get home, then.' He reached out and ruffled Edith's hair. Still the little girl bounced, her energy unmatched. 'See you in a minute, Marn.'

'Bye, love!'

They stood and watched the van as it drove towards the car park.

'Do you think Pop might like to see Minty?'

Marnie stopped short on the pavement and stared at the child. 'Please tell me you're not thinking of digging her up, are you, Edith?' She kept her tone stern, her gaze level.

'Course I'm not!' They walked on in silence, approaching the concrete steps that would eventually take them up to their floor. 'But if I did, I'd probably be able to get my sock back . . .'

Chapter One

Edith-Madeleine – who, aged twenty-nine, chose to be known simply as Madeleine – stared at her reflection in the vast gilt-framed mirror that filled the space between the marble sink and the ceiling. Turning first to the left, then right, she studied her profile in the flattering light, liking the slight curve of her bust inside her ivory silk shirt, which sat crisply over her lace bra. The top two buttons were undone to reveal her bronzed décolletage. Next came close-up scrutiny of her understated make-up, using the tip of her French-manicured finger to remove a fleck of mascara that had found its way to her highlighted cheekbone, and carefully wiping the corners of her mouth to make sure no spit or matt 'café au lait' had gathered there. Her teeth were white – *white* white. Her chestnut hair hung in artful waves around her face and her navy cigarette pants, paired with nude heels, elongated her slender legs.

She smiled twice, and laughed once, making a mental note not to open her mouth too widely or to wrinkle her nose – both habits she had worked hard to eradicate. Next, she moved closer to the mirror and whispered, 'Nyor-keeee. Nyo-kee. Nyoki. I'll have the gnocchi. No!' She shook her head, and took a beat. 'The gnocchi for me, please.'

As the door opened, allowing noise from the restaurant to filter in, she straightened and reached into her Lulu Guinness clutch for her perfume – Angelique Noir by Guerlain. The bottle felt reassuringly expensive as she spritzed her wrists and behind her ears.

A glossy blonde woman walked in and halted. 'Oh! Your scent! That's utterly divine! Love it!' She inhaled deeply.

Madeleine gave her customary half-shrug of indifference while inside firecrackers of joy exploded in her gut.

She walked quickly from the bathroom, making her way back to the front of the restaurant, where she waited in the marble-floored foyer. The maître d' approached, as she had known he would, having been so accommodating when she'd rushed in and asked to use the loo before taking her table.

'Hello again, madam.' He gave a slight bow; she liked it.

'Hello.' She glanced at his face before looking past him into the dining room, where intimate tables were set with starched white linen and silverware. The whole place carried an air of refined sophistication.

'And you're having lunch with us?'

'Yes.' She looked back at him. 'Table for two, under the name Woods – Madeleine Woods.'

He walked to the lectern, where a bespectacled girl stood with a pen in her hand and carried an air of authority. The gatekeeper. Ignoring his colleague, he ran his finger down the computer screen and beamed up at her, as if she'd won a prize.

'Please follow me.' Again that slight bow with the incline of the head.

He paused at a table that was sat in front of the bar – almost a thoroughfare, and not where she wanted to sit. Not at all.

'No, thank you. Erm . . . we'll take that one.' She pointed to a table set perfectly for two by the window.

'Of course, madam.' He did his best but failed to control the twitch of irritation under his left eye. 'May we get you some water for the table?' He clasped his hands at his chest, as if in prayer.

'Yes. Sparkling, thank you.'

She glanced at him briefly before he walked away, keeping her smile small and her attitude professional, just like her ex-boss and mentor, Rebecca Swinton, would have done. Madeleine, having watched her every move in social situations, now understood that to allow people to flourish and perform it was best not to be over-friendly, to not break the boundary that kept everyone feeling secure. To do differently only smudged the lines of operation and muddled your responses. She took her seat and placed her bag on the windowsill, moving the cutlery to her right, to give her and her guest more space. She studied the small, printed menu in front of her, already knowing what she was going to choose, having looked up the options online this morning.

'Madeleine!'

Nico called her name, unabashed and confident as he walked towards the table, two steps behind the maître d'. There was the unmistakable flare of attraction in her gut that she'd felt the first time they'd seen each other across the boardroom table at Field and Gray – the lawyers who advised the agency on all manner of property law, both here and abroad. Nico's mother, Belinda Yannis, was a partner; his maternal grandfather, Horatio Gray, one of the founders; and Nico was, according to the gossip flying around the bar of The Ned for their post-meeting analysis, being prepped to take over the reins when his mother retired – if she ever retired. From what Madeleine could tell, the immaculately groomed, wrinkle-free Belinda was more likely to collapse while poring over contracts in her office than bow out gracefully to tend to her garden or join the bowls club. Madeleine had been in awe and petrified of her in equal measure, noting the way she delicately and loosely rested her hands in front of her – Cartier tank catching the light, palms steady, wrists relaxed, no hint of tension – as if to sit at the head of the highly polished table was her absolute right, which of course, as Horatio Gray's daughter, it was. Madeleine had taken a deep, slow breath, knowing that if this was the way the woman conducted herself, she would find any overt nerves in others less than attractive.

Nico didn't have his mother's stern presence. He was as handsome as she'd remembered, with short dark hair and brown eyes that crinkled at the sides as he smiled. His easy-going expression and manner were most alluring. His presence and initial interaction confirmed the connection between them that had been immediate and thrilling. It would also be a lie if she were to say that the stature and status of a man like this didn't hold its very own attraction.

'Lunch!' He sat opposite her and leaned back in the chair, clearly comfortable in these surroundings, and picked up the menu, giving it only the briefest of considerations.

'Yep, lunch!'

'I must admit, my invitations to dinner don't usually get demoted to lunch.' He shook his head.

'Is that right? Interesting you see it as a demotion. I much prefer lunch.'

'How come?' He sat forward, interested, as he placed the menu flat on the table.

'Because if I'd said yes to dinner, and you were dull company or we didn't get on, or you had some truly terrible habits that turned my stomach, then not only would I be trapped with you for hours, but it'd be a waste of a precious free evening. Whereas lunch . . . What do you reckon, hour and a half, tops?'

'Absolute tops,' he agreed.

14

'I can put up with just about anything for that short window. So if this turns out to be a disaster, the day is not entirely lost. And if we *do* get on – and you don't reveal your horrid habits and you're not a complete bore – we can progress to dinner. Whereas if we start there, we have nowhere to go.'

'It feels like a test.' He pulled a face.

'I guess it is, for us both.' She liked their level of eye contact, the ease of conversation, the shared humour, the way she set the rules and he went along with it, falling into step as she played hard to get. A ploy that she felt only enhanced her attractiveness.

'Here's the thing: based on our very flirty texts, I already like you. It's been fun.' He sounded sincere and she took the compliment, unwilling to admit that she'd read and re-read their exchanges before falling asleep for the last couple of nights.

'Well, you should have said! We could have carried on texting and saved ourselves the price of lunch! This is probably a good time to point out that we're going Dutch, just to make sure there's no sense of obligation on either of our parts.'

'Dutch it is, perfect.' He laughed. 'And you raise a good point, but, just so you know, I do think there's somewhere to go if dinner goes well. I usually like to progress to a weekend at my cottage.'

'Usually? So you do this a lot?' she half-teased.

'Actually, I really don't.' He dropped the humour and his expression became intense. She felt a shiver of longing ripple through her bones.

'Hmmm, interesting. You see, I think a weekend away after one dinner is too big a leap for me, but a weekend away after one lunch and two dinners is just about acceptable.'

'I can see you've given it some thought.'

'I have,' she admitted, 'and this is also probably as good a time as any to tell you that I'm leaving for LA in two weeks. So don't get too attached, as I'll be jetting off into the sunset for the foreseeable future. I'm sure it's going to be just like *La La Land* and I'll probably get whisked off my feet by a budding actor, who ultimately will make it big and buy me diamonds.'

'I can buy you diamonds right now.'

'I don't even like diamonds! Plus, I could buy my own,' she emphasised.

'Touché.' He beamed. 'I like LA. Maybe I'll come visit you.'

'Too soon! We haven't finished lunch number one yet. We absolutely cannot be making those kinds of plans!' She widened her eyes in mock horror, although her stomach flipped in excitement at the prospect, more than a little enamoured by the fact he could indeed come visit and buy diamonds – one of these a significantly more exciting prospect than the other. Diamonds – in fact baubles of any kind – had never impressed her.

'Shall we order? I'm starving.' He clapped his hands together.

She liked his honesty and his humour. She raised her hand and the waiter came over.

'Madam?' The moustachioed man stared at her.

'The gnocchi for me, please.' She ordered with confidence.

'Oh, good shout. Yes, for me too, please.'

'Certainly. And to drink?'

'Just the water. Sparkling.' She reminded the man of her drinks order, which was yet to materialise.

'For me too.' Nico smiled.

'Copycat.'

The waiter walked away.

'Oh God, have I failed already?' Nico laughed.

'No, you won't know if you've failed or progressed to the next round until we leave. If it's been great, I'll text you a thumbs-up, and if it's been rubbish then I won't text you at all.'

'Harsh!' he fired back.

'Yet clear, and I think clarity is important, don't you?'

'I do. And I shall adopt the same. A thumbs-up means you did well and no text . . . well, means you'll be back to swiping right.'

She laughed at his cheek, and they shared a moment – a lingering look, both aware of how they were using humour to further break the ice, relax, get over any nerves, and to see if the instant attraction might have anything more substantial behind it.

It was typical of her luck. She had been on numerous dates over the last year with people who had all held promise until she actually spent time with them. It had helped her realise that she often preferred the idea of spending time with someone to the reality of it. Not that she considered herself to be overly picky or demanding, just that her standards were high and her list of traits in a potential partner non-negotiable. The fact that it was a long and complicated list was neither here nor there.

An image of Richard entered her mind – gorgeous, funny Richard, who had shown much potential until he'd flashed her his tattoo of Dolly Parton, smack bang in the middle of his chest. Madeleine loved a blast of 'Jolene' as much as the next person, but a tattoo on his chest? The thought of being in a semi-naked state, staring down at the perfect curves of Dolly, against whom no woman could compare . . . She'd blocked his number shortly after. Then there was Quentin, who was fabulous and flirty. A silver fox dentist with a classic Porsche who smelled as if his pores actually secreted Tom Ford's Tobacco Vanille. She could have happily sat and sniffed him for hours. That was until she realised he started most sentences with, 'I am not lying when I say . . .' or 'To tell you the truth . . .' and 'I swear to God . . .' which gave her the distinct impression that he was indeed lying, not telling her the truth and about to let God down badly. It put her right off. She had been with him in Covent Garden when she had bumped into her old best friend Trina, who she hadn't seen for a while. It was a little awkward, yet still Trina knew her well enough to text her immediately with a thumbs-down symbol.

It told her all she needed to know. So yes, typical of her luck to feel this attracted to Nico when she was about to fly across the pond for good. Not that it was going to stop her enjoying her time with him until she left. She would, she figured, be mad not to.

It was easy to make light of her dating disasters, simpler to concentrate on the frivolous. The truth, she suspected, when it came to her lack of success, was far more about not being able to be herself, not fully. Having to play a part and be wary – always wary – of when she would have to pull off her mask and tell all.

'Have you been here before?' She let her eyes rove the ornate dining hall with the frescoed walls and busy tables where men in tailored, starched, button-down shirts sipped wine, and the laughter was loud, bullish.

'Yes. But only ever for working lunches.'

'Me too.'

'My parents are big foodies. My dad's Greek, so food and wine are in our blood – big feasts for every celebration, and nearly everything warrants a celebration. My mother, who you have met *of course* . . .'

'I have indeed.'

She noticed how he paused for a second, as if inviting or expecting her to offer an opinion on Belinda Yannis, which *of course* she did not.

'Yes, so my mother comes from a farming family.'

Madeleine was aware of the farm. Rumour had it that it covered most of the South Downs, and also that it was no ramshackle cottage in which they brewed tea and discussed their day, but rather a vast country house plonked in the middle of the estate. A house that came with a title, as far as she recalled.

'She grew up hunting, fishing and foraging – eating what they caught, what they found, growing fruit and vegetables and baking for great parties.'

'It sounds idyllic. So you grew up on the farm?'

18

'Not really. I visited it.' He raised his hand and smiled in acknowledgement of the bottle of sparkling water deposited on their table and the two tall glasses with ice, mouthing, 'Thank you.' She liked his respect for the waiter. Things like that were important to her. 'But I spent most of my time away at school. During the holidays, which, thank goodness, felt endless, we went to Skiathos, where my father's family has a home. It's on a cliff with the most incredible view of the sea and sky I've ever seen. If you took me there blindfolded, I'd know it by the scent alone.' He closed his eyes and took a deep breath. 'The pine forests, the rosemary and thyme that's abundant, ripe mandarins, the woody-scented bark of the olive trees, eucalyptus leaves – all underpinned with the fragrant incense and oils from the church. It's like nothing else.' He breathed in through his nose and she envied him the memory.

'It sounds glorious.'

'It really is.' He nodded and sipped his water. 'A special place.'

'My upbringing was a little different. Not quite so privileged.'

The waft of dog shit on the breeze, the diesel fumes, the ripe fruit chucked off the roof by bored kids just to watch the splat, the scent of the overflowing communal bins, the weed being smoked on the balconies . . . and the heady scent of piss wafting from the lift and stairwells.

She swallowed. Here it was. The thought that was always waiting in the wings. The awareness that if this attraction developed, she would need to tell him about her past. It was all a question of timing, and something she relished – it felt good to detail just how far she had come – yet dreaded in equal measure, knowing she had never once shared her story and not felt the sharp lance of judgement at her breast. It was, however, going to be hard to avoid if he stuck around; she felt the need to speak the truth, which she was certain would either see him scurrying for the hills or applauding her achievements, as if she were a shining example of rags to riches . . . not that she was by Nico's standards rich, but she was certainly comfortable. And not that she'd be telling him anything today – far, far too early in developments to be shedding skin.

'But happy? A happy upbringing?' he asked, with such a look of concern it was almost as if anything other than this would be hard for him to imagine, and even harder for him to bear.

'Yes, happy.' She quickly buried the pang of sadness that sprang up when she considered how things had changed.

'And that's all we can ask for, right?' he asked softly.

She smiled and sipped her water, as the *nyor-keeee / nyo-kee* arrived.

'God, I'm famished.' She lifted her fork.

He smiled at her as she went in.

'What?' she asked, the delicious, soft gnocchi nestling on her tongue beneath the salty tang of parmesan.

'I like a girl who eats.' He nodded, as if in approval, and reached for his fork.

'Oh, you'll like me, then. A lot.'

'I think you might be right . . .' He let this trail and her heart jumped with joy in her chest.

Eleven hours and twenty-five minutes.

That was the length of the flight from London Heathrow to LAX.

Not so long really. Not even a day.

After waving to Nico as he jumped in a cab, she texted him a thumbs-up.

It felt good, exciting, as it always did at this stage, when everything was flimsy, insubstantial, and therefore mattered little if it solidified into something more or not. It was a frivolous time in any courtship, and possibly her favourite part – without weighted conversations about the future or their wants, without deep analysis of where they were heading or whether they wanted to jump ship; without having to open up about the past, how they'd lived, how they'd got to this point and the experiences, good and bad, that had shaped them. It was enough that they wanted each other physically and that they made each other laugh. She was determined to live in the now and enjoy the moment, doing her level best not to think too far ahead – trying not to picture cosy winter walks wrapped in wide scarves as they strolled hand in hand, lazy summer days spent with the sun on their skin and cold, cold wine drunk al fresco. Of a more practical – some might say cynical – nature, she had never been a romantic and saw no reason to let her guard down now.

Dr Schoenfeld would be proud of how she remained present. Heading there now, she saw her therapist at least a couple of times a week – it was her me time, provided clarity to her jumbled thoughts, and was entirely necessary to keep her worries and anxieties in check.

Her phone beeped as Nico responded to her text in kind. She laughed loudly at the thumbs-up and swallowed the bubble of happiness that rose in her throat, feeling a lot like a giddy teen who has just heard third hand from a friend of a friend that the boy she liked might actually like her in return. The kind of moment she would have shared with Trina, if things were different. Quickly she suppressed the image of the girl who had been her best friend, her confidante, her sounding board. It happened like this sometimes – fleeting, crushing moments that reminded her of what she had lost. Not that this was a time for lament, not with things having gone so well with Nico and her so looking forward to her move to LA.

If the pavement had been empty and the street not nose-to-tail with cars, cabs, buses, and bikes, she might have skipped a little, not that she was the skipping kind, especially not in these heels. Well, that and the fact that she hadn't skipped since she was a child. But that was one helluva good lunch. And she wasn't referring to the overpriced gnocchi that had barely touched the sides.

Nico was smart, funny, and extremely attractive, and his after-shave was *utterly divine*! She *loved* it! He was the full package and the kind of man she would be foolish not to invest in for a while at least. She'd suggest dinner. Dinner and whatever followed . . . knowing she wouldn't mind seeing what lurked beneath his crisp white shirt and sharp navy suit.

Her phone rang.

'Tan, what's up?'

She and Tan Shi had blurred the lines between colleague and friend. She had even witnessed his marriage to Ramon last Christmas – the only one present who had not sobbed and smudged her mascara on the steps of the Marylebone registry office. She'd done her best to mask her cynicism, knowing that marriage was not for her. It was to her mind a bizarre and outdated contract that made little sense. Her mum and dad, Marnie and Doug, were the one exception to the rule – deeply in love, bound by constraints that were not applicable to her – the grind of a hard life and a horizon that was always within reach. As if they didn't have time or energy to question their commitment, far too busy earning enough to put bread on the table and never having to contend with the bigger life questions of promotion, exploration, and risk. Like goldfish. Happy, contented goldfish who never looked up and just kept on swimming. As a teenager, she didn't know whether to pity or admire them, and that was the truth. As an adult, she only hoped that she might find a love so steadfast and unrelenting, knowing the kind of stability that could bring to a life, but she'd do so without putting on a big frock and organising a buffet. Theirs was indeed a steadfast and unrelenting love that they were happy to share with the little girl who sat at the centre of their world. Her wonderful, wonderful mum and dad . . .

'Couple of things.' Tan broke her thoughts. 'First, Stern has come back and he likes the chandelier!'

'That's great news!'

She felt a familiar flush of joy that their client had approved the expensive option, knowing it would make all the difference to the final appearance, and their bottom line. The mark-up was hefty. The ornate, coloured glass had a slight dapple and was almost iridescent – the perfect centrepiece for the open-plan foyer of the high-end apartments that would sit on top of the retail space of the renovated factory complex, only a stone's throw from central Manchester. It was also vital she leave the agency, which specialised in the redevelopment and regeneration of commercial premises, on a high. This was her last commission before she took up the new position offered by her old boss, Rebecca Swinton, who was now based in LA. Madeleine couldn't wait to fix up her new apartment, let the heat of the Californian sun warm her muscles, and wander the coast or hike the mountains of a weekend. A whole new life in a different environment. She was beyond excited.

'I'm glad he likes it. We can talk about it when I get back – shan't be much longer, an hour or so. What was the other thing?' She came to a halt outside the narrow white stucco building with its grand Palladian-inspired porch and waited to end the call.

'How did it go with Nico?'

'Again, we can talk about it when I get back, but . . . good.' She smiled; their time together might be short, her flights already booked, but that didn't mean she and Nico couldn't have an amazing couple of weeks. Not to mention the fact her mind kept returning to the idea that it wasn't beyond the realms of possibility that a man like Nico Yannis would pop up in LA now and then, although she tried not to get ahead of herself. It was, after all, only one lunch.

'So when you say it was good, do you mean good or *good* good?' he pushed.

'Bye, Tan!' She ended the call, and shook her head. He was such a gossip, a nosy gossip, but she loved him regardless.

December

5.50 A.M.

Madeleine woke in the bedroom of her grotty shared flat on the Old Kent Road to a grumbling pain in her stomach and a strong desire to vomit. It was as surprising as it was annoying. She was never ill. Never. Quite unlike some of her peers, who delighted in a mild affliction that meant a duvet day, any illness was for her an irritation – an inconvenience she did not have time for. She rarely wanted to slow down, and thankfully it had been her very fortunate experience to have never been so encumbered by a condition she couldn't shake off. While her school mates, and now colleagues, rammed tissues under leaking noses or necked syrups, potions, and pills to try to stave off whatever bug had inveigled their system, she merely drank water, took deep breaths, walked briskly, had an early night, and managed to halt any and all potential ailments in their tracks. Her gran had been the same; her mum too.

'The Woods women have the constitution of an ox and a hide about as thick!'

This was the family saying that only added to the self-belief that to get sick was for other people.

At twenty-two, she had been in her role as an assistant to the creative team for the large commercial renovation company for almost a year and was desperate to make her mark. She devoured interior design magazines and was drawn to any form and shape that thrilled her: it might be a vase or a view or even the contents of spaghetti hoops tipped on to a plate – it all fascinated her and she studied them accordingly.

The term 'assistant' had been loosely mooted at her interview and it transpired that her job entailed doing anything that the esteemed designers didn't fancy doing themselves. This included, but was not limited to, fetching coffee and dry cleaning (unless it was a sunny day when miraculously those who deemed the task beyond them in the rain suddenly found their walking shoes), making endless copies, picking up items from the printers across town, redistributing mail that had ended up on the wrong desk, staying after hours to supervise contractors, calling plumbers when the loo got blocked, grabbing sushi orders, doing the sandwich run, watering plants, answering a phone at an empty desk when the person calling was determined to stay connected, ordering flowers, buying birthday cards, booking taxis, restaurants, hotels and flights, and best of all, taking Captain the pug for a shite as and when the need arose. Captain was the beloved flat-faced beast of Rebecca, her boss. *The* boss.

The irony wasn't lost on her that Captain owned a wardrobe with more designer labels than she had seen on any human and was hand-fed poached chicken and filet mignon while she struggled to afford pasta. Thrice daily, she'd parade Captain on a thin stretch of grass along the pavement near the office, whispering gentle words of encouragement to help him go. These were not her finest moments. Especially when he was wearing his favoured sailor top and tourists insisted on snapping him mid-toilette.

It was humiliating for them both.

She was, however, determined that this would not always be her life, and wanted one day to eat poached chicken and filet mignon herself, although she'd draw the line at someone hand-feeding it to her while she sat on a monogrammed velvet cushion . . . and similarly would rather they didn't watch her poo afterwards and collect her waste in a biodegradable bag while the world looked on.

Having never been in a position to go to university, aware of the cost and petrified by the prospect of student debt, she had decided to carve her own path and had finally landed this position, her first foray into the world of commercial design. She was ecstatic to be working in the office of the terrifyingly organised and neurotic perfectionist Rebecca Swinton.

As was often the case, Madeleine had a grand plan, a vision of where she wanted to get to, and could see herself riding a wave of future success. She spent endless hours imagining how she'd decorate her bougie apartment, the incredible choice of shoes in her walk-in closet, the holidays booked spontaneously, and the way it might feel sitting in the big chair and making the rules. Freedom that she suspected would largely be dictated by having a bank account in the black. A bank account where every dime was hard earned by her alone. The trouble was, she wasn't really sure of how to bring it to fruition, hoping one day the intricacies of her life map would become clear. Right now, her main objective was to work hard and learn as much as she could. Without the qualifications that saw some of her peers awarded tasty projects or interesting assignments, she made it her mission to arrive early, leave late, eat lunch at her desk, show up, volunteer, make great coffee, fuss over Captain, and generally do whatever she could to get noticed. Having days off to be 'sick' was most definitely not part of her plan.

And now this: an unusual level of discomfort some ten minutes before her alarm went off. Sitting up in her bed, she wrapped her arms around her stomach, breathing slowly and deeply, as if this might be enough to stop the pain.

It wasn't.

She lay down and rubbed the affected area, wondering if this might help as she ran through possible diagnoses in her head. Had she eaten something dodgy? Nothing came to mind: a sandwich for lunch, toast for supper last night and three oranges. The cramped kitchen she shared with Luciano, Meredith and Liesl wasn't exactly super clean – they were all busy working people – and had now reached that point where no one wanted to do more than their fair share of housework and it therefore felt easier not to bleach the floors and scrub the fridge, but food poisoning? It seemed unlikely.

Six a.m. came and went. She felt the spike of fever, but sincerely hoped a cool shower might restore her enough for work.

'God, you look awful!' Liesl spied her from the sofa, where she sat smoking and applying eyeliner simultaneously.

'Cheers!' She gave a weak thumbs-up.

'Can I get you anything? Do you want some tea?'

'No, but thanks.' She appreciated her kindness on this day that had started so badly. 'I'm thinking a shower might sort me out.'

'Mmm . . .'

The look Liesl gave her told her she thought this most unlikely.

'I feel like shite!' she exhaled.

'As I might have mentioned, you look it. Are you at the café tonight?'

Madeleine had an evening job to supplement her meagre income at the agency. It was in fact how she'd met Luciano, who also worked there, and how she'd heard about the spare room that was now hers.

'No, night off, thank God. I'm knackered.'

'In that case, can you pick some eggs up, please, honey? We're out again.' She pointed towards Meredith's bedroom door and made a fist. She knew how to make her laugh, even when she felt this rough.

'Sure. Might not be back till late, though.'

'As long as they're here for my midnight omelette, that's fine.' Liesl did a double take, and took a drag on her cigarette. 'You know, you really do look awful.'

'Way to build my confidence!' Madeleine headed for the shower, praying it might do the trick.

Chapter Two

Madeleine ran her fingers through her hair and took a deep breath, trying to find the neutral face that she felt best for her appointment with Dr Orna Schoenfeld. It was part of the game, she figured, to hide her emotions, not wanting to give her therapist a clue. They had a regular weekly slot, but the doctor was also on hand as and when Madeleine felt the need to talk, and she felt the need often. Therapy had felt like a dirty secret when she had first considered it, but now, two years in, she viewed Dr Schoenfeld like a safety valve on a boiler – something practical she could reach for to let off steam whenever necessary, vital to prevent overheating and or explosion. She smiled at the analogy as she pressed the buzzer for entry.

After all this time, the hallways and stairwells still smacked her around the chops with disappointment. With the façade being so very grand, the semi-elliptical fan light above the front door hinting at former glory, her expectations were always high, as if the management company might have snuck in since her last visit and given the place a dramatic and necessary makeover. The light was good and the space wide with infinite possibilities, yet everything about the décor was professionally depressing. The carpet was grey and hardwearing with deep, dark stains here and there. The stairs were edged in aluminium, the walls were magnolia – the laziest of colour choices in her considered opinion, artless and uninspiring. The overhead lighting was harsh, coming from neon strips that hung low on chains. The whole place felt industrial, impersonal, and tepid. It was the very opposite of Dr Schoenfeld's consulting room, which was warm – the honey-coloured oak flooring enhanced by a thick Berber rug in neutral tones, a deep, oak-toned leather couch that she could sink into, and large olive-green lamps with gold linen shades that stood like sentinels at either end of a blond sideboard which housed a couple of arty books and boxes of tissues, which she suspected were used hungrily in this space. Although not by her.

There was probably some deeply insightful reason for the overly naff communal space. Maybe it was so that a client, who might leave the clinic in a state of high emotion, would be reminded to snap out of it and put on a suitable public-facing expression as soon as they hit the hallway, which felt municipal at best, brutalist at worst.

'Madeleine!' her therapist called from the open door, where she rested against the frame. A stylish woman who pulled off the green needlecord pinafore and yellow tights in the way that only a quirky academic could. Her wild hair was chopped about her chin and her eyes looked enormous behind her dark, heavy-framed specs. 'Maximum points for taking the stairs. Most of my clients wait for the lift, which takes an age.'

'I'm burning off lunch.' She exhaled as she walked into the room and put her bag on the sofa before sitting down, so practised was she in the routine.

'Where did you go? Somewhere nice? I like to live my lunches vicariously through others, as for me it's always a floppy sandwich – with tomato that makes the bread soggy before its time – and the yoghurt that's going out of date the quickest grabbed from the fridge.'

'Sounds revolting!' She pulled a face.

'It is, but it's made with love. My partner insists on doing this one thing for me, an act of pure kindness, and so I don't have the heart to tell him that what I sometimes crave is a greasy handful of crisps washed down with a can of pop or a couple of chocolate bars, eaten on the fly, and counteracted by strong coffee.'

The therapist sat on the couch opposite and picked up her leather-bound folder and favoured pen.

'And yet you remind me weekly of the need for honesty,' Madeleine teased.

'I do.' She grinned. 'What is it they say? The cobbler's children have no shoes?'

'Who says that?' Madeleine stared at the woman quizzically.

'We're getting off topic.' Orna unscrewed the lid from her fountain pen. 'What did you have for lunch?'

'Gernocky. No – neyorki. Damn! I've forgotten how to say it!' She felt her cheeks blush and coughed to clear the embarrassment from her throat.

'Gnocchi!'

'That's the one.' She pointed at the woman and made a clicking noise with her tongue. 'I love eating at nice restaurants.'

'Who doesn't?'

'I guess no one, but for me it's a real marker.'

'How so?'

She noted how the doctor sat forward, changing the atmosphere in the room, baiting the hook, wanting to explore the theme in the way they did and was now comfortable – or if not comfortable, then certainly less excruciating than it used to be. Madeleine had thought therapy would be different: she had imagined lying on a chaise and being shown ink blots while someone in a white coat nodded sagely and laid out the answers to all the questions, doubts and worries that spun around her mind as if they rode a wall of death. It wasn't like that at all. The biggest surprise was that she did most of the talking.

'As you know, I grew up in a council block in the shadow of the City. We were at one end of the street and at the other bankers turned the Georgian terraces into multimillion-pound homes – yet it was the same postcode.' She shook her head at the fact that still blew her mind. And one that she had not shared the detail of until today. Why she felt the time was right would be hard to say, but maybe the softening of her bones after such a lovely hour and a half spent with Nico might have had something to do with it, where the topic of her upbringing had been touched upon, opening a box that had been closed for the longest time. Plus, after two years of getting together, Orna, she felt, had very much smudged the line between friend and therapist.

'Was that difficult for you?'

'Erm, I think it was only difficult when I noticed how different our lives were. When I was very small, I liked to look in the windows of the fancy-pants houses.' She stopped speaking and smiled, remembering how she felt compelled to point them out on the way home from school – a habit, a ritual. 'They were fascinating to me – so beautiful! In our flat, every penny was accounted for and hard won, and the thought of replacing the tatty old sofa or buying an item purely for aesthetics just didn't occur. Everything in it was either very worn or second-hand junk.' She recalled asking for her bedroom to be redecorated and the blank looks that greeted her, as if it was an impossible and pointless task.

'Do you think this influenced your choice of career?'

'It must have done in some way. I now get to decorate and renovate the most extraordinary spaces with someone else's money, and usually with no expense spared. I'd not really thought about it, but, yes, I guess it did. It was only when I hit my teens that I realised things were possible for people at the fancy end of the street because they had money and those same things were off limits for me because I was poor. There was a beauty that came with having money; they were able to *buy* those things, *buy* that kind of life. They had choices. They had time. Things that had no place in my world had *importance* in theirs. It struck me as really unfair.'

'What things specifically?'

'All of it!' She gave a short, dry laugh. 'Glitter! Sparkle! Soft interiors. Spare things – spare chairs, cushions, lamps. The objects in their home didn't have to be functional or earn their place. They could be there for no other reason than because they were pretty. Things in those houses could be replaced because the owner grew tired of them or wanted to change things up, not necessarily because the thing was worn out or defunct. I just couldn't imagine it. And, as I touched on earlier, eating in restaurants!' She chuckled at the thought of Marnie's macaroni cheese, baked in huge slabs, congealing in the fridge, to be livened up under a hot grill each night until it was gone. Not that she'd minded or noticed, and never once did she go to bed hungry. Never. She was loved – so loved. It was contradictory and confusing still; the fact that she was adored and yet grew up quite unable to adore the surroundings that she felt tied her hands behind her back and urged her to stay in her lane. It was conflicting for so many reasons, but primarily because it raised the question of whether it was the best way to raise a child, or if she deserved more.

Madeleine gathered herself.

'I don't think we ever went to a restaurant, apart from cafés, on the odd occasion when I was helping out on the market stall with my dad, and we'd go for egg on toast if things were slack or it was cold.' She remembered with fondness those mornings, the windows of the café steamed up, the smell of bacon permeating the

33

air as it crisped under the grill, being given a chipped mug full of tea, which felt very adult. The cross-table chatter, the comradery, the laughter loud and dripping with affection. To sit among it had felt like being in the middle of a cosy cocoon where she was safe and she was loved . . . and with this thought she felt warmth ripple through her; there were far, far worse environments for a little girl to reside. 'Yes, we went to the café occasionally or we went for a burger, but never a restaurant. We had a lot of picnics. Or what Marnie called picnics.' She bit her lip.

'What was it about the picnics that didn't make you happy?'

She guessed her face said it all.

'Erm, I suppose they were another sharp reminder of how we lived. I'd read about picnics – I was an avid reader – and they were always sedate affairs with checked tablecloths spread out on lush grass, doorstep sandwiches, dainty cakes, and bottles of squash, all eaten with a view of something wonderful.'

'I'm thinking you were reading The Famous Five?'

Dr Schoenfeld had obviously read the same.

'Possibly. Our picnics were nothing like that. We'd go to the bench in the park that was on a slight hill with a view over the estate and we'd eat leftovers. I think I knew, even then, that I wanted a life that was more than eating yesterday's beefburgers wrapped in foil. Cold potatoes in Tupperware, that kind of thing. Marnie wasn't averse to bringing cold shepherd's pie or cooled bread pudding and water in a bloody sippy cup!' She shook her head.

'How old would you have been, when this dire al fresco experience was foisted upon you?'

Madeleine appreciated the hint of sarcasm; it made it easier to chat when it didn't feel forced.

'I don't know, six, maybe seven . . .'

'You were quite discerning for a little one.'

'I suppose I was.' She pictured her younger self, listening to the conversations between the grown-ups, taking it all in, aware of the struggle, the schemes, the ideas, and musings, all wrapped in love. Drenched in love!

Her therapist shifted in her seat and pulled the skirt of her pinafore down over her knees. 'I guess we always think the grass is a little greener. It's human nature, right?'

'That's the thing, Orna.' She held her gaze. 'I *knew* the grass was greener and I knew I wanted to taste it, see it, live it—'

'And you do,' the doctor interrupted.

'And I do.' Madeleine looked down at her fingers, taking a second to admire her manicure, immaculate and understated as ever. 'It wasn't actually about being poor or not having stuff.' She caught the woman's expression of incredulity. 'It really wasn't.'

'I didn't say anything!' Orna threw her hand in the air.

'You didn't have to. I read your face. But it's true. It wasn't about money or a lack of, it was more about not knowing the right way to do things and not recognising the wrong way to do things because my family didn't have the experience, didn't know any better.' She pictured Marnie painting her nails on the bus, Doug shouting loudly in the street because a cat had shat on the bonnet of his van, hollering into the ether – for what? Their behaviour was the equivalent of waving flags or carrying wide placards for the whole world to see that read, 'THIS IS WHO WE ARE AND WE CAN'T EVEN SEE YOU JUDGING US! AND EVEN IF WE DID THEN WE WOULDN'T CARE!!!'

But Edith-Madeleine cared.

She cared a lot.

She had learned not to be so overt, so loud, understanding that it wasn't necessary to voice her entire interior monologue as if giving the world a running commentary on her life, as Marnie did.

'I wasn't ashamed of them – never, ever that. I just wanted a seat at that table with the view. I wanted spare chairs, and a nice picnic.'

'Did you want them to want it too?'

It was a fair question but one that made her pulse jump, nonetheless.

She shook her head.

'No. I only wanted them to be happy and they were – they are. I just . . .' She shrugged. 'I just knew *I* wouldn't be happy if I didn't get to sample it all. Like I was wired differently to them.'

'That must have been alienating – lonely even?'

'I guess.' She picked at an invisible piece of lint on the thigh of her navy trousers. Picturing the little girl who had been plonked in that environment. 'As a kid, if someone gave me a coin, any coin, it was such an amazing thing. I was interested in money, fascinated by it and what it could do. My dad could do one trick, make a coin appear from behind my ear – I was transfixed and elated every time!'

'How old were you?'

'Twenty-three.' She tutted. 'What do you think? Like, five . . . six.' It was her turn for sarcasm. 'He'd reach around my head, and there'd be a shiny coin in his hand, and I'd leap about! Just so excited because I understood that money made the world go around and money was the thing we chased in order to survive and money was what bought food and paid rent and made everything possible. I knew we never had enough of it and that it was hard won and precious.'

She remembered him coming home with little bundles of cash wrapped in elastic bands, his takings. He'd hand it over to his wife in its entirety – the trust implicit, the two of them working as one. And she'd watch Marnie peel the notes away one at a time to pay the bills and buy pasta, until the money was gone. 'It took me years to learn how to be around money, not to flinch if my boss said it's going to cost a hundred grand, a million, ten million. I had to become familiar with these sums and not show my shock at how easily such numbers were discussed, quoted, thrown out to a room, as if it was second nature to me. As if I wasn't used to counting pennies that I'd found in a random pocket, hoping it was enough for the bus fare or that I might be able to get chips.'

'I would imagine that the number of people in the world who are comfortable talking about those sums and those amounts are few.'

'They're plentiful in my world. The world I now move in.' It was fact.

'So, how did you get used to it? How did you become more at ease?'

'I studied those that were already comfortable. I watched their mannerisms, studied their habits, their reactions, their phrases, the way they spoke, the way they interacted, the topics they covered, the clothes they wore and I . . . I copied them . . . I copy them.'

Nee-swas . . . Nih-swaaaaas . . . Salad Niçoise . . . Nyo-kee . . . It came back to her now.

'You still do this?' Orna asked with a flicker of concern.

Madeleine nodded. It felt a lot like giving away a secret, opening up.

'It sounds like hard work.'

She shrugged again.

It *was* hard work – bloody exhausting, in fact, but she'd always done it. Always known she needed to shed the skin she'd grown while living under Marnie and Doug's cramped roof on the seventh floor of the Brenton Park estate, and that if she were ever to stretch her wings and fly, she needed to put the work in.

'When I first moved out, I worked as a waitress at a café of an evening. I had a few jobs, but this was my evening job and the best paid. It was a diner kind of thing. Menus were written on boards and nearly everything was served with French fries. We had this customer in the restaurant, Mr Griffin. I'll never forget him. He thought he was the bee's knees. He'd come in for his supper and make a great show of looking around the room, greeting us all, wanting us to wave, to let everyone else know he was a regular, as if it gave him status. He'd bring in other men who looked just like him: old and grey, bad teeth, wearing spectacles and cheap blue suits with striped ties. They'd eat and laugh and drink fizzy pop and order huge desserts that made them chuckle when we put them on the table, as if they were kids. He'd tip heavily, making a real point of pulling out the note – ten quid, always ten quid. It was a lot of money. He'd call me over and hold it in his fingers, making me wait. And every time he did it, I wanted to shout in his face, "Keep your money! Keep your filthy tenner!"'

'Why? That was a good tip!'

'Because . . . because in those moments when he held the money and I was hoping he'd give it to me, thinking of how it would bolster my savings or what I could buy with it, he owned me, he held me in his sway – the *power* of that money and my desire for it. I felt it and I hated it; I hated how I went along with it.'

'Do you think he was aware of his power in that moment?'

Madeleine considered this. 'Maybe, maybe not, but either way the delay between him getting it out of his wallet and giving it to me made me feel powerless, made me aware of how much I needed him and people like him, because no matter how hard I worked or what decisions I made or the path I took, there was always some arsehole like Mr Griffin and his horrible mates giving me the roles, offering me choices, putting up the signposts.'

'Is your life any different now?'

Madeleine laughed. 'Er, just a bit!' She pulled a face. 'I wouldn't stand waiting for him or anyone to peel off a tenner and tease me with it.'

'But you still work for other people?'

'I am very well compensated, don't worry.' She was aware of the snippy tone and regretted it.

'I don't worry. I'm just trying to clarify – it was the amount of money that bothered you? And because you are now *very well compensated*, you put up with it?'

'No!' Why couldn't this woman get it? 'It's different!'

'How?'

'Because . . .' She fought the desire to shout and walk out, knowing that was not how therapy worked – not that she was entirely sure how it worked. 'Because I choose my own path. It's still within a framework, yes, and a framework that is, as you point out, controlled by other people – the people I work for. But I can quit, change roles, go to a rival at any time. I'm in control. I'm not desperate. I have choices.'

'Huh.' Dr Schoenfeld pushed out her bottom lip and made a note in her little book, an act Madeleine found no less infuriating even after all this time. 'Do you tip?'

'Yes.'

'Big tipper?'

'Depends on the level of service and quality of food and what-ever, but, in case you're wondering, I never wave money or make anyone wait. I put the cash discreetly under a napkin or on the edge of the table and I never mention it. I want the person to feel empowered because they've earned it. A silent transaction not in any way diminishing or humiliating. A fair offer of compensation for the job they've done.'

'You've obviously given it a lot of thought.'

'I guess. My old boss – and, in fact, my soon-to-be new boss – had a great influence on me. Always understated in her dress, she moves gently and has more grace than I've ever seen on anyone. I learned a lot from her about being classy.'

Madeleine held the image of the elegant woman in her mind, her neat gloves, a single string of vintage pearls on occasion. Her pulse raced in excited anticipation that in just two weeks she'd be back working with her mentor. It was an incredible opportunity in LA. *LA!*

Her therapist crossed her legs and stared at her, her gaze felt intense and critical. Madeleine didn't like it one bit.

'I guess there's a question I want to ask you – if that's okay?'

'Sure.' She hated when Dr Schoenfeld did that, held her chin, spoke slowly, made her *feel* like she was in therapy – the kind of therapy you saw in the movies where there's a leather couch and muted colours on the wall and a scented candle giving off a fragrance no doubt designed to help relaxation . . . Madeleine shifted on the leather sofa, her movement causing the candle on the low table to fizz a little, sending oud-scented flickers to lick the pale honey-coloured décor.

'Are you happy, Madeleine?'

'What kind of question is that?'

Again that half-laugh. 'It's one that interests me. It's what most of my clients hope for, or try for, or pray for – happiness.'

Madeleine shook her head. 'Are you kidding me? Look at my life!' She threw her arms wide. 'I have the career of my dreams, a penthouse apartment in Clerkenwell, money in the bank, a travel budget bigger than most people's mortgages, a twenty-five-inch waist, pert boobs, private gym membership, interest from any number of eligible men . . .' She pictured Nico's face. 'And I'm on first-name terms with the best aesthetician in the city. How can I not be happy?'

Dr Schoenfeld stared at her and, quite unexpectedly, Madeleine felt the bloom of tears. Standing up, she grabbed for a tissue from the box, and dabbed at her eyes.

'I guess, Madeleine, that's the real question.'

Her phone buzzed in her bag. There was a beat or two of silence that was awkward, a forerunner perhaps to a conversation she did not want to have.

'I . . . I have a meeting I need to . . . That'll have to be it for today. But thank you, Orna. Thanks.' She gathered her handbag, and looked back at her therapist as she reached the tall wooden door with the stylized chrome handle – on this side at least. 'I am happy.' She nodded, cursing the tears that still coursed down her face.

'Okay.' Her therapist closed her notebook and stared at her.

'I am happy.' She offered one last time, before heading into the grim, austere hallway.

I am happy . . .

This she whispered as she trod the stairs and repeated it all the way along the street to her office.

I am . . .

December

7.40 A.M.

'Morning, Mum.'

It was an odd thing; no matter how old Madeleine got or what was going on in her life, if anything went wrong or – as was the case this morning when she had woken feeling under the weather – her instinct was to call Marnie. The pull of the umbilical cord was strong!

'You okay, love? You don't usually call this early. Not that it isn't smashing to hear from you, it is – any time!'

She heard the message loud and clear, the one lurking between the spoken words: *call more, your mother worries!* It bothered her that Marnie just didn't get that her job was not the same as her mum's. Marnie worked at the local community college doing something she loved – doling out food to the students, listening to their chatter, the snippets they dropped as they queued with their plastic trays to collect portions of chicken curry or generously filled sandwiches or bags of crisps and pieces of fruit. She had told Madeleine in the past that this daily contact felt like they shared their lives with her, and she loved to be among it, considered it a privilege to listen to their conversations, to see their eager faces, to receive their thanks, confirming her view that each generation had something wonderful to offer the world. It was an optimism Madeleine didn't necessarily share and a set routine she could only imagine. Marnie started at ten in the morning and finished at three in the afternoon come rain or shine. Madeleine's life was busy! Too busy! Early starts, late finishes and pressure coming at her from all angles. Admittedly it was an internal pressure, determined as she was to save money while rising up the corporate ladder, to have one of the fancy offices with a view and not to have to take Captain for a dump whenever he whimpered and pawed at her leg . . . She could but dream.

Not that she didn't love her parents – she did, very much, and called or visited home whenever she was able. Distance wasn't the problem. It was a short tube ride from her shared flat on the Old Kent Road to her family home in East London – a little over half an hour on a good day with only one change. It was more a case of trying to fit it in. She worked all week with early starts, rising early to ensure her hair, make-up and clothes were on point. Evenings were spent at the diner, and on the weekends she worked hard to build a life away from the Brenton Park estate – a different life, a fun life! Heading out to clubs with Meredith, Luciano and Liesl, who were attractive to her based on no more than their different life experiences. Meredith came from money, Luciano had travelled the world, and Liesl pulled off a droll indifference to life that made Madeleine laugh out loud. On Sundays she slept off her hangover and slept off her fatigue and slept off worry over how she was going to get out of the blocks and get noticed at work.

It was exhausting.

There was the odd Saturday when she fell into bed with the intention of heading out to see her parents the very next day, planned to invite Trina – her best friend since school – over so they could catch up, but when her eyes opened and her head pounded and her bed was warm and soft, it was an easy decision to put it off until the following weekend. Plus – not that it was an easy thing to admit – but she had been kind of avoiding Trina, wary of letting it slip that her last relationship – or rather fling – had been with Jimmy. Jimmy who her best friend had held a candle for a while back. Madeleine wasn't entirely sure that flame was extinguished and couldn't risk the fallout of such an admission. Especially not now when it was done and dusted, never to be mentioned again.

Craig Fallon – Jimmy to everyone – had been in her school year. A nice boy about whom she'd known very little, other than his mother was Malaysian, his dad wasn't on the scene, and that he was an incredible artist. A boy who ran his own race and danced to his own tune, which had never been appealing when she was a kid. Yet when she bumped into him on Oxford Street of all places, a year or so ago, with the residue of a handful of rum and Cokes sloshing in her system, she had felt an odd stirring – a potent mixture of lust and nostalgia that had carried them along on a wave of hook-ups and laughter for six months. Theirs had been a physical attraction, or at least that was how she saw it. Until that fateful night when, under a full moon and with stars twinkling overhead, he had presented her with a drawing of a cottage in a garden with a pond where ducks swam, all set beneath a blue, blue sky, headed with the words 'Our Forever Home' written in biro. It had put the fear of God into her – the artistic equivalent of taking a knife to the stays that bound them and cutting himself loose.

She shivered to recall it. Jimmy was handsome, attractive, calm, and sweet, but a bloody cottage with a duck pond? Good Lord, she was planning world domination in a pair of snakeskin Jimmy Choos, not trundling around a garden in a pair of wellington boots! She didn't even own any wellington boots!

It hadn't ended well, and she hadn't seen him since – about six months ago now.

'I don't feel too good,' she whispered.

'That's not like you. How do you feel exactly?' Marnie's tone was one of concern.

'I've got a tummy ache, bit sicky, slight fever. I don't know really how else to describe it. I've showered, thought that might help, but I still feel grim. Not sure what to do.'

'Do you want me to come over, love? I can call in and they'll get Dara to cover my shift. I can pick you up some tonic water or—'

'No, no, Mum, you don't need to do that.' It warmed her heart that her lovely mum was only ever a phone call away. This thought bookended by guilt that she hadn't made it home for a while now. 'I might go to the doctor's.'

'Do you have a doctor?' Marnie was familiar with her stance on illness.

'There's, erm, a drop-in centre not far from the flat.' She had passed it hundreds of times on her walk to and from the station. 'You don't need an appointment. I might go there. I just want them to give me something so I can get back to work.'

'What you need to do is listen to your body, Edith-Madeleine! You need to rest and drink water and sleep and let it pass. Please don't rush back to work. They can do without you for a day or so, I'm sure. The place won't fall down. And if they can't manage without you, then they need to change their ways!'

Her mother just didn't get it.

'Yep, well, I'll see what the doctor says.'

'Promise me you'll rest, my love.'

'I promise,' she replied, with her index and middle finger crossed.

'And let me know how you get on at the doctor's!'

'I will.'

Again she crossed her fingers and threw in an eye roll for good measure.

Chapter Three

Madeleine put her key into the front door of her apartment –
almost an entire floor of a mansion house that had had its guts
ripped out and now offered a serene, spacious, open-plan kitchen
with a vast living room that thrilled her every time she stepped
inside. She hoped the couple who would be renting it in a few
weeks would appreciate its qualities, and liked to think she was
leaving it in the best hands. Tonight, however, far from the sense
of serenity and well-being that she had anticipated, her pulse raced
as she stared at the walls. Ditching her soft leather tote on the sofa
and shrugging her arms free of her jacket, which she dropped on
the pale marble countertop, she took a step closer and narrowed
her gaze, until her nose was only inches from the low wall that part-
divided the kitchen from the eating space. Grabbing her phone, she
took a deep breath, trying to control her breathing.

'Garth, what on earth?'

Her decorator picked up almost immediately.

'Madeleine, I guessed you were going to call.'

'You did?'

'I told Micky you'd notice. He said you wouldn't, and here we are!'

'You thought I wouldn't notice? Come on, mate!'

It was astounding to her, especially as Garth was a contractor she used professionally. He therefore knew she was a designer, a stylist, a creator with an eye for detail and that the devil was always, always in the detail. Her heart sank as she ran her fingers over the wall, as if this might help in some way. The paint samples had sat on her walls for months and now with only two weeks until she shipped her life to the other side of the world, this!

She had refused to be hurried, understanding the importance of getting the detail absolutely right. Or at least it was important to her. It was what she had touched upon earlier with Orna, being brought up in a flat with scuff marks on the paint, peeling wallpaper and no consideration for colour schemes or design. This level of detail was a mark of her success, a standard to which she held herself accountable. A standard that meant her clients were always left with total satisfaction at a job well done.

Hours had been spent studying the way the light fell on each potential shade at various times of the day as the sun travelled from east to west, taking note of how the different tones looked alongside the kitchen cabinets and chamfered oak flooring. When she finally felt able to make a confident decision, she had been bold and insistent. Chantilly! That was the colour she had chosen after much deliberation. Chantilly. It was the palest cream with the vaguest hint of vanilla that warmed the space while not detracting from the neutrality of her considered interior palette. What she now stared at, despite her strident instructions to Garth and his team, was something closer to popcorn – cream with base notes of ochre.

'I . . . I don't know what to say.' She heard him swallow. 'It was the industrial radio. It's a great clunking thing – heavy. We were just packing up and Micky dropped it and I don't know how, but something caught the fridge door and . . .' She was aware of him gabbling, and immediately turned one hundred and eighty degrees to stare at the door of her Meneghini la Cambusa refrigeration unit, imported at great, great expense . . . Her heart sank as a sound that was part wail, part sharp intake of breath left her throat. Her fridge! Her beautiful, beautiful fridge had a two-inch scratch on the door that was now the only thing she could see. It was ugly, brutal and it destroyed the flawless design of this iconic piece of furniture that was the feature of her kitchen.

'Oh no . . .' She found it hard to find the words, knowing that even if they got the paint right, this scratch would be the one thing that drew her eye each time she walked into the room. How could she fix it? How could she sleep? This imperfection was enough to put a splinter in her dreams, so strong was her drive for perfection when it came to such matters. It was that standards thing again.

'Micky spat on it to see if he could polish it out, but—'

'He *spat* on it?' She could barely disguise her dismay as Garth continued to reveal more about their disastrous day.

'I'll have a look around and see what I can find, like a paint or glue or filler-type thing.'

'It's a Meneghini la Cambusa!'

'A what?' This time she detected a hint of laughter.

Pinching the bridge of her nose, she closed her eyes and did her best to remain calm. 'And actually, just to add insult to injury, the reason I called was because you have used the wrong paint, Garth.'

'The wrong paint?' This was apparently news to him. 'It's the colour and range you wrote down.'

'It's really not. It's not Chantilly. That's the colour I wanted. The colour I chose.'

'Okay, Madeleine. Look, let's keep calm.' She knew he meant that *she* had to keep calm, and felt her pulse race accordingly. Why did men do that? She found it beyond irritating. 'It's best I come over in the morning and we talk about how we get this resolved.'

'No, don't come over in the morning, I'll be in the office. And how we get this resolved is simple: I need you to source the paint I wanted and repaint the walls.'

She heard his sharp intake of breath. 'That's going to blow my profit on the job.'

Madeleine knew she was a sucker when it came to things like this but couldn't allow him to do the work for nothing, his mistake or not.

'I'll pay for the new paint.'

'You, Madeleine, are what we call a diamond!'

'And I'll pay you a day rate as well.' Garth was a decent bloke and a great decorator; it would be a shame to sour their working relationship.

'Actually, make that a rare diamond!'

'Mmmn.' She smiled in spite of herself, remembering her conversation with Nico. 'Is there anything else you need to tell me, other than the fact that you've messed up my walls and destroyed my beautiful fridge?'

'Micky nicked one of your Diet Cokes and a Diarylea triangle from your . . . fridge thing.'

'Tell Micky not to worry, I mean, in the grand scheme of things . . .'

'Gotta go, Madeleine, football is starting.'

He ended the call and she staggered to the oversized sofa that was covered in linen the colour of biscuit, sinking down into the soft cushions, where she lay for a moment. It was a pain having to get the walls repainted, but she reminded herself of the good stuff that had happened that day; she was safe and warm inside her beautiful apartment, her lunch with Nico, his thumbs-up text, the okay from Stern on the chandelier for the Manchester project, and her chat with Dr Schoenfeld. This small gratitude ritual was a technique she used for self-calming when things felt a little overwhelming. She laughed at the thought of Micky snaffling a Dairylea triangle, the one snack she knew she would have devoured as a child.

'Those bloody picnics!'

She smiled, thinking about her conversation with Orna and how she used to sit on the bench with Marnie, who unpacked all manner of cold and congealed dinner remnants from plastic containers, food they would pick at as they nattered away the hours. She wondered if they still did that . . .

Gnocchi . . . Gnocchi . . . Again she practised, locking it in for the next time she wanted to order it.

Her phone buzzed.

It was a Facetime call from Nico. She was more than a little taken aback. It felt unusual, to say the least. A text, sure. A call, maybe. But a visual? She sat up straight and adjusted the collar of her shirt and fixed her hair before accepting the call.

He beamed. 'Hi!'

'Hi.' She smiled back, deciding to let him do the running.

'I liked our lunch.' He cut straight to it, as if this were a prearranged thing, a usual thing, which did instantly normalise it.

'Me too, actually.'

'Actually? That makes it sound like you expected the worst!'

'I did,' she lied.

'Well, I thought the décor was good, company first class but the food was a bit stingy. I mean, it tasted good, yes, but wasn't one of those meals that can see you through to bedtime.'

'That's very interesting, but I have to ask, did you mean to be writing this in a review instead of telling it to me?'

'No, I wanted to tell you because I figured if I was hungry, you might be hungry.'

As if on cue her stomach gave a delicate rumble.

'I could eat.' The mention of food turned her attention back to her fridge, wondering not only what she might have inside it, but now focused on the scratch on the front.

'Do you like sushi?' he asked.

'I love sushi. Why?' She wondered which restaurant he was about to recommend, knowing she'd say yes, and simultaneously thinking about what she could shove on that might be suitable for a future sushi date.

It was then he lifted a tray into view with his one free hand – a large, covered tray showing an artful display of sushi.

'Well, lucky old you!'

'Lucky old *us*, actually. I'm outside your apartment.'

'What?' She jumped up from the sofa and walked to the wide Crittall bifold doors that led out to a small terrace that ran the width of the building. Levering the handle, she walked outside and looked down. There he was, standing by the sycamore tree with his phone in one hand and the sushi in the other.

'I don't know how I feel about this.' She liked him, of that there was no doubt, but this felt fast – too fast. If they leapfrogged to a sleepover, then what? The open conversation about life that for her was about as comfortable as the thought of ripping off a Band-Aid? She hated the complexity of what should have been a simple get-together for sushi. It was always this way, the unsettling feeling when her worlds threatened to collide.

'Okay, I could always go get pizza or kebabs.' He pointed up the street.

'No, Nico, not your supper choice.'

'Phew,' he interrupted.

'I don't know how I feel about you turning up at my home. It's . . . it's a lot.'

'It is a lot. I am fully aware. And please don't ask me how I got your address.'

'How did you get my address?'

'From my mother.'

'I see. And do you do this often? Pitching up at people's homes after a handful of texts and one lunch?'

'Nope, I've never done it before, but here's the thing.' He paused, took a breath. 'I can't stop thinking about you. Not since I first saw you in that meeting ten days ago. And I didn't want our lunch to end today, and I've not been able to concentrate all afternoon, replaying in my head our conversation, the way you tuck your hair behind your ears, your gentle laugh, your shyness.'

'I'm not shy.'

'I think you are a bit. And I know you are heading off to LA in a couple of weeks, and rather than see that as an ending, I've decided not to waste what little time we have. This is after all the foundation-building stage and will determine what happens when you're away. Don't you think?'

'I don't know what to think right now!' This was an understatement. While she had to admit to being hugely flattered and also a little moved, was this really happening? This level of vulnerability was not what she was used to. It was as scary as it was thrilling.

'I guess the point is, I didn't want to have to wait until next week or when you had a suitable window in your calendar. I wanted to see you right now, and so I jumped in a cab and bought sushi. Actually, technically, I bought sushi then jumped in a cab, but that's just semantics.'

'I . . .' She couldn't decide if this was a wonderful act, his spontaneity, his openness, or whether he was seven kinds of crazy.

'Madeleine, don't worry.' His tone softened. 'I'm not going to come up to your apartment. I just wanted to bring you sushi and I wanted to see you, to look you in the eye and see if I can figure out why are you living in my thoughts right now. Day and night.'

'Okay.' She stepped back from the wrought iron balustrade. 'I'll come get my sushi.'

Grabbing her keys from the countertop, she trod the wide sweep of the staircase and opened the heavy front door. Nico leaned on the frame, sushi in hand.

'Hi.' He looked good, fresh from a shower, and again, he smelled so good! Her gut rolled with joy at the sight of him. 'Sushi delivery.' He handed her the box and took a step backwards.

'That's a lot of sushi.' She eyed the rows of glossy salmon strips, and delicate splayed prawns all resting on the plump, sticky rice of the nigiri. Just the sight of the sesame-edged California rolls, their centres stuffed with pale shredded crab and chunks of avocado, made her mouth water. Best of all were the little pots of fresh ginger, wasabi, and dark soy, which she would smother each morsel in.

'It is a lot of sushi,' he agreed.

'Too much for one person?' she suggested.

'I'm not so sure. I saw how you put that gnocchi away over lunch. I reckon if I hadn't been quick, you might have made a dash for mine too.'

'That's possibly true, and I definitely would have had pudding if you hadn't been there,' she confessed.

'Oh my God!' he laughed. 'Me too!'

'The tiramisu.'

'The tiramisu!'

They spoke in unison and were then quiet for a beat, a moment for her to make a decision, one she hoped she wouldn't regret.

'You wanna come share this with me?' She raised the platter in her hand.

'Only if you're sure.' He kept his gaze down, his tone soft, and far from her initial fear at having to entertain this relative stranger in her apartment, she felt warmed by the prospect of sharing supper with him, and maybe a glass or two of something chilled.

'You can either come up . . .' She stood back against the wall, allowing enough space for him to pass. 'Or I could go upstairs, put half of it on a plate and lower the rest of the platter down on a rope or in a basket. I'd work it out. A pulley system or something.'

'Sounds messy. Probably easier if I just come up.'

'Probably.'

He walked up the stairs behind her and she inhaled his fabulous scent.

'You have to take me as you find me.' She looked over her shoulder as he stood in the grand open-plan space of her home and stared up into the bone-coloured rafters of the double-height ceiling.

'It's immaculate!' He threw his arms up in the air.

'Mmmn.' She chose not to point out the irritating paint mix-up or the infuriating scratch on her prized fridge. 'I'm glad you think so. I'm a bit of a perfectionist when it comes to my living space.'

'I can see that.' He looked around as she placed the tray of sushi on the table.

Having collected the chilled bottle of dry white from the wine fridge and two glasses, she joined him on the sofa and poured two generous measures. Nico took one.

'I too have my peculiarities, things I need in place so that I can feel comfortable, and things that make my brain itch.'

'Like?' She was curious.

'Like I can't bear anyone touching my feet and the thought of touching someone else's feet is just . . .' He stuck out his tongue and shuddered.

'Okay, so no feet, got it. And don't worry, I've got so many quirks, oddities, habits, superstitions, that if I actually listed them, you'd be out of that door quicker than you could shout, "Taxi for Yannis!"'

'Okay, now I'm suitably terrified.'

'You should be!' She sipped the crisp white that was doing much to lubricate her nerves and her tongue.

'Try me.'

He turned and rested his arm along the back cushions, propping his handsome head on his palm. He looked very relaxed and at home. She was relieved that his presence felt comforting rather than invasive.

'Come on, Miss Woods, tell me one thing that you consider a . . . a quirk, and let me judge.'

'Yes, of course, because that's comfortable, telling you my strange habits so you can hold them up for scrutiny!' She rolled her eyes and he laughed.

'I'm serious! I find things are often far worse in your head or when you don't share them. It's possible that your oddities are in fact entirely normal – or more common than you might think – but you'll only know that if you share them.'

'You sound like my therapist.'

'You have a therapist?'

'I do. I literally have her on speed dial and see her when the need arises.' She held his eye, noting the slight flicker of his gaze. What was that? Concern? Approval?

'Does the need arise a lot?'

'It varies, but a couple of times a week, sometimes more, often less.' She figured he might as well know it all, as she'd taken the lid off that particular box.

'I too have a therapist. And I also have her on speed dial. You see, that's one thing shared that we have now normalised.'

She sank back on the sofa, feeling the tension over the great Chantilly debacle slip almost entirely from her mind.

'Okay.' She swallowed and waved her hand in a circle over her head. This was part of her lie, telling him something small, something palatable, almost comical, while the big things stayed firmly shut away. Testing him almost; testing herself. 'As you can see, I am rather fond of a neutral palette when it comes to décor. I like order. I like clean lines, dust-free corners, no clutter, nothing that isn't functional or beautiful.'

'I can see, and it's very chic. But I would expect no less from someone with your eye.'

She smiled at the compliment from this man who knew a luxury interior when he saw it, doubting that he'd ever lived with anything else. An image of the peach woodchip wallpaper of her childhood room flashed in her mind.

'There's a bit more to it than just wanting it to look good.' She took a sip. 'It's more about anything that jars with my motif.' She struggled to find the words. Her mouth moved but it was a while until the sound followed. 'I can't stand it! I mean, like, literally. I couldn't sleep if someone, for example, bought me a garish bouquet. You know the ones – harsh oranges or even things dyed blue or bright pinks or a mishmash of all three.' She wrinkled her nose in distaste. 'To have that on my soft wood table against the pale wall would make it hard for me to sleep.'

'Really?'

'Yes, really.' She took her time, feeling oddly comfortable in opening up to this man, wanting to build a bridge, to get closer to him. 'And that's not the worst of it.'

'Do go on!' He finished his glass and placed it on the table, staring at her, as if fascinated and amused in equal measure.

Instinctively, she covered her face with her free hand and spoke through the gaps in her fingers. 'I can't say it out loud! It's quite a big thing, actually.' There was a fleeting moment when she practised the words in her head, as her heart raced, feeling at once overwhelmed and excited by the prospect of being transparent with him.

It's rare for me to talk about it. Not something I ordinarily mention and certainly not this early on in proceedings, but here's the thing . . . And just like that, she snapped back to reality, far too soon to be an open book.

'Oh, come on! There's no way you can leave that there! Come on, spill the beans!'

He broke her thoughts, as he pulled her palm from her face and laced his fingers with hers, letting their hands rest, joined on the sofa between them. She could feel his pulse against her skin, and her heart beat quickly. It was a delicious moment of contact that held promise and, not wanting to spoil it, Madeleine smiled at his beautiful face and chose another story altogether.

'All right, then. I was seeing this guy – we'd had a couple of dates,' she qualified, 'but he was nice. Things were on track and it was good.'

'Nice?' he scoffed. 'That's got to be the most insipid compliment a person can get. Please don't ever describe me as nice.'

'What would you prefer?' she laughed.

'I'd prefer "spectacular", as in, "He is absolutely spectacular!" But I digress. Then what happened?'

'I invited him over.'

'Did he sit here, right here where I'm now sitting? Do you do this a lot? Invite men over? You're not making me feel very special!' he smarted.

'Technically, I didn't invite you over, and, yes – yes, he did, he sat right there. The problem was, he turned up in a Fair Isle sweater. Not a crime in itself, I grant you, but it was like a loud Fair Isle sweater. The yoke was orange and yellow and the background green. It might have looked cute on a hanger, but he sat there and it was such a clash with my décor . . .' There, she'd said it.

'Oh my God! Are you telling me that you ditched a guy because his sweater didn't go with the colour scheme of your lounge?'

'Well, that sounds harsh, but . . .'

'But yes! You did! I honestly don't know what to say! You're a monster!' He released her hand and grabbed a cushion to his chest. 'Thank goodness I went for white shirt and jeans. I mean, are the jeans okay? Not too blue?'

'You said you wouldn't judge me!'

'No, I said I *would* judge you! And frankly I find you to be a shocking horror of a human being!' He grabbed his phone and shouted into it, 'Taxi for Yannis, please – immediately, like immediately! Right now!'

They roared their laughter. What happened next was swift, comfortable, and felt like the most natural thing in the world as he pulled her into his arms and kissed her softly. With her wine glass hastily deposited on the tabletop next to his, they slipped down on to the deep pile of the rug, and with the lighting low, they forgot all about the sushi and shed their clothes.

As the night crept towards dawn and with the neutral-shaded raffia cushions as pillows, they took pleasure from each other before falling into a deep and satisfied slumber.

It was rare for her to sleep in this way, deeply, and without a care in the world . . .

December

EIGHT YEARS BEFORE

9.00 A.M.

'Madeleine Woods?' the doctor called from the open door of the consulting room. Madeleine identified her by the stethoscope hanging like a shiny success symbol around her neck. She bet the woman wore it everywhere – the supermarket, swimming pool . . .

'Yes, hi.'

She grabbed her bag and walked in, glad to be progressing from the crowded waiting room, where she was sure she could almost see the germs and bugs swirling in the stuffy, overly warm air. Happy, finally, to be away from the motley snivel-nosed crew who occupied the chairs placed uncomfortably close to each other around the walls of the square room.

'Sorry for the wait. I'm Doctor Khan. What can I do for you today?' Dr Khan indicated for her to sit while asking the question and taking her own seat at the desk, in what was clearly a well-rehearsed routine. The only clue to the hectic pace of proceedings was her rather hurried tone.

'I'm not feeling great. I have stomach pain and I feel sick and just a bit . . . bleurgh!' She shrugged.

'Okay.' The doctor gave a condescending smile, clearly underwhelmed by her description. 'And apart from today, I can see you're usually fit and healthy.' The doctor scanned the questionnaire she had filled out on arrival.

'Yep. I'm never ill, never taken a day sick from work.'

'Could you describe your stomach pain? Is it sharp, or gripping, or an ache?'

'Erm . . .' Now it wasn't quite so acute it was hard to put into words. 'All of the above, I guess . . .'

'Right, I think it best you pop up on the couch and let me have a look at your tum, is that okay?'

'Sure.'

'Just ease your jeans down over your hips and pull up your top.'

The doctor tapped into her keyboard and, with precision timing, turned as Madeleine assumed the position and lay on the narrow couch lined with paper, her jeans pulled down and her top up. Her neon-pink knickers made quite the statement. The doctor however didn't seem to notice and laid her hand on the base of her stomach, pushing slightly.

'Does that hurt?'

'Not really. A bit, maybe.'

'When was the date of your last menstrual cycle?' The doctor studied her face.

'Not sure.' She tried to picture when she'd last bought tampons. 'I'm on the pill and so it's never heavy, and I don't always have a proper period, but . . .' She tried and failed to recall when she had last bled.

'Is there any chance you could be pregnant?' the doctor asked softly.

Madeleine sprayed her laughter into the atmosphere and felt instantly embarrassed.

'Erm, no, absolutely none. I'm not in a relationship and haven't, you know, seen anyone for a while. Not for five or six months, maybe a bit longer.'

She tried to do the math, already logging the detail in her mind for retelling to her flatmates later – this would make them howl! Her having to admit that she was experiencing a sexual drought while in her prime – oh, the shame of it! The simple truth was that she was too focused on working her jobs and too exhausted of late to put herself out there. Falling into bed alone was, in recent times, her preferred option. Jimmy was the last person she had slept with. Sweet, good-looking Jimmy, who had drawn her a picture of a cottage with a sodding duck pond on it!

'I think it might be worth doing a pregnancy test, just to make sure. Won't take a minute, you just pee into—'

'Yes, I know what to do, but there's really no point.'

'As I say, just to make sure.' Dr Khan's voice was clipped.

It would be hard, she figured, to find a woman of her age who had not partaken in this ritual. There had been a moment a couple of years back when she and Quentin the dentist had spent a drunken weekend at his brother's wedding, only for her to remember that she'd forgotten to take her pill. The sweet, sweet relief at the sight of the 'not pregnant' message was a gift. Thinking about it now, it might have played as much a part in her decision to bin him as the feeling that he was a right Tom Pepper.

'Right, hop off the couch, the bathroom is next door. If you could pee into this cup.' The doctor tapped the small plastic tub no bigger than a shallow shot glass and left it on the table.

'I will, but I mean, I'm not pregnant. There's no way I can be, so—'

61

'Let's just exclude it then as a possibility, and we can have a think about what comes next.' The woman avoided making eye contact and Madeleine wondered why she had bothered coming here in the first place. It was a complete waste of time. What she had hoped for was a quick diagnosis, a prescription to ease her tum, and – hey presto – back to work!

She opened the door of the exam room to the expectant eyes of everyone in the waiting room, feeling her face turn puce as she made her way into the small bathroom with her pee cup in her hand. The collective sigh of disappointment that she was not freeing up the doctor for her next appointment was almost audible.

'This is a joke!' She closed her eyes and tutted as she did her best to manoeuvre the impossibly tiny cup under her stream of pee. She half-filled it and soaked the cuff of her sweater in the process. 'Perfect!' She ground her teeth.

Doing her best to ignore the eyes that now followed her from the bathroom back to the consulting room, she held her cup of pee aloft and marched in.

'Pop it on the table, please.' The doctor indicated and donned plastic gloves before removing a strip of some sort from its protective foil wrapping and popping it into Madeleine's hastily collected, still-warm pee.

'I don't think it's food poisoning. I mean, it could be – our kitchen's a bit grim. But yesterday I only had a tuna sandwich and a banana at work, then toast and Marmite when I got in, and three oranges which I thought might be going off. But when I woke up, I also felt as if I'd hit a wall – like really tired, too tired to stand up and get cracking, which is not like me at all, and—'

'Madeleine,' the doctor interrupted her nervous babble and sat in her chair, leaning forward. Joining her hands on the desk in front of her, she took her time, as if knowing that what she had to say would need to percolate. 'Your pregnancy test has come back positive.'

'Positive?'

There was a split second where she couldn't remember if positive was a good thing or not. Did that mean she was pregnant or not? Not that she could be, it just wasn't possible. It was as if her mind skipped a beat and, as the room spun, she knew that if she weren't sitting down, she might well have fallen over.

Positive?

Positive!

'That's . . . no, erm.' She felt a little winded. 'That's not possible.' It was embarrassing how this so-called professional could have got it so wrong. She gave the doctor a wide-eyed smile, showing she was friendly and wasn't about to kick off when the obvious error was revealed.

'I know that sometimes this news is surprising, a shock, and it will take you a while to wrap your head around the situation before you can figure out what comes next.'

'Mwhae . . .' She tried to respond, but what left her mouth was more of a garbled groan than tangible words.

'Do you have support, Madeleine?'

She pictured her mum and dad going about their day. Her mum, so pleased to have heard from her earlier. And Trina, her best friend, who she hadn't seen for a few weeks. In that moment she missed her more than anything, this wrapped in the guilt she felt over sleeping with Jimmy, swiftly followed by a wave of regret.

She nodded. 'Yes.'

'That's good, it makes processing this news easier when you have a support network.'

'I need to go to work. Umm . . .' Her thoughts were jumbled and she was finding it hard to take a full breath. 'Are you *sure*?'

'Yes.' Dr Khan's tone was unwavering, her gaze steady. 'I think, given the length of time since you had sexual relations and the uncertainty about your last cycle dates, it would be a good idea for you to have a scan.'

'Right.' She suppressed the desire to laugh, waiting for someone to jump out of the cupboard and tell her she'd been pranked real good!

'I can organise that right now. What would be your local hospital?'

Instantly, she pictured her childhood bedroom and felt a longing to be right there, under the duvet, with her dad whistling in the bathroom as he shaved his face before bed, and her mum's laughter floating along the hallway from the lounge while she watched her quiz shows and the re-runs of *Friends* that she so loved.

'Newham would be my local hospital.'

'Righto, let me get a message to them and I'll give you a slip of paper to take along and then you just turn up at the pregnancy clinic and they'll direct you where to go for an ultrasound.'

Pregnancy clinic! It was so bizarre. Again she wanted to giggle. 'Right now?'

'Yes, if you just make your way there.' The doctor's tight-lipped smile suggested it was a matter of urgency. 'They'll be able to tell you how far along you are, how things are progressing, that kind of thing.' The doctor coughed.

What kind of thing? she wondered, as she walked from the surgery with the slip of paper in her pocket and headed for the Tube. She texted her manager, a picky woman called 'Suzy with a Y!' When Madeleine had done this very impersonation to Luciano, he'd replied, 'Yuzy? That's odd!'

She laughed now at the memory as she walked along the street, head down, doing her best to avoid the morning crowds all trying to get somewhere, and all, it seemed, heading in the opposite

64

direction to her. Her laughter unexpectedly turned to tears as she trembled with fear.

It felt surreal. Her world was unravelling and yet it felt like a dream. Her legs felt oddly detached from her body. Staring at her feet, she did her best to concentrate on her steps, knowing this was key to staying upright, not thinking too hard or letting her worries run ahead.

'I don't know what's happening.' She whispered under her breath. It felt as if the world turned quickly while she had slowed. It was odd and unnerving. She did her best to keep her pulse steady and not pay attention to the bombs that exploded left, right and centre in her thoughts, blowing up her plans, shattering her dreams, and knocking her life so far off course she felt entirely winded by it.

Chapter Four

Present Day

Madeleine couldn't remember the last time she'd eaten breakfast in her apartment with a man. Her usual MO was to usher her gentleman guests, who were few and far between, out the door in the early hours, allowing her to sleep in her bed like a starfish and without the embarrassment of the post-date-post-wine-comedown regret that often felt inevitable. There was, she felt, nothing worse than having to make awkward small talk with one eye on the clock, wishing someone would leave. This felt different, however. Entirely different. She liked it, watching him navigate the unfamiliar kitchen and managing to make her a decent espresso, and then toast, drizzled with honey from Fortnum's.

'I'm liking this.' Nico appeared to mirror her thoughts. 'I mean, we're still early days, but so far so good. Reckon I could make an equally good breakfast in LA. In fact, better! I think I'm more efficient in the sunshine. I'm certainly happier in the sunshine.'

She gave him a double thumbs-up and he laughed. It felt good to have a shared thing, a sign, building a history. And this wasn't the first time he'd mentioned LA. Maybe he *could* visit.

'I think this is the good bit, don't you? Getting to know each other, and I don't mean the big stuff, the obvious things, but the small details.' He bit his toast. 'That's what I find most interesting. Tiny building blocks.'

It was something of a revelation to her. Ordinarily, the merest suggestion of a man wanting to get close to her and she'd head for the hills with her scent still lingering on his collar. Wary, always wary, of letting anyone get close to her. With Nico, however, she couldn't quite put it into words, but the thought didn't horrify her, not at all. Or maybe it was because she was safe in the knowledge that in two short weeks she'd be leaving on a jet plane, and so what was the harm at playing grown-ups for a while . . .

'Small details like?' She was curious as to what detail he was chasing.

'Like . . . I don't know.' He threw his hands in the air, before wiping crumbs with the back of his hand from his mouth. 'Did you have a pet? Who was your first crush, your favourite childhood biscuits or snacks, star sign, what scared you?'

'No pets. My first proper crush was probably Zayn from One Direction, who, incidentally, I would still run away with if he were to knock on my door.'

'Noted.' He gave a single nod.

'And my favourite biscuits were – indeed, are – Malted Milk.' She interrupted herself and grinned. 'Hands down, no question: Malted Milk. And I don't follow star signs, I think it's total bunkum.'

'Ah, that cynicism – classic Scorpio trait.' They both laughed. 'And as for Malted Milks, I've never heard of them.'

'You've never *heard* of Malted Milks? You've never *eaten* a Malted Milk? Where have you been?' she squealed.

'Mainly in the Sporades – where we ate home-made baklava and not Malty Milks or whatever!'

'They have cows on them!' she enthused. 'So it wasn't just that they were moreish and fabulous, but they had little cows on them. *Cows!* I thought they were things of wonder! I still do.'

'You still eat these cookies?'

'Oh no, my friend, they're not *cookies*.' This she felt was a vital point of difference, her tone deadly serious. 'Cookies for me are something big and squidgy with lumps. These are biscuits. They snap, they're thin. I haven't had one for years, but I swear if there was a packet here, I'd go through the lot, right now!'

'I knew you were a biscuit snaffler!'

'There's no shame in that.' She sipped her coffee.

'And what scared you?'

'Erm . . .'

They fell silent. The comfortable kind of quiet where neither felt the need to fill the spaces in conversation with idle noise to mask unease. The comfortable kind of quiet that usually took time to perfect. It gave her time to think.

'I was scared by the thought that things might be as good as it was ever going to get. That I might be stuck in that life for ever. Scared that I might never do all the things I dreamed of or go to the places I wanted to and that my life would be . . . small.'

'Your life seems anything but small.' He spoke softly.

'I kind of mentioned to you before, I grew up quite poor.' Saying it out loud was at once cathartic and terrifying. The timing was a surprise to her, justified with the one simple thought that it felt right. Like ripping off a Band-Aid to reveal something unpleasant and festering beneath. He didn't respond but stilled, coffee in hand, as if sensing that she had more to say. 'Poor, but full of love and warmth from my parents.' It always felt important to add this, to dispel the myth that 'poor' might mean 'abusive' or 'traumatic' or 'desperate'. It was none of those things. A little smothering from Marnie, sure, but Madeleine was pretty certain this would have been her mother's parenting style whatever their bank balance. 'And so a packet of biscuits was the best thing. A treat.'

'Are you close to your parents?'

'Am I close to them?' She thought about how best to answer. How to respond to that simple question that was anything but simple. 'I love them both very much. I don't know if "close" is how I'd describe our relationship now. We lead very different lives and sometimes I've got my head down and I'm crazy busy and I suddenly realise I haven't spoken to them for a couple of weeks. Then I feel guilty and so I call them and it's a little tense, like we're all pretending everything is fine but actually they're pissed that I haven't called, and I'm pissed that they're making me feel that way when all I've been doing is working, and so it's complicated. More than complicated.'

'It always is with parents.'

'Yours too?' It felt nice, sharing in this way – another thing in common, another shared secret.

He gave a wry laugh and wiped his mouth. 'My mum is, erm, quite a character, and my dad is so laid back.'

'They say opposites attract.' She threw in the mollifier.

'They do, and it's true most of the time for them. When they're in sync it's wonderful, attractive, and fun, but there's been the odd occasion when they clash more than attract, and then it's like thunderbolts! An explosion! The icy tail wind after such a bust-up can blow for weeks. And since I was a kid, I've often found myself caught in the middle, reeling from the fallout. When it's like that, I can't please either of them. I think they'd like me to pick a side, even now, and because I don't . . .' He pulled a face and looked downwards.

'Families, eh?'

'Yep, families.' He sounded resigned. 'It makes me think about the kind of parent I want to be.'

She felt her heart race; was this it? The 'children' conversation already? Where to begin . . . It was a topic she shied away from at all costs.

'I mean, not that I'm thinking of that in any meaningful way or planning for it or anything remotely like it.' Madeleine thought he pressed in a way that suggested he might protesteth just a tad too much. 'But I'm aware of how I think you should parent. So I guess I'll pick the bits of how I was parented that worked and try my best to avoid the things that didn't.'

'Isn't that what we all think?' She blinked, not enjoying the topic at all, feeling her face blush.

'I guess.'

'I think you're a nice person, Nico. A good man.'

'Did you just call me nice?' He screwed his eyes shut.

'I meant to say, spectacular! You are a spectacular person!'

'That's better.' He opened his eyes. 'I try really hard to be a decent human. I'm aware that most people expect me to be an arsehole. I mean, how can I not be, growing up with all that dosh?'

'I mean, yes, I get that! You do give off powerful arsehole vibes.'

He ruffled her hair, teasingly, playfully, and she liked it.

'I'd give it all up you know.' His tone was sincere.

'You'd give what up?'

'The . . . the money, the job, the cars, all of it. I'd give it all up to be with that one person who made my whole day feel better. The One. Happiness.'

'Nico, you old romantic!' This too was a state of affairs that would ordinarily make her cringe, but not with Nico, not with him. The idea that she might be falling for him was a terrifying one. She might have little control over the way her heart jolted at the sight of him, but as for being ready for romance, she was pretty sure she was not. She had a new life in LA to get to, a job to do, and needed to remain focused.

'It's the truth. I would.' There was another moment of quiet before he asked, 'Wouldn't you?'

She looked into the middle distance. 'I don't think it's that straightforward. I know what it's like to want more. I know what it's like to live a life hemmed in by barriers that keep your horizon from view. To wake each day handcuffed by restraints only you can see and feel. It doesn't feel good. It feels like you're suffocating and silently screaming with a burning rage in the base of your gut and no idea how to calm it. It wasn't easy.'

'So, you're saying shacking up in a tent for love wouldn't cut it for you?'

His question was so close to the bone it pained her.

'Tent? When did a tent creep into the equation?' She deflected his comment with humour. 'And, actually, if you threw in my biscuits, I'd consider it.'

'Malted Milks.' He let go of her hand.

'Them's the ones!'

The way he stood and now busied himself at the sink suggested that he might not be satisfied with her response, embarrassed almost that she had not matched his declarations. Not that there was much she could do about it now, glad the moment had passed and the pressure felt lifted.

'Right, I'd better get going.' She necked the remainder of her coffee.

'Me too.' He turned to face her, drying his hands on her dish towel. 'This is good, isn't it?'

They shared a lingering look that was as meaningful as the words they exchanged. She felt the intensity of his question, asking if they were on the same track. It felt easy then, as she stared at his beautiful face.

'It is, Nico. It's really good.'

◆ ◆ ◆

She hummed as she walked to the Tube, smiled as she sauntered into the office, and felt like a giddy schoolgirl as she received a thumbs-up from Nico, just before her morning meeting.

'The floor is yours, Nathaniel.' Madeleine gestured to the top of the large table and the space on the carpet in front of the drop screen.

'Th-thank you.' The man stood and pushed his glasses up on to the bridge of his nose from where they'd slipped. 'I . . . I don't have a presentation as such, but just wanted to talk through a few ideas that . . . that I've been mulling over.'

'Great!' She clapped and nodded knowingly at Tan, her colleague, who she knew would be cringing in anticipation as much as her right now. Nathaniel had an 'alternative' view on most things – great as a sounding board for ethics and green issues, but in terms of practicality and delivering client satisfaction, his suggestions were usually unworkable. She admired his tenacity, the way he never went off script, and knew his passion was genuine, but that didn't make sessions like this easier when time was tight and he was, no doubt, about to deliver one of his championing speeches. Not that she was going to intervene. With only a few weeks left in this office and wanting to leave the project in the best possible shape before she shipped off to LA, it was all about ironing out the wrinkles.

'I just feel . . .'

She glanced again at Tan, knowing he was aware that she was not a fan of feelings in the boardroom. Or feelings in general, truth be told, yet still feeling the warm flush of happiness at the way her day had started.

'That we could be doing things a little differently, a little better.'

'Okay, so let's be specific. What things? And differently how?' she urged, keen to rush him to the point.

'The . . . the Stern project.'

'Yes.'

'I don't think it's future proof.'

'Future proof how?' She sat forward, as did at least three of her three colleagues.

'The . . . the . . .' Again he pushed his specs up on his greasy nose, his top lip peppered with sweat. 'Well . . .' He took a slow breath and she tapped her pen on her leather-bound jotter. 'The generator that's been selected is good for now – great for now – but . . . but with the expansion required over the next decade, the next phase of the build – based on the projected figures from Stern – the generator will need replacing within three years to cope with the demand, and that's an extra million or so right now, and who knows what it might be then.'

Tan, she noticed now, stared at Nathaniel, his cheeks a little flushed.

'That feels like an oversight. But I'm sure the client can swallow a million.' She paused, knowing it was something she would, none-theless, have to raise with the developer, with whom they worked closely. All involved kept a keen eye on the financials. 'Anything else?'

'Yes.' He took a breath and seemed to grow in stature and confidence now he had her attention. 'The jetty next to the landing space for river access, also great for the next two to three years – the first phase previously mentioned. But with the estimated resident numbers, river traffic, and commuters too, it'll get a lot more wear and tear and could need replacing or repairs, and that's costly, and—'

'Nathaniel.' She waited for him to make eye contact. 'It sounds like you have a few other suggestions – ideas that might mean the cost of build, choice of services, hardware, and construction might be a little off?' All aspects that had a direct impact on their part of the project.

He shook his head as he spoke. 'A *little* off, yes.'

'What's the difference, between the bottom line given to Stern and the areas of concern that you have picked up on?'

'Potential areas of concern,' Tan clarified, and his defensiveness bothered her.

She ignored him. 'What's the figure, Nathaniel?'

'I can't give a specific fig—'

'Ballpark.' She cut him short. 'What's the ballpark figure?'

'The difference?' It was his turn to clarify.

'The difference.' She felt her leg jump under the table; she was as impatient as ever.

'About forty million.'

There was the audible gasp of breath around the table and she locked Nathaniel in a gaze.

'That's quite a gap.' She smiled, knowing it was a mouth smile that didn't reach her eyes, designed to intimidate.

'Maybe fifty. In fact, definitely fifty.'

'I see.' She tapped her fountain pen on to the jotter – on it the scrawled reminders for her ever-growing to-do list.

'I'd be more than happy to take you through it in more detail.'

'Yes, speak to Nadia and arrange some time over the next couple of days.'

'I will.' Nathaniel beamed like he'd won something, and Tan, she noticed, picked up a pen and buried his face in note writing.

She did her best to hide her concern. This was the last thing she needed – the proverbial spanner in the works at the eleventh hour. It would hurt both her pride and her professionalism to leave the agency with her flawless reputation dented by such an oversight. The thought of handing the project over to Aarushi, her successor, with issues to be dealt with, was more than she could handle. And the clock was ticking.

The boardroom door opened.

'Madeleine?' It was an unexpected and unprofessional interruption. These meetings were sacrosanct. Dorian, Allan Goodwin's PA, poked her head into the boardroom. Allan was on the board of directors and was currently in Portugal playing golf.

'Yes?' She turned.

'So sorry, but there's a call waiting for you. Nadia is at lunch and it came through to me.'

'Oh, right, could you take a message and number and I'll give them a shout in a mo.' *Basics . . . Dorian . . . basics . . .*

The woman gave a slight shake of her head. 'No, erm, I mean, I could of course, but it's . . . It's your father on the phone.'

'My . . . ?' She swallowed, wondering if she'd misheard.

'Your father. He says he needs to speak to you.'

Aware of all eyes now on her, and equally how unusual it was for the smallest detail about her private life to be revealed, she stood on shaking legs and tucked her hair behind her ears, standing straight, doing her best to keep her composure while her heart thundered.

'Do excuse me, everyone.'

There was a muttered chorus of, 'Of course!'

'Tan, if you could handle AOB and any housekeeping. Nathaniel, I look forward to catching up. Thanks, everyone.' Gathering her laptop, jotter, water bottle and belongings, she followed Dorian from the room.

'Will you take it in your office, Madeleine?' The woman looked both nervous and on high alert.

'Please.' She nodded and took her place in the leather chair behind her immaculate desk, where two carefully placed onyx lamps gave just the right amount of light to allow the modern workspace to feel cosy.

She stared at the phone, waiting for the winking transfer light, her cue to pick up.

It felt like an age for the call to come through and she was torn – feeling intense waves of frustration at Dorian's lack of speed, yet also glad of the chance to breathe, to prepare. It had to be something bad, something that couldn't wait – why else would he be calling at work? Her heart skipped and she swallowed, as her composure briefly slipped. It was rare for her two worlds to collide. Without time for further analysis, the small light flashed and, trying to control the tremor to her hand, she lifted the receiver.

'This is Madeleine.'

She regretted the line the moment she said it. It was automatic, yet no less officious, and there was no need for that, knowing that would be viewed as antagonistic, especially when this might be the most difficult of conversations – it was not well thought out. This wasn't a client or a colleague, this was her dad, her daddy . . .

'This is your dad.'

He mimicked with a softness and humour that was not only familiar and comforting but was also the biggest relief. She was confident that had the very worst thing happened to her mum or anyone else at home, he wouldn't start like this – there would be more urgency, more . . . panic. Of that she was sure.

'Hey, Dad.' Holding the phone close to her face, she closed her eyes, knowing they were connected, that hearing his voice was enough to cause a small ball of emotion to settle at the base of her throat. It happened like this. It was true what they said – out of sight, out of mind . . . She was a master. But to hear his voice, to listen now to him breathing, was like opening a heavy door behind which she kept a tsunami of feelings at bay.

'Sorry to call you at work.'

'That's fine, really.'

'It's just that Mum's got your mobile number on her phone and you know I don't like the bloody things.'

She smiled to hear he was still railing against mobile phones, as he did with all manner of technology, seeing it as an infringement on his peace rather than an asset to his life.

'I do know that.' She paused, not wanting him to feel rushed, but keen to discover the reason for the call. 'Is everything okay, Dad?'

'Not . . . not really, love.' The quaver to his voice was alarming and she felt her own breath stutter in her throat.

'What's happened?'

'It's . . . it's your mum.'

'Is she . . .' Her voice was thin and the words disappeared on her tongue.

'She's in Newham General.'

'Oh no! Dad! What's happened?' she repeated, wanting him to get to the point.

Her mother, as the family saying went, was as strong as an ox and with a hide that was just as thick. For her to be hospitalised, was, she knew, not without good reason.

'It's, erm . . .' He took a slow breath. The anticipation was killing her! 'It's her heart. They said she had a heart attack.'

'Oh, Christ.' She sat back hard, sinking into the chair, her hand over her eyes.

'Yep, bit of a shocker. She was heading to work on the bus. She was with Trina – it was her who got hold of me. Her neighbour's a security guard up the market and so she called him and he came and found me as I was unloading. I'm all over the place, I can tell you.'

'I bet.' She could hear his distress, the underlying warble to his tone. 'Where are you now, Dad?'

'At home. I went to the hospital, but they said best to let her sleep or whatnot, and I'm going back in after lunch.'

'Is she going to be okay? What did they say?' She spoke gently, coaxing, as if he were the child.

There was the tiniest pause that suggested it was hard for him to consider.

'They seem to think so. Lucky, really, that she was with Trina. And I'm winding down Fridays, only got a couple left. I've given up my Friday pitch, but I'll do Sundays instead, I take more on a Sunday . . .'

A wave of sadness swept over her. Sunday, their day of rest, about to be conceded in the face of financial need. Madeleine decided to speak to her mum again about using the money she sent each month. Bookending the sadness was an unpalatable tang of envy at the fact that Trina Watkin had been with her mother, spending time with her mother, and was right there when her mother needed help. Trina, who Madeleine rarely saw and when she did it was not by design. It was misplaced jealousy that she was aware she should swap for gratitude. Madeleine knew she had no right to consider or even hanker after a life that she had discarded. She knew that no one could have it all.

'Did . . . did they say why she'd had a heart attack or anything?' Just what she was hoping to hear she was unsure, but it felt like the right thing to say.

'Not yet, love. They're doing tests, but she's in the best hands. The NHS is marvellous, always said so.' Again that wobble to his voice, the sniff of his distress. It tore at her breast.

'Do you need me to come over right now? I can. I can be there in under an hour.' Mentally she visualised her calendar, figuring out how she could rejuggle her day.

'No, no, not at all. She's asleep. I'm just going to have me sandwich and then head back over to see her.'

'I'll go to the hospital, then. I'll come after I've tied up a few loose ends here. When's visiting time?'

'You have to leave by eight at night, but I think you can pitch up when you want on her ward. I think that's what they said.'

'Right, don't worry, I'll check, Dad. Do . . . do you guys need anything?' She swallowed. What was she asking? The details of arrangements that really were nothing to do with her, the well-oiled logistics of a life lived in harmony. The mechanics of a routine that functioned perfectly well without her.

'No, love. We're fine. Might see you later, or we might go in tomorrow if you're there tonight. Don't want to overload her. But I do want to see her. I'm worried sick, love.'

'Of course you are.' She swallowed, dreading and looking forward to the visit in equal measure. 'But it'll all be okay, Dad. As you say, she's in the very best hands.'

'Yes, she is.'

'And you'll go and fetch—'

Her sentence was curtailed as Tan knocked on the glass door of her office and stared at her.

'Yes, yes, don't worry. As I say, we have everything under control.'

'Okay.' She took a beat. 'Dad, I've got to go. I'll speak to you later, keep . . . keep in touch. Let me know if there are any developments. And we'll speak in a bit. See you later.' Her heart flexed at the thought of seeing her lovely dad, who she knew would flounder without Marnie by his side, even if it was only temporary.

'Will do, my little sausage.' He put the phone down and with Tan walking in there was no time to dwell on the name her dad had been calling her since she was young. No time to pay heed to the sadness that swelled at the fact her mum had been taken ill, nor the worry of what might happen next.

'All okay?' Tan asked, approaching her desk with caution.

'Yes.' She looked up. 'I'll need to leave early today.' She was keen to get to the hospital.

'Of course.' He bowed his head slightly. 'Anything else?'

'Actually, yes. Would you mind telling me how there can be an oversight to the tune of fifty million pounds? How does that happen, Tan? You have full sight of the spreadsheets, you're supposed to be one step ahead of the budgets, to keep an eye on mitigating risks, costs, future-proofing – the very things that Nathaniel was talking about. If Stern gets the wind up him over costs, where do you think he'll make cuts? It won't be the generator or the jetty, but it might be goodbye to my customised chandelier or the bespoke artwork for the reception, and that could hurt us.' *Could hurt me . . .* 'I've worked so hard to get things to this point. I just want to hand it over to Aarushi in good shape. It's important to me.'

She watched her colleague, who was also her friend, sink into the chair in front of her desk, as she leaned back in hers. This was no time for emotion.

She had a job to do.

December

11.00 a.m.

Madeleine wasn't fond of hospitals. Without the best sense of direction, she found the signage confusing and, being rather squeamish, was overly worried about seeing an injury. Her stomach rolled at the thought. Still, her presence here – and, in fact, the whole morning – felt surreal. Her mind focused on the minutiae of life; she hoped Captain was being adequately tended to in her absence, and wondered if 'Suzy with a Y' or anyone else in the team would comment on her absence. She thought about the reason she'd give for not going into work this morning – a dicky tum, she decided was the best catch-all. She also wished Marnie were with her, but was simultaneously glad she wasn't, unsure how that conversation would go and knowing that any premature panicking from her mother would make the already farcical situation quite unbearable.

Nausea leaped in her throat. Supposing this wasn't a mistake, supposing . . . *No, nope!* She shook her head, unable to entertain the idea. The doctor's strip of magic paper dipped in a thimble-ful of pee was surely defunct, and what a fiasco! A day wasted for that. The whole idea of her being up the duff was as preposterous as it was petrifying. She hadn't slept with anyone for over six or seven months; if she was pregnant, she would know – there'd be signs! She decided there and then to write a strong-worded letter of complaint to the health centre when this was all over. It was unacceptable – putting people through this ordeal due to human error. She didn't want an apology but would certainly like them to tighten procedures so that no other unsuspecting soul would have to experience the same thing.

Eventually, after wandering aimlessly around corridors, and more from luck than judgement, she found herself at the pregnancy clinic, checked in at the desk, handed in her slip of paper, and took a seat in the waiting area. Looking up, Madeleine saw that she was surrounded by very pregnant women wearing loose tunics. Women who rubbed their backs, cradled their stomachs, and sat with legs slightly splayed. Women whose signs of pregnancy were obvious – more than obvious! She looked and felt like a fraud among them and was entirely thankful for that. A couple of dishevelled-looking partners whose expressions suggested they'd rather be anywhere else ran around after toddlers who seemed intent on putting the corners of dog-eared books and various plastic toys into their mouths – items they'd fished from a lidded box. She felt her nose wrinkle at the germ swamp that must lie in that toy chest. That, and the fact she was entirely unable to fathom why on earth, if you were already in receipt of one of the sticky-faced, chubby-wristed humans who seemed intent on causing mayhem, you would have another one?

She thought children were a bit like a large water feature in a small garden – a novelty at first, something to show your friends and family, but when there was no room for a sun lounger, if and when the current bun showed its face, and no budget for a holiday as the cost of purchase and installation had been huge, buyer's remorse would set in. Although, given the choice right now, without hesitation she'd choose an elaborate leaping dolphin fountain over one of the kids racing around the table with a full nappy.

'This is a right pain, isn't it? Parking is a bloody nightmare!' A woman with a space hopper up her jumper chuckled in her direction.

'Yep.' She nodded, looking down and hoping that her reply and manner, which verged on curt, would be enough to dissuade the woman from trying to engage with her further. She wasn't in the mood for chitchat, and just wanted to get the whole mess cleared up sooner rather than later. The chatty woman was rounded, voluptuous, engorged with impending motherhood and glowing with a radiant beauty that was the exact opposite of her own grey pallor and flat chest.

'How far are you?' the woman asked.

'Oh, oh, I'm not . . . not actually . . . I don't . . . no, no, I'm not . . .' She pushed her palms between her thighs and rounded her shoulders, trying her level best to disappear inside the plastic chair on which she sat.

The woman stared at her, her expression a little perplexed, and Madeleine could entirely relate. She too was a little perplexed, to put it mildly.

'Madeleine Woods!' A perky woman wearing pink scrubs beamed from over the rim of her clipboard.

'Here!' She put her hand up and called out, instantly regretting the word, as it sounded like she was answering the register at school.

The small room was overly warm and, for the second time that day, she was asked to hop on a narrow coach lined with a flimsy strip of paper. Only this time she was to remove her jeans and neon-pink knickeroos.

'Okay, so this is how an ultrasound works.' The sonographer spoke slowly and deliberately as if Madeleine were a dumdum. It irritated her. After a simple explanation, the woman coated her stomach with a viscous gel and stared at the wide screen.

Her thoughts wandered.

It'll take me a good forty minutes to get to work. Which is actually fine. I'll be there in time for lunch. In fact, that might work out quite well as people will be busy or out of the office and I can slip behind my desk, as if I've been there all morning. Poor old Captain, though. Hope someone else has taken him out or he'll have his legs crossed . . . What do I fancy for lunch? I actually feel a bit better . . . Maybe a sandwich . . . or pasta salad . . .

Madeleine heard the noise before she saw the shape.

A loud, distinct *boom, boom . . . boom, boom . . .* The unmistakable sound of a heartbeat.

Whipping her head towards the screen, it was as if *her* heart skipped and the breath stopped in her throat.

She knew she would never be able to describe the utter shock, the terror at the sight that greeted her. There it was: the undeniable, distinct shape of a head, and a body, and scrunched-up arms and legs. Scrunched-up arms and legs *inside* her body . . .

She thought she might vomit and gripped the sides of the trolley.

'That's . . .' She pointed towards the screen.

'This is your first scan?' Perky woman obviously hadn't read her notes, or maybe there were no notes to read. Either way . . .

Madeleine nodded.

'Well, you have *one* baby. And we have a good, strong heartbeat and everything looks great.'

'How much pregnant . . . ? I mean, how . . . how old is the . . .' Shock didn't aid the fact that she was unsure of the language, unsure of everything.

There it was. Right in front of her, the indisputable proof: an image on a screen of the alien-shaped thing that had taken up residence in her womb. She stared at it, unable to look away, knowing that if she didn't see it, absorb the fact, and stare at it some more, committing it to memory, she would not believe it was true. Was it true?

How? How could it be true?

It was as the sonographer seemed to be taking measurements from the screen by clicking a mouse that she asked the question that occurred to her, a get-out-of-jail-free card, a reason for the mix-up.

'And is this . . . this is a . . . a live feed? Is that . . . I mean . . . are you absolutely sure that's my . . . my picture . . . my body?'

The woman turned to face her. Her voice was soft, her smile genuine, and this time Madeleine was grateful for her slow, considered tone, because it helped the facts sink in. It helped her, the dumdum who hadn't known she was pregnant, get her head around the situation.

'Yes. I am one hundred per cent sure. This is your body, your womb. Your pregnancy. You are approximately twenty-four weeks pregnant.'

'Twenty-four weeks, that's . . .' She didn't know much, but knew that the average pregnancy was about nine months long, give or take. What was that in months? Again her brain ticked a few beats slower than usual.

'Seven months.'

'Seven months?' she asked as the sonographer spoke.

Seven months!

'How?' She lifted her head to get a better view of the screen. 'How did this happen?'

The woman looked aghast, and Madeleine realised that it wasn't quite the question she had intended to ask.

'I mean, I know *how* it happens,' she added hastily. The woman's shoulders visibly dropped. 'But how can I be this much pregnant and not know? I'm on the pill!'

The woman took her time.

'It's not as uncommon as you might think. A lot depends on your build, where the baby is positioned, how it's lying, how regular your cycle is – and the pill isn't foolproof. Forgetting to take it, sickness, diarrhoea – lots of things can affect the contraceptive. I've seen women who only know they're pregnant when they go into labour and arrive via A&E.'

'Fucking hell!' She spoke without thought, horrified and petrified at the same time.

'You haven't done anything wrong.' The woman was being sweet, offering comfort. 'Do you want to the know the sex or do you want the surprise?'

Madeleine stared at her. What *did* she want?

'I can't believe this is happening.' She spoke her thoughts. 'The father of this baby is no more than a friend, really – a guy from school who I first slept with because we were drunk. *That* was a surprise. The fact I'm pregnant? That's a big, big surprise. The thought of not working, even for a short while and having to give up my flat, my freedom, all the bloody shite that comes with something like this – the fact that I'm in this bloody situation at all! It's all one big, terrible surprise!' She raised her voice with a half-laugh, 'Not living the life I planned – *big* surprise – and so, no, I don't need another surp— Just tell me what it is . . . please.'

'A girl. It's a girl.'

'Thank you.'

'You're welcome.'

'So what happens next?' She hardly dared ask.

Miss Perky had handed her a wad of tissue to wipe the viscous jelly from her stomach.

'You should tell your GP and probably anyone else you would want to know.'

Madeleine hopped down from the couch. It was a very good point. Who did she want to know?

Having walked briskly from the building, she leaned on the wall outside and with shaking fingers, took her phone from her pocket.

'Mate! Hello!'

It was only when she tried to speak that she realised that she was crying. Her words tried to navigate the lump of distress at the base of her throat, which made coherent speech almost impossible.

'Mads? Mads, what's wrong? Where are you?'

'T-Trina . . . I . . . I need you.'

Chapter Five

Present Day

Madeleine paid the cabbie and climbed out on to the pavement in front of Newham hospital. Just the sight of the building was enough to pull memories to the fore that she tried hard to keep buried in the dark crevices of her mind, knowing it did her no good to allow them to surface. They were distracting at best, distressing at worst. Reminders of a time when her whole world had spiralled out of control.

She'd got away from the office as early as she was able and was happy to have arrived before rush hour. All she wanted was to spend some time with Marnie, to confirm she was alive and as well as could be expected, rather than waste minutes sitting in nose-to-tail traffic, knowing she would only stop worrying when she'd seen her mother, spoken to her. She also wanted to be there for her dad. He'd sounded old on the phone, frail in a way that she had never considered before, understanding how a shock like this could do that to a person.

Do you want to the know the sex or do you want the surprise? She shook the words from her mind.

Tan had quietly acknowledged her long digital to-do list and had done so without so much as a hint of dissent. She had left him in no doubt that she wasn't best pleased with Nathaniel's revelations. It was a cock-up. It was important to her that she left the Stern project in impeccable shape when she got on that plane to LA, knowing that when it came to her professional reputation, you were only as good as your last commission. Rebecca was demanding, with the highest of expectations, and Madeleine wanted to deliver.

The truth was no matter what she achieved, she always felt she was one wrong move away from being let go and having to return to the bottom rung of the ladder – the ladder she concentrated every day on climbing diligently. Her confidence, when flagging, let her believe her achievements were no more than a fluke and she would, at any moment, be found out and told to get back to the Brenton Park estate where she belonged.

Her plan, although not yet voiced to anyone, was that after LA she would open her own agency. With one more international high-profile project under her belt, she felt that the time would be right. There was a file on her laptop, a secret folder crammed full of ideas, thoughts, and musings; everything from the entwined M and W that would be her gold logo on a navy background, to images of the kind of loft-style premises she favoured, and trusted supplier contact details she had gathered over the years. She collected pictures of colour palettes, stylish images of commercial makeovers that had caught her eye. And her very favourite sub-folder, entitled 'Frippery' for photographs of jewel-coloured chandeliers, industrial light switches, the perfect aged patina on a piece of wood, a shell or two – anything that made her heart race with the sheer beauty of the design. It was a dream that had felt a very long way off the last time she had entered this hospital and yet right now, some eight years later, it felt within touching distance.

Inhaling the scent of this wintery afternoon, she watched the streetlamps come on in anticipation of dusk. Hitching her soft bag over her shoulder, she ran her fingers through her hair and looked up at the pale façade. She had always been a bit squeamish when it came to illness – anything medical, in fact – and took a deep breath.

'Mads!'

She froze on the spot. There were only two people in the whole world who had ever called her that. It was a blast from her past that caused a jolt of anxiety as she turned on her heel. Trina raised her hand in a wave as she walked towards her, holding a punnet of grapes, a bottle of orange juice and a magazine. It hadn't occurred to her to stock up on goodies for Marnie and even before a word was spoken she felt a little deflated, on the back foot. It had been six months or so since she'd seen Trina last, and that had been a short and uncomfortable encounter on the walkway outside her parents' flat as she had arrived and Trina was leaving.

'Hi!'

'Hi!'

'I'm just leaving.'

'Okay, well, see you soon!'

'Take care!'

'You too!'

Trina, it seemed, had been as keen to be gone as Madeleine was for her to leave. Their eye contact minimal, tone false, demeanour hurried. That meeting was an indicator of how far they had fallen. And not without poignancy, as it took place on the very walkway they used to run along after school, keen to get to the sofa, share a packet of biscuits and debrief their day. Malted Milks, of course, their biscuit of choice. The same walkway where they would prop each other up when, as eighteen-year-olds, topped up with Bacardi Breezers, they'd arrive home late, trying not to disturb the neighbourhood as they accidentally kicked milk bottles, dropped their keys, and let the front door bang shut behind them, before waking

Marnie and Doug with their loud recollections of a night well spent, and Madeleine howled her laughter into the night because *everything* was funny and the world felt full of infinite possibilities!

As ever, the sight of the woman she had grown up with left her riddled with a range of complex emotions. It was wonderful to see her in some ways, always wonderful; their shared history was often a comfortable place for her memories to idle. This, however, was tinged with an awkwardness at how they had grown apart, chosen different paths, and was a discomfort that was hard to neutralise. Madeleine smiled as broadly as she was able while clenching her fists inside the pockets of her navy cashmere overcoat.

'Trina, hi!'

'You off to see Marn?' Her ex best friend gestured towards the entrance of the hospital with the magazine in her hand.

The old Madeleine would have made a joke – *'No, I just happen to be loitering outside the very place where she's laid up right now, probably won't bother going in . . .'* – but she didn't, hating how every encounter was now wrapped with a formality that was still, even after all this time, as uncomfortable as it was alien. This girl who had been the sister she had never had, with whom she shared everything.

'Yes, just arrived. Dad said you were with her this morning when she got ill?'

'Yeah.' Trina exhaled through bloated cheeks. 'It was bloody horrible.'

'I bet. What happened?' She wanted the detail.

'I was already on the bus when your mum got on, and she came and sat next to me. It was lovely to catch up. We just spoke about the usual rubbish, the weather and what have you, then right before the bus got to Mile End, she said she wasn't feeling the ticket and put her hand on her chest. I asked her if she was okay and she told me she felt sick and a bit light-headed. It was all so quick; I didn't really know what was happening. Then she stood up, rang the bell, and said she wanted to get off the bus.'

'Poor Mum.' She knew what it was like to feel unwell and out of sorts in a public place. It was scary, disorienting, and overwhelming. The memories came thick and fast now, all unwelcome and leaving her feeling a little wobbly.

'I could tell she just wanted to be outside – to get fresh air or be sick, I wasn't sure – but she'd gone a funny colour, kind of grey. And then the next thing I knew, she grabbed her chest and sort of toppled backwards in the aisle. She was really sweating and I just started yelling, "Stop the bus! Call an ambulance!" And that was that.'

'Thank goodness you were with her.'

'It's weird, Mads. I haven't caught that bus in an age.'

'Marnie said she hadn't seen you for a while.' She knew her mum and Trina shared a bus route to and from work, and recalled Marnie mentioning her absence in passing.

'Yep. They moved me from my regular branch up to one in Woolwich for a bit. But I'm back in the area now, so . . .'

Trina, she knew, worked in data administration for a bank. She had always imagined her friend might lead a more adventurous life, do something fun – the girl who used to wear halter-neck tops and short shorts and paint her face in extraordinary designs to go clubbing. Her spirits lifted a little at the thought of the happiest times before the axe had fallen on all she took for granted.

'You look . . .' Trina eyed her up and down. 'You look lovely. Fancy! But lovely.'

'Just come from work.' This her justification, masking the self-consciousness Trina made her feel, as if drawing attention to her designer labels and well-thought-out ensemble, like she had over-done it or was trying too hard. It bothered her.

'Me too.'

It might have been her imagination or an over-sensitivity on her part, but she noted the set of her friend's chin, as she stood with her hair scraped up into a messy knot. Her face still pretty, her skin, once dogged with the acne of youth, now clear, and make-up free. Trina's whole deportment was that of someone who had vaulted the line from teen to woman, gaining confidence as she did so. A confidence that screamed: *This is me! Take it or leave it!*

Trina – her very best friend throughout school, who had morphed from someone who was on the edge of erratic, a little unpredictable, to this woman with life etched in her face, who now carried herself with purpose and gave off a vibe that suggested she did not want to be challenged. A woman who was proud of how she looked and how little she seemed to care. Beneath her flared slacks poked the toes of her trainers and just the sight of them was enough to send a throb of discomfort to the balls of Madeleine's feet, as she teetered in her Jimmy Choos. She envied her that.

'It's been a while since I saw you too, mate.'

'It has.' She smiled, not sure what else to add. 'How's *your* mum doing?'

'Oh, all right.' Trina's tone was cool. 'You know, plodding on. One disaster to the next.' She crossed her eyes in the way she always used to, and it made Madeleine laugh, just as it always had. It was nice, easy – a natural and familiar response, and she was glad of it. These moments were when they healed a little; tiny stitches that helped pull them back together. It seemed there was an unspoken agreement that Marnie being ill was hard enough without any additional drama lurking around the edges.

Madeleine *did* know what it felt like to plod along – it was how she used to live, putting one foot in front of the other and doing her best to seek out the little pocketfuls of glitter that made the dark days worthwhile. Just as Marnie had taught her. It was precisely this life that Madeleine had wanted to escape: the life of the

Brenton Park estate, where her future had felt precarious, economically unstable, and surrounded by people who felt safer telling tales of the past rather than looking ahead. As though the best place they could mentally linger was among the funny and dramatic moments that dotted their memories: the celebrations and events that were markers, highlights in the grey mundanity of their existence. Births, christenings, weddings, funerals, days of high drama or disaster . . . times of communal gathering and buffets, and the laughter and tears that accompanied each.

Even thinking of it was enough to make her skin itch! She still, when her thoughts dwelled on all she had escaped, felt the hand of her class boundary, reaching for her throat and squeezing tight. She swallowed.

'Is she still with her fella?' Marnie had told her a while back that a man had moved in and that Mrs Watkin seemed keen.

'Which one?' Trina rolled her eyes. 'I don't bother learning their names anymore. They all look the same, sound the same, and it always ends the same: her crying into her Prosecco, an empty closet with hangers clanging together, and her bank account a few quid lighter. She never learns.'

Madeleine couldn't imagine growing up in a house like that. It was a state of affairs that was as sad as it was unimaginable to her: a life without the constancy of her parents' marriage. Marnie, she knew without hesitation, would go and live in a tent with the man she loved.

'Shall we go in?' She wanted to get to Marnie.

'Yep.'

The two walked side by side, through the wide automatic doors and into the foyer of the hospital. They called, waited for, and entered the lift with some of their original awkwardness melted away. Madeleine's hands unclenched inside her pockets.

'You look taller.' Trina observed as the lift juddered to a stop.

'Heels.' She kicked up her foot.

'How the bloody hell do you walk in them all day?'

'Practice.' She winked.

'You got over Zayn leaving yet?' Trina asked as they left the lift.

'Nope.' It made her smile, another reminder of how easily Trina could do this.

A memory came to her now – the two of them sitting on the kitchen countertop in their school uniform, laughing and eating toast with One Direction blaring out of the radio.

'If you had to marry one of them, which one would you pick?' Madeleine had laughed.

'Harry. He's cute,' Trina answered without hesitation. 'What about you?'

'Zayn.'

This followed by their giggling and embarrassment at a topic that was so grown-up and unthinkable.

'You'd have cute babies.' Trina beamed.

'Urgh!' The sound she made was almost instinctive. 'Nope. Never. Not for me.'

And just like that they stopped laughing. It was true that on her life journey she was still very much feeling her way, but when it came to having babies, of this one thing she was certain. The thought was almost repugnant to her. And it wasn't the babies per se, but more the idea of being tethered, her choices limited, her time not her own, her budget accounted for and her plans curtailed. She'd seen enough examples where she lived of women worn, weary and weeping, as they pushed their snot-nosed bundles along the cold, grey pavements, on the forage for sliced white bread and cheap milk, to know that she wanted more – wanted different.

'Oh, you say that now,' Marnie called out, clearly listening in to their chat.

'Actually, I'll say that always!' She felt the flare of conviction in her veins. It irked her; why would no one listen? 'I know me and I know I don't want kids.'

'You can't *know* that.' Trina sided with Marnie, and this irked her even more! 'You might *think* you know that, but you don't know how you're going to feel in the future. You might meet someone so fabulous who wants kids and they might convince you it's a great idea. Or you might just change your mind.'

'I might.' She curled her top lip. 'But equally I might not! And I find it really odd how everyone, like *everyone*, as soon as I say anything about not wanting kids, tries to tell me how I will feel differently when I'm older or how kids are the "best thing that's ever happened to them!"' This she aimed unapologetically at Marnie. 'And I don't understand why it bothers people so much, why can't they just accept my decision, my view and say, "Fair enough!"'

'Because . . .' Trina's face suggested confusion. 'Because it's what we're supposed to do, isn't it?'

'Who gets to say what we're supposed to do? God, Trina! Just, no!'

'All right! All right! Keep your hair on!'

'Well, it's just so bloody . . .' She let out a small growl of frustration. 'So bloody annoying!'

Trina had opened her mouth, suggesting she had more to say on the topic, before closing it again, as if thinking better of it.

It felt simultaneously like a blink and a lifetime ago. Never could she have imagined that in just a few short years from that moment in the kitchen, she would have taken a path that all but excluded Trina from her life, made decisions that came with the toughest of consequences and would be spending her days in a world that was as far from her childhood experience as was possible.

'This way.' Trina, it seemed, remembered Madeleine's appalling lack of navigational skill, and pointed along the corridor, where they walked the linoleum-covered floor.

The ward, when they found it, was a large square room with four beds, each positioned in a corner and with an identical over-bed table and nightstand by each. Pale blue curtains on rails gave some semblance of privacy. Marnie was in the far corner, asleep by the look of things, and tethered to a machine by wires that appeared to be stuck to her chest. On the end of her index finger was a plastic cap with a light on it, this too attached to goodness only knew what.

'Bless her.' Trina placed the gifts she'd brought on the over-bed table and spoke softly. Madeleine could only nod, feeling a little overwhelmed by the sight of her mum so incapacitated.

Marnie looked old and small, both aspects that tore at her heart. She only ever pictured the woman upright, robust, laughing – always doing something, active and engaged. The sight of her now was a reminder that Marnie, like everyone, was not invincible. Two of the other three beds were occupied. In the one opposite Marnie, an older lady slept with her head tipped back, her long grey hair cascading over the pillow and the lacy pink edge of her nightgown open to reveal tubes and wires affixed to a machine that beeped in time and seemed to be keeping track of something. In the bed next to Marnie, a woman – in her forties, if she had to guess – was engrossed in her iPad with headphones on, and laughed heartily, as if she were alone. It was the strangest of environments. Three strangers, all in night clothes or gowns, in such close proximity.

Madeleine shivered at the thought of having to spend another night here, remembering how glad she had been to make her exit all those years ago.

'We should let her sleep.'

'Yep, shall we sit outside the room?'

She liked Trina's suggestion and had earlier eyed seats just outside of the door, opposite the nurses' station. Nerves flared in her stomach. Her and Trina, sitting side by side without the relief of being in transit, of passing through, almost forced to stop and confront the fact that they were estranged. It had been a while.

'Do you ladies need anything?' A kindly nurse looked up from the computer screen.

'Just didn't want to wake my mum. Mrs Woods?' Madeleine pointed over her shoulder.

'Righto. Yes, it's good she sleeps. I'll let you know when she wakes up. I can see her from here.' The nurse nodded through the open doors of the ward.

'Thank you.'

The two women sat back in the creaking plastic chairs that were about as uncomfortable as they had looked.

'You seen Jimmy?' Trina asked, as her cheeks took on a rosy hue, as they had her whole life at the mention of the man. She had done it, brought up the topic that Madeleine had hoped they might avoid. There had been no lead up to it, just *bam!* Like a gunshot, and just as powerful. His name was out and that was that. It was probably for the best, she figured, to get it over and done with and not let it become a subject they left simmering while both waited for it to boil over. The anticipation in this already charged environment might have been more than either of them could handle.

'Erm, not for a while, but I hear he's doing great. Marnie likes to fill me in, of course.'

'I bump into him occasionally. It's always the same; he pootles by in his van. Have you seen his van?' Trina faced her.

'No. No, I haven't.'

'It's really cool, a beautiful thing. Last time we chatted was when I saw him in Asda. His business is doing *so* well.'

'It's great, isn't it? Woodwork and stuff. Mum said.'

'Yes. He's really clever. The things he makes.' Trina sighed in the way that someone who was still obviously in awe and smitten would.

Madeleine recalled the stunning pictures Marnie had shown her of ornate staircases, hand-built sash windows, fire surrounds, hearths and more, all posted on his website. His skill was a gift and his patient nature, she was certain, an aid to his art. It was the kind of craftsmanship that she appreciated both personally and professionally. Maybe she'd pop his details in her secret contacts file for her new business venture.

'He was always smart at school, wasn't he? But adamant he didn't fancy university and would rather use his hands than have to wear a tie. I think that's still the worst thing he could think of.' Madeleine recalled this exact conversation as they walked along the canal after school.

'And he's not wrong; I work with a lot of tie-wearing men at the bank, and they're all bloody miserable.' Trina laughed at this truth. 'It must be so nice to spend your life doing something you love. He just wants to be outdoors – gets up to all sorts of adventures when he's not collecting and chopping wood. Like frogspawn spotting, or drying wildflowers, foraging for goodness only knows what and making all kinds of funny food – like nettle brew!' Her friend pulled a face, suggesting it wasn't her cup of tea, literally.

'Are you seeing anyone?' Madeleine kept her tone casual, wondering if some lucky man had usurped Jimmy in her friend's affections, because he would be lucky, and also sticking her beak in, thinking how lovely it would be if they did get together. Ease her guilt . . .

'Nope.' Trina shook her head. 'You?'

'Well, I've kind of met someone, but it's all brand new and so we're at that point when it will either bloom or fizzle, and I'm not sure which right now.' She felt a surge of longing for Nico, excited to see him again, to inhale that glorious scent. 'But I'm going away in a couple of weeks so . . .' No matter how flippant she tried to sound, the truth was she liked him – spectacular Nico . . .

'Marnie said you're off to America?'

'Mmm, yep, a project in LA.' It was odd how uncomfortable she felt talking about the life that was so different to Trina's. She had also been rather vague in giving Marnie the details and hadn't yet found the courage to explain that it wasn't just a trip but was in fact a permanent move. This in turn fed her guilt, especially today, at the thought that Trina would be around to pop in for a cup of tea if she was close, and how it would bring joy to Marnie and Doug; all three casualties of her ambition. An ambition that drove her. When it had been no more than a goal, it seemed to be something they held in admiration, yet now, in practice, she knew her life was unfathomable to them. 'Do you still like Jimmy?' She twisted to look her friend in the eye. It felt fair, as Trina had raised it. She too could do candid if Trina was willing.

Her friend snorted laughter and looked down. 'Do I still like Jimmy?' Her response was slow in coming. 'I never really talk about it, but I suppose my question is, would it make a difference if I did? I think he's only ever seen me as a friend, and I don't know how to change that. I'm like something comfortable and familiar in your house that's always been there and likely always will be, but it no longer excites you and you no longer notice it really. Like a knackered cushion on the spare bed or your nan's old Teasmade.'

'Did you just compare yourself to an old cushion or your nan's Teasmade?'

'I think I did.'

They both sighed.

'Have you ever . . . I mean, have you told him that you'd like more than friendship?' she pried.

'What do you think?' Trina's words dripped with sarcasm. 'You remember what I was like – what I'm still like! He pitches up and I get my words fuddled. He never sees the best of me, just this gibbering idiot.'

'I think, knowing Jimmy – not that I really *know* him, but what I used to know,' she clarified, 'he's the type of person who might need a little nudge, might need something more obvious than a hint or a subtle longing for him from afar.'

'A subtle longing for him from afar? What's that, Shakespeare? God, Mads, you talk some utter bollocks!'

Madeleine laughed out loud before remembering where she was and putting her hand over her mouth. The nurse gave her a hard stare, in reply to which she mouthed, '*Sorry!*' She couldn't remember the last time someone had spoken to her like that. Trina's particular brand of humour had always appealed to her – yet another aspect of their friendship she missed when she stepped off the hamster wheel long enough to consider it.

'I want you to be happy, Trina. I want Jimmy to be happy too.' This she whispered. It was the truth and her words had been a long time coming.

Trina's face softened; her eyes lit up. 'Do you think it might have legs?'

'I think it could. I believe if you want something or someone, then you have to make it happen.' She pictured Nico and saw him arriving in LA, probably with sushi. 'You should turn up at his house with an armful of board games, a box of chocolates, a bottle of something fizzy.'

'Lucozade?'

'That'd do it.' She smiled at the woman who she used to know back to front and inside out. 'But take the step, build a life. Let him know you want more than to bump into him in Asda. This is our one life, Trina.'

'You always said as much.' This mention was enough to roughen up the edges of their conversation that had been smooth.

She blinked. 'Because it's true.'

'Ladies.' The nurse rose from behind her desk. 'It looks like Marnie's waking up. Just give me a minute to check how she's doing and I'll tell you when it's okay to come in.'

'Of course, thank you.'

'Cheers,' Trina added before turning to face her. 'Although, you know, Mads, I don't really think, when it comes to Jimmy, you're the person I should be taking advice from, do you?'

They sat quietly side by side. It seemed like their easy chatter had been a false dawn, as if the subject of Jimmy, now broached and explored, had opened old wounds, exposed old differences, and no matter how much time might have passed, it hurt just the same.

December

12.15 P.M.

Madeleine stirred her tea and took a bite of the fat croissant. She was hungry, her sickness gone, replaced by a much bigger worry. She looked out over the street from her vantage point on the banquette in the front booth of The Copper Kettle, happy to be in the warm café where she had idled in her teens, when funds allowed. This very booth where they had laughed and made life plans, all seemingly redundant now. This very booth where she had once got up and walked out without paying for her coffee, thinking Trina had settled the bill. An oversight rectified by the leaving of large tips here ever since. Her friend still teased her about it.

People rushed by, some loaded up with bags – evidence of Christmas shopping; others were holding hands with loved ones, and a disproportionate number of them were pregnant or pushing prams or pushchairs. Everywhere she looked she saw distended tums, smiling toddlers, cute babies nestling inside papooses. A man bustled past carrying a bulk supply of nappies. It felt like the world was conspiring to normalise her predicament, although she doubted anything about this would ever feel 'normal'.

It was a curious situation. She had seen the screen herself, knew for a fact that she was pregnant, and yet it didn't feel real. Armed with her new knowledge, she recalled that her boobs had been quite sensitive, but no more or less than when she was expecting her period. Maybe her waistbands were a smidge tighter, but she had been lax about exercising in recent weeks and was possibly indulging in more snacks than usual. She took another bite of the croissant.

The door opened and in ran her buddy – her best friend since childhood and the only person she had wanted to reach out to. It was a surprise how her tears again threatened. This was not like Madeleine. Not at all. It was a relief her mate had got there so quickly, evidently dropping whatever she was up to and heading where she was needed most.

Trina slipped into the booth and took both of Madeleine's hands into her own. 'Look at you, slumming it back over in East London!'

She nodded and bit her trembling bottom lip. It was as if she'd been holding it together but the sight of her friend meant she could let it all out.

'What on earth's wrong? I've never seen you like this.' Trina lowered her head and looked into her face. 'Is it Marnie or Dougie? Has something happened?'

'No.' She sniffed.

'Have you lost your job? Got dumped? Damaged your knock-off Gucci handbag?'

Shaking her head, she allowed herself a small smile. She did love that handbag.

'How many more guesses have I got?'

Trina referred to the game of What Am I? that they liked to play in their youth – the more random the subject, the better.

Taking a deep breath, she freed herself from Trina's hands, sat back against the leatherette seat of the upright booth and swallowed. 'I'm pregnant.'

'Oh my God! Pregnant?'

'Yep.' Saying it out loud didn't make it feel any less ludicrous.

'Have you done a test? Are . . . are you sure?'

'Yes, I did a test. The worst minute of my life. I sat there, and the result came and my whole world imploded.'

'Pregnant?' Trina studied her face as if looking for clues.

'Yes. In fact' – she wiped her nose on her napkin – 'I am very pregnant. Like, seven months pregnant.'

It was a scary thought, and equally as scary was the prospect of having to admit who the father of the baby was.

'Seven months!' Her friend's wide-eyed repetition said it all.

'Yep.'

'Mads! Oh my God! That's wonderful! Is it wonderful? I . . . I don't know what to say!'

Her friend spoke for both of them.

'No, it's not wonderful. Not for me. I only just found out – I had no idea. I can't believe it. It doesn't seem real.'

'Shit.'

She couldn't have put it better herself.

'Yes, shit.'

'Well . . .' Trina took her time. 'I don't know if it's okay to mention this, but I'm guessing your options are limited this far into your pregnancy?'

'You could say that.'

'My God, this is . . . a lot!'

'It really is.'

'In that case, Mads, you have to think of it in a positive light. This could be absolutely brilliant. It might just be the best thing that has ever happened to you. You might not have planned it, but . . .'

She shook her head and raised her hand to stop her friend from talking. To hear the dribble of clichéd claptrap did nothing to help her.

'No, no. I mean, I know I'm in shock, but I can tell you without hesitation that it is most definitely *not* the best thing that has ever happened to me, it's the worst. The very worst. A child?' She closed her eyes and breathed through her nose. 'You know this is how I've always felt. Nothing has changed. I don't want, and never have wanted, kids.'

'I thought you'd change your mind.'

Trina's forthright and automatic response was galling.

'Why do people always say that? As if they really, really hope that this might be the case, because any woman who decides she doesn't want to be a mother must have a screw loose, right? Or must be strangely wired or just doesn't get it! Whereas I think it's everyone else desperate to jump on the baby train that just doesn't get it! I've never wanted to be trapped like that, never wanted the bloody responsibility, the burden of it.'

Trina held her gaze and again reached for her hand. 'You won't be thinking straight, Mads. You need time.'

'You're right, I'm not thinking straight, but you *know* me, Trina! You know this is how I've always felt!'

'I know it's what you've always said, but . . .' Her friend's tone of disbelief was jarring.

'There is no but. It's a life for someone else! Not me! I can't stand the thought of it! I've lived around these women my whole life, women whose existences are small, women who are made old in months. You've seen them too.' She pointed out of the window, knowing several examples to prove her point would walk by at any given moment. 'Pushing their babies around in second-hand prams, meeting other mums on the bench by the swings, swapping tales of mediocrity just to have a break in their groundhog day. We only have this one life, Trina – this one life! I'm not going to waste a second of it.'

'Maybe they don't think they are wasting it – have you ever thought that they might like that life? That maybe they're happy, maybe—' her friend began.

'No, they don't! They can't! They read magazines and wonder what it would be like to look like the model smiling back at them, just for a day. They cry over soppy tunes on the radio because it takes them back to happy, carefree nights when they had choices and the life that lay ahead for them held fabulous possibilities. They plan for holidays they can't afford, fixated by the red ring on the calendar pinned up on the damp kitchen wall, living for that week when they get to escape the monotony and head to the seaside to stay in a shitty caravan and eat chips in the rain and dance at the on-site social club because it's the greatest bloody week of their lives! A week they will think about while they save up to go again. And I want more! I want a different life. I always have! I have so many plans!'

'You sound so certain, Mads, but perhaps they don't feel limited like that. Maybe, to be a parent, to make a home, to climb into bed every night and snuggle close to someone they love and who loves them back, to feel content, eat nice food, knowing they get to spend every average day wrapped in love?'

'No! No way! Why are you romanticising the shiteness of it all?' She hadn't meant to raise her voice.

'And why are you shitting on the niceness of it all?'

'What are you *talking* about?' It bothered her that Trina didn't get it. This was her best friend – they agreed on ninety-nine per cent of everything, except which member of 1D they were going to marry, but even that was probably a good thing; no one wanted you and your best mate to be in love with the same boy.

'What I'm talking about is your bloody attitude. It sucks! You sound so superior. You're never satisfied, and you've been that way since you left school – always desperate to look around the next corner because you think that's where the good stuff lurks. Never standing still, not for a single second, stopping to enjoy the view, but always with your mind on what comes next and what comes next . . . It means you'll never arrive! It means you'll never be happy! And for your information, that small existence that you hold in such scorn is exactly what I aspire to. What you describe, making a home and feeling content, is a life *I'd* like – a life *I'd* love!'

'Are you fucking kidding me?' Madeleine's voice was loud, her tone incredulous. She wasn't sure she'd ever sworn at Trina like this. Her heart flexed and her skin itched with the pain of it all.

'No, I'm not. I'm deadly serious. I look at someone like Jimmy who is kind and sweet and placid and I think I'd love to wake up to him each day, love to cook him nice food and go for walks and—'

'J-Jimmy?' Madeleine stuttered, Trina now making it clear that when it came to the boy in question, the candle she had held for him during their school days did in fact still burn brightly. She felt sick at the prospect of coming clean about their fling, admitting to the few months they'd met up secretly for sex and vodka and vodka and sex. 'Jimmy was just a school crush for you, wasn't he? One minute you fancied him, the next you were off to Southend for the day with Mark Henderson!' She tried to make light of it, tried to defuse the verbal bomb that ticked on her tongue.

'I would rather have been in Southend with Jimmy. Yes, Jimmy! And how dare you laugh? He might not be the high-earning ambitious type that you've got your sights on, someone who can buy you designer shoes and posh dinners, but I happen to think that kindness and patience are worth more than anything.'

'All right, Mother Teresa! It wasn't so long ago that I was pulling you off flat-nosed bruisers in dodgy pubs who were snogging the face off you and trying to shove their bitten fingernails inside your bra! So don't come at me with "all I want is kindness"!'

'Don't be such a cow. It's not all I want, Mads, and you know it! I just want someone who is going to show up, someone who instinctively knows what I want and when I need it, and who just shows up! And yes, kindness. And I'm sorry if that doesn't fit with your vision of a perfect man!'

She and Trina stared at each other, neither wanting to be the first to look away. When they finally averted their eyes, it was at the same time. And when they looked back up, they found themselves on either side of a widening chasm – a deep, treacherous pass with no bridge, no rope ladder, and no hope of crossing. Madeleine knew she could reach out her hands, call to her friend, beg her to find a way to jump across, but that it was futile. They now, having for most of their lives been joined at the hip, found themselves in very, very different places.

Heartbreakingly, it felt like the beginning of the end.

This would forever be the time when the friendship that had sustained her through her teens and provided her with more joy than any other relationship in her life so far began to falter. There was no fresh argument, no intensification of their row, no fight or further cross words. And actually such a rupture, a more violent occurrence, might have made things easier to accept, because deep down Madeleine knew that in the quiet moments and dark nights when she felt the ache of loss and wished she could call her sister, her beloved Trina, this was the moment that she would recall; the dull *thud, thud* as the ties that bound them fell away.

Two women, no longer kids, who at this crossroads in their lives, chose very different paths.

'Well, whatever you decide, whatever happens, you know that your mum and dad will always be there for you.' Trina swallowed, her eyes misting.

Madeleine breathed deeply as their words settled around them like a toxic dust. Her friend's implication was clear, her mum and dad would be there, but she may not . . .

Trina was hurt and Madeleine knew that what came next would be the final cut; their fate about to be sealed with six words.

Three spoken by each.

Equal in magnitude.

She was sure that the effect for Trina was the same as it was for her. Words which hit her body like fire-flaming rocks that burned through her skin and bone and came to rest in her chest where she was confident they would be lodged for a lifetime. Equally sure was she that in the future, it would take only the merest breeze of memory to fan them and the fire would roar again as surely as if she had heard them for the first time.

Six words that changed *everything.*

'It's Jimmy's baby,' she whispered.

'That's fucking perfect,' Trina had replied.

Chapter Six

The nurse took readings from the machines Marnie was hooked up to as Madeleine and Trina stood by the door, out of sight, doing their best to keep out of the way. Madeleine watched her mum blink and lift her head, looking to her left and right, suggesting it took a fraction of a second longer than was comfortable for her to remember where she was and what was going on.

Marnie glanced at her chest and her eyes widened, as if realisation dawned. Madeleine could only imagine how odd it must be for her mum; the clothes she had dressed herself in that morning were gone, and in their place the soft cotton of a medical tunic against her skin. The nurse helped lower her head back on to the pillow. Marnie's lips smacked together, suggesting her mouth was dry. She looked groggy, tired and a little weepy, which wasn't like her at all.

'How are you doing, Mrs Woods?' The nurse reached for Marnie's wrist, offering warmth and kindness with this one act of contact. Her tone was patient and Madeleine loved her for it.

'Very weak.' Her mum's voice sounded thin and she was clearly embarrassed to be tearful. 'Look at me,' Marnie tutted, 'a right old display!'

It was a phrase Marnie's mother would have used. Madeleine Macintyre might have been dead for a couple of decades, and yet it was the case for Madeleine too that when she was feeling a bit under the weather or sorry for herself, she wanted her mum. It was, it seemed, no different for Marnie. Age, she understood, did not make any allowance when it came to missing your mother.

'That's not surprising.' The nurse smiled. 'You've been through a lot. Your body has been through a lot. It's going to take a while for you to recover. So you need to try to relax and let us take care of you.'

'I'd rather be at home. I've got a pile of ironing that I've left in a laundry basket and dumped on the bedroom floor. There's defrosted mince in the fridge that needs using up – I was going to make a spaghetti Bolognese. And the breakfast things are still in the sink, waiting to be washed.'

Madeleine got it, the idea of being halted in her tracks, and the thought of all the irritating chores that would have to wait was not a pleasant one. Not to mention her to-do list, equally as bothersome to her as Marnie's defrosted mince and laundry pile. Small things to some people, but for her they were actually the big things, the markers in the day that helped a life run like clockwork. For her – and it seemed her mother too – they gave life routine, purpose, and structure.

Trina rolled her eyes and they both smiled. It was typical of Marnie to want to get cracking, giving no credence to lying idle, heart attack or not. It boded well for her recovery and Madeleine felt her muscles soften a little.

The nurse was a little sterner now. 'You need to rest and not think about everything going on outside. Concentrate on you and feeling better.'

'That's easy to say. I'd just rather be at home.'

The nurse bent low and smiled into Madeleine's mum's face. 'Between you and me, I'd rather be at home too. I've got three episodes of *Bake Off* to catch up on and the remains of an apple crumble in the fridge, but here we are, so let's make the best of it, okay? The doctor will be around later and you can ask her anything that's worrying you. Now, how about a nice cup of tea?'

'Thank you, that'd be lovely.'

'And if you're feeling up to it, you have a couple of visitors.'

'Oh?' Marnie squinted in their direction and it was then her misty eyes upgraded to a trickle of tears. 'There they are!' She reached out.

They walked forward. Madeleine stooped by the side of the bed and took her hand. 'Hey, Mum.' She grazed her mum's cheek with a kiss, giving her a slow, lingering look as if seeking confirmation that she was alive and present before reaching down to give the best hug she could manage with Marnie at such an awkward angle. They weren't the hugging kind, but it felt necessary; this situation – Marnie's illness – a hiatus to any tension, a break from self-consciousness, a reset; another reminder that life was fragile, time short, and that connection was all important.

'My girl.'

The two locked eyes. The same eyes – grey-blue in colour with glossy lashes. Eyes that woke and stared upon two different worlds. One a small and familiar world of all Marnie had ever known, and the other Madeleine's world, which she knew was beyond her mum's imagination.

'For the love of God, Marnie! Look at you! The things some people do for a rest.' Despite the humour, there was no escaping the emotion in Trina's tone.

'You scared me, Mum. And you scared Trina!'

Her friend leaned over and kissed Marnie. 'You really did,' Trina confirmed.

'I scared meself,' Marnie admitted. 'It's strange, I don't remember much about what happened. I remember being at the bus stop. I know the sky was winter blue and it was frosty and there was a line of sparkle running along the kerb that made everything look beautiful. I remember sending Dougie off with a full flask of tea. And then I know we chatted, Trina.'

'We did.' Trina leaned in. 'And if you genuinely can't remember, I lent you twenty quid.'

Marnie managed a half laugh. 'I vaguely recall being on the trolley that brought me from the ambulance and into the accident and emergency department, but everything else is a little fuzzy. I might have been here for an hour or a week . . . It's odd.'

'Marnie, we know you like your sleep, but even you couldn't sleep for a week,' Trina quipped.

'Don't you believe it.' Her mum looked into the middle distance and her brow furrowed. 'Actually, now I come to think of it, I remember Dougie was here. I know he spoke to me. He held my hand and I could tell he was crying a bit, my lovely old softy.' She stopped to wipe a fresh trickle of tears with her shaking hand. Madeleine could only imagine what her dad must have said, how distressing the situation must have been for them both. 'A young doctor came to see me in the casualty, who told me I'd had a heart attack. A *heart attack!*'

'It's scary, Marnie,' Trina empathised. 'But it could have been so much worse.'

Madeleine understood that even the words were frightening. It wasn't something she'd ever considered, not really. Her granny had slipped away after a battle with Alzheimer's, her grandad cancer, but Marnie's heart health had never entered her mind. She was after all as strong as an ox.

'It is bloody scary, and a shock! I know keeping healthy and active is important. I don't smoke, only sip booze in celebration a couple of times a year. I walk everywhere and always take the stairs instead of the lift. My weight's in check and I thought heart problems were what happen to other people.'

'How are you feeling now?' Madeleine sat on the chair by the side of the bed and placed her soft leather handbag on the floor. Trina sat next to her.

'I'm fine.' Marnie's words sounded practised.

'Course you are, Mum. I think you'd say that no matter how you were feeling. You're in hospital! It's okay to admit to feeling ropey, okay to not have it all under control.'

Marnie put her hand on her daughter's arm. 'Madeleine, my beautiful darling, if I was feeling better, I'd laugh out loud. This coming from you, who is so fixated on control it's a miracle you don't pass out with the exertion! Your dad always says you could tighten the screws of the sofa just by sitting on it!'

Trina chuckled, and Madeleine felt the love in it. The atmosphere around them was instantly lifted. A reminder of how it used to be – the ribbing, the banter, the honesty wrapped in humour – back before everyone was on guard.

'You might have a point,' she conceded.

'I'll admit it is a hard thing to talk about,' Marnie admitted. 'Your heart's important, isn't it?'

'It is.' Madeleine gave a wry smile and caught the shoulder shake from Trina. She too, it seemed, recognised the understatement.

'You know what I mean,' Marnie tutted. 'It's not like if you break a finger, lose a toe, or have a dicky tummy – you can still crack on, can't you? I mean, not easily, but everything else still works. But your heart? Your heart is everything. It's like a car with a dodgy engine – a broken engine.'

'Mum, have you ever considered a career in medicine? Your in-depth knowledge of biology is really something.' Madeleine squeezed her hand and hoped Marnie felt the love in it.

'Cheeky mare.' Marnie took a deep breath. 'You know, this is a horrible, terrible, fearsome situation, but I'd be lying if I said that it wasn't the very best kind of reward for the very worst kind of day, seeing you two sitting next to each other, chatting. It takes me right back. It makes me happy. My beloved girl and her beautiful friend. I love you both so much.'

Neither she nor Trina spoke, but both smiled politely. Madeleine sensed that her friend felt the same as she did; that even though today had felt like a breakthrough – a calming of the choppy waters – they weren't quite there yet. Marnie's words, however, made her wonder if this could be a new start for them . . . Now, wouldn't that be something?

'The doctor I saw just before they brought me up to the ward, the young woman, I think, she said I've got to have an operation.'

'What kind of operation? Did they say?' Madeleine felt the leap of concern. A heart attack was bad enough, but now surgery?

Marnie patted her daughter's hand. 'The last thing I want to do is worry everyone. She didn't give me too much detail and didn't seem overly concerned. All very routine. I'll hear more tomorrow. I think that's what she said. I do know I've got to have a little thing fitted so that if my heart stops, it'll shock it back to life. Like a battery pack. I'll be part robot. Almost bionic.' She gave a big false grin that barely hid her fear.

'Oh. Do you mean a pacemaker?' Trina asked the question before Madeleine had the chance. She knew very little about them but would of course investigate.

'No, not a pacemaker, a different thing. But it's more as a pre-caution. As I said, the doctor isn't worried and neither am I.' She embellished, but Madeleine knew her too well to be fooled by her bravado.

'Have you had any warnings, Mum? Have you been feeling ill or anything?'

Marnie shook her head. 'Not really. Bit tired, but I'm always tired.'

'I can get you some help,' Madeleine spoke with urgency. 'I can get someone to clean the—'

'I'm fine,' Marnie cut her off. 'I'm fine. We're fine. Do you know how many times I say that to you?'

'A lot.' Her daughter clicked her tongue on the roof of her mouth, as if making a point.

There was a beat of silence while the novelty of reunion settled and the practicality of the situation wrapped them.

'Did they say when they might operate or how long the surgery was or—'

'No, Madeleine, no detail. Nothing. As I said, I'll hear more tomorrow.'

'Sounds like you'll be in for a while.' Trina's addition was less than helpful.

'Oh God.' Marnie rubbed her face. 'This is the last thing we need.'

'You've got no choice, Mum, you have to rest.'

'Yes, that's what the doctor said. I just wish I could stop thinking about all that needs doing in the flat, and our life – the way we run things, I'm needed there. I worry everything will all go to rat shit without me.'

Madeleine understood how these small mental papercuts, tasks that were out of reach, had the ability to cause such agitation. She pictured the bloody scratch on the front of her Meneghini la Cambusa.

Marnie tried to sit up straighter before flopping back on the pillows that supported her. Something had snagged on the top sheet and it was this that alerted her to the fact that she was attached to machines that flashed sporadically and beeped occasionally.

'I just want to go home,' she repeated. 'Just want to get back to our little flat and the people in it who need me.' Just this thought seemed enough for those darned tears to gather again.

'Dougie will have everything under control, and I'm close by.' Trina shot Madeleine a look, as if aware that she might be treading on her toes, but this was how it had been for the last few years: Trina on hand and Madeleine popping in when she could.

'Oh, I know Doug will be fine.' Marnie smiled, as she always did when she spoke his name. 'He doesn't mind much, does he?'

It was the truth, and one of the things Madeleine most admired and adored about her shovel-handed, placid giant of a dad who she had never heard raise his voice. Never. She had asked him once why he never got angry. His reply had stayed with her.

'I grew up in an angry house.' This much she knew; her grandfather, so she had heard, had a fearsome reputation at the docks, where he'd start a fight over which way the wind blew. 'I used to dread the sound of my old man's key in the door. I lived with a knot of worry in my gut morning, noon, and night. I saw the way my mum and sister changed the moment he arrived. He'd stand in the doorway and they made themselves smaller – they went quiet and left the room or shrunk down into a chair as if they could avoid his barbs. It was horrible to watch. Terrible for us all and frustrating for me, the only other man in the house, and yet I was unable to stop him or make things better. It killed me, that. I vowed that if ever I was lucky enough to have a family, I'd make sure they looked forward to me coming home, not dread it.'

'And we do, Dad.' She had spoken the truth. 'We really do.'

'I'm blessed, little sausage. Plus, I don't see what hollering and mouthing off changes, anyway. In my experience, it doesn't really resolve anything, just makes for an unpleasant atmosphere, and I don't see the point in that.'

He had pulled her in for a hug. She could still feel the imprint of it now.

She smiled, warmed by the memory and equally the prospect of seeing him later.

Trina stood. 'Right, I'd better get going. Only wanted to check in on you, Marn, and to bring you some bits.'

'Thank you, love.' Marnie touched the grape punnet.

'Plus I'm sure you two would like some time alone.'

Marnie smiled at the woman with a slow blink of gratitude, but neither of them made any attempt to dissuade Trina from leaving. 'Oh love, you really didn't have to come in, but I'm so happy you did. You go before it gets late.'

'Are you kidding me?' Trina kissed Marnie goodbye and zipped up her coat. 'I wouldn't have been able to sleep if I hadn't seen you for myself, up and chatting. Flippin' 'eck, Marnie, you gave me a proper fright this morning.'

'As I said, I gave myself a proper fright, love.'

'I can't stop seeing it. Us chatting about nothing much and the next thing I knew you'd gone grey and clammy and then you just . . . keeled over!'

Madeleine wasn't sure rehashing it was a good idea.

'I'm proper embarrassed. Can't imagine what I looked like or who saw me. I'll never be able to show my face again on the bus.' Her mum shook her head as if floored with embarrassment.

'No one saw anything. You were very graceful.' Trina gave Madeleine a quick conspiratorial glance, sharing her unspoken intention to say the right thing, truth or not. 'Do you know, I always thought I'd be great in a crisis, calm and composed, but I just stood there calling your name and shouting for help. I was rubbish! So, next time, please make sure you're within grabbing distance of a nurse or firefighter. They'll know what to do.'

'Gawd, Trina, I hope there's not a next time. And you weren't rubbish, lovey, you were marvellous. I'm so glad you were there.'

'Me too.' Trina placed her hand on Madeleine's shoulder. 'See you soon, Mads.'

'Yes, and I can only echo what Mum said – thank goodness you were there.'

'It's what we do, isn't it? Show up in a crisis, look after each other.' Her words were considered, pointed.

'Family,' Marnie croaked.

'Yes, Marn, family.' Trina blew a final kiss and left the room.

'Don't you miss her?' Marnie's question caught her off guard. Madeleine cursed the lump that gathered in her throat.

'Sometimes.' It was all she was willing to admit. The truth was a lot harder to say, that in the dead of night or quiet times, when in a memory of something funny, or bursting to share some news, she'd either laugh or cry accordingly, and her desire to sit with her old friend, to be in her presence, to hear her voice, to lay her head on her shoulder, was almost overwhelming.

'It's true what we said – life is short, my love, and after today it's made me think about you and Trina, all the girls I love.'

She braced herself for what might follow, but Marnie was robbed of the floor by the arrival of a doctor in scrubs and a shallow hat, suggesting she might have come from surgery, her speed of speech also a big hint that she was in a hurry.

'Hello, Mrs Woods, I'm Doctor Callaghan.'

Marnie nodded.

'Hello, Doctor, this is my daughter.' The pride in her mother's gesture was unmistakeable and moving in equal measure.

'Just wanted to check in. We've had your scans back and the results of a few other tests that my colleagues ran when you first came in.'

Madeleine saw how Marnie's limbs trembled with fear. She reached for her mother's hand.

'And I'm sure you will have lots of questions and, fear not, I will be coming to see you tomorrow for a longer chat and to talk you through everything, but this is just to give you an overview and hopefully stop you worrying. You had a heart attack – I think you know that already.'

Again Marnie nodded.

'And having weighed everything up, I do think the best course of action will be to insert an ICD. Did someone already mention this to you?'

'They did, yes.'

The doctor touched her chest, presumably where this device would live. Madeleine felt a little queasy at the prospect but hid it as best she could.

'It's similar to a pacemaker and is designed to prevent cardiac arrest. It's very clever and detects abnormal electrical signals that can be an indicator that you are about to go *into* cardiac arrest and it sends an electrical shock to the heart.'

'Like a defibrill . . . thing?' Marnie questioned.

'Yes, exactly like that,' the doctor enthused. 'It reboots the heart. As I say, we can go into it in more depth tomorrow, but I just wanted to make you aware of what I'm thinking and what I believe will give you the best chance of living the fullest life while mitigating risk. How does that sound?'

Terrifying . . . unthinkable . . . disgusting . . . hopeless . . . desperate . . .

'Sounds good, doesn't it, Mum?' Madeleine kept her thoughts to herself and managed a small smile.

Marnie nodded, her face a little pale.

'Good.' The doctor gave a huge sigh, as if catching her breath. 'Right, well, I will see you tomorrow. Now rest. And that's not a suggestion, it's a necessary thing to reduce your myocardial workload.'

'Okay.'

'I'll leave you to it.' Dr Callaghan left as quickly as she'd appeared.

Marnie rubbed her chest, as if feeling the bones and skin beneath her fingertips – bones and skin that would be cut to accommodate some kind of device. The thought was horrific, and Madeleine felt a quake of fear at the prospect, not that she'd show it to Marnie, Dougie, or anyone else who asked, knowing if she kept her emotions in check, made it sound routine, they would likely take her lead.

'What a bloody carry on, Madeleine.' Marnie cried then, great gulping tears that fell down her face.

'Don't cry, Mum. Please don't cry. It's all going to be okay.' She hoped she spoke the truth.

Marnie's eyes seemed drawn to the wide double doors of the room, which were propped open. Doors that Madeleine knew promised all good things: something to eat or drink, a nurse or doctor to bring relief or company, and more importantly a route out of here – the first step towards home and recovery.

'I've not yet spent a night under this roof and already I miss my bed, my flat, my little family . . .'

This invited another burst of tears.

'I can help, Mum. Please let me just—'

'No, I've told you. I've told you a million times—'

'And I'm telling you.' Her daughter raised her voice, her turn to interrupt. 'I *can* help and I *will* help. I can pick up, drop off, do the shopping, anything that might—'

'We can manage.' Marnie wiped her eyes and sniffed her distress. 'We have always managed and we always will.'

'But—'

'Aren't you off to America soon on your trip?' Marnie cut her short.

There it was – the tone, the words, the question . . . a reminder that Madeleine lived a very different life.

'Yes. Yes, I am.' She nodded and stared at the doors herself, understanding the desire to escape. 'And actually, Mum,' – she swallowed – 'it's more than a trip. It's a move. I'm moving there. I'm going for a few years at least. I have a new job. I'm getting an apartment and everything.'

She watched her mother's face fall, her mouth set in a thin line of disapproval.

'Well, there we go.'

Marnie's words sounded finite and accusatory in equal measure. It had always been her skill; her ability to say so little and yet say so much.

December

2.00 p.m.

Madeleine watched Trina leave the café with a dark pit of despair in her gut. Her fingers twitched with the need to reach out to her; her lips moved as if tempted to call her back. But she did neither. Instead, she stared after the silhouette that was as familiar to her as her own, as her friend marched down the pavement without so much as a backward glance. Madeleine paid for her half-eaten croissant, took the last sip of tea, and headed out for the Tube. Cloaked in self-consciousness, she wondered if people could tell she was pregnant, wondered if they could see by looking at her in the way *she* could the women in the pregnancy clinic. What would happen now? Would she wake one morning to find she'd sprouted enormous bosoms and a round bump of life that was a total give-away? Would she reach eight, nine months and catch up for this rather demure start? She shuddered at the thought, frightened and repulsed in equal measure.

She didn't want this – any of it!

Lacking the desire or inclination to head back to her shared flat and wallow in her news, she decided the best thing she could do was keep busy, for now. Sorrow threatened to drown her and so she pushed it down into the base of her stomach and did her best to remain upright.

She flashed her pass and walked into the building, finding it almost impossible to understand how when she had left the office last night she was one person and now, just one cup of pee and a scan later, she was entirely another.

What am I going to do?

This was the question that pinged around her mind like a kicked can in a busy alleyway. It was just as noisy and disrupting. This job, her routine, working hard, were the things that sustained her. The thought of regressing . . . Or, worse, going back to the starting blocks, only more encumbered than she was before, trapped once again by a life that she had worked so hard to escape, when she had only just made headway enough to feel progress was within her reach . . . And now, now this unforeseen disaster that threatened to push her so far off course she didn't know how she might recover, or even if she could. To say it was unfair was an understatement. It was instead a catastrophic threat to her life plan. A disaster of epic proportions, contrary to every image she had ever held in her mind of her future. But only if she allowed it to be. This was the time she needed to dig deep and find a solution, something that would allow her to get back on track, as if it had never happened.

Her pulse was already calmer, her manner less flustered, as she settled behind her desk and flicked through the emails that had arrived during her absence. Nothing of great interest. It seemed her mum was right: they could do without her for a day or two. The place had not fallen down.

The design team were in a meeting and the corner of the vast open-plan office where she and her colleagues resided was almost empty.

Rebecca's fabulous workspace, separated from the hoi polloi by a glass and brass bifold door, was similarly deserted, and Captain's velvet cushion was without him in residence.

Digging into her bag, she pulled out the leaflets, a slip confirming her next hospital appointment and the scan picture, before placing them on her desk. Her eyes flicked over the information but it was hard to take in – impossible to accept as truth, no matter the evidence in front of her. To think at all was like mentally wading through treacle – slow, cumbersome, and without clarity of vision of what lay ahead. Her temples pulsed with the beginnings of a headache.

She opened the project file on her Mac, studying the images for a new hotel foyer that was being bolted on to an existing building in the heart of Old Berlin. It was her responsibility to keep the master file up to date with images and amendments, distributing it to everyone before meetings.

She hadn't heard Rebecca approach, and nearly jumped out of her seat as the woman's voice spoke over her shoulder. She turned to see Captain resting on his mother's arm. He looked happy, his soft body lolloping, little legs dangling.

'Hello, Captain, have you missed me?'

Rebecca and Captain both ignored the question.

'So, what do you think?'

'Oh! Of what?' She was instantly flustered, terrified to be conversing one to one with the scary legend who kept multiple global projects running like clockwork, and just as wary that she had no business looking at the images right now, other than out of curiosity. 'What do I think of . . .' Again she prompted.

'Of the pitches for the foyer?' Rebecca pointed at the screen with her neutrally manicured finger.

'I . . . I . . .' It was as if Madeleine understood that this was a pivotal moment in her career. A split second when she had to make a choice. Was it better to comply and win the woman's approval or should she be brave and speak the truth? If today had taught her one thing, it was that life turned on a penny, and who knew what tomorrow would bring. She sat up straight. 'I don't like them.'

'You don't *like* them?' Rebecca's brows knitted, whether in fury or fascination, it was hard to tell.

Madeleine's stomach dropped to her boots and she realised that if she was going to get fired or professionally squashed, she might as well be hung for a sheep as a lamb, as the saying went. It was moments like this that reminded her that there was no safety net – no parent with contacts on the board who could put a good word in, no first-class degree to waft in front of potential employers. No degree at all. This was it. This was her life. Her and her smarts, trying to make on-the-spot decisions that she could only hope helped propel her towards the life she craved.

'I thought they were disappointing.'

'I see. Did you tell anyone of your disappointment?' The woman's tone dripped with sarcasm.

'Oh, no! I just make copies, get the coffee, answer calls, I didn't think I should . . . erm . . .'

'What don't you like about them?' Rebecca pulled out the chair next to her and plonked Captain on the floor before she sat down, elbows on the table, fixated by the six prospective designs on the screen.

'I . . . I think they're good, all of them – bright, modern, eye-catching.'

'I thought you didn't like them?' The woman held her gaze quizzically and folded her arms.

'I was going add, but they aren't right for Berlin. *Old* Berlin. This one, for example, I can see in New York.' She touched the screen on the gold and onyx light-filled image. 'This one in an upmarket resort, somewhere like Dubai.' The colours were green and busy, tropical undertones with hot pink accent tones.

'Have you been?'

'No. I've not really been anywhere, but I study travel magazines, follow bloggers, and the same with anything to do with architecture and interiors. I like to match an object or a theme to a place. I think the two things need to work in harmony. Then it's like a building or an interior has sprung from the place, with roots that give it authenticity and age, even though it might be brand new. I think the best thing a passer-by could ask is, "Hasn't that always been there?"'

Rebecca turned to stare at her. Madeleine was still unsure if she was a friend or a foe. She felt the very real quake of fear in her boots, quite unable to discern the woman's neutral expression. Losing her job today would be the shittiest cherry on top of the shittiest cake imaginable. It felt a little late, however, to back down now.

'So how do you see the Berlin job, if you had to describe it?'

'Well, the hotel is quite dark.' She clicked a document and the current façade popped up. 'I wouldn't bother trying to bring light. It's a cobbled street and the frontage doesn't get any sun, so I'd go *with* the dark – embrace the gloom! But make it spacious, so it's not claustrophobic. I'd use the lack of light for atmospherics – smoked glass, black metal window frames, eclectic modern clustered lighting, a dark wood reception with glass lamps, like an old library. But with an air of mystery, of decadence. Round velvet sofas in bottle green with vast potted palms in oversized brass planters. The sharp lines of a cool warehouse but with the vibe of the cabaret. Nostalgic yet modern. I see a small bistro-style bar with a rail and sit-up stools, just for good coffee. A place to gather. A destination, not just a foyer. Dark enough for illicit lovers to remain incognito and cool enough to people watch.'

As her words flowed, so her clarity of vision increased, fuelled by her passion for such things and an image now so vivid she could walk through it in her mind, noting every last detail.

Rebecca held her eyeline, before Madeleine looked to the floor, her heart sinking as she mentally located her bag, figuring she might be asked to leave pronto and wanting to be able to make a hasty exit if this were the case. Instead, something quite remarkable happened. The woman laughed.

'I don't like them either. And you're exactly right.' She stood. 'Draw me your vision, just as you've explained it, and get it to me after the Christmas break.'

'Really?' Her smile split her face and just for a second she forgot the news that had cleaved open her plans.

'I never joke when it comes to business.'

And just like that Rebecca Swinton stood and swept past her, disappearing into her hallowed office like a Chanel-wearing spectre of opportunity. A Chanel-wearing spectre of opportunity who had no idea of the day Madeleine had had or how her whole life had been sent into freefall.

Captain pawed at her leg and she sighed.

'All right, Captain. I'll go grab the poo bags.'

Chapter Seven

Marnie's words settled around them like dust. Her curt, bitter insinuation that Madeleine was running away, abandoning them all, and maybe she was. Trying to figure out what to say next, she stared at the double doors of the ward when a sound made them both jolt.

They looked towards the noise that entirely splintered the air. 'Mu-mmy!'

It was jarring to hear such a racket in the quiet, considered environment of the hospital. Even the old lady in the pink nightie, who hadn't stirred before, opened her eyes suddenly.

It was a shriek, no less. A loud, loud combination of excitement and surprise.

Madeleine could feel Marnie now staring at her, no doubt picking up the almost involuntary smile that lifted Madeleine's mouth at the corners. And she understood; it had always been this way. And would more than likely always be this way. Marnie, staring, hoping that Madeleine's expression of deep joy at seeing her child might be tinged with enough regret to stoke the embers of regret and galvanise her into action, even rethink her life.

She knew that Marnie's one wish was that Madeleine might one day come to realise that being a parent was golden and that little Edith was such a gift. Her mother had said as much to her on more occasions than she could count, the words indelibly etched in her thoughts.

'I hope, Madeleine, that one day you might feel the pull of motherhood, might understand that it's never too late to step in and take the reins . . .'

And Madeleine would have to remind Marnie that she had been expressing a desire to the contrary her whole life, and that this situation was of both their making and that there were consequences. It was an ongoing battle and one she suspected would rage on for the rest of their lives, not that this understanding made it any easier to navigate. The words and these thoughts, however, pulled out of shape by the punch to her gut just to see the little girl, to hear her, be near her . . . It didn't get any easier.

'There she is!' Marnie beamed at her granddaughter.

Edith broke free of Dougie's hand and raced across the linoleum floor, her shoes squeaking as she did so. One sock bunched around her ankle, a new bruise on her knee. Her dark, dark hair flying.

'Mind Nanny's chest!' Dougie shouted as Marnie tensed, almost in anticipation of the little human hurricane that was her granddaughter landing on the bed. Madeleine well-judged the situation and stood, catching Edith as she jumped up into her arms.

And there they stood.

Almost nose to nose.

Mother and daughter.

Daughter and mother.

Madeleine and Edith.

Edith and Madeleine.

One named after her grandmothers.

One named after her great-grandmothers.

Reunited after three months apart.

What Madeleine felt in that moment would be hard to describe. It always was. Delight, on some level, to be close to the child. Happy, to see her smiling face. Relief, that the little girl was still too young to bring fire to her door with questions about rejection or her less than conventional start in life. And guilt. Armfuls and armfuls of it.

'My mummy's heeeeere!' Edith shook her long fringe from her face and shouted to her grandad, who followed her into the ward.

Marnie, suddenly teary, looked away. Madeleine suspected that she would never get used to the fact that for Edith to see her mummy was a rarity. But for her and her daughter, it was of course quite standard.

'I can see that.' Doug smiled. 'Hello, little sausage.' He planted a kiss on her cheek in greeting, before taking the chair Madeleine had only just vacated, as he reached for Marnie's hand.

His wife, his priority, always. His one true love. His other half.

Marnie seemed to soften, relax. The fact that he was there clearly made her feel better. Instantly better. It was just how it was. How it had always been. And how the sight of them gladdened Madeleine's heart.

Marnie scooched further up the bed. Madeleine could see that just the smallest movement was surprisingly challenging. She looked exhausted, a reminder of what she had endured, that her mum's body was broken and that there was no quick fix.

'Grandad picked me up from school and we got a McDonald's, but don't tell Nanny!' Edith did her best to whisper. Her little girl's breath against her face felt a bit invasive. Madeleine had to remind herself that this was the norm with small children – the complete disregard for personal space and a glorious lack of self-consciousness.

'I heard nothing!' Marnie smiled.

'Well, lucky old you!' Madeleine beamed into her daughter's ketchup-smeared mouth. 'How do you think Mum looks, Dad? Compared to when you saw her earlier?' She asked as if Marnie wasn't present. Transparency was, she knew, important, the very first thing she and Marnie had agreed when she had come home pregnant.

We are honest with this child from the start. Any lack of transparency would only lead to heartache further down the line . . .

And they had stuck to it. Until now that was, when the fact that Madeleine was moving to LA had yet to be broached. She was dreading telling her daughter, dreading it as much now as she had over the last couple of months, chickening out of the discussion on more than one occasion. Not that it was a topic for tonight. Edith had enough going on. They all did.

Doug studied his wife's face and she saw her own heightened emotion reflected in his expression.

'She has a little more colour and she's awake, thank God.' He kissed the back of Marnie's hand. 'I've been worried sick. Didn't know what to do with meself. When I got that call this morning' – his breath stuttered in the unfamiliar rhythm of distress – 'I felt like the ground had opened up in front of me. I can cope with anything – anything. But I can't cope with anything happening to you.' He addressed his wife directly, unashamed and unabashed, and Madeleine loved him for it. 'You're my girl, aren't you? You've always been my girl.'

'I am, and I'm fine,' Marnie piped up, clearly hoping her words were enough to reassure them all. 'I'm fine.'

'Course you are.' He winked at her.

'I think you've grown.' Madeleine spoke into her child's hair as the little one held her mamma close, cheek to cheek, reconnecting. It was always this way, the strength of feeling quite overwhelming and instantly smothered with the blanket of guilt at the fact that part of her wanted to walk away. To leave and let them all get on with the life they had built without her interference or presence often felt like the easiest option.

'I have.' Edith nodded quickly, as if this was some kind of conscious achievement. 'And I think you've grown!' She pointed at her mother's head, as if aware that this compliment was something others seemed to delight in and therefore wanting to say a nice thing.

Madeleine looked at Marnie and they shared a knowing look. Edith was funny; she'd always been funny.

'Are you okay, Nanny?' Edith squirmed to get out of Madeleine's arms and walked to the bed. Reaching up, she gently ran her fingers over the wires that dangled over the side of the top sheet.

'I'm all good, little darling. This is a bit funny, isn't it? Your nan lying here in a nightie having a rest.' Marnie did her best to make light of it, smooth any concerns for her granddaughter before they became worries.

'Grandad said you were poorly.'

'I got a bug!' Marnie sucked her teeth. 'I'll stay here for a little bit and then I'll be good as new and I'll come home to make your tea and run your bath and listen to you read.' She winked. Clearly not all topics were to be approached with transparency.

'Who's taking me to school tomorrow?'

It tore at Madeleine's heart to see the slight wobble to Edith's bottom lip.

'Well . . .' Marnie looked up at Doug, and Madeleine knew this would be another tiny papercut that her mum could well do without.

'I'll go to the market late.' Her dad took her lead, doing what they had always done – making it up as they went along. 'I'll call Tony later and tell him not to give away my pitch, then, erm . . .' He clicked his fingers. 'I'll ask Amir to watch things while I go fetch her, and then she can stay with me until—'

'I can take her to school.' Madeleine spoke up.

She was aware of her parents' collective sharp intake of breath and the brief moment of silence, as if a little stunned by the suggestion. She had never offered to get this involved. For a reason. It was potentially too confusing for Edith, and not what they had agreed. The kind of involvement she had been keen to avoid, not wanting Edith to rely on her in that way, knowing she was, in fact, unreliable. The help she proffered, at every opportunity, was nearly always of the financial kind. This, however, was a moment of reckoning. She saw the conflict on Marnie's face – delighted and concerned in equal measure. Madeleine would never admit to feeling the same, unsure she fully understood all that went into looking after a little one. This doubt alone, painful enough in itself, flew in the face of her desire to help. Her worry, even though she would never say it out loud, was that a disastrous experience would only damage the fragile connection she and Edith shared. Plus, she wasn't sure she was up to the task. This last thought, she kept to herself.

'What, me stay at your house and then you take me to school in the morning, Mum?'

There was no mistaking the look of sheer delight on Edith's face at the prospect. It did much to bolster Madeleine's confidence.

'Well, that's a possibility, or maybe . . .' Marnie sounded conflicted, clearly trying to think of Plan B, as if doubting that Madeleine was in fact the cavalry. It smarted. Madeleine resisted the temptation to remind her mum that this was what she had always hoped for – Madeleine stepping up to the plate.

It had felt like an easy decision, to take a back seat in the face of such a sledgehammer coming down on to her life, the answering of Marnie's prayer not to place her child with strangers, not to allow that chain to be broken. Yet there was nothing easy about the consequences that she only fully understood in retrospect. Not that she regretted it – 'regret' was a strong word – and while it wasn't easy, she was almost entirely certain that in the exact same circumstances, she'd do the exact same thing again, knowing she wasn't ready, and would likely never be ready to commit to a life of bedtime stories and warming up beige food while her child did her homework at a cosy kitchen table. That was a life for someone else.

Someone like Trina . . .

Doug placed his hand on his wife's forearm and rubbed her skin with his fingertips. A subtle reminder, she was sure, to let it be. Her lovely dad, always the peacemaker.

'What do you think? Would you like that, Edith, to go home with Mummy?' he asked his granddaughter directly.

'I really, really would!' The child jumped around on the spot. It was dusk, usually a time when she was winding down, and yet here she was, full of beans.

Marnie, who had gone a little pale, turned to look at Madeleine.

'If it's too much, love . . .' she began. 'I know how busy you are, and the last thing I want is for you to feel burdened, and I don't want Edith to feel tricky – it's already an unfamiliar situation.' The last bit she whispered.

'No, it's . . . fine . . . It's . . .' She struggled to find the words to allay her mum's fears and give herself the confidence that she could do this. It was typical of Marnie, doubting she had the ability while pushing her to try. It did little to build her confidence.

'We're having a sleepover!' Edith twirled until she nearly toppled with dizziness.

'It's fine. It is. It'll be fine.' Madeleine painted on a smile. 'If Edith comes home with me, then you guys can have some time alone right now and I'll drop her at school in the morning.'

'Do you know where to—'

'Yes, Mum.' Madeleine cut her short, her manner a little sharper than was necessary, as embarrassment flared. She wasn't entirely sure which class Edith was in and knew the place had been remodelled a little since her day, but how hard could it be? 'I know where.'

'Of course you do. Can you wash her uniform?' As usual, the little girl looked like she'd been rolling in dirt.

'Mum, please, of course I can wash her uniform. I even have a spare toothbrush. It'll be fine. I'll call you when she's gone in tomorrow, so you know I haven't mislaid her and that she survived the night.'

'What does *mislaid* mean?' Edith piped up.

'Lost, it means to lose something, so I'm going to call Nanny in the morning to prove I haven't lost you.'

Edith looked wide-eyed.

'Mummy is joking!' Marnie did her best to chuckle. The exertion showed on her face.

'Come on, you. Say goodbye to Nanny and Grandad and you'll see them tomorrow.'

Edith blew her nan a kiss. Madeleine looked on as Doug ruffled her hair. A reminder of how deeply they cared for their granddaughter, how they had taken her into their lives and loved her unconditionally, as was their wish.

She could feel her parents watching her leave, their stares burning into her back, as they headed along the corridor. It did nothing to aid her flagging confidence, wary as she was to be walking out of this building with Edith for the second time in her life. And, just like that first time, without a clue as to how best care for her, and a weight to her bones at the prospect of having to figure it all out.

'Oh no! I forgot to tell Nanny something!' Edith stopped walking and turned to run back.

'Wait, Edith!' She grabbed her arm, stalling her, as she bent down to whisper, 'We need to be quiet and not really run around, as there are lots of sick people who need to sleep.'

'Okay.' Edith gave an exaggerated nod, her thick hair again falling over her face.

They tiptoed slowly and quietly back into the ward.

Her dad was standing now, bent over the bed, holding Marnie close, her fingers gripping the fabric of his sweater, her face buried inside his neck, as she sobbed. It felt intrusive, even to observe this moment of intimacy, let alone interrupt it.

As they drew a little closer, she caught fragments of their conversation.

'. . . my love, my love!' Doug breathed against her.

'. . . scared, Doug . . . so scared . . . an operation. An operation on my *heart*.'

'. . . my girl. We'll get through it . . . the best place . . . the surgeons . . . all very routine . . . day in and day out . . . you'll be fine.'

It was heartbreaking to witness Marnie's fear first-hand; the least she could do was keep Edith from witnessing the same.

Reaching down, she gently lifted Edith into her arms. Her little girl certainly *had* grown, and to lift her from the floor was a reminder that she was heavier than Madeleine remembered. It was still lovely though, to feel the weight of her in her arms, the thought of her made real, a connection. They made it back to the corridor unseen by Doug and Marnie. Madeleine placed her gently on her feet.

'I think Nanny and Grandad are having a lovely chat. Can whatever it is you need to tell her wait until tomorrow, do you think?'

'Yes.' Edith nodded, but the protuberance to her bottom lip suggested this was far from satisfactory.

'Or maybe you can text her later from my phone or call her before bedtime, how about that?'

At this her daughter brightened and reached for her hand.

Madeleine tried to rationalise the cloak of self-consciousness that held her fast, knowing that anyone looking at her walking along with this child would likely not guess at the tangle of nerves that knotted in her gut. The responsibility of being alone with Edith weighted her down like a physical thing. She was unskilled in the task, unfamiliar with the detail, and it was petrifying. Supposing she got it wrong? Supposing Edith got hurt or sick? Supposing she did lose her? This was very different to playing board games with her at the little kitchen table in the flat, where Marnie was never more than twenty feet away, and definitely not the same as taking her to the swings for a ten-minute jaunt. This was a familiar anxiety. Whenever she saw Edith after any time apart, her initial reaction was one of sheer delight. Her little girl always seemed more capable, and more grown-up, than she remembered, and so very beautiful. It tore at her heart and was bittersweet. Edith was clearly happy at home with Marnie and Doug, and all Madeleine wanted to do was wrap her arms briefly around her, inhale the scent of her and hold her to her breast before letting her go, freeing both of them to live their lives . . .

Instead, she buried the desire to display such love, as if she had given up the right to behave in that way when she had given up the baby into the loving care of her parents and walked away, stuck in the belief that she couldn't have it all.

'I'll press the button!' Edith shouted, pulling her from her thoughts, as the little girl raced ahead and jabbed the call button for the lift. Her enthusiasm for such a mundane task brought a smile to Madeleine's face.

The lift doors opened and they stepped in.

'Hello!' Edith waved at the elderly couple who stood at the back of the lift holding a plastic bag, their faces etched with worry – a standard expression in this vast building where the human condition was spread over its floors.

'Hello.' The older woman smiled, as if relieved to be in the little girl's presence. A spark of sunshine on what might have been for them a dark day.

Ordinarily, upon entering a lift, Madeleine would have smiled briefly and stared at her phone, willing the lift to open again so she could leave without interacting with the strangers. Edith's introduction had denied her the preferred anonymity and so she stood awkwardly, feeling like she had no right to have taken the child – a kidnapper no less, and just as jumpy.

'I'm going home with my mummy!' Edith informed them with pure joy.

'Well, that's good.' The woman held her gaze, as if it would be odd if the child were not going home with her mum. Little did she know.

'I don't know where she lives, but my nanny is poorly and so she's staying here and Pop can't take me home as he has to be up early for the market and then I wouldn't be able to get to school.'

Madeleine wanted the ground to open up and swallow her, as her blush spread from her chest to the roots of her hair. It was exposing and embarrassing all at once, as Edith gave more information to the strangers than she was comfortable with.

'Well, I hope your nanny gets better soon,' the man added sincerely, seemingly as unfazed by the revelations as the girl was.

It was striking, the small act of friendship offered by a stranger that warmed her from the inside out. It was the Edith effect for sure; she now turned and waved at the couple, who walked in the opposite direction as they left the lift.

It amazed her how at ease and chatty the little girl was. Skipping along the hospital corridors, yanking Madeleine's arm up and down as she did so. Her small, sticky hand inside her own felt alien, clumsy, and she wanted to let go of it, unsure how to walk in her heels and keep pace with her daughter jumping around by her side.

It was a relief to have seen Marnie awake and talking. Still, it hurt her that there was a thin veneer of distance between them that had been present since she'd first told her she was pregnant. It had changed things. It had changed everything! At first she'd thought it was that her mother was disappointed at how she'd messed up, got pregnant when it was not part of her plan. But the moment she saw Marnie with Edith, she understood that it wasn't getting pregnant that was the problem, but the choices Madeleine made after. Not that she could do a damned thing about that now.

The cab ride from Newham hospital to her apartment was a reminder of how Edith liked to chat. Her little voice ricocheted around inside the cab, as she looked up through the glass roof of the taxi and voiced her every thought.

'Look! I can see a church! And another church! And there's a cat!'

'I like these lights!'

'Lots and lots of cars!'

'That man's eating his sandwich at the bus stop!'

'I need a wee!'

'That's the river over there. My great-grandad used to work on the river, didn't he, Mummy?'

Madeleine had nodded; it was true, he had.

'Chicken and noddles!' she read aloud.

'Noodles,' Madeleine corrected.

'Yes! Noodles!' The little girl laughed, only to start bouncing in her seat. 'My friend Travis went to the Tower of London, but I've never been.'

'Maybe I can take you.'

She liked the thought, planning a trip. They never did that, only ever meeting at Marnie and Doug's for birthday teas and Christmas dinner or if she happened to be passing. It felt easier that way, keeping it casual and abiding by Marnie's rule – not to interfere, not to confuse anyone and to allow her mum to parent with freedom in the way she saw fit. Madeleine hoped that making a plan wasn't overstepping the mark. But if she could manage a sleepover, surely a trip to the Tower of London would be a breeze, as long as she could fit it in before she hopped on a plane bound for LA.

'Yes!' Edith jumped in the seat. 'Can we go to Legoland too?'

'Oh, I'm not sure. We can think about it.' She was wary of committing to too much; not only did she not want to step on Marnie's toes, but she was after all heading off in a couple of weeks –a conversation yet to be had with Edith. In the face of today's events, she relished it even less.

The taxi pulled up outside her apartment building and as she helped Edith out of the cab, she felt her gut roll with nerves. Unsure now if it was such a good idea to bring her daughter here, wary of someone seeing them and her having to explain, and was it going to be confusing, showing her where she lived? Showing her how she lived? Deep down, she knew Edith was smart and figured once she'd seen Madeleine's life up close, it wouldn't be too long before Edith figured out that her mother had chosen that life over staying on the Brenton Park estate with her, and had a thousand questions she felt ill-equipped to answer. Not that there was anything she could do about it at this point in time on a school night.

Edith counted the stairs to her apartment as they climbed. Madeleine opened the front door and switched on the lights, watching as her little girl stepped over the threshold and surveyed the flat with her hands on her hips, looking and sounding so much like Marnie it was comical.

'Well, this is very nice!'

'You like it?' It was a lovely compliment from her child, who only spoke the truth.

'I do. It's like my school hall where we have gym and do sing-ing!' She pointed up towards the rafters of the double-height ceiling.

'I'll take it!' At least Edith seemed to understand the sheer joy of the cavernous space.

'You haven't got much stuff though, have you, Mum?'

Madeleine laughed loudly at the observation made by the child, who lived in the cosy confines of the flat where she too had grown up. The flat where knick-knacks and ornaments crowded the windowsills and dusty faux flower displays nestled on cluttered bedside tables, and where crockery that wouldn't fit into the limited cupboard space was piled up on the countertop, to be navigated every time you wanted to put the kettle on. Her apartment was luxuriously spacious and fairly bare; her life streamlined. Just the way she liked it.

'I have got stuff, I just put it away, out of sight.'

'I see.' Suddenly she placed her little hand on her forehead. 'Oh no, Mum! I haven't got my reading book. I need to read my chapter!' Edith spoke with a hint of tears, suggesting she might be a bit more overwhelmed by the day's events than she was letting on. 'It's in my book bag on the end of my bed and that means I won't have it for school tomorrow, will I?'

'Well, that's okay.' She did her best to appear calm and in con-trol, knowing that was what Edith needed right now – a steady hand on the tiller, as well as being unsure how she'd cope if the little girl lost her sunny demeanour. 'What we can do is find your book online and you can read a chapter on my tablet, and then I'll write you a note and we can give it to your teacher, explaining the situation and letting them know that you'll have your book bag for school the day after, and that you did your reading. She'll understand.'

'He. My teacher is Mr Lawal.'

'I thought it was Miss Shrapnel, or something like that?'

'Miss Shrader was my first teacher. In *baby* class.' Edith pulled a disapproving face, as if disgusted at the idea that she might still be a baby.

'Oh.' Madeleine swallowed; it didn't feel good not knowing this most basic of details. Tangible proof of how she was only on the periphery of Edith's life. 'I guess I'm rubbish when it comes to the detail.' She tried to make light of it, at the very same moment that Edith's shoulders began to go up and down and her chest heaved and a fat tear rolled down her cheek.

'Edith! No! No! No! Please don't cry! It's okay, it's all going to be okay. What's the matter? I promise I'll write a note to your teacher, and Marnie is going to be fine – she's as strong as an ox, and—'

Edith opened her mouth, as if she hadn't heard a word or if she had easily dismissed them. Her cry was as loud as it was unnerving. Madeleine dumped her handbag on the countertop and wrapped the little girl in a hug. 'Please don't cry! Please. You'll make me cry and then what will we do? What's the matter, darling? Why are you so sad? What can I do to make things better? Would you like some toast?' She hoped there was bread somewhere.

Madeleine's heart beat a little too quickly for comfort and she wished she knew what to do. Her first instinct was to call Marnie, before remembering that she was laid up in a hospital bed awaiting heart surgery – a terrifying fact that she had to keep from Edith at all costs.

'I don't want you to mislay me. I don't . . . don't want to get lost. I want . . . I want to go home now!' her daughter sobbed.

'Oh, Edith, sweetie! I won't mislay you, I never could!' How she regretted making the ill-informed comment in front of her, a rookie mistake that she was now paying the price for. 'I was only joking with Nanny. I'm right here and I'm not going anywhere. I'll watch you sleep; I'll watch you sleep all night, and in just a few short hours – quicker than a wink – I'll put your uniform on you and take you to school and then . . .' She stopped talking, unsure of the plan for the rest of Marnie's hospital stay.

'I want my dad.' Edith took stuttered breaths and pulled away from Madeleine's arms. 'I want my dad!'

Madeleine's heart sank. She hadn't seen or spoken to Jimmy for the longest time.

'I want my dad!' The wail was deep, heartfelt, and moving.

'All right, all right, love. How about we Facetime him? Would that work, do you think?'

Edith wiped her face and nodded, her crying slowed and her breath seemed to come a little easier.

'Right. I'll call him on my iPad and you guys can chat before bed. How about that?'

'Okay.' Edith nodded as she wiped her damp face on her sleeve and kicked off her shoes, before heading for the sofa. Her face trying to be brave was heartbreaking to see.

Shit! Madeleine lifted her tablet from her bag and tried to control the tremble in her fingers as she prepared to make contact with the man who had promised to love her for a lifetime . . . if not forever.

December

5.30 P.M.

Madeleine left the office and stepped out on to the pavement on this purple-hued wintry night where Christmas lights had been strung up across the street and a chill lingered in the air. Buttoning up her coat, she felt awash with a potent combination of loneliness and fatigue. Her flatmates were her friends, kind of, but they were no Trina. She shared no history with them and the prospect of putting her key in the door to be met with Luciano bitching about his colleagues in the department store, Liesl crying over her shithead of a boyfriend's latest antics, or Meredith necking wine like it was water until she passed out, was all more than she felt able to cope with right now.

Her interaction with her best friend earlier played heavily on her mind. It was a situation she didn't know how to remedy, unable to take back her words or change the fact that Trina saw her sleeping with Jimmy as a betrayal. And in the light of her friend's admission, her words of intent, the life she pictured with someone just like Jimmy . . . Madeleine could hardly blame her. It was all such a bloody mess.

As if guided by instinct and without too much forethought, she jumped on the Tube and headed out to her parents. *Home . . .* Not that it had been home for a while, but right now it was the only place she wanted to be. She needed to tell them, *wanted* to share with them this boulder of destruction that had hurtled into her life, aware that it was hurtling into their lives too.

It felt like she had to concentrate on keeping everything together, putting one foot in front of the other and not giving in to the volcano of emotion that threatened to burst from her. It was impossible for her not to picture the thing that had taken up residence in her womb. No matter how often she saw the image of the scan imprinted behind her eyelids, it still felt like a dream – or rather a nightmare – and she couldn't wait to wake up, laugh over the horror now averted, and crack on with her life.

Her bag was stuffed with leaflets about what to expect during her pregnancy, how things would progress from now on, the options around giving birth, the importance of eating right, and so on. She was fairly certain much of the wisdom and instruction was aimed at those in the early stages who could make sure they were doing everything in their power to build a healthy little specimen.

All of this was coming to her too late; her baby was only going to be cooking for another couple of months and then it was here! *She.* She was going to be here. A little girl. This was the first time she'd properly considered this, as if the news of her pregnancy had been enough to digest and, now that was bedding in, she allowed herself to think of this baby as a girl.

It was a lot.

Here too, on her journey home, every billboard, every poster, every image in every magazine, on the front of every book, and every shop window was baby related – how had she not noticed this before? Nor the preponderance of prams and buggies that cluttered up the pavements and station platforms. Babies and pregnancy bumps were everywhere! This was not going to be her life! It was not! She was going to impress Rebecca, grab her chance and make something of the opportunity that had fallen into her lap.

Arriving at the Brenton Park estate, she moved en masse with other weary workers who walked with a heavy tread from the high street, along the back alleys and short cuts to the tower blocks that Madeleine was convinced grew taller and wider the longer she was away.

Eschewing the piss-scented lift, as was always the Woods way, she walked up the concrete stairs, admiring the fresh graffiti that someone had sprayed up the wall. A vast, indecipherable tag that looked a bit like 'Hot Dog' but could have been anything. It smacked of boredom and destruction and could not have saddened her more.

Standing outside the front door, she placed her hand on the doorbell and hesitated, yet another door through which she was going to walk in as one person and leave as another.

She pressed it and stood back.

Marnie opened the door and yelled her delight.

'Oh, hello, little love! Why didn't you use your key? What a lovely surprise! I wasn't expecting you! How are you feeling? Do you want soup? I've got tomato or chicken and sweetcorn and I can do that with some toast – it'll make you feel better!'

All this before she had taken a step over the threshold.

'Hi, Mum.' She half walked, half fell into her mum's embrace. Closing her eyes against the shoulder that had always been there for her to cry on, enjoying the sensation, knowing that in just a short while things would never be the same again. Everything – *everything* – was about to change, and the only thing of which she was certain was that she didn't want it to.

'Poor little lamb, I can tell you're not feeling the ticket. Come in, you're letting all the warm out.'

Marnie pulled her inside and closed the front door behind her. They turned right into the small, square sitting room and she sank down into the chair by the window.

'Where's Dad?' It was unusual for him not to have called out in greeting when she entered, no matter where he was in their tiny flat.

'Oh, he's not here! He's gone up The Red Lion with a couple of lads from the market. They asked him out for a pint. He was quite excited to be going out, bless him! He even put some of that Lynx on I got him for Christmas a couple of years ago. He smelled lovely!'

It was a relief of sorts that he wasn't home – one less set of questions, one less face contorted with disappointment. The thought of letting her dad down, her beloved dad who worked so hard . . . it cut her heart.

'The Red Lion? Can't imagine Dad up the pub.' He had never been a boozer, bar the odd tipple at Christmas.

'I know, he said he's going to sip half a shandy and make it last. Hope he has a nice time. He works so hard.'

The love in her mum's eyes when she spoke about her husband was touching. It made Madeleine think of her earlier chat with Trina, who wanted this life. The image of her friend walking away without looking back was burned in her mind.

Marnie nestled into the corner of the sofa, clipped her pen to the front cover and folded away the word search magazine. 'So, how did you get on at the doctor's? What did they say? Did you get some antibiotics? It's all they ever seem to do up the health centre, dish out anti-bloody-biotics.'

This is it . . . She shrugged her arms from her coat and curled her legs beneath her, as she prepared to voice the unthinkable.

'I didn't get antibiotics, no. It was, erm . . . It was . . .' How to begin? What to say? She felt the pressure in her chest and fought to get a full breath.

'What is it, love?' Marnie's face twisted with worry.

'It's okay. Erm . . .' She literally couldn't find the words and looked up, hoping inspiration might fall from above.

'Madeleine, you're scaring me. Are you . . . Are you poorly, darling?' Marnie's hands balled into fists, which she now coiled against her mouth. 'What's wrong? Whatever it is, just please tell me. I can't stand the thought of you not being well. What did they say? Tell me!' Marnie's chest heaved as she no doubt ran through all the terrible possibilities.

'I'm . . . I'm pregnant.'

Her mum's mouth fell open and she emitted a long, slow breath. 'You're pregnant?' This she asked with the faint twitch of a smile on her mouth.

'Yes.'

'Are you sure?'

Madeleine pictured the image of the baby girl on the screen and nodded. It would have been hard to define the emotions that filled her up in that moment, but shame – shame was right up there – along with guilt and relief and a whole other bunch of feelings that weakened her. She sank back into the chair.

'Oh my love!' This time there was no mistaking Marnie's smile behind the hand that part-hid her mouth. 'I just . . . Oh my goodness! I don't know what to say! A baby! Well, that's a surprise! My God! Oh, Madeleine!' Her mother lurched from the sofa and came to rest on the rug in front of her. On her knees, her mother pulled her in for a warm, tight hug. It was restorative, it was comforting, and she knew it was short-lived as what she had to say next would not be so welcome.

'Oh! My little girl. Oh, my word.' Pulling away, her mum looked into her face and ran her hand over her hair. 'You look tired, but are you well, other than tired?'

She nodded and slipped free of her mum's embrace. Marnie retook her seat on the sofa. Her hands fidgeted in her lap.

'Are you in a relationship? Are you seeing someone? I haven't heard you talk about anyone, not that it's any of my business.' Marnie licked her lips. 'But are you?'

Again, she shook her head, knowing her mother was probably imagining Sunday roasts, welcoming her fella into the flat, the man who had got her daughter up the duff. 'No. No, I'm not seeing anyone.'

'Okay, okay.' She watched her mum shuffle to the edge of the sofa, the excitement in her voice barely disguised. 'Well, that's fine, we can cope with that. Plenty of people do it alone nowadays and of course you're not alone – you have us, you have Trina, you have—'

'Mum,' she began, and Marnie stopped talking. 'It's not that straightforward.'

'I know, my love, but you won't be the first and you'll certainly not be the last. And your dad might be a bit old-fashioned, but he will be over the moon once he gets used to the idea, he really will. How far are you? When can I tell people?' Her eyes were bright with joy and it almost floored her. How this woman could only see the positives, as if life were like it was in the movies, where everyone gets a happy ending.

'I didn't know I was pregnant, not until today.'

'Well, I bet it's still sinking in, but that explains you feeling a bit off colour. I remember that feeling of shock – of wonder, but a shock! I'd offer you a glass of champagne but a) you can't drink and b) I've never had a bottle of champagne in my life!'

'It is a shock, Mum. And as to how far along I am, it's a funny one, actually.'

Marnie held her gaze. 'How far are you? Can I start knitting? Or is it too soon?' Her mother beamed up at her, pushing to know the answer. 'How far are you, lovey?'

Chapter Eight

Madeleine was mentally scrabbling for solutions. She – the woman who juggled complex design projects, was responsible for teams of people, and who had her sights set on world domination. Yet here she was, sweating and fighting the desire to vomit as she weighed up her options and tried to figure out how best to get Edith through the night without crying.

Much to her delight, Edith's dad hadn't picked up when she had called earlier. She had been dreading speaking to him, with nerves bubbling in her throat, but what to do now? She had promised that Edith could make contact with Marnie but doubted the wisdom of phoning her mum at this hour. Marnie needed to sleep and there was the risk Edith might only get more upset, which meant no one would sleep, herself included. Edith, after her bath and now wearing one of Madeleine's oversized t-shirts while her uniform whizzed around the washing machine, nestled next to her on the sofa. Her soft form was warm against Madeleine, and she took comfort from it, liking how it felt a lot like building a connection.

'I was thinking, maybe it's best we *text* Nanny a goodnight message and then you can chat to her properly tomorrow. How does that sound?'

'Good.' Her daughter nodded.

'All right, then.' She reached for her phone with barely disguised relief. 'What was it you wanted to tell her?'

'I wanted to tell her that Travis and me went to visit Minty, but we couldn't find her. We looked really hard, but she wasn't there.'

'Oh dear. Who's Minty?'

'She's our mouse.' Edith stared at her, her expression blank.

'Oh, well, that explains it. Mice are proper little scamps. They're fast on those tiny feet, plus they've got four of them, so they can really motor. Minty has probably moved on, gone exploring, or she might be out with her friends. It's not surprising she's not where you last saw her.'

'Minty won't be out exploring with her friends.' Her daughter sounded adamant.

'Or maybe she moved to a new place or is working away . . .' It felt like a good segue into explaining her move to LA.

'Nope.' Edith shook her head. She was a tough nut to crack.

'You sound pretty certain!'

'I am certain, because Minty is dead.'

'Oh!' This she had not expected. 'So you were going to visit her . . . her final resting place?' She was struggling to keep up.

Edith let out a long sigh, as if having to explain was tedious. 'We went to dig her up, but don't tell Nan because she told me not to. She said it didn't matter about my sock.'

Madeleine opened her mouth to speak, trying to order the many, many questions that had sprung from this exchange, when Edith spoke instead.

'Mummy?'

153

Madeleine wondered if she'd ever get used to being called that, wondered if she'd get used to the unique taste of guilt and betrayal with soft undertones of joy that it left on her tongue. Wondered what her life might have been like if she'd not told Marnie she was pregnant, if she'd let this incredible little girl grow up without knowledge of her, in another family, all of which had been under consideration. These thoughts now, depending on her state of mind, mildly attractive or absolutely horrifying.

'Yes, Edith?'

'Can we try my dad again, please?'

'Sure.' She did her best to hide the fact that it had been nothing but sweet relief that filled her up when he had failed to answer earlier. She doubted she'd ever be free of the shiver of nerves along her limbs at the prospect of contact. On the rare occasion their paths crossed, she felt exactly as she had on the towpath the night she'd told him of her pregnancy – awash with remorse. And wishing, just a little bit, that she felt differently.

This time the Facetime call connected almost immediately and there was nowhere for her to hide and no time to practise in her head.

'Hey, Mads.'

And just like that – there he was.

His face filled the screen of her tablet. Her stomach flipped as it did when she bumped into any lover or old flame, as if her body reacted viscerally to lingering memories of lust before her brain caught up with the reality that they were an ex or an old flame for a reason. His hair was still long, sitting about his shoulders, and was as enviously thick and shiny as she'd remembered, his beard fuller than she had seen. It suited him.

'Hi, Jimmy.'

154

She smiled in the way that she knew was alluring, despite her nerves, wanting to present her profile in the best way – still, after all they had been through, hoping he saw her in the best light.

'How're you getting on? Doug called to say you'd taken the munchkin home.'

This was always his way, straight to it, focusing on their connection and always his main concern: Edith.

'Daddy!' Edith denied her the chance to respond as she jumped up, leaned on the back of the sofa, grabbed the tablet, and held it close to her face.

Madeleine was pretty sure that Jimmy would have a great close-up of their daughter's nose and mouth. She noticed how Edith's beautiful, podgy feet made dents in the cushion. It was an odd thing, how children used furniture and other objects with such disregard for how they were designed to be used. Equally surprising was that it didn't bother her as much as she might have expected, not like an overly loud jersey or the wrong shade of cream paint.

'I haven't got my book bag, Dad.'

'Well, don't worry about that tonight, pickle. I can text Mr Lawal on the class WhatsApp and let him know that Nanny isn't feeling very well. He'll understand, and you don't need to worry about it. You don't need to worry about anything. Everything is going to be okay – I promise.'

They had a WhatsApp group. That made sense. She felt the grip of inadequacy that Jimmy was not only part of this group but also knew her teacher was Mr Lawal. Judging from the relaxing in Edith's demeanour, he also knew just what to say and how to say it. His tone, his promise, left no doubt that he was a man of his word. What had Madeleine expected? He was far more present in their child's life than her, and Madeleine knew she had no right to feel even a flicker of envy. This was her choice. It was and always had been her choice. Not that these reminders were easy to swallow or made up for the feelings of inadequacy that swilled in her gut.

'Can you take me to school in the morning, Daddy?'

'Sure I can.' His response, she noted, offered without hesitation or consideration of the time pressure, hassle, or the inevitable battle in both directions against the rush hour. 'If that's what you want, my love, then I will come get you in the morning, bright and early, and I can drop you at school.'

'And, Daddy . . .' She glanced at Madeleine and then back at the screen, before whispering, her face mere millimetres from the screen, as if it might prevent Madeleine hearing or at least being offended. 'Can you please come and get me right now?'

It didn't work.

She heard and was incredibly offended, or rather hurt. Hurt would be more accurate. It cut her that her little girl didn't want to spend the night there. And left her wondering what it was she'd done wrong.

'Can you put Madeleine back on for a second, please, my love?'

Edith nodded and, now avoiding eye contact, she passed the tablet over.

'I guess you heard that.' He pulled a face.

'I did indeed.' She forced a smile.

'She's got her bedroom here with all her stuff. It's familiar so . . .' Jimmy was and always had been a kind man. Even at this late hour, and in this unique situation, he tried to placate her, to spare her feelings with the justification.

'Of course. Listen, whatever's best. I just want her to be comfortable.'

She saw him check his watch, and then he yawned. 'It's going to take me three-quarters of an hour or so to get across town, maybe less, depending on traffic, but I'll be there as soon as I can. If I call you when I'm close, I can maybe pull up outside and—'

'And I'll bring her down.' She finished the sentence, relieved he wasn't going to come into her apartment, her space. The idea of making small talk here was almost more than she could stand. 'You have my address?'

'Yes, Marnie sent it to me, just in case.'

Of course she did.

'Right, see you in a bit.' He ended the call.

'Jimmy will be here soon.' She stared at Edith, who stared back, the little girl now unafraid to hold her eye, unblinking. It was an odd moment. The two looking at the face of their past and their future. 'Your uniform will be washed and ready by the time he gets here. You can travel in my t-shirt. You can have it, in fact.'

''Kay.'

'Do you . . . Do you want something to eat?' Madeleine knew it was a while since she had had her McDonald's treat.

'Have you got any sliced chicken?'

'Sliced chicken? No. But I've got hummus, cheese, crackers, apples, vodka, all kinds of things.'

Edith shook her head, the vodka joke entirely lost on the infant.

'I'm not hungry.'

'Would you be hungry if I had sliced chicken?'

'Maybe.'

She liked the child's honesty.

'I guess we could nip to the shop and get some sliced chicken?' She felt a sudden flare of panic. What were the logistics? How did it work? Was it ever okay to leave the kid at home alone with the TV on while she nipped out? That didn't feel right. Edith was barefoot in an oversized t-shirt, ready for bed, and she wasn't sure she wanted to drag her around the streets in the darkness.

'I'm okay.'

157

She heard the echo of uncertainty in the little girl's usually chirpy demeanour, and it was crushing. This evening was quickly going from bad to worse.

'Would you like to watch something on TV?'

'Sure.' She shrugged.

Madeleine was about to grab the remote control, which she was certain was far more complicated than it needed to be, when Edith pressed the tablet to life and started scrolling. Her proficiency with the digital keypad and her comfort with the technology was super impressive. It made her heart swell with something that felt a lot like pride. The little girl gave a big yawn and settled back on the sofa. Madeleine ran her fingers over the top of her child's head, feeling her silky hair, fresh scented after her bath, glide beneath her touch. The perfect little head that she had pushed from her body.

'You're crowning! That's it, Madeleine! Keep going! You're doing a wonderful job! Nearly there, my love! Keep going!'

She didn't often think about that day. It was easier to keep it buried under a busy schedule of work and meetings and plans and designs – easier not to dwell on those moments when her world changed for ever. When Marnie's, Doug's and Jimmy's worlds changed for ever too – the day her daughter was born. The thought was enough for her to feel a pulse in her womb.

Edith, it seemed, was bored of her programme. Twisting on the sofa, she touched her little fingertip to Madeleine's cheek.

'Mummy.'

'Yes?'

'Lots of my friends live in the same house as their mummy.'

This was not an uncommon topic when they met, and Madeleine understood. It was how the little one wrapped her head around a situation that was different to that of some of her friends. Not that their set-up was unique, and Marnie had explained to her a while back that Edith understood that there were many kinds of family. In her school class alone, Melodie had two mummies, Tunde had no mum, one dad and an older sister – who was also a mummy to Tunde's nephew, who was older than him. Jonah had a mum and a stepdad and a dad and a stepmum and a half-sister, and Edith had a nan and a grandad who adored her, a dad who saw her every week, and a mum she saw sometimes. When it came to a support system, it felt like enough.

'I am sure they do. But not all families are the same, are they?'

'Nope, they are not.' Edith yawned again. 'I was thinking, Mum, you could come and live with me and Nanny and Pop, if you wanted. You could share my room. I wouldn't mind.'

Edith made the suggestion cautiously but had obviously given it thought. Madeleine stared at her, quite unsure of where or how to begin. Her daughter's words were the verbal equivalent of taking a dagger to her breast.

'I think we'd be a bit squished if we had to share that little room!'

It was cowardly, she knew, and did them both a disservice as she reverted to the flippant, the comical, rather than address the question head on, which was so much bigger than the question Edith was *actually* asking: *why don't you live in the same house as me? Why have you never lived in the same house as me?* Questions she was afraid of and felt ill-equipped to answer.

She noted that her daughter didn't suggest that they all move here to this spacious flat, clearly not seeing it as anything remotely like a home. Again, she felt the crushing blow of rejection and wondered if her child felt the same. It was like trying to figure out a puzzle with half the pieces missing and no instructions. It was a knotty wool ball of a problem and she had no clue how to start.

How did she begin to explain her choices without resigning Edith to a lifetime of therapy? An image of Orna flew into her thoughts – Orna who always pushed for honesty, reinforcing the saying that it really *was* the best policy.

Tonight, however, Madeleine decided to go with avoidance. Ostrich style. Head in the sand.

This was going to be her tactic. It was too late in the day and too much of a minefield to open the floodgates on such a complex situation. It required so much more than a quick chat while they waited for Edith's ride home.

She kissed Edith's hand, unable to think of the discussion around the little girl's impending birth: the heartache, the fights, the throats raw with emotion and enough tears collectively shed to sail away on . . .

She thought of Marnie and hoped she was comfortable, hoped her surgery wasn't going to be too gruelling, hoped Dougie was managing without her. They hadn't spoken for a while before today, almost a fortnight, in fact. Not that this was unusual – she was a busy woman – but it wasn't easy for any of them.

It felt to her that Marnie had misjudged just how tricky it would be, despite the openness that was the bedrock of their agreement, that she had underestimated the level of emotion when it came to all being in the same room.

Edith rubbed her eyes.

'I know you're tired, Edith. It's been quite a day, hasn't it?' She thought of the emails that would no doubt require her attention, that she'd have to dive into once her little girl had gone home. 'Your daddy will be here soon.'

'I can sleep in his van. I have a special cushion that goes around my chin.' She pointed to the area lest there be any doubt where her chin was.

'Ah, I know those special cushions; I have one I use sometimes on an airplane.' This felt like the time to lay the foundation, sow the seed of the idea that she was going to the States, leaving her behind.

'I've never been on an airplane.'

'Would you like to go on one?' She wondered how, logistically, she could get Edith out to LA, unwilling to admit that the thought of her being accompanied by Marnie and Doug or even Jimmy made it a whole lot less attractive as a proposition. It was that thing about her two worlds colliding again.

'Not sure.'

'Where would you go if you could go anywhere?' She was curious.

'I'd go to Manchester.'

'Manchester?' Her laugh was spontaneous; it wasn't quite what she'd expected.

'Yes, my friend Travis—'

'Travis the mouse hunter?' She was delighted to be keeping up.

'Yes, well, he got a plane to Manchester to go and stay with his other grandma.'

'I see. Did he have a nice time?'

'Not really. He said her house smelled of wee wee because her cat is old and just wee wee'd on the floor and then it did a poo in the kitchen next to the cat toilet.'

'Oh dear! That doesn't sound great. Poor cat. Poor Travis's grandma, come to think of it.'

'Yep.' Edith sighed wearily, as if she understood what it felt like to have the worry of an old cat. She was indeed a comical little thing.

'I'm going on a plane in a few weeks, actually.' *Transparency*, she reminded herself, just as Marnie had taught her.

'Where are you going?'

'I'm going to LA. Do you know what LA stands for?'

Her daughter nodded. 'Lanzarote.'

Again she felt the laugh erupt from her. This kid was great company. 'I love that! But not quite. LA is short for Los Angeles.'

'Is it *near* Lanzarote?'

'Not really. It's in America.'

'Near New York?'

Edith's eyes were wide, and she remembered feeling a similar fascination for the place when it was no more than a footnote to Christmas movies and soundbites on the news. When finally she got to visit, her fascination only intensified. It was sad that now, after so many trips, she would sigh at the thought of crowds on the 'Q' and dreaded having to navigate tourists who clustered on the paths in Central Park or stopped dead on the sidewalk to take endless selfies in Times Square. The irony wasn't lost on her that other visitors were her irritation when she was no New Yorker. The Big Apple, like anything that was overfamiliar, had lost a little of its glitter.

'I think I'd like to go to New York after I've been to Manchester.'

'It's an obvious route.'

Again she cradled her child's head in her hand, smiling, revelling in the contact, knowing the opportunities to be alone with her were few and far between. It gave her freedom of sorts – no one watching to see how she interacted, whether she did or said the wrong thing and how 'maternal' she seemed.

'Are you going there for your job?'

'I am, yes. Do you know what my job is?'

She felt the little girl, nod. 'You do decorating.'

The simplification was perfect. 'Yes, I do. I do decorating.'

'When I grow up, I want to work on the market with Pop. "Get your pots and pans here! Your buckets, your bowls, your drainers, your tea towels, your pegs!"' Edith stared at her as if expecting her to laugh; it sounded a lot like a performance, but it had the opposite effect. Edith was smart – so smart – and the thought of her not achieving her full potential, or worse, following Dougie up the market through a misplaced sense of duty because she might believe that this was what she was 'supposed to do' horrified Madeleine. The early damp starts and the days washed out by rain, trying to eke out a living by flogging buckets – all of it. Yet how could she comment when it was her who had left Edith in that environment and carried on with her life?

'Nanny laughs when I do my market shout.' Edith again looked nonplussed.

'I bet she does. The thing to remember, little one, is that you can be or do *anything* you want to, but it's important you use your brain and never regret building the life you want, okay?'

'Okay.' Edith stared at her and seemed to choose her words carefully. 'How long are you going to America for?'

And there it was, so eloquently put and so painfully insightful. The fact that Edith deduced from their chat that building the life Madeleine wanted meant going away, possibly for a very long time . . . possibly for ever.

'I'm not sure.' Again this half-truth, ostrich style. 'But we can Facetime. How does that sound?'

'Sounds okay.' Edith's response was half-hearted.

Madeleine felt the pull of something deep in her chest at the prospect of not seeing her child for a while. Knowing it sustained her, the brief catch-ups, the moments of celebration, were enough of a balm to ease her concern over the life Edith lived on the Brenton Park estate. It was easy not to worry when the little one was always full of laughter, living her best life while mouse hunting and eating macaroni cheese.

'I'm moving out of here.' She looked up at the double-height ceiling.

'Will you ever move back in? It's lovely.'

'Eventually, probably. But I've rented it out to a couple from Hong Kong who are in banking. They move here in about six weeks.'

'Trina works in the bank!'

'Yes, she does.' It was a strange sensation that Edith knew and was clearly fond of the woman who had been her confidante, her best friend, for so long. 'Trina and I were friends when we were the same age as you are now. Can you believe that?'

'Yes, then you got one whiff of the bright lights and were gone quicker than a rat up a drainpipe!'

'What?' It was a phrase that seemed alien coming from Edith's mouth. The words and tone so grown-up, she could only have heard it from an adult. If it wasn't so wounding in content, it would have been hilarious. 'The reason Trina and I aren't still close . . .' She stopped, suddenly unsure of what to say, aware not only of the complexity of the topic but also that she was talking to a seven-year-old. Why were she and Trina not close? Because her friend didn't understand her desire to chase her dreams? Because Trina felt abandoned by her? Because Trina was a little jealous of her success? Because Madeleine had slept with the boy Trina loved . . . and had kept it secret?

Edith managed a half nod, as if to confirm she was listening, and yawned again, as her eyes gave a slow blink. The certain fore-runner to sleep. Madeleine decided their chat could wait, wondering quite how she'd manage if her daughter actually fell asleep, unsure she could navigate the stairs *and* carry her slumbering form. She'd have to invite Jimmy up.

The intercom buzzer ringing loudly around the apartment gave them both a start.

'It's my dad!' The little girl perked up a little.

'Not sure it is. I didn't think he'd be here quite yet.' She made her way to the intercom and lifted the phone. It wasn't unusual for various delivery drivers to try all the intercom buzzers if one didn't respond immediately. More often than not, they then shouted gar-bled messages about pizzas or groceries that needed to be collected from the street. The panic in their voices was obvious, no doubt as they kept one eye on their vehicle usually abandoned half on the pavement.

The voice that came through loud and clear was neither garbled nor panicked and was certainly not what she had been expecting.

'This is your friendly supper delivery! I might have sushi or I might have something a lot more exciting!'

'Nico!' Her mouth ran dry.

'The very same. Open up, I'm cold and horny – I mean, cold and lonely.' He laughed.

'Just a sec . . .' Looking towards Edith, who sat on the sofa, she tried to stem the tremble to her limbs as she weighed up her options. *Hide Edith in the bedroom?* Her eyes screwed shut for a second at the abhorrent and unwelcome thought. Of course not. *Come clean?* That didn't feel like a good idea at this stage of their . . . what was it even? Hardly a relationship yet, plus with her departure to LA getting closer, why was she even investing in this . . . whatever *it* was?

'I'm sorry, Nico, you've caught me off guard. I just, I don't feel . . .'

'Are you okay?' With all joviality now wiped from his tone, his concern caused her gut to bunch with guilt.

'I've been on the loo.' She winced at the imagery he would no doubt conjure. 'Don't want to go into detail, but don't want to give it to you either.'

Her heart raced. She kept her eyes closed. Lying. Lying to Nico. It didn't feel good.

'No, no, oh God, I should have called first. Ah, I'm an idiot! I thought I was being spontaneous and interesting.'

With her eyes closed, she gripped the phone of the intercom to her face. He was so lovely. Spontaneous, interesting, and lovely in every way.

'I'll call you.'

She wanted him gone so that she could end the farce. And she wanted him gone so there was no question of him running into Jimmy or seeing Edith – not that she was ashamed of her, not that. It was more that it required a bigger conversation than a quick introduction on the fly. Not that it mattered in the grand scheme of things – she was after all, jetting off very soon. At the thought of boarding the plane and flying away from this man, away from the little girl who was scrunched in a heap on the sofa wearing her t-shirt, she felt a flicker of sadness. Meeting him and spending this time with Edith was certainly going to make it a little harder to simply pack up and go.

'Yep. Look, if you need anything, anything at all . . .' He let this trail, and his sweet goodbye, offering help, being there for her, only made her feel worse.

'Bye – and thank you,' she whispered, trying to sound ill. It was as uncomfortable as it was cowardly.

'Who was that on your phone thing?' Edith asked. She opened her eyes and noticed the little girl had left the sofa and was sitting on the floor close to her, her hair mussed, her eyes heavy. Beautiful. It happened like this sometimes, when Madeleine would catch a glimpse of her and feel the stir of deep, deep love. The connection, almost visceral, reminding her that she had made this incredible human. It really was some achievement. Her best, in fact.

'That was a friend of mine.'

'Is he your boyfriend?'

'What do you know about boyfriends?' She sat on the floor opposite her child.

'My friend Melodie loves Olly but he doesn't love her back. He loves me and Jonah.'

'I see, and do you love Olly?'

'No. I don't want a boyfriend. I'm too busy!' This she spoke with her palms upturned, as if she really did have one heck of a schedule.

'I hear ya.' She knew she'd remember this glorious chat when she was working late in LA or hiking those trails and, when she did, it would be with a papercut of sorrow that she could not see Edith in that moment. 'I guess love can be complicated.'

'That's what Nanny Marnie said.'

'She's right.'

'So *is* he your boyfriend?' Edith looked up at her with a wrinkle to the top of her nose and a persistence she recognised.

'No. But he's nice. A nice man.' A *spectacular* man!

'He *sounded* nice.'

This assessment made her smile. This kid was smart and aware and wonderful. All the things she'd hoped she would be and yet the thought of this being her norm, of having this responsibility, this role, every day of her life? It still felt like more than she was equipped to handle. So why did the prospect of leaving her and going so far away hurt a little? And as for Nico, he was so very wonderful, but she was not the kind of person to hitch her wagon to a man's and spend cosy nights in with sushi. She had an empire to build! A brand to launch! These motivational thoughts were easy in her mind yet paid no heed to the lurch in her chest at the thought of having lied to him.

Her phone beeped with a text. It was from Jimmy.

FEW MINUTES AWAY!

'Right, that's Jimmy. He's nearly here and so in a bit we'll go downstairs.'

'Okay. So, would you like the nice man to be your boyfriend?'

This kid was tenacious.

'Erm, it's not that straightforward.'

Edith rested her chin on her palm, her elbow propped on her leg, as if settling in for a long conversation.

'I mean, he is certainly boyfriend material. He probably has everything I look for, but I agree with you, Edith – I'm too busy!'

'My daddy was your boyfriend, wasn't he? That's what he said.'

'Oh, well, yes, he was.' She felt the film of discomfort slide over her skin. Where was this heading and what was the right thing to say? Madeleine felt woefully unprepared for any questions that might come her way.

'Did he buy you chocolates and stuff?'

'He might have done; I can't really remember. I know he was lovely.' *And has always been very good to me.* 'So are you saying that you might let Olly be your boyfriend if he got you chocolates?'

'No, I prefer sliced chicken.' Edith spoke without an ounce of irony and not for the first time it made Madeleine laugh out loud.

Her buzzer rang again.

'That'll be your dad.'

'Yes!' Edith scrabbled to her feet. 'Do you think I'll come back here, Mum?'

She nodded, swallowing the lump in her throat. 'I think you will, one day. Yes.'

Jumping up, she grabbed her goose-down-filled coat from the concealed cupboard by the front door and bundled Edith into it. It was massive but, when zipped up, the smile on Edith's face suggested she was quite happy to be ensconced inside it.

'I can't walk in this!' As if proof were needed, the little girl waddled from side to side on the wooden floor like a drunk, and threatened to tumble.

'I'll carry you, if you hold on around my neck. Don't move for a sec. I'll just go grab your uniform.'

With the warm garments pulled from the dryer and folded inside a Dean & Deluca tote, she hooked it over her arm and picked Edith up. She made for a bulky parcel, the thick layers of coat a warm cushion on to which she held tight.

It was as they were about to leave the apartment that the buzzer went again.

'Your dad is very impatient!' she clucked. 'I'm coming! I'm coming!'

She hoped her words might float down the wide stairs and through the front door.

It felt, as she opened the front door with her one free hand, and Edith draped over her shoulder like an enormous earthworm, that the two things happened simultaneously. The grass-green van with gold vintage script on the side which read, 'Woodwork and Renovation from The Old Lock-keeper's Cottage' pulled to the kerb with the hazard lights on, and Jimmy lifted his hand in a wave. Trina was right, the van was really cool – a beautiful thing.

And at the same time, Nico stood one step back from the front door, beaming at first, and in his hands an array of stomach-settling medications, a bunch of white carnations and, most touchingly, a packet of Malted Milk biscuits. All no doubt grabbed from the nearest Tesco Express.

She was aware of the fight or flight phenomenon but had never fully understood it until that second; with Edith hoisted on to her shoulder, and faced with the prospect of her two worlds colliding, she honestly considered slamming the front door and retreating back up the stairs. Her hastily considered plan was then to bolt the door of her apartment, unhook the phone and hide until everyone had gone away. This wasn't like her, not at all. Her reputation was as a problem solver, a calm but proactive leader – a trailblazer! Yet the thought of sinking down on to the sofa with her padded earthworm had never felt so attractive.

'Oh!'

She watched the smile fall from Nico's face, replaced with something close to utter bewilderment, and her heart sank down to her boots.

'Ma-Madeleine,' he faltered. 'I'm so sorry to, erm, to disturb you. I was just . . . just going to drop off some . . .' He made as if to thrust the items he'd bought into her arms, before deciding against it at the realisation that she had her hands full, in more ways than one. 'I'm not . . . not staying.' He swallowed. 'I just—'

'Nico, I . . .' She didn't know what to say in response to the fact that she was evidently not ill, evidently not stuck on the loo, and evidently not alone.

'No, no, it's fine. My fault, I shouldn't have, erm . . .'

He kept his gaze averted and it spoke volumes. His expression and demeanour all in response to her deceit and the strange and unchartered dynamic in which they now found themselves. She felt rooted to the spot while wishing she could run away. It was awful. Everything about it was just awful.

'You . . . you're obviously busy, so, erm, I'll go. I hope you feel . . .' he babbled.

'Mummy?' Edith lifted her head and hooked one padded arm under her chin.

'*Mummy?*' Nico stared at her now. His eyes searched her face as if seeing her for the first time. 'You know, all that talk about openness and honesty, you could have told me you were divorced or . . . whatever . . .' He kept his tone low as if whispering to her alone. This was most definitely not the time for that conversation.

'This is Edith.' She smiled at her daughter, hoping it might dispel any awkwardness her child might feel, not wanting that for her, not ever.

'Hi.' It was almost instinctive, the way Nico stepped further back on the pavement.

'It's my daddy!' Edith called, and tried to wriggle down as Jimmy stepped from the van.

Nico turned to face Jimmy and actually gave a wry laugh and bit his bottom lip, as if a little overwhelmed by the utter absurdity of the situation. Still he clutched his assortment of medications, the wilting carnations, and the packet of biscuits.

'Can I have one of those?' Edith had spotted the Malted Milks and pointed at them. 'I wanted some sliced chicken but Mummy didn't have any.'

'Sure.' He handed her the packet.

'Whoa! I'll take those!' Jimmy walked forward, arm out-stretched, to intervene. 'She's not allowed biscuits at this time of night, not that it doesn't stop her trying.' He smiled at Nico, as was his way, friendly and nice. 'I'm Jimmy.' He held out his hand.

'Nico.'

Watching the two shake hands was a strange thing. Her past and present coming face to face. She looked away as it was almost unbearable to witness.

'I was just heading off, so . . . Nice to meet you.'

Nico pointed down the street in an obvious hurry to escape the pantomime into which he had stumbled. Her instinct was to dissuade him from leaving, to ask him to stay and give her the chance to explain the situation, to tell him of her history, her story, and the choices she had made so she could live the life she wanted. But of course she wasn't about to say anything of the sort in front of Jimmy and Edith.

'Bye, everyone.' He barely glanced at her before heading off, still with his booty nestling in his arm.

'Cheers!' Jimmy's goodbye was jovial and genuine. He looked well, very well. His signature dark, dark hair, and slow smile unchanged. Still in his work clothes – mustard-coloured corduroys that were dotted with glue and paint, a quilted waxed jacket that was similarly adorned, and battered pale Timberland boots with the laces loose.

'Thanks for coming to get her.'

He reached for the bundle of Edith and held her with ease on his forearm. The little girl kissed his cheek and looped her arms around his neck, nestling against him.

'I've told her that no matter how old she gets or wherever she is in the world, if she asks me to, I will always, always come and find her and bring her home. It's important.'

His sentiment was so beautiful and spoken with such conviction she felt a thickening in the base of her throat. To have such a safety net . . . it was a wonderful thing.

'Right, you, say goodbye to your mum.' He jostled the child who she could see was minutes away from sleep.

'Bye, Mummy.' Her small hand crept from the voluminous sleeve.

Madeleine reached out and squeezed her little fingers. Kissing them would have been her preference but, as ever, when in front of Marnie or Jimmy or anyone really, she held back, unsure of the protocol.

'Hope Marnie's okay. Bit of a shocker for everyone.' He looked concerned. It was another jab in the ribs, a reminder that he had a relationship with her parents, saw them with more regularity than she did.

'I'm sure she'll be fine.'

'I'll check in on Dougie, of course.'

Of course.

'Will you come and see us on Sunday?' Edith spoke softly, rubbing her tired eyes.

'Sunday?' She thought how best to answer. It was conflicting; she wanted to see Edith on Sunday, but was equally anxious, feeling the swirl of unsettling sediment that had been stirred up today, and wary that seeing her on Sunday would only make parting that much harder for everyone.

'I have her every Sunday and Sunday night. It gives Marnie and Doug a break and, honestly, it's the highlight of my week.' His expression told her he meant it. 'Come out, Mads.' No one called her Mads anymore, or Maddie, or any of the other affectionate nicknames that had sprung up in her youth. 'Come see us at the cottage. It'll be nice for you to spend some time with her. And we can give you back your bag and coat.'

'Mummy's going to Lanzarote.' Edith yawned.

'On Sunday?' He looked confused.

'No, no, not for a while.' She was aware of the ticking clock that would spirit her away soon enough. 'Sure, yes, why not? I'd love to come and see you guys on Sunday.'

The decision was made.

'Great, after lunch? You know where it is.'

Nodding, she pictured the dilapidated wreck that had been a blot on the towpath for as long as she could remember. She was half dreading setting foot inside the place, and prayed it wasn't damp or disgusting. Her memories of it were fairly grim. Her parents had kept her up to date with his renovation project, but they were, she knew, prone to exaggeration in their desire to paint Jimmy in the best light. It was as if on some level they wanted to remind her that it was not too late to snare the 'one that got away!' or maybe they just wanted to reinforce their decision to let him play such a big part in Edith's life. Either way . . .

'See you then.' He backed away.

She noted how he studied the façade of her building as he reached into his pocket for his keys, taking it all in and no doubt remembering how she had been the girl who wanted more, while he had looked at her with an expression of bewilderment – the boy who only wanted enough.

December

6.00 P.M.

Madeleine took a deep breath, knowing she had to say it, but not sure how to get the words out.

'Come on! Don't keep me in suspense! How far are you?' Marnie pushed.

'I'm seven months pregnant, Mum. Twenty-four weeks. Seven months.' She spoke clearly, bracing herself for the fallout.

Her mother sprayed her laughter into the room, like blowing a raspberry – childish, a reflex almost – and she understood. Because despite having had the test, seen the scan, and heard that powerful *boom-boom*, *boom-boom* of a heartbeat, she too found the whole concept to be unimaginable.

'What d'you mean, seven months?' Marnie asked when finally able to compose herself.

'I mean, I woke up feeling sick and horrible. I went to the doctor, who did a test that came back positive. I then had a scan which confirmed that I am seven months pregnant.'

'You're not joking?' The crease at the top of her mum's nose spoke of her confusion.

'I'm not joking, no.'

'But . . .' Marnie seemed to study her.

'I know, I don't look it. I had no clue – none. And I certainly don't feel pregnant, or at least I didn't until I saw her image on the scan.'

'Oh!' Marnie briefly buried her face in her hands. 'A little girl! You're having a little girl! That's wonderful!'

'Mum.' This had gone too far. She needed to level with her mother, make her intentions clear. 'I don't think I can. I mean, I can't . . . I can't . . .' She tried to get the words out, the words that stuck like pins in her throat, words that she knew would unleash a whole world of pain and wipe the joy from her mother's face. Neither of which she relished. Marnie clearly wasn't listening as the words rushed from her, as if the ideas formed and out of her mouth they popped.

'I'm going to knit! I'm going to knit her a little matinee jacket just like your Nana Edith did for you, and a matching bonnet and—'

'Mum.' She spoke louder now.

'What, my love? Do you need anything? A cup of tea? Foot rub?'

'I'm not sure I'm going to keep her.'

This was a lie; she was almost entirely certain she was not going to keep her.

Madeleine had heard the expression of going as white as a sheet but had never seen it until that moment. Marnie's high colour disappeared from her cheeks and her pallor, in an instant, was almost grey.

'It's . . . It's all new and I'm still processing it, but if I had to make the call right now, I'd say that I wouldn't keep her. I don't see how I can. And, crucially, I really don't want to.'

'But . . . surely not! No! Of course you want to keep her! It will all work out, it will. It will all come good in the end. I . . .' Her mum's mouth moved but no more words came.

They sat quietly for a beat. It felt like they were both trying to figure out the best route forward and were simultaneously exhausted in advance at the prospect.

'I just don't know what to say right now, Madeleine. I don't know what to do!' Marnie wrung her hands, her anguish visible. 'This has gone from being one of the best moments of my life to the very worst. I can feel it in my stomach – this terrible, terrible sense of grief at the very idea that you—'

'This is not about you, Mum.'

It was typical. The way her mother harnessed a situation and steered it in the direction that suited her, as if she knew best – as if she always knew best. It didn't matter so much when the issue was what to have for supper, the best way to iron a shirt, the quickest bus routes, but this . . . Madeleine knew it was nothing so frivolous. She had to find the strength in her weakened and confused state to stand her ground.

'I know that. I just don't want you to act in haste. I *do* know that, I just . . .' Marnie hesitated, wary, it seemed, of saying the wrong thing. Madeleine hated that she had put her in this position. Her mum was remarkable. She knew that not every mother would receive the news of their daughter's pregnancy out of the blue and welcome it so fully, digesting it quickly.

Madeleine also knew her well enough to understand how she would have let the facts settle and swiftly found the pocketful of sunshine. *A baby! A grandchild!* This glorious news that would allow Marnie's mind to leap ahead, forming pictures of a life she would embrace – no doubt imagining the little one's first Christmas, first steps, first tooth, starting school, nativity plays, crudely drawn pictures stuck to the fridge doors, and the sheer joy of watching her family tree grow deeper roots and higher branches, under which they could all rest in their dotage. But Madeleine knew this was a falsehood, aware that her plans had taken a scythe to that pocketful of sunshine and left it sitting forlornly in a pile somewhere.

'As I said, I'm still processing everything, I'm not sure what I'm going to do. But I'm also aware that this baby will be here in a couple of months. I'm considering all my options.'

'What do you mean, your *options*? You have no options!' Marnie raised her voice a little. 'Motherhood is only a *choice* before you are seven months bloody pregnant!' It was obvious she regretted how she'd shouted; her hand flew over her mouth and Madeleine under-stood how easy it was to lose control when fear guided the words from your throat. When Marnie spoke again, it was with a calmer tone, pleading almost. 'Talk to me. What is it, love? I can imagine how scared you must be. Of course you are, because it is scary and a shock! But I meant what I said: your dad and I are here for you, always. We'll help you. We can put things in place, we'll—'

'You're just not listening to me!' she shouted, standing now, then pacing the small lounge in her socks, her trousers clinging to her slender legs and without even the slightest of bulges, despite her advanced stage, beneath her pale grey sweater. The one with the sleeve that smelled of dried pee.

'I'm trying to listen, but you're not saying anything that makes sense to me!' At last the truth from Marnie's mouth.

She turned sharply and stared at her mum; her eyes carried a desperate glaze of sorrow and confusion that to Madeleine felt like nothing but pressure.

'You never understand my choices, Mum. You don't under-stand *me*!' The crack in her voice was hard to control.

'What do you mean?'

What *did* she mean? The times when Marnie had given her a similar look of sorrow and confusion were many. Each one burned in her memory, there for perfect recall that was either motivating or heart-rending depending on Madeleine's mood. Every suggestion from her mother was designed, it felt, to keep her daughter close, to maintain the boundaries that kept her firmly in her place, ensuring that she lived a life close by, a life just like her mother's.

'No, Mum. It does matter that I do my homework. We can go shopping another time. I need to get this done.'

'No, Mum. That's not true, people do care about grades. At least, I care about grades . . .'

'No, Mum. It's very kind of you to have had a word, but I don't want to enrol at catering college. I want to work in central London . . .'

'No, Mum. I'm not going to stay here and let you help me save up. I want to move into a shared flat, spread my wings . . .'

'No, Mum. I'm not going out with Billy from the block opposite. I never want to end up like Billy's mum, stuck here on the estate, counting the pennies. I want a different life, a fancy-pants life. I don't want to end up as a woman like that.'

Her implication, whether intentional or not had been clear: *a woman like you* . . .

'I mean' – she drew breath – 'that sometimes I think you find it hard to see things from my point of view. You only think about what's right for you and not what's right for me.'

'Of course I do! You're my child, my only child and you were hard won, we never thought—'

'Oh, I know! I know!' Madeleine placed her hands in her hair and looked skyward. 'I know how you longed for a baby! I *know* what you went through – we all do! I've heard it my whole life. I understand that you saw every doctor this side of the Thames, who all told you there was no reason, no medical barrier, and yet . . .' She let her arms fall and took a deep breath. She was exhausted. 'I know it was when you *stopped* fretting, *stopped* panicking, that you fell pregnant with me. I know having me was like walking around

178

with a pocketful of bloody sunshine that could brighten your world on even the dullest, darkest day.'

'It was. It is.' Marnie gave a small smile at this truth, a fact that was obviously still so wonderful to her.

Madeleine gave in to the tiredness that pulled at her muscles and slumped once more back into the chair in the corner, next to the window that looked out over the walkway, shrouded by the net curtains that her mum washed monthly with a scoop of bicarb to keep them bright. She clasped her hands over her stomach and pictured the baby girl that lurked within. 'But I am not you, Mum.'

'I know that! I've never—'

'You *don't* know that!' She sat forward, her tone impassioned, as pleas, distress and cutting honesty dripped down the walls and pooled on the floor, giving off fumes that were so potent she could breathe little else. 'You really *don't* know, Mum. You never have, and it's evident in every suggestion you make. I don't know how to make you understand that I'm not you; I've never been you. And instead of a pocketful of sunshine' – she prodded her stomach – 'I feel like I've got a heavy rock in my gut. One that is weighing me down, dragging me to the floor and tethering me to a life I know I don't want.' Tears unexpectedly sheeted her face and Marnie looked conflicted, as if her heart was shredded at the sight of such turmoil, while her brain ran the reality this way and that, trying to make sense of what Madeleine was saying to her. 'And if further proof were needed, it's in the fact that before you even asked what my plans were or what I thought I might do, you are planning what to knit! I mean, sweet Jesus!'

'So what *do* you want?'

Marnie ran her tongue over her top lip, trying to catch her tears that fell. Madeleine felt split in two, already pulled in one direction by loyalty, devotion and tradition to her mum and dad and the life they wanted for her, and knowing that the life she wanted was within reach – a life of freedom, a life of success. So close she could taste it! She wiped her face and did her best to halt her tears.

'Not this. Definitely not this.'

She ran her palm over her waistband and did her best to hide the flicker of something close to horror that leaped inside her.

'So what now, then? What happens next?'

'Adoption.' Madeleine held Marnie's eyeline, the word spoken without any of the emotion or hesitancy she thought might accompany it. She was aware of the weight of it, and that it was surely a knife in Marnie's heart. But this was her life, not her mother's. That was the one thing she did know. 'But, as I say, it's all new – all so bloody shocking! I need time to think about it, to understand how it all works.' It was easy to sound confident, even though the prospect felt more than a little overwhelming.

Marnie sat back in her seat, looking as if someone had punched her in the gut so hard she couldn't get a full breath. She shook her head.

'The idea that a stranger might get to raise this child, our own flesh and blood! It's unthinkable. And I know he's not here, but I know it's what your dad would say.'

'God, Mum, it's such a bloody awful mess.' Madeleine wiped her face with her hands and shrugged at the understatement.

'It doesn't have to be.' Again Marnie was on her knees in front of her. 'What about . . . What about if your dad and I raised the baby?' Her face was again animated, some semblance of colour returned to her cheeks.

'No, no, that sounds . . .' She shook her head. It sounded awful and involved and wasn't what she wanted at all. The thought of being confronted by the child every time she came home would mean this nightmare lingered for . . . for ever! Her wish was that her life might carry on as if this had never happened. Yes, she would inevitably be changed, but ultimately she believed it possible. Also, did she really want to consign a baby girl to repeat her childhood, where the walls felt like they were closing in and everything that sparkled felt just out of reach?

'Sounds what?' Marnie's voice was stretched thin with emotion.

'Sounds complicated. Too complicated.'

'Jesus Christ! Every bit of this is complicated! But letting my granddaughter be adopted doesn't make it less complicated. I can't even imagine that.'

'And I can't imagine coming home for Christmas or the odd weekend and watching you play with my daughter-sister! It's weird!'

'We'd make it not weird. We'd make it normal, and it would be for her.' It was as if ideas formed on her tongue. Marnie spoke rapidly and nervously.

'And how exactly would we do that, Mum?'

'By . . . by telling her the truth from day one – that I was her nan and Dougie was her pop, and that we'd love her for ever like a mum and dad. Just like we do her mummy.'

Madeleine stared out of the window, looking up towards the glimpse of evening sky visible through the curtains, considering this very thing, trying to imagine the scenario. The thought of the little girl sleeping in her bed, eating her tea with Dougie in the way she had liked to, battling with Marnie, perhaps, just as she had. She didn't think she could do it – was almost certain it was a non-starter for a million different reasons, but if it *was* feasible . . . would that make it an easier transition? Might it be that to let the child live a life Madeleine knew and understood could be the key to future peace? Would it be the best thing to quieten any fears around the unknown, any doubts over whether the little girl was loved, cared for, happy? Might it also appease the guilt she knew was waiting in the wings, already prodding her conscience?

'I could send money when I get on my feet, when I get promoted.' She thought about the images she was going to draw for Rebecca.

Marnie shook her head, her eyes flashed with indignancy. 'No, love. We wouldn't need your money.' She sucked her teeth. 'We've always managed and we always will. Kids don't need diamonds and steak, none of us do. We need love, attention, a cuddle at the end of a difficult day, someone to talk to and a place to be – a safe haven.'

'But . . .' Confusion rolled in her mind like thunder. What if she wanted her child to aspire to steak and diamonds?

'No.' Marnie stared at her with red-glazed eyes. 'If we do this, and I'm hoping you change your mind, praying you come to see what a blessing this little one is, hoping you might feel differently when you hold her . . .' This, Madeleine knew, would be her mother's absolute wish, the same sentiment Trina had expressed, as if both refused to believe she would see it through. 'If we do this, then I would have three conditions.'

'What are they?'

'The first I've said: that we are honest with this child from the start. Any lack of transparency would only lead to heartache further down the line. A secret like that would be like living above a trap door, and I couldn't exist knowing that at any second it could give way.' Madeleine wondered what it might feel like, having to face her daughter, who would know the circumstances of her birth and how she had effectively given her up. 'Second: you don't pay us or contribute. We've raised you just fine and I'd never want the little one to think there was any financial gain for us. *I* wouldn't want that either, even the smallest suggestion that we were being paid to have her, instead of doing it for love.' Marnie visibly shuddered. 'That wouldn't feel right to me.'

'What's the third one?' Her hands fidgeted in her lap.

'That you tell the father.'

Madeleine shook her head. 'No. No way. Why would I? It's nothing to do with him! How would that chat go? Oh, hi, mate, I know I haven't seen you for six months, but guess what? I'm about to have a baby and it's yours!'

'But it *is* something to do with him, whether you like it or not.'

'Not!' she fired back, suddenly remembering that she'd told Trina who the father was, and now unsure if she could trust her with a secret like that. Her gut bunched with nervous sickness. She instinctively placed her hand on her stomach, as if to calm the little girl who now lived there.

'That's the thing about life, my love – no matter how much you want everything to be neatly boxed and labelled, it isn't. It can't be. Because much of it is dealing with humans, and we are complicated and unpredictable and spontaneous and all the other things that make us wonderful!'

Not for the first time, she felt the enormity of the news swamp her. She stood, as Marnie walked over and wrapped her in a tight hug.

'I love you,' her mum whispered into her hair. 'I love you so much. Always have, always will. I don't have to understand you and you don't have to understand me. But you are, and always will be, my pocketful of sunshine.'

'I love you too, Mum.'

'There's one more thing. If you let us have her, I'd need to know that I'd be free to raise her in the only way I know. I need to be relaxed and not worrying that you might tell me off or want things done differently. I can only parent her how I parented you, otherwise it wouldn't be natural, and that would be stressful and horrible for us all, her included.'

She pulled away and looked at Marnie, their faces inches apart. Her mother sounded so confident it gave her faith that this might actually be an option. And if it delighted Marnie in the way she suspected it would, might that mean that they could build a bridge over this one life-changing event and carry on? She hated to think of what might happen between her and her parents if the child went to strangers. The thought of losing her mum and dad altogether was more painful than she could stand.

'That's four things. Do you think there might be more? Is this a list that's going to keep growing?'

Marnie kissed her button, freckled nose. 'Without doubt, my darling. Without doubt.'

It was as they stood holding each other that they heard the front door open and close, and her dad call from the hallway.

'Hello? Anyone home?'

He poked his head around the sitting room door and beamed. Madeleine's heart jumped, knowing what came next.

'Hello, little sausage! I wasn't expecting to see you. What a lovely surprise!'

Both she and Marnie turned to look at him, their faces betraying the tears that had fallen.

'Crying? Now, now, we can't have that! What have I missed?'

Marnie let go of her and turned to Dougie. 'You'd better sit down, my love . . .'

Chapter Nine

Present Day

Madeleine texted Tan to let him know she'd be in the office by mid-morning. It wasn't unusual for her to go and see her therapist at short notice; what was unusual was for her to leave the office early on one day and arrive late the next. These were not, however, normal circumstances. Her life felt it was moving a little too fast and she needed it to go slower, to rationalise her thoughts and talk to the one person with whom she didn't have to hold back – the one person who didn't openly judge or make snarky comments or make her feel guilty or interrupt. Well, not often, anyway. The person who kept her on an even keel and had done for the last couple of years.

She was grateful Dr Schoenfeld could see her.

Her sleep had been fitful and her pulse raced. Tossing and turning in her Egyptian cotton sheets as thoughts of Marnie in hospital, her earlier chat with Trina, Edith heading off with Jimmy, and Nico's face as he walked away all now interspersed with the things that usually preoccupied her musings in the early hours: the Stern project, her move to LA, the scratch on her fridge, the incorrect paint colour on her walls. One thought, however, hammered inside her skull louder than all others: why the hell hadn't she stocked up on sliced chicken?

It wasn't the best way to start the day – a little frazzled, a little fraught. And that was before she plucked up the courage to contact Nico. Each time she pictured him on the doorstep with his bottles of antacid and the cheap flowers in his arm, his face full of joy at seeing her and then his expression instantly falling when he saw the padded earthworm over her shoulder, it made her stomach roll with anxiety. It was also most unlike her to keep checking her phone like an overly keen teen with the explicit hope that he had called or texted – a simple thumbs-up would have been enough to quell her worries – yet this was precisely what she did, over and over. But nothing. So far it was radio silence from Nico Spectacular.

She wanted to call him directly, but wondered if giving him space was the right thing to do, allowing him to calm down and get the questions straight in his head, which she would answer willingly. Or maybe she'd never hear from him again. This too felt like a possibility. His assuming she was divorced, or in fact whatever he deduced, didn't really matter. It was all irrelevant if he simply decided she was too much of a gamble, carrying too much baggage, secretive, or just not for him. Could she really see Belinda Yannis welcoming Edith for a play date? Of course not. What had she been thinking? She and Nico were from different worlds. No matter how fancy the restaurant she booked or how plush her apartment, she was a girl from the Brenton Park estate who had royally messed up, and he was son and heir to Field and Grey, with a few minor titles thrown in for good measure. She swallowed, embarrassed to have thought for a moment that things might have been different.

With the beginning of a headache pulsing in her temples, she rang the buzzer and trudged up the dreary stairs to find Dr Schoenfeld waiting by her open door, her curly hair still damp about her shoulders.

'Morning, Madeleine.' She stood back to let her pass, closing the door behind her.

'Thanks for seeing me.'

'That's my job.' Orna sipped coffee from a pretty pottery mug. 'You want one?'

'Please.' She watched her therapist pop a pod into the noisy machine and press a couple of buttons before handing her a coffee.

It tasted surprisingly good, restorative; she sipped as she dumped her bag and sat on the sofa.

'How was your evening?' Orna took her chair and unscrewed her pen lid, notepad at the ready.

'Hectic.'

Her therapist stared at her – this Madeleine's cue to expand.

'My mum's in the hospital. She had a heart attack.'

'I'm so sorry to hear that. How is she doing?'

Madeleine waved her hand. 'Okay, I think. My dad's all over the place. But that's not . . .' She took a breath. 'I mean, it *is* what I'm worried about, of course it is, but that's not what's on my mind. I mean, it *is* on my mind, the both of them, but there's more. It's like . . .' She hated when she got flustered like this.

'No need to rush, Madeleine. We have time. Take some deep breaths.'

It was the simplest of instructions that often had the biggest impact. Today was no exception. With her eyes closed and shoulders relaxed, she did as she was asked: in through her nose and out through her mouth. There was something about being in this calm space, this safe place, away from the hustle and bustle, the busyness of life, that was cathartic. It was all about her, a pause from the race, somewhere she was permitted to offload. She was fairly certain that even if she and Orna stayed silent and she did nothing but sit on this couch and breathe, inhaling the sweet earthy scent of the candle, wrapped in the warm lamp light, she would feel better. Having a relationship with Orna didn't make up for losing the ear of a friend like Trina, but her therapist certainly helped plug some of the gaps. It had felt entirely necessary to come and see her this morning. Her thoughts were a turbulent rage when what she needed to function best was calm waters. She was, to put it mildly, unsettled. Unsettled by being plunged back into Marnie's world, unsettled by spending time with Edith and knowing she hadn't exactly got it right as the kid wanted to bolt the moment they'd arrived. Unsettled by seeing Jimmy, which was never easy for her – he the other player in this drama that had bound them for the longest time – and unsettled by what had happened with Nico. Nico, who, it seemed, had slipped through her fingers. It was an awful lot to process.

'When you're ready.' Her therapist's soft voice encouraged her to speak, her gentle rhythm inviting a response that matched.

'I remember when Mum asked me if it was okay for Jimmy to be more involved in our daughter's life. I mean, he'd met her, of course he had. And I knew what Marnie was asking: could he hang out, play with her, maybe take her to his mum's or out for a walk, whatever.'

She remembered the day clearly. She'd gone to visit her parents and was in the kitchen with Marnie, chopping parsley as she helped with supper. Edith, about six months old, was asleep in her bassinet on the sofa next to Dougie, who liked to watch her sleep. Liked to watch her, full stop. The new apple of his eye. That hadn't bothered Madeleine. Not as much as she thought it might. She was just grateful for their devotion and for her freedom.

The conversation had been brief.

'You don't mind if Jimmy spends more time with the little one, do you?' her mum had asked almost casually, as Madeleine switched her attention to slicing courgettes on the plastic chopping board with a burn mark on it in the cramped kitchen.

'What?' She'd held the knife still, and stopped slicing. 'Has he asked to spend more time with her? Why are you even asking me that?'

'You're right, why *am* I asking you? We have an agreement that I raise her how I think is right and asking you for permission is not how we do things!'

'Just a second, Mum.' She'd concentrated on keeping her voice steady, on letting go of the stream of angry expletives that were lined up on her tongue. 'There's no need to come down on me like that!'

It was a familiar battle, but no less wearing for that. If anything, the inevitability of it only made the whole exchange more loaded. This was the way it had been since Edith's birth; Marnie fluctuating between expressing her admiration and love for Madeleine, holding her close when she saw her, smoothing her hair and repeating how proud she was of her and her bravery – and curtly offering up cutting remarks as she still tried to fathom how her only child could choose *not* to be with Edith, could give up parenting the most beautiful baby girl. Behaviour that was, she liked to remind Madeleine, quite unlike that of any other mother she knew.

It didn't help.

It made her feel useless and had paved the way for further estrangement. Over time, Madeleine chose not to put herself through the guilt bath that her mum verbally immersed her in every time she went home. Not that it felt like home then, and not that it had felt like home since. It was easier to stay away, not to endure, and leave cloaked in inadequacy and confusion, pulled in two different directions by her feelings of guilt over leaving Edith and her desperation to walk away from the nappies and bottles to pursue her career.

Orna gave a subtle cough, a reminder that she was there.

'I didn't object to him seeing more of her – why would I? But I guess I thought he'd be on the periphery of her life. Dipping in, like . . . like . . .'

'Like you do?' Orna finished her sentence, her tone neutral.

Madeleine nodded. It sounded horrible and accusatory, and she didn't like it. She didn't need her inadequacy pointed out by Orna, who was supposed to be on her side. The therapist's expression, however, told her this was not how she had intended it.

'But it's become more than that, more than a peripheral thing?' Orna gripped her pen.

'Yes, much more.' She shifted on the sofa. 'Our daughter is always so *delighted* to see him or talk to him, so . . . excited!'

My daddy!

'Is that hard for you?'

'No.' She shook her head. 'Maybe a little.' *Maybe more than a little . . .* But this she knew was a feeling she had no right to. 'And perhaps this sounds ridiculous, but she was supposed to stay at my flat last night, for the first time, but instead she called her dad and he came to fetch her. She didn't want to stay with me.'

The emotion that now gathered as her eyes misted was as surprising as it was embarrassing. She didn't want to cry over this. It was ridiculous!

'It's like, every time I see her, I have to start over. Slowly getting her to trust me. When she leaves, she seems keen to see me again, but then the next time there's this . . . this thin veneer of mistrust. I can sense it. I'm not sure how it's supposed to feel, how it's supposed to be, but it doesn't feel like either of us truly relaxes.'

'She's nervous with you? Hesitant?'

'No, not exactly.' She pictured Edith jumping into her arms, curling her little arms around her neck. 'No, not nervous, it's more like . . . I don't know. Like we don't *know* each other that well, and she's a smart kid – really smart. And all the while I'm staring at her, figuring out what to talk about, whether it's okay to . . .'

'To what?' The doctor sat forward.

'To touch her, cuddle her, in the way that seems second nature for my parents and for her dad.' She clicked her tongue on the roof of her mouth; it wasn't easy to say. 'But for me, it's like I forfeited that right and I never know where to start. I don't know how to get close to her.'

'Children are very astute, and if she senses your hesitation, your nervousness, that might be why she prefers to stay at her dad's, perhaps?'

'Yep.' This was obvious. 'He makes it look easy. They all do.'

'I guess it's just practice, right?'

It was Madeleine's turn to nod. 'I guess so. And he's had a lot of practice. I kind of . . .' She took her time. 'I kind of stayed away a lot when she was a toddler. I was always working, and when I did see her, I felt so uncomfortable, so . . . ill at ease. And Marnie would make such a big deal of dumping her in my arms and watching me. I'm not sure if she was on high alert in case I dropped her or to see if I broke down and begged to be her full-time mum. I couldn't stand it.'

'Does your mother know this? Are you able to talk to her about it?'

'It's not easy. She tends to take everything personally and chooses to cherry-pick the bits of the conversation that resonate most, which aren't necessarily the things I want to talk about or resolve.'

'That can't be easy.'

'It's not. I remember I went to see our daughter on her third birthday. I'd bought balloons and gifts and whatnot. We were in the lounge at my parents and Jimmy walked in and the baby went nuts! So happy to see him!' She took a sharp breath at the memory. 'It was the first time I'd seen it. And I realised that he'd made different choices to me. He showed up. And he's still showing up.'

'It must be a difficult day for you on her birthday.'

Madeleine looked at the floor. 'It is. And even though she's now seven, I still don't . . .' She hesitated, wary of what unboxing this particular thought might unleash.

'You still don't what?' her therapist coaxed.

'I still don't always feel like it's real.' Her voice no more than a whisper.

'You don't feel like what's real?'

'Her being here! *My* child! *My* baby!'

'Because of your late pregnancy reveal or . . .'

'Because I don't feel like a mother. I don't feel like *her* mother. I'm fond of her, more than fond – I love her. I can see she's this fabulous, beautiful child, but I know it's not for me. It's like I was tricked. And in being tricked, I had to make the hardest of decisions and as a result of those decisions, I lost my . . .' Her breath caught in her throat. 'I lost my family.'

'You didn't lose them. But they have had to shift their priorities. Would that be fair to say?'

'Yes.'

'And would it be fair to say that you exclude yourself?'

'It's jealousy, Orna. I know it. It's not easy for me to say.'

'Jealousy of?'

'Jealousy of this little girl who came along and blew up my life! And stole my parents and even stole my honesty. I now live with this . . . this big secret. The fact that she is mine, the fact that she exists at all! And jealous of how she chooses others over me, chooses anyone over me, which I understand. Even though I don't like it.' She thought again of Nico. 'What kind of person does that make me?'

192

'An honest one, actually. And it's that honesty that will help you find your answers.'

This was the first time Madeleine had said any of this out loud. It was scary and cathartic in equal measure. It was her truth; she felt seven flames of envy flare in her gut, fanned by a wind of disloyalty whenever the baby she had given birth to reached for Marnie, or wanted to go sleep at her dad's house rather than spend one night under her roof. And the hardest thing was that Madeleine knew, had Edith wanted to live with her, be with her, she would have felt her blood run cold. What was wrong with her?

'I mean, what was Marnie thinking? Letting him get so close to her, letting him *parent* her? I don't get to do that and he does? What kind of messed-up thinking is that? It's like it's part of my punishment.'

'But it was your choice. It *is* your choice?'

'Yes, it was my choice.' *Thank you for the reminder!* '*Is* my choice, but does that make it okay that Marnie allowed this relationship to foster, without me . . . without my . . . my . . . blessing?' She was breathing hard and sat back on the sofa, knowing she needed to calm down. 'Not that she needs my blessing, of course.' And there it was again, that punch in the throat that reminded her of the deal. 'And I suppose what you're thinking is that shouldn't I just be happy that the little one is happy? Shouldn't I be delighted that she has Jimmy to lean on for those times when one of her pillars crumbles away? Shouldn't *I* be thankful that this is the case? Because let's face it, I can't do it, can I? I just can't do it!'

'You never say her name.'

'Sorry?' She'd heard perfectly but wanted the chance to think over her possible responses.

'I said, you never say her name when you talk to me about her. You say, "my daughter", "the little one" or "my little girl" or "the baby".'

'And your point is?'

'Just an observation, but I wondered if it's difficult for you to say her name out loud, because that makes her real.'

'Difficult?' She laughed, as she did when nervous or wanting to deflect.

'Is it difficult?' her therapist asked with her typically deadpan expression. 'To say her name out loud? To refer to her by her name?'

'It's not difficult, no.'

'Really?'

It felt a little like goading and she took a deep breath, finding that place of control that she had mastered over the years, to curb her spontaneity, to dull her temper, to control her vowels, to speak clearly, to fit in. To shake off Mads Woods from the Brenton Park estate who, just like every other girl she saw wandering the walkways reluctantly pushing a second-hand pram, had royally fucked up her life!

Knee-swars . . . gnocchi . . . gnocchi . . .

'Her name' – she held the woman's eyeline and spoke slowly – 'is Edith-Madeleine. She was named after her grannies, as was I.' And without warning, to say her name, to picture her dancing on the grass with daisies on her dress, was enough to bring her to tears, which she swiped angrily from her highlighted cheeks.

'Did you choose her name?'

Madeleine found it hard to get the words out and wiped her mouth on her sleeve.

Dr Schoenfeld pulled a tissue from the box that was always within reach, but which Madeleine rarely required the service of. Until recently.

'Can we please talk about something else?' She coughed to clear the croak from her throat.

'Sure. I will say this though. I think you need to give yourself permission to freely give love and demonstrate love to Edith. And that doesn't mean being her full-time mother or comparing how you wish to parent with how Jimmy or Marnie does it. It's between you and Edith. I also think part of that permission should start with you talking to Marnie, expressing how you feel.'

'You make it . . . make it all sound so easy.' She hiccupped, knowing the dread she felt at having to talk openly with Edith was as powerful now as it always had been, and she suspected would only grow stronger as her child hit her teens.

'If it was easy, Madeleine, I doubt you'd be sitting here right now. No, it's not easy' – Orna reached for her coffee and took a sip – 'but valuable. So valuable. And the outcome I believe could change things for you – for you all.'

Having hailed a taxi, Madeleine slid into the back seat, gave her destination, and called the office.

'Tan, it's me.'

'Good morning, Miss Madeleine. How are we on this dull, grey day?'

'I am dull and grey, so quite fitting, really.'

'Darling, you could never be dull and grey. And there's a little something that has just arrived and is sitting on your desk that will be sure to lift your mood. And, trust me, they are neither dull nor grey, but more a rampant display of rose pink, apple green and pale lilac all interspersed with Baby's Breath and the most delicate of feathery ferns. A glorious, glorious display! Must have cost an arm and a leg.'

She loved this vulgar aside, knowing it was horribly crass to put a price on a gift or gesture.

'Flowers?' Her smile was wide and her spirits instantly lifted. Nico had sent her flowers! This was far, far better than a comic thumbs-up. 'Are they tasteful?' she whispered, aware that the cabbie was within earshot and not wanting him to think she was one of those women who would rather not have flowers than have nasty flowers. Even though she was precisely that kind of woman. And, actually, when it came to Nico, she would right now happily receive any flowers, even the shoddy garage forecourt ones, the thought of which usually gave her hives.

'Fret not, they are exquisite, abundant, and filling the whole space with the most delicate of perfume.'

'Is there a card?'

'Of course – sealed and awaiting your return.'

Her stomach bunched with excitement. It spoke volumes, the kindest gesture that was conciliatory, forgiving and held promise.

'Wonderful, and actually it's about my return that I'm calling. I'm going to the hospital to see my mum and so should be with you just before lunch or just after. Either way, I'll be in later. I'm on my phone for any emergency, and ask Nadia to check my diary and shift any meetings, etc. She knows what to do.'

'Of course. Take your time and don't worry about a thing. I can hold the fort.'

'I know that.'

'Hope your mum's okay.'

'Thanks, Tan. See you shortly.'

She opened her phone to send a text to Nico. Her finger hovered over the keyboard, what to put? She settled on one word.

HAPPY X

She would send another when she'd read the card and arranged her beautiful bouquet. It was exciting, and comforting – a stay of execution! Maybe he did want her after all. Maybe having had a chance for his thoughts to percolate, he had decided that she was worth the investment – baggage and all. The thought of sitting down with him and filling in the blanks, of coming clean and the two of them continuing without the burden of her secret weighing her down, a chance to explain what had happened and how her life was now structured, felt as if a weight had been lifted from her shoulders.

She smiled broadly as excitement rose in her gut.

Forgiveness was certainly healing and there was no better way to say it than with flowers . . .

December

7.00 P.M.

Madeleine wanted to leave the flat. The sound of her mum alternately crying and then coming up with wild suggestions on how she would make the perfect substitute parent was doing nothing to aid her clarity of thought. The feeling of otherworldliness persisted; she fully expected to wake up at any second. Her dad kept stealing glances at her, as if seeing her in a different light, and it hurt her. She could cope with most things, but the thought that she'd disappointed her lovely dad; it was too much and felt a lot like the shine had fallen away from his image of her, leaving her in some way tarnished.

The way she and Trina had parted earlier preyed on her mind. Not only did hurt ripple through her, but what if her friend reached out to Jimmy and told him what she knew? What if that morsel of information was just too good not to share – not only a way to get back at her friend, balance the hurt, but also information that meant a discussion, a secret shared, a way to ingratiate herself with

Jimmy? Madeleine now knew Trina had a soft spot for him, just as she had all the way through school, not that anything had ever come of it. And when Madeleine had bumped into him on that drunken night out, Trina was the last thing on her mind. She had figured that if Trina and Jimmy were ever going to be a thing they'd have made it happen in the intervening years. Plus, she and Trina had both harboured ridiculous crushes that had never materialised; it hadn't felt like a reason not to let the gorgeous man whisk her off her feet for a while.

How's that working out for ya?

This she asked herself as she crossed the footbridge over the A-road that led to the estate where Jimmy lived with his mother. Traffic thundered underneath. Juggernauts made the structure shudder. She paused for a second, staring headlong into the traffic, and allowing her eyes to go fuzzy in the dazzling glare of headlights. She felt herself sway and gripped the handrail.

'Hello, mate – just off to visit me mum.' She hadn't seen the man approach from the other side, recognising the voice in the dusk as that of Bradley, Mrs Nelson's son – their neighbours.

'Hi, Brad.'

'You all right, Mads?'

'Yeah, I'm fine.' She gave a weak smile.

'Good.' He carried on walking past with his newspaper tucked under his arm. 'In that case, cheer up, love, it might never 'appen!'

Her heart hammered in her chest and she watched him leave the bridge, knowing it was too late; it had already happened. She looked back along the route she'd taken, still unsure if this was a good idea. The thought of having to tell Jimmy made her retch. The simple fact was she didn't have the luxury of time. It wasn't as if they had nine months to get used to the idea or endless evenings on their sofa, hand in hand with a fire smouldering in the grate and excitement fizzing in their veins as they discussed the joy of impending parenthood before examining their latest haul of cute baby clothes. Nothing like that. They were instead up against the clock. He just didn't know it. No more than mere weeks until this baby was born, and in that time she had to wrap her head around the fact that she was pregnant, plan the next steps for her and this child, knowing one thing to be true: she did not want and was not ready for parenthood.

Madeleine had never been so nervous in her life as she walked the narrow tarmac path towards his mother's ground-floor flat. This wasn't her first visit. They had returned here one Saturday afternoon during their fling, his mother gone to visit her sister in Bromley. With the place to himself, Jimmy had cooked her a delicious nasi goreng – a Malaysian rice dish that tingled her tastebuds. They'd demolished two bottles of plonk, danced in the kitchen to hits of the eighties and had sex on the sofa, before pulling a throw over their naked bodies where they slept for the night. A memory flashed in her thoughts. That night . . . she'd drunk too much, they'd had sex, she'd vomited – due to the wine, not the sex . . . Could that have been the night that she conceived? Not that it mattered now, the end result was just the same. Plus, it wasn't as if she'd ever have the conversation with the child about their conception. *Oh, I was so sloshed I could hardly stand. Your father and I smooched to ABC's 'The Look of Love' and I don't remember the sex very well, but I know I spent at least ten minutes in the early hours with my face in your grandmother's toilet bowl, ridding my body of contraception . . .*

'You idiot, Edith-Madeleine,' she whispered into the night as, with a trembling finger, she rang the doorbell. The hall light came on and she heard movement.

Her wait on the step felt interminable, her heart pounding, her stomach barely risen inside her jumper and words cued up on her tongue that felt like lies no matter how many times she practised them in her head. She looked along the path that ran across the low-rise block of flats. It was dusk, cold and the uniform streetlamps gave off an eerie glow that pooled on the damp pavement still slick from earlier rain. Her limbs shook and she felt light-headed with nerves as her breath blew smoke into the atmosphere.

Hi, there! Good to see you again. What have I been up to? Nothing much. Oh, by the way, I'm pregnant . . .

Hey, Jimmy, remember me? Well, guess what? I'm pregnant!

Jimmy! Sorry for not calling you back. You won't believe what's happened . . .

Jimmy, hi! So here's a funny thing . . .

'Can you get the door, lovey?' his mother, she assumed, called out. And there she stood, wanting the meeting to be over and hoping – praying – that he wouldn't make things any more difficult than they needed to be, that he wouldn't try to complicate an already complicated situation. His mother, who lived in the same postcode as her family, her accent like Marnie's, sounded familiar, and her heart bunched for all she was bringing to her door – quite literally. The woman who had no idea she was about to become a grandmother – and maybe she never would. Who knew what Jimmy was about to say? How he'd react? Who he'd tell? Would he and Trina discuss it? Judge her? Again she shivered.

Jimmy opened the door and his face instantly split into that easy smile. He looked good, his straight, almost black, hair longer than she recalled, and it suited him.

'Hey, stranger.'

He held her eyeline, his stance a little awkward, but there was no doubt he was pleased to see her. His face lit up at the sight of her – he shoved his hands in his jeans pockets, shoulders hunched, hair falling messily over his handsome face, self-conscious in the way that was hard to disguise when you liked someone and weren't sure how to hide it.

'Hi, Jimmy.'

'It's good to see you. Wow! You are, like, the last person I expected to see.'

'It's good to see you too. Sorry to turn up so randomly.'

'No, it's all good.' His words were a green light, his way of telling her she was forgiven for whatever might have transgressed and how they had ended, opening a door that he was seemingly willing to walk through. 'You wanna come in?' He stood back against the wall.

'Actually, can we talk?' She pointed down the street.

'Sure. Just nipping out, Mum!' he called over his shoulder as he slipped his feet into boots that were unlaced on the welcome mat, before following her out into the cold of early evening. He walked in step with her and her heart sank as he initiated small talk.

'So, what have you been up to?' he asked.

'Not much.' Felt safest. She was aware it came across as rude, but all she wanted to do was buy time until she could come clean, get to the point, and leave.

It was the very last thing she wanted – to discuss the weather, football, his latest music craze, a party he'd been to, or plants. She remembered he had a thing about plants.

It seemed he got the hint, and they walked the four hundred metres in silence, until they reached the edge of the canal, made their way along the towpath, and sat on a bench that was lit by one of the old cast-iron Victorian streetlamps that were dotted along the path. There were some slats missing on the bench. The seat was slimy, damp. Not that she cared. She sat down hard. He followed suit. She had already figured it would be easy to talk openly if they sat side by side and she didn't have to look him in the eye.

'So,' she began, 'I need to talk to you.'

'So you said.' He stretched his long legs out in front of him and put his hands inside the kangaroo pocket of his caramel-coloured fleece top.

She exhaled.

'You seem nervous, Mads.'

'I am, a bit. A lot, actually, I'm nervous . . . a lot,' she stuttered.

'Well, don't be. We've known each other a long time and so anything you want to say or ask me, I can almost guarantee a favourable response, unless it's a request for money. I don't have a whole lot of that.' He tried to make light of the situation, speaking in his slow, slightly intense way, that she had always found quite attractive.

'It's not easy to know where to start,' she began.

'So take your time. And for the record, I'm really pleased to see you.'

Oh God! It occurred to her then that he might think she was there seeking reconciliation or with the hope of picking up where they had left off. It was the jolt she needed to cut to the chase, to put them both out of their misery.

'I came to tell you something – something that's not very easy for me to say.'

'Right.' She felt him stiffen slightly beside her, as he sat up straight.

'Oh, Jimmy . . . God . . . I'm just going to say it.' She drew breath.

'Please do.' He licked his lip nervously.

'I'm pregnant.'

'Oh!' He made a small noise that was part astonishment and part relief. 'I thought you might be about to give me really bad news, like, "Jimmy I've got three weeks to live!" Or similar.'

She turned on the bench to face him.

'Truthfully, I'm finding it hard to read your face.' He toned down his enthusiasm. 'I don't know what to say next. Are congratulations in order? How do you feel about it? Are you excited, happy, scared? All of the above, I bet.' She liked his honesty. 'Are you being supported? I guess you're seeing someone. How do they feel about it all?'

She realised they could go around the houses in this way for some time and decided to grasp the nettle.

'It's your baby, Jimmy. You're the father.'

He laughed then, a nervous guffaw that saw him rock forward and then back.

'Okay, you got me!' He put his hands up. 'Not funny! Not really, but very well done! Jesus, Mads!' He placed his hand over his heart.

'It's not a joke.' She studied his face and watched his smile slowly fall away.

'Okay, so, I think we all know that school wasn't really my thing.' He coughed to clear his throat. 'But even I know that we slept together over half a year ago, and so, by my reckoning, if it were true, you'd be very, very pregnant by now. So what's going on? What's this all about?' He clasped his hands between his thighs.

'I had no idea, none. But I can promise you I'm not joking.'

'For real? You are honestly pregnant?'

'Yes. I only found out today. I got a test this morning and then a scan.'

'But . . .' His look of bewilderment was entirely relatable.

'I know it's a lot. It's a lot for me too.' And now for the kicker. 'I'm seven months pregnant.'

'You can't be!'

'I am.'

'You don't look it.'

'I know!' She pushed her fingers into her forehead, hoping this might relieve some of the pressure she could feel building. 'I guess that's why it didn't occur to me.'

'And you were on the pill?'

'I was. I am. I was.' She pictured the foil pack in her bedside cabinet, which was of course now redundant.

'Then how? Mads, help me out here!' His voice shook with emotion.

'I was sick once or twice, and that can affect it. I'm still trying to get my head around it, but I thought you should know.'

She didn't think it prudent to mention that it was actually Marnie who thought he should know, having to admit that right now there was no small sense of relief that whatever Trina chose to divulge, it was Madeleine who was in control of how the information was given.

'It's definitely mine? I don't know if it's okay to ask . . .'

It was a fair question. They weren't even a couple.

'I haven't slept with anyone since you,' she admitted, and noted the lift to the corner of his mouth, suggesting the idea delighted him. It bothered her. He was not what she wanted, not now. Not ever. He was what Trina wanted, and in that moment she felt a smack of remorse around her face at how she had hurt the girl she so loved.

'Seven months! So that means you have the baby in . . .'

'She's due on January twenty-sixth.'

'She?'

'Yes, a little girl. Do you want to see the scan picture?'

He nodded. She hadn't shown it to her mum, understanding that if this child was possibly not going to be part of their family, aware of the huge undertaking and the slim chance that her parents might have second thoughts, then to see the image and start to bond with the baby would only lead to greater heartache when it came to saying goodbye. But with Jimmy, in that moment, it felt like his right. To see this baby they had made together.

Reaching into her jacket pocket, she pulled out the black and white photograph and handed it to him. It was the first time she'd seen it since she left the hospital that morning, finding it too hard to look at, until now. There she was. Intact, perfect, and coiled in her nest. The sight of her had a curious effect: tears welled up and clogged her nose and throat, spilling down her face, as she struggled to take a breath.

Jimmy skirted across the bench and took her in his arms, rocking her and whispering gently into her scalp. 'It'll all be okay. I promise, whatever happens, it will all be okay. Please don't cry.'

His words were moving, his kindness no less than she had expected of him. He was wonderful. She could see how Trina was still smitten.

'I'm scared, Jimmy. So scared.'

'We've got this.' He kissed the top of her head, and in that moment she understood that they might have very different ideas of what might represent a successful outcome when it came to this pregnancy. Even the vaguest suggestion that they were in it together was something she could not allow to foster. She felt the same level of wariness she'd felt when he gave her a picture of the cottage with a duck pond, suggesting they might live there.

He was undoubtedly the very best kind of human being, beautiful inside and out, but he was not what she wanted. Just like becoming a mother was not what she wanted. And being tied to a life that she had fought so hard to be free of was most definitely not what she wanted.

'Nothing is insurmountable.' He tried to reach for her hand and she folded her arms across her chest to keep them out of reach, leaning out of his grip, until he sat back on the bench. 'You need to remember that no story is about how you start, Mads. It's always about how you finish.' His eyes were bright, as if a plan was forming, and it hurt her to hear. 'You have no idea how happy I was to see you on the doorstep tonight. I've thought you about a lot.

206

Like, a *lot*. And I think you're remarkable and beautiful and funny and smart and—'

'Please, don't, Jimmy.' She cut him off and sniffed the last of her tears. 'There's no point.' Her were words harsh, direct and she knew the kindest in the long run. 'Nothing lasts for ever. Nothing, Jimmy.'

He stopped talking and his head hung forward a little. 'This might really be something for us! We were having such a good time – it was brilliant! You sabotaged a really good thing. A *really* good thing,' he whispered. 'You just stopped answering your phone, disappeared! And now this' – he flicked the photograph into the palm of his other hand – 'this could be something wonderful. A baby!'

'You just don't get it, do you?' She turned to face him, he looked right at her, and she was forced to face the situation head on. It was every bit as difficult as she had imagined. 'It's only ever a *really, really* good thing if two people feel the same, and I didn't! And I don't, Jimmy. I don't want any of this!' She brushed her stomach with her palm. 'None of it. I just want to pick up with my life as if this had never happened. I'm on track to achieve all the things I want. It's my chance to live an incredible life. I don't want to be a mother and I don't want a baby, not now – maybe not ever, but definitely not now! I can't and won't do this. I can't keep her. I want someone else to have her.'

'Adopted?' His face crumpled, and she thought for a terrible moment that he might cry.

'Yes. Kind of.'

'Jesus Christ!' He put his hand over his mouth.

It seemed obvious to her in that moment; the solution that Marnie had suggested came even more sharply into focus. It meant the baby would be brought up close to him, close to her if that was what she wanted, to know her a little, to loiter on the edges of her life like a really good auntie or friend, and yet she would be free. And what she wanted more than anything was her freedom.

'Or maybe something less formal than adoption to strangers. My . . . my mum and dad said they'd take her, bring her up. And you'd know where she is if you wanted to see her occasionally, or not, I don't know. I'm just making this up as I go along, Jimmy, it's all . . . new.'

He stared at her, eyes narrowed, as if seeing her for the first time, and judging by his expression, what he saw wasn't to his liking. It made her feel small.

'I can't imagine thinking there's only one option – one life and that's the path you have to follow, no matter what. I believe life drops boulders in our way and we have to find a way to climb over them, or go around them, or tunnel through them, but sometimes they are the very best things – these surprises that pop up – because they help you find a new route or they help you look at the world in a different way.' He paused. 'Would my mum and I be as close if my dad had stuck around? Probably not. Things happen, and even though they seem like the end of the world, often they're not. They might just be the obstacles that bring you more joy and fulfilment than you knew was possible. *That* to me would be an incredible life.'

'Well, that sounds like some deep hippie shit to me and confirms that we are very different people. I'm a lot more practical, Jimmy. I don't think anything lasts for ever and that's why you have to grab opportunity when it comes along.'

She pictured Rebecca walking away from her desk, having offered her a chance . . .

'I couldn't agree more.' He took a deep breath. 'I guess the only difference is what we define as an opportunity.'

'Not this.' She pointed to him and then her chest. 'Not us.'

'Well, you've made that very clear.'

'Don't you want more?' She gestured behind her to the blocks of flats that towered above them and stole their horizon.

'I think' – he paused – 'that I don't want *more* necessarily. I only want enough, and I know that enough will make me happy. But as you said, we're very different people.'

He stood then, his eyes roving her face, taking in every bit of her. It felt a lot like goodbye and there was no denying the jump in her gut at the thought. They were, after all, now irrevocably connected. Or maybe it was simply her little one reacting to their daddy as he left. He tried to hand her the scan picture; she shook her head – he could keep it. When he next spoke, his tone was steady, his manner calm.

'I'll do whatever you need or want me to. I will be as involved or as absent as you think is right. I want to be involved, but I will take your lead.'

She let out a long sigh of relief. He wasn't done, however.

'And you're right, Madeleine.' He spoke with an unmistakeable note of sadness as he turned to walk along the towpath. 'Nothing lasts for ever. But I always figured that we don't need a love that lasts for ever – we only need it to last for our lifetime. And even though it's you who is calling the shots, I would like this little girl to know that I'll be here for whatever you need, whatever she needs, whenever she needs it. Always.'

Love? It was the first time he'd used the word and it struck her like a tiny knife in her chest. It was as she considered how best to reply that she looked up, and he was already walking away.

The man who was beautiful inside and out, the man her beloved best friend had always loved . . .

Chapter Ten

PRESENT DAY

It already felt a lot like routine, Madeleine's second visit to the hospital in so many days – not that it endeared her to the place any more. Nerves still rattled her bones as she stepped inside.

She found Marnie sitting upright in the bed against a pillow pile, looking weary, but so much better than she had the previous day. It was a relief.

'Madeleine! What are you doing here, love? I don't want you to get into trouble. Shouldn't you be at work?' Despite her voiced concerns, her mum's face lit up at the sight of her. It was a reminder that she was sunshine in Marnie's life, sunshine that would soon be hot-footing it across the Atlantic. This thought cloaked her in remorse, like she was running out on them for the second time, leaving them all to figure out how to go forward.

'I'll go in later. I wanted to come and see you.'

'Thank you, my love. Just seeing your lovely face, it warms my heart. This dodgy old heart that's let me down a little. That's going to carry its very own device around to shock it back to life! Can you believe that? How is it even a thing?' She placed her hand on her chest. 'It's a very strange thought.'

'You won't even notice it after a while, I'm sure.' She took the seat next to the bed. 'How are you feeling? You look a bit rosier in the cheek.'

'I'd say I'm calmer today, but so tired. Your dad stayed until the very last minute yesterday. He didn't want to leave and I didn't want him to go.'

'Did you manage to sleep?'

'Not well. Goodness only knows how anyone manages to rest in here. The strip light in the corridor kept me awake, not to mention beeps from all the machines in the ward, and the nurses, bless them, popping in to run checks throughout the night, chattering outside the door, a phone ringing, ambulance sirens . . . It's like Piccadilly bloody Circus!'

'Maybe try to rest today, Mum. I won't stay long.'

'Oh, you stay as long as you want, my love. Once you're all the way over in America, it won't be possible, will it? So you stay as long as you want.'

She couldn't decide whether this was offered as a barb or in acceptance.

'I'll come back to visit, of course I will.'

Marnie reached for her hand, their physical contact not quite as easy as it had been yesterday when the emergency and novelty had oiled the interaction. Today, holding hands was already a slightly forced thing, a little uncomfortable for her. As if she were overly aware of her mother's hand in hers. But then, as Dr Schoenfeld had reminded her, sometimes the things that were most valuable were not always easy.

She understood how hard it might be for Marnie to settle, remembering what it had been like to first sleep away from the flat on the Brenton Park estate in her new abode with her three rather eclectic flatmates, including the wonderful Luciano, whom she had adored, her colleague from the diner who had told her of a room to rent. She hadn't seen him for the longest time – didn't see anyone really – with work and sleep her sole occupations. Until Nico came along. She pictured those early days in the flat on the Old Kent Road, and how it had taken a while to get used to sleeping in a strange bed, without the noises that had cocooned her every night of her life in that little room where every inch of walls and ceiling was familiar. It had been thrilling and terrifying in equal measure. A new life. Memories of her childhood bedroom were warm and cosy – the room that was now Edith's, and where Peppa Pig was immortalised on the curtains.

'Truth is, love, I can't sleep properly without Dougie by my side. We're not used to being apart. Although he did send me a text this morning saying he was trying to hoover up all the sequins that the dancing girls had left on the carpet. Just hope he gets them all up before I get home.'

It was good to hear Marnie joking, more like her old self.

'I can't imagine being with one person for all that time, and still feeling how you guys feel about each other.'

'I never know whether it's wonderful or pathetic that, after thirty-odd years of marriage, I only settle at night when I feel him sink down on to the mattress.'

'I think wonderful.'

And she did, especially having seen the strength and comfort Marnie gleaned from her husband, the image of the two of them holding each other tight as they spoke of their fears still fresh in her mind; her mum clinging to his back the previous night as she cried her worries into the fabric of his sweater.

'Yeah, me too. Can't sleep unless he says, "Night, night. Love you." I've heard that every night since I met him, rain or shine, in good times and bad. It's what I want for you, Madeleine – that kind of love, that kind of security.'

'I guess I make my own security.'

'You know what I mean, and it's nothing to do with money. I've always said people don't need diamonds and steak, none of us do – we need love, attention, a cuddle at the end of a difficult day, someone to talk to and a place to be – a safe haven. It's knowing there's someone at home who worries about you, who thinks about you. It gives you purpose.'

She nodded rather than challenge Marnie with the concept that her purpose came from climbing the corporate ladder and her plans to open her own agency, which after LA would be tantalisingly close. As for having someone at home, she might not be willing to admit it, but it was thrilling to know there was a bouquet waiting for her on her desk from a very, very nice man. A man with whom, if this strength of feeling continued in the same vein that it had begun, she could possibly see a future with. Although it was far too early to express this publicly.

'Anyway, I'm dying to know, how did you get on with Edith last night? Did you drop her off okay this morning? She's a little pickle, isn't she! I bet all the other parents were wondering who this glamorous lady was!'

There was no mistaking the joy in her mum's eye, the delight in her tone, as well as the oblivious nature of her comment. She was sure Marnie meant it as a compliment, but instead it reinforced the fact that no one at Edith's school would have the first clue who she was, and why would they? This only bolstered the idea that she had no right to be there, even if she had turned up.

'And I have to say,' Marnie continued, placing her hand over her heart, as though comforted by its steady beat beneath her fingers, 'that yesterday might have been the absolute worst, with everything I take for granted thrown into chaos, but seeing you leave the ward with Edith . . .' She swallowed, as if it was almost too much for her to express. 'It was wonderful – so wonderful. You took to it like a duck to water. I've never felt so proud, so confident that—'

'Well, you might want to hold your horses for a mo.' Madeleine removed her hand from under her mum's. In the wake of her mother's misplaced praise, she felt the weight of dread about having to explain that she had in fact failed again, and that Edith had not stayed over with her. Orna's voice now echoed in her thoughts, encouraging her to communicate. It was as she was about to explain what had happened that Marnie's phone beeped – a Facetime call.

'Oh, look, it's Jimmy!'

Marnie took the call, while Madeleine dug deep to find a smiley face, knowing it would translate in her demeanour, and wondering how his version of events might sound.

'Hello, mate!'

'Morning! How are you feeling, Marn?'

'Oh, I'm fine. I've got Madeleine here!' She twisted the screen, forcing Madeleine to lift her hand in an awkward wave; he responded in kind.

'Ah, so I expect you've had the run-down on last night?' he began.

'No.' Marnie looked anxiously from her back to the screen. 'What happened last night?'

'Edith called and said she wanted to sleep at my house, so . . .'

'Oh no! Was she upset? What did you do?' This she fired at Madeleine, without giving her the chance to respond. 'I can't stand the thought of her being unsettled!'

This was how it was; her mum going from zero to a hundred miles an hour in a matter of seconds.

'She wasn't upset,' she interjected.

'No, she wasn't upset at all.' Jimmy backed her up. 'Mads called me just before bedtime and Edith said she'd rather come to mine, so I nipped over and picked her up. It was no big deal.' Madeleine loved how he made the laborious round-trip sound easy, reminded now of how he promised to pick Edith up from anywhere, any time. Lovely, lovely Jimmy. 'She slept all the way home. And this morning she was on cloud nine. She's wolfed down banana pancakes and apple juice for breakfast and I've sent her off with a packed lunch.'

'Wowsers!' Marnie beamed. 'She's having the best adventure. And she went into school all right?'

'Yep, right as rain. Olly's mum said she's happy to take her home if we're stuck on any days, but I don't think that'll be necessary. I can shift things around, make sure I'm there to collect her. She's perfectly happy about that, so don't worry, Marn.'

'I won't, Jimmy. You're a marvel. What would we do without you?'

Indeed, what would we do? Thank God for Jimmy! There to pick up the pieces of everything Madeleine dropped . . . And pancakes? How did anyone know how to make banana pancakes? This she kept to herself, knowing it was both mean and undeserved.

'Oh, you and Dougie more than have everything under control. She's a lucky little pup.'

'Bless you, Jimmy, and thank you, sweetheart.' Marnie looked lovingly at the screen.

'Obviously I'll pick her up from school from now on and hang on to her until we know what's what. You know I'm always happy to have her. Right, I'd better crack on, but I'll get her to call you later, Marn. And, Mads, Edith says can you say thank you to the nice man for the biscuits. And that she'll see you on Sunday. She made me promise to pass that on, and you know she'll check!'

'Yep, cheers.' She waved again, through sheer embarrassment, and watched as Marnie ended the call.

'What's happening on Sunday?'

'Oh, I'm going to visit them and to collect my coat and bag. Jimmy asked, and it felt like the right thing to do, to accept.'

215

Especially as Edith was so keen to be free of my company last night. I want to see her before I go away, make sure we're good. This she kept to herself.

'Mmmm . . .' Her mum looked deep in thought. 'You know Trina likes him, don't you?'

'Jesus Christ!' Marnie's assumption was as irritating as it was false. 'I'm going to have a cup of tea and collect my coat and bag, not move in! And for your information, I told Trina to tell Jimmy how she feels, and I hope she does.'

'Me too,' her mum echoed. 'And there's no need to *snap* at me.' She crossed her arms indignantly.

'And there's no need for you to make a *snap* judgement that because I'm going to visit Jimmy I must be interested in him! You know that's not me.'

It bothered her that it had to be this way, the underlying tension that had the ability to flare from the smallest of embers. It always put her on edge and was part of the reason she avoided contact. At least in LA she wasn't going to have to face it.

They both drew breath. It was Marnie who broke the impasse.

'So, what happened at your place? Why did Edith suddenly want to leave?'

I shouted at her and put her in a cupboard . . .

'Nothing happened, and it wasn't sudden. I think she was out of sorts. My flat was strange to her and she was missing you and she just wanted her dad – that was it. Nothing *happened*! There was no incident,' Madeleine pressed. 'She was quite jolly, chatty throughout the whole thing. It was fine.'

She wasn't so sure it was fine, certainly not for her at any rate, but what would be the benefit in sharing this with Marnie?

'I guess she had a lot to get her head around yesterday. And little ones don't like their routine being upset, not really. It just felt so right, though, you taking her. An opportunity.'

216

'Yes, I thought so too.'

'You see, Madeleine, I *know* how quickly time flies. One minute you were a toddler and the next you were putting on heels and lipstick, and it happened quicker than my dodgy heart could catch up. It's the same with Edith, and I guess I don't want you to miss a second of it. We're all running out of time, whether we like to admit it or not.'

There it was: the regular reminder to get her act together. Although the setting for this latest verbal prod certainly added poignancy to it, it didn't get any easier to be at the receiving end of her mother's judgement.

'I think it might be a bit late for that, Mum. I've already missed a lot. And . . . and I'm going to miss a lot more, aren't I?' Her legs jumped.

'Yes, yes, you are. How long are you planning to stay in America exactly?' Marnie sat up straighter, as if reading between the lines, sensing her daughter's discomfort around the topic.

'Hard to say, but as I mentioned, I'm . . . I'm renting out my flat and have taken an apartment, and the job is . . . is fairly permanent.'

'Fairly permanent?' Marnie scoffed at the mixed metaphor. 'I see.' Madeleine felt her cheeks flame, reduced with no more than two words to a child being scorned. It didn't feel good. It never did. 'And what about Edith? How does she fit into this fairly permanent move to the other side of the bloody world? How is she supposed to navigate that? How am I? How are you? Won't you miss us?'

Madeleine bit her lip, deciding not to point out that she and Marnie saw each other sporadically and both managed just fine. But Edith, that was a whole other matter. Last night had opened a door into a world that she had peered into, and she'd be lying if she said she didn't want to visit that world more. She was excited for Sunday, possibly because it came without a particular pressure – what did it

217

matter if she royally messed things up? She was going to be leaving soon for LA.

'I will figure things out with Edith. It's enough for me to know that she's happy and smart, and—'

Marnie shifted to face her. 'Don't give up on her. Don't run away. It's *not* too late for you to make amends, to learn how to—'

'Oh my God! I'm not running away!' She raised her voice and the woman with the tablet looked up from her programme. Aware and embarrassed, remembering where she was, Madeleine lowered her tone. '*You* never give up, do you? You never miss a chance to remind me of what you think I should be doing, how you think I should live.'

'Because I will never, ever, until my dying day be able to fathom it, love. Never.' Marnie twisted her lower jaw and pulled the indignant face Madeleine had grown used to.

'And this is why I told you taking her would be difficult, and this is what I tried to explain to you in the weeks leading up to it and every bloody week since! It's an action that comes with consequences. These are the things I'm talking about, Mum. This right here! This disconnect between you and me – the friction! The huge gap between us! The lack of closeness, the awkwardness, the pressure!' She threw her arms into the air.

'Don't exaggerate – that child has a lovely life, a wonderful life. She's happy, she's—'

'I'm not talking about Edith. I'm talking about you and me.' And just like that, she took Orna's advice and opened the can of worms that she had been kicking ahead of her on the pavement for as long as she could remember. 'It's easy to say it's all worked out, Mum, but can't you see that further down the line I'm the one who's going to have to hash it out with Edith? You're right – she's a smart cookie. Last night she said I could come and live with you all, said she'd share her room with me.'

'Oh, that's heartbreaking!' Marnie took a breath and shook her head. 'Absolutely heartbreaking. What did you say?'

Looking at her shoes, Madeleine felt the tight grip of inadequacy, knowing she had chickened out, taken the coward's way. 'I kind of made light of it.'

Marnie stared at her open-mouthed and Madeleine was actually grateful not to hear the rebuke that she could have guessed at. *Made light of it? What kind of response is that?*

'This is exactly what I mean by consequences. You don't think there are questions building up in her mind that, when she feels ready, she is going to fire at me with rejection and possibly venom? That's the price I will have to pay, Mum! "Why *did* you give me to Nanny?", "Why *did* you not live with me?", "Why *did* you choose not to be my mum every day?"'

'And she'd be right! Why did you choose those things, Madeleine? Why did you?'

Marnie's response was automatic, speedily delivered without hesitation and landed like blades in her chest. Looking down, she tried to keep her expression neutral and not react to the blood-seeping wounds she fully expected to see at her breast, as her mother's words and the manner of their delivery wounded her as surely as knives. She sat backwards in the chair and felt the air leak from her lungs, all at once deflated, winded and sucker-punched.

'I didn't mean—' Marnie began.

'Yes, you did.' She kept her eyes downcast and her voice low, knowing she needed to keep control. 'And I think therein lies the heart of it. It's like, at some level, whether consciously or not, you want me punished. Like you understand that things between Edith and me are never going to be smooth because of how we live, because of the choices I made.'

'How can you say that! How can you *think* it?' Distress made Marnie's words warble.

'I don't know, Mum, but sometimes I do.' She nodded at this truth that was as hard to swallow as it was to say. 'I don't want you to be upset. You're in hospital, for God's sake, but I also know that you're right – we're all running out of time.'

'I want you to want her,' Marnie whispered, and there it was, the truth, her driving belief, distilled.

'And I do want her' – she leaned her elbows on the side of the bed, and buried her head in her hands – 'but I think that means different things to you and me. I want to see her and know she's doing well, but I don't need her hanging off my hip twenty-four-seven. I don't need to be one of those women at the school gates. I don't even know how to make basic pancakes, let alone banana ones! I'm not like you!'

'What are you talking about bloody pancakes for? I don't expect you to be like me.'

'No? I think you thought I'd come round to your way of thinking when I gave birth.'

'Maybe.'

It was an admission Madeleine was thankful for, validation that showed she wasn't making crazy assumptions.

'The thing is, Mum, and what I believe is at the heart of our . . . lack of closeness' – she didn't know how else to phrase it – 'is that you gave me an ultimatum when I was vulnerable.'

'What the . . . How dare—' Marnie turned to face her.

'I don't want us to fight. I honestly don't. It kills me. But I do need us to be able to talk about it.'

Her mother settled back on the pillows and gave an almost imperceptible nod.

'I came to you that day, sat on your sofa, and there was no real discussion. No thought about the longer term. You were adamant. "That can't happen! This can't happen! I will take the baby!" You

220

didn't ask me; you didn't *hear* me!' She felt her vocal cords pull taut with all they tried to contain.

'So what are you saying? That you would have *liked* her to go to strangers?' Marnie's voice too was almost strangled with emotion.

Sometimes, a little bit, maybe . . .

'No.' It was still impossible to voice this dark thought, *her* truth, aware that it was also unthinkable to Marnie. Edith was not a notion, an idea, the suggestion of a person, or the dark shadow on a scanned image. She was a wonderful, beautiful, life-enriching living thing, and so how could *any* decent human prefer the thought of her not being in their lives . . . Madeleine knew she wasn't a decent human, because these thoughts, no matter how unpalatable, crept into her mind on the odd occasion. And that she could never share, with anyone.

Not even Dr Schoenfeld.

And certainly not Marnie.

It felt like an ugly quirk deep inside her that bled into her whole life. It drove her in her chosen career because she knew this was her thing. While other women spoke with pride about their little ones, she would have her achievements on her CV and a bank balance to reflect it, because work for her was easy, being a mother was not, and it was just how she was.

'So then why are you bringing it up? Why mention it all? You talk about punishment – well, this feels a lot like you wanting to punish me.'

'No, Mum. But I hate how you can't see that you're part of the problem. I absolutely know you have the best of intentions and your actions are rooted in love and loyalty, but you have always manipulated me to try and come around to your way of thinking, putting thoughts in my head and volunteering facts that are nothing of the sort.'

'That's simply not true, Madeleine!'

'But it is true! It is! On the day I came to you when I was pregnant, you said to me, "Of course you want to keep her! It will all work out, it will. It will all come good in the end." As if there was no other discussion, no other choice. And I hit a wall. How was I supposed to have any meaningful discussion when that was your standpoint, your default? And I needed your advice, your protection. Instead I just had to let you lead and I followed.'

'You have never followed!' Marnie let a small, dry laugh escape her mouth. 'You have never, ever followed! If I say it's green, you'd argue it was red. If I say it makes four, you'd argue for five! You go against me at every turn.'

'That's not true, that's only how you think it is. But it's not. You don't see me, Mum! And you don't hear me! And I've never felt I could tell you that I think much of what you say, the way you try to coat everything in glitter, is detrimental – like we are both reciting lines in a crappy play where none of the players has been told the ending. It's not real. Your sunny outlook and "let's have another cup of tea and everything will be fine" – it's not real! It's not helpful. It just creates confusion! Like spraying perfume over a turd in a cupboard, it might mask things for a minute, but the next time you open the cupboard, the turd is still there.'

'I actually think my attitude makes life better.'

'Well, I don't.' Madeleine shook her head. 'Encouragement, yes. Kind words, yes. But not "A little smile can turn a bad day into a good one!" "If we wish hard enough, good things can happen!" "Don't let a bad thought spoil a pretty day!"'

'I happen to believe all of those things.' Marnie stood her ground.

'It didn't help me, it just confused me. I wanted a better life, and I wanted you to acknowledge that it was okay for me to want a better life.'

'We were always so proud of you – always.'

It felt like she just didn't get it.

'It's not about you being proud! There was dog shit on the walkways and you made a little song up: "Don't step on the poo poo, that just won't do do!" And I remember Bryan the junkie passed out in the lift with a needle sticking out of his hand and you smiled at me and said, "Shhhh . . . We mustn't wake Bryan up, he looks like he's having a lovely dream!" Did you never want to scream from the rooftops, "We're living in a nightmare and this place is in the depths of hell! We deserve better! We want better! And I want better for you, Madeleine!"'

Marnie took her time, composing herself. 'Yes, Madeleine, I thought that every single day, and every single day I still want to scream from the rooftops!'

'Me too! That's why I left, why I built a different life. And I never wanted to drag Edith into it. It doesn't feel good, it feels the opposite of good! I escaped, and yet part of me, my little girl, is still in it. History repeating itself!'

'You think it'd be easy for me and your dad to build a different life, to "escape", as you call it? And actually, Madeleine, you know what? It's a great idea. I wonder why we never thought of it! What do you suggest? That Dougie gives up his buckets and pots and retrains as a lawyer? Or maybe he could become a surgeon and we could get that villa in Tuscany with staff . . .'

'That's unfair. I have nothing but respect for how you and Dad have worked, cared for me and for Edith, how you've given us chances.'

'Really? It's just that it always feels a bit like you resent having to come and see us.'

'I never resent it, but it's not easy, is it?'

'We're your family, it should be the easiest thing!'

'Yes, it should, but for a million different reasons it's not. And this shouldn't be a surprise – I *told* you when you said you wanted to take her that it wouldn't be easy, that it'd change things between all of us, I *told you* that. And it has, in more ways than I could have imagined.'

'You did.' Marnie's tone was unapologetically sarcastic and she did nothing to amend it. 'And you were right. So you're vindicated! And yet whenever you see Edith, I can see you feel guilty, and whether you admit it or not, your tone is sometimes resentful.' Marnie looked a little startled, as if she didn't know where the words had come from, but once they were out they were out.

'You're right. You got me!' Her daughter nodded. 'Sometimes . . . sometimes a little resentful, and always guilty, and most of the time a potent combination of the two. And I knew it was going to be this way, but you wouldn't listen – you didn't listen! You only thought about how *you* would make space for her and love her, and it's like it didn't occur to you that the flipside of that decision was going to affect me. You were solely focused on how this baby was going to fit into *your* life.'

'You have no idea about my life! None at all.' Marnie's smile was fake, her eyes now misty.

Madeleine reached for her hand, and this time it sat against her mum's palm with ease.

'What are you talking about? You're my mum; of course I know about your life.'

'No, Madeleine, no. You only know about my life from the point at which you came into it. And from what I show you.'

'So what don't I know, Mum? What don't you show me? Tell me.' This felt a lot like progress.

'You're not the only one,' Marnie began. Nerves made her words quiet.

'Not the only one who what?'

'I was smart. Not smart like you, but smarter than the kids in my class – smart enough to be aware of the life I had and the life I wanted and that they weren't necessarily the same thing. But I had no choices.' Marnie wiped her mouth. 'And every time it looked like I might be coming to a crossroads where I could make a choice, something came along and wiped it out, meaning I could only go where I was needed or told. Firefighting, plodding and trying very hard to find the pocketsful of sunshine that you find so irritating, just to keep going.'

'What are you saying? What do you mean by that exactly? What things came along?'

She wanted the detail. Wanted to understand this woman who was at once her mother, her protector, her saviour, and her nemesis. Marnie took a beat and the air around them stilled.

'I love you, Edith-Madeleine. I love you. You are without a shadow of doubt the best thing that ever happened to me.' Her voice faltered with emotion. 'But the way you talk about ambition and drive and climbing the career ladder, as if you're the only one ever to have thought about it—'

'I don't think that.'

'It seems like you do, love.' Marnie squeezed her hand. 'It sometimes feels like you believe you invented ambition.'

'I don't think that, Mum.' Her words were hurtful.

'Good, because you didn't. I was always ambitious. Always. I lived close to the bright lights, just like you, and I wanted to be among them. I wanted to—' She swallowed the sadness that seemed lodged in her throat.

'What did you want to do?'

'I wanted to go to college.' Her expression was one of embarrassment at the admission, even after all this time. 'I wanted to study.'

'What did you want to study?'

Marnie shook her head, licked her dry lips. 'Anything! I don't know. I thought maybe teaching.' She looked down as the bloom

225

of awkwardness spread on her chest, an admission that Madeleine knew to her mum would sound lofty and so far out of her reach it was almost laughable. 'I just thought that if I had qualifications then I'd get a decent job, and I remember what your Granny Edith always said to me – that I'd get on in life because I was good with people, and if I got a job, then people would want to spend time with me and that was how I'd advance, and I believed her.' She wiped her eyes. 'I believed her.'

'So what happened?'

'What happened?' Marnie gave a short, sarcastic laugh. 'Life! Life is what happened! We were fixated on having a baby to no avail, and I accepted it. I was heartbroken, but I accepted it. Then when my dad died, my mum was already wheelchair bound, and so I took over where he left off and became her carer – not that I minded, and I would honestly do it all over again. When you lose your mum, if you were lucky enough to be close to her, there isn't anything you wouldn't give to have one more day with her. Even those days where she was struggling and I was tired and I just wanted to fall into bed, I loved them, I loved her . . .' Madeleine noted the tremble to her mum's bottom lip, as if it cut deep and hurt still, even just expressing this truth. 'Then when she got worse and there was more help available, I got pregnant with you. Which was wonderful, the most wonderful event, but it made things difficult. There wasn't enough of me to go around, not enough of anything.'

'So it's my fault?'

Marnie gave her a sharp look. 'First, this is not about you, it's about me right now. And second, I would have given my last breath for a shot at being your mum. You are everything – everything! And then, as you got older, and Doug and I thought it might be *our* time . . .'

Edith came along . . . Madeleine filled in the blanks.

'I'm just trying to explain to you, love, how no one gets the life they think they will or the life they think they deserve. Every single one of us has to compromise and sidestep the cracks and jump over the lava and cling on the best we can because that is just life, and you are no different. None of us gets it all, Madeleine. There is a price to pay for every choice, always. What you can't do is make a choice, then moan about the price, because that's just shitty.'

'Good morning, Mrs Woods!'

'Morning, Doctor Callahan.'

Marnie sat up straight as if in school, and patted her hair, looking uncomfortably self-conscious. It was Madeleine's turn to squeeze her mum's hand. Not that the doctor seemed to give a fig about the aesthetics; she was engrossed in her tablet, reading something, and only glancing up from it to smile in a practised manner. She had interrupted them, and now stood at the foot of the bed. In much the same vein as her first visit, she was in scrubs with her hair scraped back and an air of urgency about her, as if she was supposed to be somewhere else.

'Right, we are scheduling your surgery for the week after next and, in all honesty, there is no point in keeping you here in the lead up to that.'

'I can go home?' There was no mistaking the delight in Marnie's tone.

'What I propose is that, as long as your stats hold up and you continue not to give us any cause for concern, then yes, we'll send you home tomorrow, and you can come back in for your operation. How does that sound?'

'I'd much rather be at home, definitely.'

'You don't live alone?' The doctor scanned the notes.

'No, I live with my husband and my . . . my granddaughter.' She glanced at Madeleine.

'Good, right then! Just rest up, listen to your body, sleep. The nurse will explain your new drug regimen and tell you about your home visits, and what to expect when you come back in and whatnot, and I'll look forward to seeing you the week after next.'

'Thank you, Doctor.'

'My pleasure.'

And with that she was gone from the room, hurrying to wherever her attention was required next.

'Well, that's good news, Mum. Not too long to wait for your surgery, and you get to go home.'

'I've got a lot of questions, but I didn't want to keep her. Do you think they'll give me a leaflet or something?'

'I'm sure they will.'

Madeleine felt the hard ball of regret nestle in her stomach. She wished she had waited to have this conversation, and at the same time was floored by the idea of Marnie making sacrifices she had been unprepared to make. It was a mess, a bloody mess.

'I just need to know how quickly my life can get back to normal, that's all I can think about.'

Madeleine thought about that day when her pregnancy was confirmed and knew that this too was her overriding thought. *When will my life get back to normal . . . ?*

It was probably a good thing that she hadn't been given an answer.

Never. The response came to her now. *Your life was never going to go back to normal.*

The question she now wrangled with was this: did she want it to? Did she want less of Edith in her life, to go back to those carefree days when she wasn't dogged by guilt, didn't carry the secret, her world cleaved in two?

Marnie sank back on the pillows. The two of them were quiet, as the echo of their conversation rang around them, both taking a beat to calm a little.

'Who is the nice man Edith was talking about, and why did he bring you biscuits?'

She'd wondered how long it would be until they circled back to that.

'Just a friend.' She smiled at the thought of what message of reconciliation might lie in the card, pinned to her exquisite bouquet.

The train ride up west was a nice trip down memory lane. It had been a while since she'd done it. Nothing much had changed, bar a few new low-rise blocks of flats which had sprung up along the track, packed tightly together with minute balconies barely big enough to hold a plant pot. And the towering cranes, further out, heralding the building of bigger developments that rose high into the sky. Hers was a city that was ever evolving; she wondered what the skyline in LA might look like and felt a pang of longing for London, even though she hadn't yet left. With it came the realisation that it wasn't so much the city or its skyline she was going to miss, but rather the people in it. Marnie was right; there was a price to pay for every choice.

Walking back to the office, she entered the building and raced to her desk, not only keen to arrive and make up the hours she'd lost that morning, but also desperate to rip open that little card and see what Nico had written. She wanted to be reminded of the good thing they had shared, wanted to feel more like herself – happy with her lot in life and with a plan laid out in front of her. These last couple of days had thrown her somewhat; it felt like she walked on a soft surface, wobbly and uncertain.

Tan waved from his desk, where he was engrossed in a call. Nadia was at lunch. Closing the office door behind her, she ran her fingertips over the blousy-headed blooms that filled the air with their glorious bouquet. Tan had been right – the composition, colour and variety had all been put together with impeccable taste. Taking the small brown envelope that had been clipped to the side of the bouquet, she carefully opened it to reveal a simple off-white card, edged in gold.

She read and re-read the message, doing her best to swallow the bitter tang of disappointment that filled her mouth.

Madam Marcia and I are very much looking forward

to seeing you soon in sunny Los Angeles!

Much love, doll.

Safe travels.

R x

The flowers were beautiful. The intention lovely. And yet as she sank down into the chair behind her desk and opened her computer, it would have been hard to describe the feeling of dread that engulfed her. The LA project was her dream, working with Rebecca again her professional ambition, and yet at the thought of leaving Edith, her parents and even Nico, she felt an uncomfortable flicker of doubt that it was the wisest choice.

That, and she sincerely hoped that she would not, at this stage of her career, be expected to take Madam Marcia, Rebecca's new pug, for hesitant walks along the nearest strip of grass.

Tan knocked as he entered. 'Aren't they lovely?' He nodded at the bouquet.

'Yes. What have I missed?' She cut to the chase.

'I'm glad you're sitting down.' He looked nervous.

'Why? Just say it, Tan.' She was in no mood for games.

'Stern's been on the phone.'

'And?'

'He's not happy.'

Not happy . . . Well, that makes two of us.

This too she kept to herself.

December

9.00 P.M.

The words of her conversation with Jimmy still echoed in her thoughts as Madeleine hopped off the train and made her way back to her flat. Her phone beeped as a text came in from Marnie.

ALL OKAY DARLING? X

It was nearly nine o'clock and she was exhausted. Wiped out. It had been a long day – the longest. Her brain was fuddled.

HEADING BACK TO MY FLAT. I'LL CALL YOU TOMORROW MUM X

Marnie's reply was instant.

YOUR DAD AND I ARE HERE FOR YOU, ALWAYS. WE LOVE YOU. PLEASE LET ME KNOW HOW

YOU'RE FEELING IN THE MORNING. CAN I
CALL YOU AFTER WORK TOMORROW? IF YOU
NEED ANYTHING, ANYTHING AT ALL, JUST
SHOUT. AND PLEASE, PLEASE THINK ABOUT
WHAT WE SAID X

And so it began . . .

It was almost farcical. As if she could think about anything else.

She put the key in the door and was hit by the loud music coming from Meredith's room, which was a sure indicator her flatmate had been on the sauce.

Liesl was on the sofa, flicking through the channels before settling on a documentary about coral reefs. Her greeting: 'Did you get the eggs?'

'I forgot.'

Slipping off her shoes, Madeleine sat down on the opposite end of the sofa and put her feet on the coffee table littered with the witness marks of wet coffee cups, burn marks from careless cigarettes left to smoulder, several ratty, smeared napkins, and an old pizza box. It was disgusting. Realisation dawned that it was no place to see out her pregnancy, and not a great idea to spend money on rent when she'd be at her parents' flat before she gave birth and no doubt immediately afterwards. Her decision came to her as she voiced it.

'I'm moving out.'

'Oh my God, no! Don't worry about the eggs, I can do without my omelette! I'll have cheese on toast instead. Do we have cheese?'

'I don't know. And I'm not moving out because of your eggs. I need to go back to my mum and dad's for a bit.'

'No, no, don't do it, babes. That's never a good idea!' Liesl pulled a face and Madeleine laughed for the first time that day.

'Maybe not, but I need to go home, get myself together for a few months and then . . .'

And then what, Edith-Madeleine? That was the million-dollar question.

'Please don't leave me with Luciano and Meredith, they are literally some of the worst human beings I've ever met. Luciano leaves hair in the sink and Meredith steals my moisturiser, and licks the teaspoons, I've seen her.'

Again Madeleine laughed. 'You'll survive. And who knows? Whoever takes my place might be your new best friend.'

'Darling, *everyone* is my new best friend until I get to know them.' Liesl took a drag on her cigarette. 'And then I pretty much hate them. I hate everyone. But not you. You're fabulous! That's why you can't leave me.'

'I don't feel very fabulous.'

'Well, you should. What's up, chick? You don't seem yourself. And not just the leaving the flat thing. You seem . . . down.'

'I am a bit. But I have a plan and I know I won't always feel this way.'

'That's the spirit! Set yourself a time limit and wallow until then, it works for me.' She winked.

'January the twenty-sixth. That's the date or thereabouts. I think I'll wallow until then.' She bit her lip and tried to stem the emotion that threatened.

'Flippin' 'eck, that's an age away! Nearly two whole months of sadness – do you know how long two months is?'

'I do.'

Eight weeks of a pregnancy . . . a little over twenty per cent of my gestation . . . the end of the third trimester . . .

'And you reckon you can survive that?'

'I reckon, Liesl, that I can survive just about anything.'

She hoped she sounded convincing.

'Atta girl!' Liesl blew her a kiss as she left the sofa and Madeleine headed for her room.

There was some peace to be found in her decision to go back to the Brenton Park estate, to live at home and be close to Marnie, closer to the hospital. It made sense for appointments, check-ups, and the birth itself. She shivered to think of it. And as for what came after the baby was born? Maybe it could work, letting Marnie and Doug raise her. Maybe her mum was right – it was for the best. Or if not the best, then certainly the least worst decision to help them all move forward. She could take leave from work, or work from home and return to the office after the baby was born, as if nothing had happened. Nothing at all . . .

Having changed into her softest pyjamas and a pair of warm socks, she climbed beneath her duvet and opened her laptop, before googling: *what happens when you have a baby?* The images that filled the screen made her gasp. Quickly she closed it down, knowing that any level of detail was more than she could cope with tonight. It was after all only this morning that she found out she was pregnant. It was, as Trina had pointed out, a lot.

Trina . . . How she wished she could call her.

Despite her physical fatigue, her thoughts whirred and she knew sleep would not be forthcoming. With her hair scraped back into a scrunchie, she opened up a new folder and named it 'Old Berlin/New Foyer'. Her pulse raced as she scoured images with which she would start to build her mood board. And just like that she was in her happy place, studying wallpaper, lamps, paint, and furniture to build her vision.

The movement in her stomach was sudden, unexpected, and bizarre – a flutter almost, and she now understood it wasn't the first time she had felt it. The difference was she now understood it wasn't an undigested burrito, gas, the rumbling of a gut trying to break down a pie that was well past its sell-by date, or a reminder to eat more fibre . . . She now knew it was her baby girl getting comfortable.

'It's okay. It's okay, little one, go to sleep.'

Madeleine cried then, great gulping tears that robbed her breath of rhythm and left her feeling spent. Reaching down, she placed her hand on her stomach where her baby girl was nestled and palmed small circles on her skin.

'I'm sorry, little one. I'm so sorry. I'm sorry you chose me, but your dad was right – it'll all be okay. I promise, whatever happens, it will all be okay.'

Sinking further down into the pillow, she closed her eyes, hoping beyond hope that this was true.

Chapter Eleven

PRESENT DAY

Madeleine laughed at the texts her dad had sent from Marnie's phone. Her mum had arrived home via ambulance and was transported to the flat in a wheelchair. He had snapped a picture of her in the lift – the lift! – looking none too impressed. Oh, the indignation of it – this the woman who prided herself on climbing the stairs in all weathers. The next picture showed her sleeping on the sofa under a soft blanket, and he was wearing her apron, so all good. It was great that Marnie was home, where she would no doubt instruct Dougie on the chores that needed doing and sleep well at night, knowing he was by her side. Finally her mum could stop worrying about the mince in the fridge and the laundry pile.

The flowers Madeleine had sent would arrive in the morning; she hoped Marnie liked them. Her mind flew to the bouquet from Rebecca and then of course to Nico. She cringed to recall the text she had sent him.

HAPPY X

The message that, as indicated by the two small blue ticks that sat alongside it, he had read and chosen not to respond to. She winced every time she thought of it, wondering if he still needed time to order his thoughts or had decided that to invest in her complicated life was simply not a price worth paying. Her heart hurt at the thought of the latter, but she understood. Of course she did. It was no surprise that a man like Nico would not want a woman like her with her many quirks, oddities, habits, and superstitions. And that was before he knew of the ugliest quirk of all, the one deep inside her that she kept hidden. The one where other women slipped into motherhood as if it was the natural order of things, as if it was what was expected, while she railed against it, knowing it was just not how she was built.

Madeleine didn't know how she felt about her and Marnie's chat in the hospital. It had felt like the beginning of a wider conversation, if not the conclusion she'd been hoping for, but it was a start. Next time, she figured it might be more successful if she could voice exactly what she wanted and a plan of how they might achieve it; those two things, so easy to say, were the goal. It sounded simple now she thought about it: she wanted Marnie to support her choices and not make her feel bad about them; she wanted to feel at ease when she saw her mother and not constantly waiting for the barbed judgement to drop from her tongue. She wanted to visit Edith without the gut-churning nerves at how she might still, even after all these years, be getting it wrong.

She would have been lying if she said she wasn't nervous to be heading to Jimmy's place. The old lock-keeper's cottage was a place she'd passed more times than she could count – a building that was part of the fabric of her childhood. The towpath had been their whole countryside when she was growing up on the Brenton Park estate. She and Trina would walk along it for hours in the summer evenings, practising smoking, which thankfully neither of them mastered. The rest of the time they hoped to see boys and giggled over specific boys, like Jake Dowdeswell – a boy in their class. He was *that* guy – a great footballer with a good smile and blond hair; everyone loved Jake. Jake who ended up with Andrew Lewis, leaving many broken hearts in the wake of their nuptials.

Sometimes the chatter was just of boys in general – the kind of man they wanted to end up with. She often expressed her desire for someone with a decent car, an extensive wardrobe, someone who earned enough for travel to exotic places and a healthy budget for fine dining. Even as a teen, she knew the life she wanted – that extra life with spare chairs and pretty things. A fancy-pants kind of life. Trina was not quite so prescriptive; she wanted someone who was nice, kind, and funny. Madeleine remembered stopping on the path and staring at her friend.

'I want someone who is nice, kind, and funny too! Doesn't everyone? I thought that was a given. I mean, have you ever heard someone say, "Oh, I'd like to end up with a mean arsehole who has zero sense of humour!" I mean, dur! But wanting them to be successful is okay too! And I want my success to match his so I never have to wait for him to hand over a roll of banknotes wrapped in a plastic band. I want to pay for myself. I want it all!'

'Yeah, you do.' Her friend had shaken her head like a disapproving mamma, and they had dropped the subject for the evening.

The towpath around the now defunct lock was also where she had told Jimmy she was pregnant. The details of that night were ingrained in her memory: the damp, slimy bench, the way he had walked away, his silhouette disappearing into the darkness, and how she had never felt so alone. Today, though, in the winter sunshine, where the sky was blue and the air still, she hoped it might feel like another place entirely.

The lock-keeper's cottage had in her lifetime been occupied by an old man who she could recall sitting outside the front door in a camping chair on warm nights. After his death, the place had fallen into ruin. Windows were then smashed by vandals, the walls daubed with illegible, mindless graffiti and a large penis had been sprayed on the front door. Twists of determined ivy had roped their way around the window frames and covered the once pretty red-brick exterior. The small garden grew wild and consumed the spear-headed railings that were its boundary. Vast woody-trunked lilacs grew strong and high until they almost hid the cottage from view entirely. Years ago, to add insult to injury, someone had lit a fire – whether looking for warmth or simply with malintent it was impossible to know, but the result was just the same: a blackened hole in the red-tiled roof and damage to the front corner of the property. It had saddened her to see the place destroyed and, worse, as it was then utilised as a rubbish dump for items too cumbersome or troublesome to have removed legitimately. Hence the collection of old mattresses, a rusted fridge, and piles of builders' rubble that were all visible within its broken walls.

She'd had to ask three times when Marnie told her Jimmy had bought the place. 'The old lock-keeper's cottage?'

'Yes, love.'

'What, the one up on the towpath? The derelict one?'

'Yes, he said he can see its potential.'

'The one up by the old lock, the burnt-out one with the penis?'

'Madeleine!' her mother had shouted. 'For the love of God! How many bloody lock-keeper's cottages do you know of around here? Yes, that one!'

'Well, I hope he's not planning on taking Edith there!' She could think of a thousand hazards that might befall the child in such a grotty place.

'He's a good dad. The best.'

And just like that they were silent.

Marnie's words were so much more than the sum of their parts. As ever she felt them land like ticks burrowing into her skin, and they hurt just as much. She got the message. *He's a good dad . . .* and would do nothing to harm her. *He's a good dad . . .* and I trust him. *He's a good dad . . .* and you are in no position to judge, bearing in mind that you're not exactly mother of the year . . . At least, that's how Madeleine took it.

Marnie had kept her up to speed with Jimmy's renovation project over the last couple of years.

'Oh, you should see it! A proper oasis. He's a clever man – done all of it himself.'

Madeleine was pleased for him, but also felt a little disappointed that the grotty little dwelling on the edge of the canal was his home. She had wanted more for him, better. How he could settle a stone's throw from his mother's flat when there was a whole wide world to explore was beyond her.

The cab dropped her by the lock and, doing her best to avoid the muddy puddles that pitted the cobbled stone pathway that ran alongside the canal, she was glad she'd opted for her hiking boots. It was only the second time she'd worn them – the perfect opportunity to break them in before she hit the trails of LA on her downtime. With her mini Louis Vuitton backpack over her shoulders, she set off.

It was nice to be back here – nicer than she'd thought – as nostalgia warmed her from the inside out. Memories of walking along hand in hand with her dad, the crappiest of picnics with Marnie, smooching with Jimmy during their fling, as the days grew longer, the sun shone higher and life felt full of the infinite possibilities that her youth, and lack of insight, allowed to flourish. And Trina, of course – all those hours she walked with Trina, idling by the water, drawn by the change of scenery, a place to breathe. A calm space in this urban sprawl they called home; lobbing small stones from the bank as their feet dangled over the edge, just for the joy of seeing the ripples grow wider and spread further.

It had been lovely to see her again at the hospital, to chat to her, in the way it did when someone was so familiar. Despite their obvious awkwardness, there was still a spark there. The shared humour, timing and ribbing that had been the mainstay of their chatter. It was jarring to realise just how much she missed her. There was something about that friend you grew up with that no new relationship could emulate.

And here she was, walking tentatively over the cobbles to reach the cottage where Jimmy now lived. How she hoped he'd scrubbed the elaborate penis from the front d—

Madeleine drew closer and stopped in her tracks.

'What the . . . ?' She placed her hand at her throat and took a moment to take it all in, feeling almost light-headed at the sight that greeted her.

If she hadn't been entirely sure of the location, she wouldn't have believed it to be the same place. The old lock-keeper's cottage with its collapsed roof, overrun garden, graffiti and neglect had been transformed into something quite beautiful.

It was picture-postcard pretty, and more so because behind it stood the towering blocks of flats that were anything but. The contrast only served to illuminate its cosy perfection. It was like a bright wildflower that caught your eye on a neglected verge, a piece of stunning sea glass on a bland pebble beach, a double-ended rainbow that cut through the gloom of a rainy day. It was something loved and nurtured in a world of decay. It was a slice of countryside right there in the middle of the city.

The glossy grass-green front door in the middle of the building matched the painted railings and woodwork of the four wide sash windows. Two at the top and two at the bottom, they sat in perfect harmony next to the scrubbed and restored red-brick exterior. The patch of front garden was neat. Atop the pale gravel, bisected by a flagstone path, sat railway sleeper troughs that even at this time of the year held grasses and ferns that prospered. An open-fronted porch with a climber snaking over its roof had been added and gave the whole place a feeling of cosy-cottage warmth that had previously been absent. Inside the porch, her eyes were drawn to an iron welly rack with two pairs of wellingtons upended on to the poles. One large green pair with a leather binding around the top and the other pair . . . She swallowed the feelings that flared at the sight of them. Pink glittery wellingtons with a purple sole and tiny unicorns on the side. Wellington boots inside which Edith's tiny feet must nestle as she no doubt puddle jumped and splished in mud.

A wide raffia basket stashed by the front door to the left side of the porch held piles of kindling and what looked to be gathered twigs. She raised her fist to lift the brass knocker, which was embellished with two acorns, and hesitated.

It was an odd thing, how she could command a boardroom, make confident suggestions to clients like Stern, whom she'd spent an hour calming only yesterday. His rage over the budgetary slip-up was incendiary. He threatened to fire her and her entire team, asking how she could justify such exorbitant sums for art installations when he was being shafted over the price of a jetty! By the time they ended the call, he had increased his request for art and agreed to another two paintings at an equally exorbitant sum, which made her bottom line positively glow! It was a skill. She could even stand up to the formidable Rebecca Swinton when the need arose. All of this she could do with confidence in her gaze and a steady voice.

Yet the thought of walking into Jimmy's home, the home where Edith liked to spend time with her dad, the home where memories were made that excluded her, routines were adhered to and of which she had no knowledge, the place where life carried on perfectly without her presence – just the thought was enough for her legs to tremble inside her designer jeans.

Your choice, Madeleine! Always your choice! She heard Marnie's words as if she were standing next to her.

Edith, who must have been alerted by her silhouette through the glass, called loud enough for her to hear, 'Mummy's here! My mummy's here!'

Folding her hand into her jacket pocket, Madeleine painted on a practised smile and took a deep breath.

The moment the door opened, her senses were overloaded. Jimmy looked great, relaxed, as was to be expected in his home environment, but in his jeans, soft brown corduroy shirt and hand-knitted socks, with his beard trimmed and his lustrous locks pushed behind his ears, he looked like a poster boy for outdoor living. The smell that hit her nose was a cosy combination of real fires and amber-and-oud-scented incense that was quite intoxicating. Her mouth watered as the aroma of baked gingerbread wafted from the kitchen.

'We've been baking.' He looked pleased with himself.

'We made gingerbread people and we've given some of them boobies!' Madeleine peeped inside as Edith ran headlong into a long patchwork chesterfield that took up most of one wall and crashed face-down into it, her hysteria, it seemed, at the mere explanation of boobies on gingerbread more than she could stand.

'How wonderful!'

The sound of a fire popping and spitting enticed her in.

Placing her hand on the inner wall of the porch, her fingers touched the rough stone that gave the lower half of the porch shelter, before it opened up into a sturdy oak frame that met the portico roof.

'Would you mind kicking your boots off?' Jimmy pointed to the wellie rack and, slightly embarrassed not to have thought of it, she took a step backwards.

'Sure! Of course!' Bending low, she untied her boots, stepped out of and upended them, placing them on the welly spikes, where they sat next to his large boots and Edith's dainty ones. There was something about the sight of them that stirred the silt of loss in her veins. It happened this way sometimes when glimpses of a life that could have been hers caught her off guard. A *Sliding Doors* moment . . .

Stepping over the waxed flagstones that acted as a wide step, she was truly astonished at the home he had created.

'Jimmy! Oh my goodness! This place is incredible!' She looked up at the beamed ceiling, where wood and plaster were both painted white – Old School white, if she'd had to guess. It was TARDIS-like in that it seemed much more spacious on the inside than it looked from the outside.

'Thanks.' He smiled. 'I love it when people see it for the first time.' His pride was evident and she more than understood, knowing how she took delight from someone stepping into her neutral apartment and being similarly impressed. 'I knocked down the walls – well, that's not strictly true, only some of the walls were still standing – and I moved the staircase to the back on the side, so it's kind of hidden behind the kitchen.'

He pointed to the other side of the property. The kitchen she could see – a large room the same size as the sitting room, the two spaces separated by an ornate, green-glazed wood burner whose pipe went straight up and along the ceiling.

'That's beautiful!' She stood in front of it, almost dazzled by the orange flames that leaped and danced to a music she wished she could hear.

'It's very old – Dutch. I found a place that restores and sells them. I kind of designed the whole of the downstairs around it. That's . . . that's probably daft.'

He faltered as if remembering what she did for a living.

'No! It's not daft at all. It's a great principle for design; one thing, one element, that is all important or a focus, like a trunk, and then your branches, leaves, fruit and whatnot grow from it.'

She felt the blush on her cheeks; she didn't want to sound like a know-all or an arsehole.

'I didn't picture it as open plan, but when I started to spend time here, it kind of made sense. I couldn't imagine putting walls up and making it smaller. It's all about how I wanted to use the space. It used to have a narrow entrance hall at the front, and another corridor between the rooms – just wasted space. She loves it.' He pointed at Edith, who finally took her head out of the sofa. 'She can run around, use her roller boots, twirl. She's big on twirling and then falling over.'

'I love to spiiiiiin!' And just like that their daughter was off, turning quickly in a circle with her arms out until she teetered and tumbled down on to a bright, multi-coloured deep-pile rug that part covered the wooden floor in front of the sofa. Her pink t-shirt rose up to reveal her rounded tum. Her green leggings were embroidered in pink hearts, and with heart-covered socks to match, she looked adorable.

'She's a bit excited,' he whispered. 'She'll calm down in a bit. I hope.' He raised his crossed fingers.

His words were a poignant reminder that Madeleine's presence here was unusual. She was a guest, a visitor, and was not part of this little family, this little life.

Your choice . . . She batted the air by her head as if this might help remove Marnie's words of rebuke.

'Do you remember what it was like before?' he asked, as she followed him into the kitchen, which was a neat cottage style, with handy butchers' hooks beneath sturdy wooden shelves on which pottery mugs and cream jugs were hung. The worktops were slate and the cupboards either side of a gleaming enamel range were rough wood with heavy ironmongery for latches and hinges. It reminded her of a cabin, an escape. She liked it.

'I do! Trees growing out of the windows and a big knob on the front door.' She pulled a face as they both laughed at the double entendre.

'Oh, in that case, you'll like this!' He beckoned her over to a rear archway that led to a glass-roofed extension that ran the width of the house and took up most of the rear garden. The walls were stone and glass, the window frames black, and a very soft oversized denim-blue sofa with elaborately embroidered cushions scattered on it sat in the middle of the room on a large jute rug. Positioned, she could see, to take advantage of the shifting light, the change of seasons and the sight of the big, big sky overhead. His taste was warm, eclectic, and yet sophisticated. 'Here!' He pointed to a large piece of modern artwork that hung on the only solid stone wall. It was hard to make out what it was at first. She stood closer and studied it, able now to recognise the damaged brick, a broken window, the twist of an interloping climber and the pale curve of purple paint, no more than a hint that she knew was in fact part of the rather gross work of vandalism that had been the cause of many giggles as they walked past the spooky old cottage.

She turned to Jimmy and smiled. 'I know what this is!'

'I took lots of snaps throughout the renovation, but it felt a bit sad to have one framed. I didn't want to be reminded of the decay. Then I had the idea of disguising the whole, but offering a hint, this mega close-up, but only those that knew the place will know the place. If you get what I mean. This little corner.'

'I do know what you mean.' She liked his subtlety, his cleverness.

'Can you read me a story?' Edith ran at her and thrust the book into her hands.

'Oh, yes, I guess so.'

'We like to read here.' He pointed at the big blue sofa and clicked on a large ceramic ochre lamp with an oversized shade that flooded the room with a golden glow. 'I'll go and make tea. How do you have it?'

'Erm.' It struck her as the most bizarre of things. This man with whom she had created a child, this man with whom she would be connected for their whole lives because they shared Edith, this man who didn't know how she took her tea. 'Just a bit of milk. No sugar.'

'I only have oat milk, is that okay?'

'Sure.' She smiled.

Sinking back into the soft cushions, it was a wonderfully comfortable place to sit. Edith sat against her, curled into her, as was her way. It was a feeling like no other and one she knew would keep her warm on the coldest of nights when she looked out of her picture window over a view of LA, palm trees and all. Opening the book, she stared into the garden. The tall trees cast shadows over the honey-wood floor and in this warm, gingerbread-scented cocoon, it was hard to believe that just a few feet the other side of the rear-garden wall, sat the flats where she had grown up.

They were three pages in when Jimmy returned with a rattan tray loaded up with two mugs of tea, a cup of orange juice and a plate piled high with gingerbread, some sporting rather badly drawn boobies in icing.

It was only when he handed her a mug and placed his finger on his lips that she realised Edith was asleep.

'She's absolutely zonked.' He pulled a soft teal blanket, edged with pink stitching, from a wicker basket and placed it over his little girl, and took a seat on the other side of her sleeping form. Caring, attentive and lovely, as he had always been.

She sipped her tea and confessed, 'It feels strange being here.'

'It does, yes, for me too. Having you here.' He readily agreed and she was reminded of his candour.

'How have you been?' She didn't know how to chat to him casually; this felt like as good a place as any to start.

'How have I been? What, since you broke my heart, left me holding the baby and buggered off to chase the bright lights and the big bucks?'

'Jimmy, I—'

'I'm kidding!' He ran his fingers through his hair and gave that easy smile. 'Although if you talk to my mother anytime soon, that is her exact version of events.'

She could well imagine.

'First, I've spoken to you a million times since Edith was born, and second, I didn't run off and leave you holding the baby.'

'No, you ran off and it was up to me to go and find the baby and become part of her life.'

'Is that what your mother thinks?'

'No, it's what I think.' He turned his body on the sofa to face her.

'What do you want me to say?' She hated every part of this conversation; she wasn't good at handling the blanket of shame that covered her as surely as the one under which Edith now slumbered. Her little mouth, moving in the gentlest of snores. 'You sound like you want to get stuff off your chest, so do it! Go for it!' She kept her voice low so to not wake Edith.

What could be the harm? She was leaving in two weeks and to have this situation also resolved could be no bad thing. She'd simply do what she always did – take the flak, button up her big-girl britches and carry on.

'I'm not angry with you, Maddie.'

'Good.' She raised her chin and held her ground; he had no right to be angry with her. She was, after all, free to make her choices and had done everything that Marnie had asked.

Everything.

January 29

6.00 A.M.

Madeleine had been given permission to work from home, to deal
with a medical emergency. She'd promised to be back on site and on
top of her game in no time. Thankfully, her request had been met
without too many questions or lengthy interviews to ascertain why.
And for the last week she had been ensconced in her childhood
bedroom in her parents' flat. Surprisingly, it proved to be condu-
cive to work – without a commute, the many tasks assigned by the
design team, and being at Captain's beck and call, she had more
time and used it to harness streaks of super-productivity. Sitting
against the velour, foam-covered headboard with her laptop on her
knees, she poured her time and energies into the Old Berlin project.
During any low moments when the reality of why she was there at
all nudged out excitement over the job she had been tasked with,
she would go deeper into her creative space and the hours would
fly by, yielding results that she knew would both please and impress
Rebecca – two things that motivated her.

It did her good to think about her boss's reaction when she first showed her the mood board and her idea for the revamp, presented, as instructed, after the Christmas break. At first, the woman said nothing, but placed her palm on her chin and her gold-framed spectacles on her nose, studying the images as if she were looking at art or trying to figure out a puzzle, tilting her head this way and that. Eventually, she removed her glasses and turned her attention to Madeleine.

'You're very good.'

These the three words that saw the kindling of ambition she had carried roar into a fire that warmed her body and awoke her soul!

'Really? I . . . I don't know what to say!'

'Okay.' Rebecca nodded. 'Let's give it a go. You can join the design team. Shadow Suzy, ask lots of questions. I'll show her these and square it away.'

'Really? Are you joking right now? I can't believe it!'

She hadn't meant to cry. In fact it was the last thing she wanted to do in front of Rebecca, who was as cool as ice.

'But, but I . . . Only, I can't . . .'

'Okay, I'm going to give you some advice, Madeleine.' It was the first time she'd used her name, and there was a particular thrill in it. 'Never feel unworthy of an opportunity that's offered to you. Always raise your chin, retain eye contact, and simply say, "Thank you," confirming not only that it's your right and that you are capable, but also reassuring the person making the offer that they've made a smart move.'

Gathering herself, Madeleine sat up straight and, retaining eye contact, lifted her chin.

'Thank you.'

'You'll be an asset, I'm sure.'

'Thank you.' It was easier, the second time. 'There is one thing I need to ask.'

'Never be afraid to ask questions.'

Madeleine nodded and swallowed the nerves that threatened to wash away any poise.

'I will need to work from home for a bit – not long, a . . . a couple of weeks or so. Or I can take it as leave, around the end of January. Unpaid, of course, and I wouldn't ask if it weren't unavoidable, but I can work from home – I *want* to work from home, it will keep me sane.'

Rebecca gave her a hard stare and Madeleine thought she might have blown it. Her heart sank.

'If you are working from home, then why would you suggest we don't pay you? Lesson two, value your craft, and understand that what you do is of importance. There will be people throughout your career who will want to cut you down or devalue your efforts. Remember this speaks volumes about them and not you. But don't aid them, rise above, keep your cool and always know your worth.'

Her words had resonated with Madeleine. She was determined, in a work setting, to always keep her cool and to know her worth.

Having returned home, it was odd how in such a short space of time the dynamics of her relationship with her mum and dad had so changed. Marnie was nervous around her, fluctuating between love-bombing her, smothering her with affection, bringing her soup and fruit, and sobbing into her hankie every time she saw her, as if the whole world were coming to an end.

Her quiet dad was harder to read – the man who wanted a calm, happy house. He was clearly torn, outwardly and willingly supporting his wife through her tears, but his side glances and stolen tight-lipped smiles suggested he was on Madeleine's side. Not that there were sides to be taken. But she certainly loved him all the more for his unconditional love and acceptance. She wanted to explain to her mother during her bouts of hysteria that her reaction was far less helpful, and to remind her that this was not a situation Madeleine had manufactured or designed. Marnie's meltdowns didn't make Madeleine question her plan, which she was certain was her mother's intention, but only served to make the atmosphere even more strained and made drifting off to sleep trickier than it needed to be. *Technically* the blame lay with her, of course it did, but had she planned for this, engineered it? It was in fact about as far from her intention, her dream, and the idea of her future as it was possible to be.

She might have had eight short weeks to get her head around the situation, but she had failed miserably. No matter how frequently she studied the leaflets, devoured blogs, and posts online and read accounts of people like her who had experienced what was known as a "stealth pregnancy" or a "cryptic pregnancy", she still did not fully believe that at the end of the whole episode she would be giving birth to a small human.

It did, however, make her feel marginally less stupid to know it wasn't as uncommon as she had imagined. The response, from the few people she *had* told – her parents, Trina, Jimmy, and a woman in the queue behind her at the checkout in Tesco who had smiled as the day caught up with Madeleine and she'd blurted out her whole sorry situation – whilst sympathetic had certainly, if only briefly, carried expressions of a querying nature, as if she *must* surely have known but had simply chosen to keep it secret. Her question to them, had they been brave enough to ask such a thing outright, would have been why in the world would she? The situation in which she now found herself was preposterous, unimaginable and the scariest thing she had ever had to face.

Her body had changed a little, but no one looking at her would guess she was pregnant, let alone had reached her due date. Tiredness was the one giveaway, the bone-deep fatigue that dogged her every waking moment. Jimmy hadn't been to see her, not that she wanted or expected him to, but he had phoned to see how she was doing and once again had offered to assist or be there for whatever she might need. It had taken all her strength not to ask if he might be able to build a time machine so she could go back to a day in May and not drink too much and vomit up her contraception. Or better still, go a little further back and not bump into him on Oxford Street when – with her rum goggles firmly attached – she'd taken one look at his luscious locks, his muscled arms and hey presto! Her pants had fallen off. Instead, she thanked him kindly and agreed to keep him posted. The thanks were sincere, but as for keeping him posted? She wasn't so sure.

The conversation with him had once again ripped open the wound she felt at having hurt Trina. Her best friend had popped in only once and it had been awful. So much so that when the girl left after their stilted conversation in the hallway, her desire for a speedy exit obvious from the fact that they had barely been able to look each other in the eye, Madeleine very much wished that she hadn't bothered. It was worse somehow, confirmation that their once beautiful friendship was now no more than cobwebs; frail, insubstantial and something that with one clean sweep would be gone for good. If she hadn't had much bigger things to worry about, her devastation at the fact would have hit her even harder.

It was one of the only times she had given in to the self-pity that she largely managed to keep at bay. No sooner had she watched Trina walk through the door, heading out into the world without the burden that was Madeleine's alone to bear, than she stumbled into her room, coiled on the bed, and cried great hot tears that left her feeling spent. She had woken in the early hours with a desperate need to pee, a red, puffy face, sore eyes and a feeling of loneliness that sat like a dark hole in the glorious future she envisaged, once she'd got over this hump.

Marnie had insisted she stay home near her due date. And here she was, holed up in the flat, trapped, lonely and staring at the walls. Despite her initial reluctance to be cloistered inside the peach woodchip of her old room, in these latter stages of her confinement, she was thankful for it. Having her mum and dad within hollering distance made the whole prospect slightly less daunting, but only slightly.

It was also hard to navigate the kind words of encouragement and hopeful looks that Marnie threw her way, refusing to believe, even at this late hour and despite her claims to the contrary, that Madeleine would give birth and hand the baby over.

And maybe she was right. What kind of woman could do that?

A woman like me . . . came the answer. *A woman like me . . .*

It felt easier to stay in her room and while away the days. Sleeping, daydreaming, trying to get comfortable, working on the glorious Old Berlin project, and nesting the tiniest of bumps, while both dreading and thrilled by the prospect that soon the whole ordeal would be over and she could pick up where she had left off and go build her life.

She woke early to the sound of a car revving its engine in the car park below and the slam of a car door. Someone, it seemed, who wasn't best pleased to be up at this ungodly hour had decided that the rest of the estate should suffer as a result.

Something felt a little off and instantly she was aware of and horrified by the wet patch that soaked her pyjamas. Relief was instant when she touched her fingers to the damp and found that it wasn't blood. This realisation was quickly followed by the low rumble of an ache that intensified as she threw back the duvet and stood. A bit like menstrual cramps, it was an ache that flashed to pain once or twice but was bearable. Pleasant, almost, as it spoke of nearing the end.

Filled with something close to excitement – not for the arrival of her child, not that, but to know that it was nearly over – she knocked gently on her parents' bedroom door. She did so with a scrunched-up nose, knowing she had to wake them, but feeling far from good about doing so and the disruption to their day.

'Mum . . . Mum . . .' she whispered, a little louder the second time.

'Youallrightlove?' Her mum came to, head barely lifted from the pillow, hair mussed, and in the throes of semi-sleep slurred her words.

'Yes, sorry to wake you. I just, erm . . . I think it's . . . it's happening.'

Chapter Twelve

Present Day

Madeleine coiled her feet beneath her on Jimmy's denim sofa and faced him, Edith still asleep between them. She sipped her tea.

'I'm really not angry with you, Maddie, not anymore.'

'So you were?' she fished.

He drew breath. '"Let down" is better. I felt let down.'

'What are you, my *dad*? I feel like we're one step away from you telling me how disappointing my life choices have been for you.'

He didn't reply and she hated the silent implication that this might be the truth.

'Why does everyone feel they have the right to judge me, Jimmy? How come everyone has an opinion?' she pushed.

'I guess because your choices are . . .' He took his time. 'Unconventional.'

'Not to me they're not!' This felt important. 'And I'll happily explain my choices to anyone who wants me to, but, jeez, it's wearing.'

'You sound defensive.'

'Can you blame me?' she fired back.

'I just mean it's odd considering you got what you wanted, the life you want.'

'Oh my God, who gets the life they want?' She sniffed.

'Didn't you?' He held her eyeline.

She took a second to get the words right. 'I did, but then there's that big fork in the road that I come up to time and again, and I'm forced to check my route, weigh up the options, look back at the path I've taken. I have to decide if I want to keep forging on; I have to keep evaluating, checking it was all worth it. Do you know what I mean?' She had a lot running through her head – Marnie's illness, Nico . . . Little Edith sleeping right there between them. The blob of human glue that would forever connect her to this man.

'I guess I don't really know what you mean.' He spoke plainly.

'And I guess that's the issue.'

Edith moved her head and murmured.

'She's tired. Early night, I think, after I've fed her.'

'I want to talk to her, Jimmy. I need to tell her that my trip to the States is not just a holiday.' This she whispered, aware of Edith's proximity, sleeping or not.

'Yeah, Marnie said.'

Of course she did . . .

'I don't want to keep it from her. I've been waiting for the right time.'

'And that time is now?' he asked, and sipped his tea.

'I guess so.'

'You'll know when the time is right – far better it happens organically. Kids are smart and Edith will know if a topic is set up.'

Not for the first time it struck her how confident he was with their daughter, aware of her needs in a way she couldn't imagine.

'It's good we talk, Jimmy, clear the air. My therapist has been saying as much for the longest time.'

'What's a therapist?' Edith woke then from her doze. Her question was succinct, and like all her observations, tinged with humour by the confidence and eloquence of such a little girl.

Jimmy smiled. 'Over to you!'

'Well, it's like a doctor. Well, mine *is* a doctor, but a doctor you *talk* to rather than one you go and see because you are *physically* hurt or have a sickness or whatever, like a tummy ache, but they help me sort out all the things I'm thinking about.'

'A doctor you talk to?' Edith sat up straight, restored by her nap. 'Yes.'

'What do you talk to him about?'

'Her. I talk to her about anything that's bothering me, things that might be taking up too much space in my head. It helps me understand my own thoughts better. Helps me make sense of anything troubling me.' She hoped that was clear.

Edith stared at her, her little nose adorably wrinkled, as she was wont to do when she was in deep thought. Madeleine knew because she did something similar. It was funny how this whole nature thing asserted itself.

'Why don't you just talk to your friends?'

It was a fair question. Madeleine stared at the child and struggled to find the answer to that.

Maybe because I don't have that many friends. Maybe because I work with Tan too and therefore don't want him to know the clutter that fills my head. Maybe because the only friend I would have spoken to about anything and everything was Trina, but she's barely my friend anymore. And maybe because I don't have a partner, a soulmate, no Dougie to my Marnie, no one that I can open up to in that way, and maybe because I'm so wary of sharing what goes on in my head with anyone that I'd not want a friend to know all the secrets and confusion I carry around with me . . .

She pictured lovely Nico making toast and honey in her kitchen and again felt the throb of sadness that the bouquet she'd received was from Rebecca.

'I don't know.' Felt like the safest cop-out.

'I talk to my friends and they make me feel better,' Edith offered sweetly, as if this might be a solution. It sure would save her a fortune on Orna's fees!

'Edith has great friends,' Jimmy added, another small reminder of a life she had little connection to, unaware of who her daughter's friends were, just like she hadn't known the name of her teacher. The basics.

'Who are the friends you talk to, Edith?'

'I talk to everyone in my school.' This was good to know, that their child was sociable, confident. 'But my best friends are Travis, Olly, Jonah, Melodie, Tunde, Sandra—'

'Sandra?' Madeleine hadn't meant to laugh out loud, but the idea of this being how the class register might be called made her chuckle.

'Oh boy, you've done it now!' Jimmy pulled a face.

'Yes, Sandra,' Edith responded indignantly. 'She's my dinner lady, but she's also my friend. She gives me extra when it's chocolate sponge and she never counts my sweet potato fries, but everyone else only gets seven. I think it's a rule.'

'Wow, that sounds like some menu. It's good to have friends in high places.'

'I *love* Sandra. She smells like flowers and chips.'

Madeleine stared at her, this funny little thing who was as hard to fathom as any puzzle she'd ever seen.

'Sandra has a daughter, Chelsea, who is forty-eight, and she's married to Carl, who is work-shy.'

Again laughter burbled from her lips, and Jimmy joined in.

'Poor Carl!' he cut in.

'Poor Chelsea!' she countered.

'It's not funny!' Edith stood on the rug and put her hands on her hips. 'Chelsea has to do *everything* in that house!'

'How *old* are you?' Madeleine laughed, delighted by the child's mimicry, and wondering just how much time she spent with Sandra, and more than a little concerned at how freely the woman spoke in front of her.

Edith let her hands fall to her sides and her expression was one that verged on horror.

'What's the matter, pickle?' Jimmy, no longer laughing, studied Edith's face, leaning towards her so they were eye to eye, clearly worried, as was she, at what could have caused this sea change in her demeanour.

'Mummy doesn't know how old I am!' The wobble to her bottom lip was apparent and sent a jolt of guilt through Madeleine's core.

'Oh God! Of course I do!' She reached for her small hand. 'You're seven! You are *seven*. I always know how old you are.'

Edith's shoulders dropped, suggesting she'd been holding tension in them.

'You're my mummy.'

She felt her little fingers coil against her palm.

'I am.' She wondered if this would ever get easier, feeling the oppressive scarf of guilt and shame wrap around her throat. The thought of coming clean about her move to LA was dreadful.

'You send me things on my . . . on my birthday.'

'I do.'

'And . . . and Nanny always tells me that it was a very special day. The day I was born.' She let go of Madeleine's hand.

Sitting back against the sofa with her legs folded beneath her, Madeleine nodded. 'It *was* a very special day. The twenty-ninth of January.'

Edith smiled, wriggled on to Jimmy's lap, facing her, happy, it seemed, to have the mutually significant date confirmed.

'I was born in Newham hospital.'

'You were, indeed.' She tucked her palms between her thighs, hiding their slight tremble. It didn't get any easier, reliving that day – the day that changed everything. Well, *one* of the days that changed everything. The first being approximately two hundred and eighty days prior, but that was a whole other story. 'You were born at ten past eleven in the morning.'

'Did you have any breakfast before you had me?'

'Oh, did I have breakfast? I'm trying to remember.' She did just that, replaying the day in her head. 'No, I don't think I did. I remember we left the flat very early. It was dark, and I didn't eat anything there. I might have had a banana while I was waiting for you to arrive. In fact, yes, I did, I had a banana.'

'Waiting for me to pop out of your tummy!' Edith gestured dramatically, as if birth were an explosion not dissimilar to the famous scene from *Alien*.

'Yep, that's it.' She shared a knowing look with Jimmy. Edith might have had a great friend who was in her late sixties, and was even au fait with the vague location of boobies, but it seemed the rudimentary details of giving birth still escaped her, and Madeleine was much relieved for that.

'Nanny said the day I was born was the best in her whole life! She said she remembers everything about it.'

'It was the best day of her life, for sure. And as for remembering everything . . . It was a while ago.' She pictured Marnie's face, beaming with a joy she found hard to emulate.

'Was it the best day in your whole life too?'

She noticed how Jimmy studied her face, as if he too was interested in her response.

'It was certainly memorable!' she laughed, embarrassed to have been put on the spot and not sure how to respond.

'And then you went to live somewhere else.' Edith kept her eyes averted, toying with the edge of her t-shirt, as if cloaked in her own shame at such a simple fact, and it tore at Madeleine's heart. She didn't know what to say.

Jimmy, as ever, came to the rescue, as he verbally swooped in with his words and manner, both a diversion and a balm.

'Right, how about I make us some supper? We've got soup and soda bread, how does that sound, Mads?'

'Oh.' Madeleine was thankful to him, and equally as surprised to have been asked to stay for food on this chilly winter's day. Soup sounded perfect. 'That would be lovely, thank you.' Not for the first time she was startled by his kindness.

I'll do whatever you need or want me to. I will be as involved or as absent as you think is right. I want to be involved, but I will take your lead.

'I can set the table!' Edith leaped from the sofa, keen to help. The diversion had worked. Madeleine watched as she grabbed the woven jute tablemats from the drawer of an aged green armoire that stood by a wall, the doorframes that she suspected once held glass now with chicken wire over them revealing throws, blankets, tablecloths, and other vintage linens. She liked Jimmy's eye, the way he put things together. It all smacked of Scandi chic with just the right amount of cosy. Edith retrieved deep-bowled soup spoons from glazed utensil pots that sat on the lip of the dresser.

It was the first time she, Jimmy and Edith had sat together, just the three of them at a dinner table, yet there was a relaxed atmosphere, as if it were no big deal. It was hard not to think that this was what life might have been like, a daily occurrence if she had let him build her that cottage with a duck pond. He carried a large earthenware tureen from the stove top and placed it on the table.

'That smells incredible!' Her mouth watered.

'Homemade carrot, ginger and sweet potato, with enough garlic to keep the vampires away for months.'

He returned with three soup bowls and a worn breadboard weighted down with a dark soda bread, and a butter dish loaded up with thick golden butter.

Pulling a hunk from the loaf, he used a rounded, pearlescent-handled knife to pull a generous curl and buttered the bread, handing it to Edith, who tucked in. Steam rose from the fresh bread, as the butter melted on it and ran down Edith's chin.

'Help yourself!' He pushed the board towards her.

She ripped a chunk and dived in with the knife to the butter, the handle still warm from his touch. The first bite was heavenly – nutty and dense – but the melting butter made it something else.

'Oh my goodness! This is *so* good!' She took another bite, only understanding when she started eating just how hungry she was, as her brain caught up with her stomach.

'It's my mum's recipe.' He ladled thick soup into a bowl and pushed it towards Edith. 'You know the drill – stir and blow until it cools down.'

He ladled twice the amount into a bowl for her with no such instruction. The soup was thick, flavoursome, and unctuous; as good as any she had had.

'Oh my God, Jimmy! This is delicious!' Immediately she went back in with her spoon.

'Good. You have to dip the bread in to get the full effect.' He did just that.

'Oh no!' Edith put her head on her hand and looked a little crestfallen.

'What's the matter?' Jimmy asked, his look one of concern.

'My soup is nearly at the right temperature and now I need a poo!'

Madeleine stared, as Edith hopped down from her chair and made her way upstairs to the bathroom.

'And people ask me how I remain so trim.' He put the spoon back in the bowl.

'She's lucky to have you.' It slipped out. She hadn't meant to draw comment or make the observation.

'I'm very lucky to have her. And it's a choice, isn't it? Whether you choose to be part of a family, whether that family chooses to let you in, whether you choose to stay.'

'I guess.'

'I'm thankful that Marnie and Doug chose to let me in. It'd be hard if it was just Edith and I, but it's not – we're a little co-operative, a funny little family, and it works.'

'I can see that.' It was hard not to take his comments personally, as if pointing out that she had chosen not to be part of it, chosen not to stay.

'Daaa-aaad, I can't reach the loo roll!' The call hollered down the stairs.

'As I said' – he rose from the table – 'this is why I remain so trim.'

And just like that, alone at the table, Madeleine stared at her reflection in the window that looked out over the garden. She cut a solitary figure, a sight that doused her in sadness. Staring back at her, in shadow, alone at the table with two abandoned bowls, was someone she didn't recognise. Spoon in hand, she dined alone.

'What happened to me? Why am I on my own?' she asked softly, wishing the reply, the answer, might land in her ear. But it did not.

◆ ◆ ◆

With the supper things cleared away and Edith dancing in her pyjamas to Jimmy's rather eclectic playlist, Madeleine folded the dishcloth and placed it on the handle of the range where she'd found it.

'I guess I'd better think about hitting the road. Thank you for a lovely afternoon and for supper. It was great.'

'Sure, any time.' His smile, like his words, were sincere. 'You didn't speak to Edith about the move?'

'I'm not really sure how to start,' she confided.

'My advice would be not to overthink it.' He made it sound easy, and not for the first time she envied his natural aptitude when it came to parenting. 'When are you off?'

'In a couple of weeks – bit less than that, actually.' The upheaval of Marnie's hospitalisation, spending time with Edith, events with Nico . . . she'd kind of lost track of time, but was painfully aware right now that it was moving quickly.

'How long are you there for?'

'Erm, it depends a lot on the project, and I guess I'll see what happens. But it's a permanent move. I've let my flat and rented an apartment.' Her plan to open her own agency was still very much under wraps; she hadn't told a soul.

He nodded and his mouth twisted in a smile that smacked of disapproval. 'I see. Well, there we are then.' She felt the cooling in his tone and it bothered and embarrassed her in equal measure, stoking the shame, the guilt, the discomfort that was ever present when it came to discussions around her child. 'I'll get Edith to Facetime you when you're away if you'd like.'

'I would like. I suggested that to her when we were at my place. She didn't seem averse.' She stared at the little girl, who twirled and danced and jumped with abandon. 'She's so lovely, a wonder to me.' *And a mystery* . . . Madeleine felt the pull of sadness in her breast, knowing she would miss this kid.

'She is.'

'Come and dance with me, people!' Edith ran in and grabbed them both by the hand, dragging them to the rug, where, as luck would have it – or not, depending on your musical taste – Cypress Hill's 'Jump Around' filled the air.

Jimmy and Edith, it seemed, were not hampered in the way she was by self-consciousness and, as instructed, they jumped, jumped! She had no choice but to join in, awkward at first, with the dust of Jimmy's slight disapproval settling on her shoulders, but tethered to Edith as she gripped her hand, it felt easier to go with the flow. And there on the rug, the three went for it, dancing, shaking, and leaping as the air grew warm around them and they sweated out their soup. It was the most exhilarating, heart-pounding, chuckle-inducing three and a half minutes she could remember, and when the song finished, they fell into a heap on to the patchwork sofa, each laughing at the spontaneous outburst that had felt as unifying as it had fun.

'Can Mummy tuck me in?' Edith managed as they all caught their breath.

'Wow, you're honoured!' Jimmy acknowledged.

'I'd love to, if that's okay?' She deferred to him, not wanting to overstep the mark or outstay her welcome but recognising the perfect opportunity to talk to the little girl about going away.

'Of course! I'll finish up in the kitchen and get your night drink. Edith, you can show Mummy your room.'

Madeleine followed her daughter as she clumped up the stairs and into a small square hallway. She was again in awe of the clever design of the place. Almost the entire footprint of the upstairs was divided into two bedrooms. Jimmy's room, she could see, was minimal in design. A large wrought-iron bed sat on a pale tapestry rug and the room had the same vast picture window as the addition downstairs, offering the most incredible view. The tower blocks, now in darkness, twinkled like a thousand stars. The lights from the apartment windows, softened in the winter mist, looked otherworldly and alluring. They were beautiful in a way she had never considered.

Directly opposite the staircase was a small family bathroom and to the right sat Edith's room.

'Oh my word!'

'It's my fairytale room.'

Edith whispered, and she understood, feeling that to talk loudly might just break the spell that lingered within the walls. Three were painted in a warm mustard, one wall was navy, and all were adorned with large, hand-painted Amish barn stars in a variety of colours from tangerine through to lime. The bed was a cubby, cleverly built inside a frame on the navy wall. The deep mattress was set inside a part-curtained recess; the curtain was gold and edged with hot-pink bobble trim, and the whole space was lined with velvet pillows also in bright colours.

The lighting was soft and low and came from the myriad LED bulbs hiding behind stars in the false ceiling.

'I think this is possibly the best bedroom I've ever been in!' She felt the swell of tears at the sight of it.

'My daddy made it for me. He made it *all*.' Edith wrinkled her nose with delight and hopped into the bed, falling and sinking into the mattress surrounded by the pillows. It looked divinely comfortable.

'It's amazing!' She meant it, in awe of the carved and painted wood frame that made it look like Edith slept in a den that was safe and cosy, a million miles away from the dilapidated cottage that used to dwell on this very site. She now understood how sleeping here was preferable to trying to nod off in the all-white spare room of her apartment. There was no comparison.

It wasn't too extreme to say the sight and feel of the room was shocking. The whole cottage and the work Jimmy had put in was a revelation. The oasis he'd created in the middle of the urban sprawl was really something, but this room, Edith's room, it was even more than that. Madeleine had grown up thinking the world was divided into two halves: the haves and the have nots, rich and poor. A fancy-pants life, and macaroni-cheese life. People who were happy, or sad; those without opportunity and hope, and those with it. Extremes, always the extremes, two sides of every coin. But this room, the magical place he had created, was something quite beautiful, but not just that. It was safe and nurturing – an insight into the overlap of all worlds. It was a pocket of pure joy that paid no heed to what went on out outside. What had Marnie always said? *Kids don't need diamonds and steak, none of us do. We need love, attention, a cuddle at the end of a difficult day, someone to talk to and a place to be – a safe haven.*

That was the definition of this room, this cottage: a safe, safe haven. Conflicting emotions fought for space in her thoughts: relief that this was how her little girl was nurtured in this warm nest, an easing of the guilt that dogged her, happiness for all Edith got to enjoy, and something very close to regret at the fact that, if she had been a different kind of person, one without her flaws and quirks, one a lot more like Trina, then this too might be her life, and every day she could look forward to coming home to a safe, safe haven just like this.

'Here we are, one drink of water for the night.' Jimmy pulled her from her musings and reached over as he handed Edith her night flask with a sippy straw. He bent low and kissed her forehead, before positioning a large soft sloth by her pillow. 'You know the rule, just call if you wake up and feel like a chat or if you need anything. Just shout out and I'll be here.'

'I will, Daddy.' Edith gave a long, noisy yawn and placed her arms around her sloth, as Madeleine perched on the side of her bed. 'Can Mummy sit with me for a bit?'

'Sure she can. I'll leave you guys to it.' The latter he addressed to Madeleine, and she acknowledged his generosity, his inclusion, and the unspoken suggestion that this was the time to talk, as he slipped from the room.

'Do you like my toadstool nightlight?' Edith pointed to the red-capped, white-dotted fungus that gave off a magical glow from the little shelf inside her cubby, filling the bed with gentle light that only added to the fairytale atmosphere.

'I really do.' She smoothed her little girl's hair and watched her eyelids grow heavy.

'You won't be here in the morning, will you?'

'No. I'll be in my apartment, then heading off to work.' She swallowed the lump in her throat, unsure why this truth was so affecting when it was their norm.

'Will you take me to the Tower of London and Legoland before you go to America?' Edith's voice was no more than a whisper.

'Well, I would like to . . .' The reality was it was going to be hard to find the time before she left – another disappointment, another way to let Edith down. Only this was worse than not having sliced chicken in the fridge because she had kind of promised. 'But I'm not sure if we're going to be able to fit it in.'

'Okay.' Her daughter's quiet voice, the small sigh of acceptance, as if she'd expected nothing different, was as wounding as it was accurate.

'I would like to, it's just that I leave in less than a fortnight and I've got so much to do.'

Edith stared at her, eyes that seemed to see more than her silence let on. It was uncomfortable.

This was it. The right time to talk detail, to give clarity.

'My trip to LA that we spoke about, it's not just a holiday,' she began. 'I have a new job there. I have a new apartment there.'

'You're renting your flat to people who work in banking.'

271

'Yes, I am.' It seemed the little girl had taken in more than she realised.

'Will you . . . will you be here for my birthday?'

'I'm not sure. I would like to be here for it, I really would, but it's a long way.'

Edith nodded and gripped her sloth.

'You know you don't have to live with someone to love them, don't you? You know you don't have to be with someone to think about them *every* day? You know that, don't you, Edith?' She did her best to control the note of desperation in her words, so keen for her child to understand this very important point.

'Night, night . . . my mummy . . .' The little girl spoke softly in a way that was both calm and dismissive, and it tore at her breast. Edith's eyes closed as the day caught up with her and her tummy rose and fell, as her sweet mouth purred with the gentlest of snores.

Madeleine again felt the slip of tears. She couldn't remember the last time she'd had the privilege of watching her daughter fall asleep – maybe not since she'd held her in her arms in the days after she gave birth, before she walked away.

Her words when they came were quietly delivered, hoping they might permeate the thoughts of her sleeping baby and settle somewhere deep inside where they might live for whenever Edith might need to hear them.

'That wasn't quite true earlier. I remember every single second of the day you were born. Every single second.' She pushed her nose to try in vain to stop the tears that threatened. 'On the day I had you, the moment I first held you, on that cold, cold day with frost on the ground, I knew warmth. And for those few hours when I held you in my arms, you were like a secret. It was just you and me, Edith-Madeleine. And I thought about another life, a life where I didn't follow my dreams and didn't go after all the things I knew I could to make something of myself.' She sniffed. 'A life where I got to be your mummy and hold your hand when you fall asleep and bake with you, and shop with you, and help you with your homework, and I would know your friends and who your teacher was, and you'd run to me if you cried or you needed to feel loved, and you'd . . . you'd know that no matter what, I was your safety net, I was the person who would catch you if you fell. It never occurred to me, sweet girl, that I could have everything. I thought I had to choose.'

'So what happened?'

She spun around towards the door, hadn't realised that Jimmy was close by listening.

Standing quickly, she wiped her face, mortified that he had seen her so distressed and had heard her words. She walked past him and down the staircase into the cosy sitting room, where embers glowed red in the vintage glazed grate, and logs were stacked in a basket on the hearth.

He sat on the patchwork sofa and she followed suit.

'What happened, Jimmy, is that I made that choice. The sun rose and I reminded myself that there was so much I had to achieve, and that I had made a pact with my mother not to let her go to another family, but to instead have the baby and walk away. To give her to her nan, who would raise her with love. And I did. I switched it all off, Jimmy.' She clicked her fingers. 'I switched it all off and I put myself first, which is something men do every single day, and no one questions it, no one. But for me, a mother who has dared to say she wants a different life, a life unburdened by the routine, the struggle, the responsibility, while I strive to be the very best I can, for some reason, that invites judgement.'

'I don't judge you, Mads, I just—'

'You just what, *Dad*?' She bit the inside of her cheek; it was never easy having this type of conversation, confronting that day, and even harder when it was with Jimmy, the father of that baby.

'I guess, and I don't know how to say it without it sounding mean, but . . .' She noticed the slight twitch under his eye; he was nervous, which was quite infectious. 'I feel a bit sorry for you.'

'You feel sorry for *me*?' This was not what she had expected to hear.

'Yes.' He glanced at her face, then away again. 'I feel sorry that you think it's an either-or choice, feel sad that you don't get to spend time with Edith like I do. Because that warmth you talk about, the way you felt when you first held her, that's what it's like for me every time I see her, every time I tuck her in for the night or read her a story or we just get to hang out. It warms my soul – it makes me happy, the happiest! She makes me happy.'

This she understood and saw evidence of in every interaction he had with Edith, every choice *he* made, from the cottage he had built to the perfect fairytale bedroom he had created for her. It was unpleasant to realise this thought was bookended with something close to envy at all she had missed, and all she would miss.

'And I'm pleased for you, genuinely I am. I'm pleased for you both. What you have is magical. Especially being here in this beautiful little bubble. You've created a magical, safe home for her. A haven, a refuge.'

Jimmy held her eyeline. 'Do you . . . do you remember the drawing I did for you?'

'Drawing?'

'Yeah.' He ran his fingers through his hair and settled back into the sofa, pulling a cushion over his chest as if this shield might protect him from further blows, as if he too recalled the way things unravelled when he made the bold declaration with a piece of art. 'It was of a . . . a cottage, a place I wanted to live someday.'

'No, no, I don't remember it at all,' she lied, figuring it was easier that way, easier than rehashing the whole awkward evening when she had decided to call it quits, sparing him the embarrassment.

His face, the way he had looked, so heartsick, she wanted to spare him it all.

He stared at her. 'Would you have told me you were pregnant if you hadn't had to? If . . . if you'd found out earlier and not kept her?' His voice was thin, his breath coming fast. It was a question that came out of the blue and one he had never asked, one she hoped he never would, knowing she owed him nothing but the truth.

'No.' She lifted her chin and told him the truth. 'I wouldn't have told you, Jimmy.'

His eyes seemed to glaze and his shoulders and head dropped as if someone had thrown a hood of disappointment over him.

'Trina said that would have been the case, but I wasn't so sure.'

'I think Trina knew I didn't see kids in my future.'

'And now?'

She took her time, her mouth dry with nerves. 'I love Edith. In my own way, I love her and I always will.' She shook her head. 'But can I see me doing the school run and making soup?' She pointed towards the kitchen. 'I just . . . I don't know.'

'You lobbed rocks into our lives, Mads. You lobbed rocks that created ripples and then you swanned off into the sunset.'

The criticism coming from someone as generous-hearted as Jimmy was hard to hear. He wasn't done.

'I would never for a minute not want to be her dad, never. She's the best thing that ever happened to me, but the moment she arrived, my life was without certain choices. I was never going to be able to fall in love and for that person and I to embark on parenthood together for the first time, because I was already a dad.'

'But you love being a dad.'

'I do.' His tone was steady. 'I do, but financially, socially, my whole world revolves around Edith, and that was a path you set me on. Someone had to pick up the slack. I didn't have choices.

Because of the type of person I am I never come to that fork in the road you talk about, I just keep ploughing on.' He gestured with his hand turned sideways, as if giving directions.

'I see, and reading between the lines, I guess what you're saying is that the situation I find myself in is because of the type of person I am not.'

'That's not what I'm saying.'

'So what are you saying?' She hated the catch to her voice.

'What I've already said! That I had no choice.'

Madeleine picked up her bag from the floor and retrieved her padded coat from the hook by the porch, the one she had wrapped her earthworm in, before heading out to grab her boots from the rack where they sat next to the tiny unicorn wellingtons.

'You weren't the only one with no choice, Jimmy. But no one seemed to want to listen to me, and if you think I haven't lost too, then you'd be wrong.' She pictured Edith dismissing her with a 'night, night' before reaching for her sloth, not that she deserved anything more.

'I don't want you to be upset, but you did say we needed to talk about everything . . .'

'You're a remarkable man and a wonderful dad. Any woman would be so very, very lucky to have you there making soup for them. And what you said is true: the woman who falls in love with you may not get to be the first when it comes to parenthood, but every choice comes with a price and you are one of the good guys – the best. To have someone put a blanket over you while you sleep and to dance with on the rug . . . There are far worse ways to live.' She thought of Trina and hoped her friend found the courage to speak to him.

'Well, that might be true, but if that's the case, the universe is doing a great job of keeping her just out of reach. It gets lonely when Edith's not here.'

She nodded, understanding this. 'Maybe she's closer than you think. There, that's another rock lobbed into your life – food for thought. I hope the ripples it creates are good ones, because you deserve it, Jimmy. You deserve the fairytale.'

Trina does too.

She blew a kiss up to the room where her little girl slept and made her way along the towpath, while calling a cab.

January 29

12.00 P.M.

Marnie and Doug had finally gone home. Madeleine had been too tired and more than a little overwhelmed to object to their pandering and fussing in the maternity ward where she was now settled. One of six occupants, all with newborns alongside them, all she wanted to do was rest, gather her thoughts and mentally focus. The penny seemed to drop for her parents when her eyes had fallen shut mid-sentence and she slept for a second before jolting awake.

'Perhaps we should go home and let you doze, love?' Marnie asked with her perma-grin fixed, as she took constant glimpses of the sleeping baby.

Ya think?

'Yes, okay,' she'd whispered, her voice thin.

Shifting her bottom, she did her best to sit comfortably in the bed, wanting – needing, actually – to rest her bones, which felt pulled, and her muscles, which felt stretched, sore, and trying to regroup under her skin. Every fibre of her being was doing its best to nestle back into position and to calm after what had been an exertion. She felt at once superhuman and entirely broken. Exhilarated and defeated. Relieved and wrapped in trepidation. The prospect of being left alone was an attractive one, but being left alone with the baby, of being solely responsible for her, not so much.

It was the oddest of sensations, staring at the plastic bassinet on wheels next to her hospital bed and studying the little pink face peering out from within the soft white blankets inside which she was swaddled. A healthy little specimen if ever she'd seen one. Beautiful and delicate with ten tiny toes, ten little fingers, all her bits and pieces present and correct, and with Jimmy's dark, dark hair sitting like a cap on her perfectly shaped head. It was unreal that this little human had, only an hour or so before, been residing inside her body and was now outside of her body. It was almost impossible to comprehend.

Marnie, throughout the labour and birth, had kept repeating, 'Oh, she's cold, she's trembling with cold. Can we please get an extra blanket for my daughter?'

But Madeleine wasn't cold. Her trembling was not due to a chill in the air, but rather because she was petrified, and no matter how many blankets they piled on top of her, it wasn't going to help alleviate her all-consuming fear.

The moment her labour accelerated, she wished she'd stuck with the antenatal classes. She'd popped along to one session, walked into the hall, taken one look at the couples sitting closely together, all beaming with excited anticipation, and had turned right around and left. It hadn't felt like such an unwise decision then.

During the birth, she had felt slightly detached, as if the rigmarole, still at this very late hour, might be revealed to be a hoax. Even up until the point of delivery, she half expected the midwife to howl her laughter. 'Well, will you look at that? No more than extreme gas! No baby at all! Off you go!'

It became real, very real, however, when Marnie gripped her hand tightly and her tears flowed as a nurse called out, 'You're crowning! That's it, Madeleine! Keep going! You're doing a wonderful job! Nearly there, my love! Keep going!'

A head. A head was visible. And that meant only one thing: a baby was without doubt about to be expelled from her body. Things had happened relatively quickly after that – one or two big pushes, the sharp bite of fear that she might become damaged during the process, and then a sweet, satisfying slithering as the child was delivered. Her body sang with relief!

A girl.

Her girl.

Edith-Madeleine.

Seven pounds, two ounces.

The midwife had placed the tiny tot with grasping fingers and a scrunched-up face on to her chest and she had felt . . . conflicted. Drawn to the little thing. Fascinated and in awe of her, emotional in the face of such a marvel of nature, but attached to her? Responsible for her? Wanting to hold her close and never let her go? The instant and all-consuming love that she had read about online? Nothing like that. Not even close.

Her parents left slowly. Going back to hold her close, smooth her hair, to tell her they'd return later. They hovered by the cot, burbling high-pitched lamentations of adoration and awe into the baby's tiny ears, telling her how beautiful she was, how happy they were that she had arrived safely and that they loved her, yes, *loved!* It threw her a little, but maybe they were experiencing the instant and all-consuming magic that others had phrased so eloquently and which she could only begin to imagine.

The moment Marnie and Doug left, she became aware of the others in the room – all it seemed in various states of euphoria and/or exhaustion. All with partners, either dozing in the chair with their newborns on their chest or in their arms, and one couple who lay on the bed, entwined, resting, as if unified by this one incredible thing and oblivious to the rest of the world. Another was feeding her wife what looked to be pasta salad, flatbread, pickles, and cubes of charred halloumi – pre-prepared and in a bento box, forking delicious morsels of gorgeousness that made Madeleine's stomach rumble with want.

She felt lonely and yet wanted to be alone. It wasn't straightforward. And what might be the cure to that loneliness? To call Jimmy? Hardly. Or Trina? Their one dissatisfying get-together lingered in her thoughts; the memory of it pained her as a measure of how far apart they had sprung.

Closing her eyes, she sat back against the pillow and allowed her breathing to slow, concentrating on the throb of discomfort below her waist and the tenderness to her stomach; the rage of a womb that had worked hard and delivered. Sleep called to her and she responded, wanting the bliss of oblivion, just for a while.

She had thought that to deliver this baby would mean the beginning of the end, but as the child cried and the other parents stared at her, focusing on her inaction, their eyes pleading with her to do something, anything, she understood this was not the beginning of the end. Not at all. As the baby howled, disrupting the atmosphere, and they held their own offspring closer, unable to imagine not lunging for them the very second they stirred, Madeleine turned back the blanket and pulled the bassinet closer to her. She understood in that moment that this child, and her connection to it, whether she saw it or not, and the judgement of others who had a view on how she should or might do things differently, was actually for ever.

For ever . . .

Chapter Thirteen

Present Day

Madeleine had been solemn on the cab ride home, thoughtful, as she replayed the afternoon's events and her conversation with Jimmy, unsure whether they had made progress or had regressed. She had swapped text messages with Marnie, who, unsurprisingly, was keen to hear all about her visit – of which she gave her a potted summary – and equally keen to detail how well Dougie was looking after her, even managing to cook a chicken and roast a couple of spuds.

> *I'M BEING SPOILED AND FEEL QUITE GOOD. RESTING.*

Her final reply was short and sweet.

> *GOOD X*

Walking through the busy London borough, the street where she lived seemed particularly noisy. This awareness, no doubt, following her afternoon spent cloistered in the quiet cottage on the towpath. The contrast was striking. The hallway echoed as she entered and the wide front door clanged shut. There was nothing soft or particularly cosy about the grand foyer and entrance hall and she wondered how she might soften the space. A project post-LA, whenever that might be. An image of a willow basket filled with wool blankets and that stunning green vintage log burner filled her mind.

Her apartment was in darkness, and in the dark she felt the mournful echo of loneliness. She switched on the lamp and walked over to the far wall. Garth had texted that morning to say that her Chantilly had arrived and that they would be painting it today, even though it was Sunday. He also let her know that Micky had put a can of Diet Coke in her fridge and a Dairylea triangle to replace the one he'd borrowed. On any other day, she might have found this funny. She cast her eyes over the fresh coat of paint and was only mildly satisfied by the rectification. Strangely, it didn't seem quite so important now. She was after all going to LA soon enough and the flat would ring with the sounds of the new tenants, who probably, with hindsight, would neither care nor notice the particular paint colour. There were far more important things, she was discovering, than the perfection of her décor. Like dancing on a Sunday afternoon and reading stories on a comfy couch with a tummy full of home-made soup.

She was tired – overly tired. Her feet hurt, her back twinged and she felt the beginnings of a headache. It was as she ran the cold tap for a glass of water that the intercom rang. She ambled over, ready to direct another lost or befuddled delivery driver to a different apartment.

'Hello?'

'Madeleine.' She'd almost forgotten the soothing nature of his tone and how much she liked him. She felt like crying at no more than the sound of his voice, which she hadn't heard for a couple of days. Time enough, it seemed, for him to gather his thoughts and decide how he wanted to go forward.

Nico . . . the very nice man.

'Nico, hello. Please come up.'

She pressed the button to release the front door, wanting him to step inside before he changed his mind or any discussion could take place over the intercom. She was also nervous, wary of what he might want to say and how he might say it. This was a new position for her, one where a potential future love-interest was aware of her child, aware of Edith. She took a deep breath and opened her door.

Gone was the confident manner of when he had last set foot in her home. That glorious morning when he'd cooked breakfast and they had laughed and kissed as she sat on the countertop, and he'd pulled her back to bed for ten minutes before he absolutely had to leave to get to the office. This was different. His tread was hesitant, his skin a little pale with dark circles of fatigue looped under his eyes. He held back, unsure of his welcome, and she matched him, hesitant glance for hesitant glance. His reticence was sweet, endearing, and she felt it put them on an even footing, which was reassuring. There was nothing aggressive, assumptive, or resolute about his actions, suggesting he came without an agenda, and for this she was thankful.

'Hi.' She smiled nervously.

'Hi. Hope it's okay just to pitch up.' His hands stayed close to his body, neither expressive nor reaching for her as they had before.

'Of course, I've only just got back, but I'm . . . I'm pleased to see you.'

He nodded and took a step further inside.

'Would you like a drink, Nico? I'm going to have one.'

'A cup of tea would be lovely.'

'Just what I was thinking.' She switched on another lamp in the kitchen and filled the kettle, a very different dynamic to his last evening here, when they'd guzzled wine and shed their clothes.

'I nearly didn't come. Right up until I knocked on your door, I nearly didn't come.'

'I'm really glad you did,' she reiterated. 'That text I sent you, the one saying, "happy" – I should explain.'

'It was meant for someone else?' he interjected.

'Oh God, no, no!' She grabbed two mugs and threw teabags into them. 'I thought that you'd sent me some, erm, some flowers.' She was embarrassed, as if this had been her expectation; naive at best and, at worst, assumptive. 'Kind of like a forgiveness thing, or if not forgiveness then a "We're good!" kind of thing.'

'I see.'

'But they were from someone else, obviously.'

'From Edith's dad?'

'Jimmy?' She pulled a face. 'No, no, I don't think he's ever sent me flowers.' She poured on the hot water, agitated the teabags with a spoon and opened the door of her scratched Meneghini la Cambusa to fetch the milk. 'But he did make me soup today. Well, technically he'd made soup anyway and offered me some.' She babbled as her discomfort at the topic guided her tongue.

'Are you guys married, or were you? If it's okay to ask.' He licked his lips; his mouth sounded a little sticky with nerves. 'I'm trying to piece together the . . . situation. I mean, it's none of my business, the detail, but I'm aware of how you spoke about clarity and the importance of it.'

She got the message loud and clear and picked up on his slightly irked tone, not that she had lied – apart from about being ill. It was more that she'd not confided in him, totally different, and why would she, after one measly date and one night spent together?

'Of course it's okay to ask. Shall we sit down and drink this while it's hot?' She handed him a mug and he followed her to the large sofa, which was still in semi-darkness. The soft light from the kitchen area was all she could cope with, thinking it would be easier to talk openly with some of her expression shaded – a privacy of sorts.

He took a seat in the corner where they had spent time together – chatting, sipping wine, and learning the shape of each other, as they spoke words full of promise and let excitement fuel their touch.

'Don't know where to begin really.'

'Me either.' She hoped this was some consolation, if not comfort.

'I . . . I guess I just wanted to see you, to say . . . I don't know . . . just . . .' He sighed and looked towards the ceiling as if this was where the words might lurk. 'I don't know what to say now I'm here. Not sure how I should feel about it all.'

'Well, the short answer is it's nothing to do with you, not really. We've had one lunch date, one night together and a bit of flirtation. It didn't really give me a chance to build up to giving you my history.'

'And I absolutely understand that, but . . .' He paused. 'I suppose, what I've found tricky, is that we did open up to each other, spoke about the important stuff, and you never thought it might be a good idea to mention you had a daughter?'

'When would you suggest I did that?' This was what she did, put up the screen, spoke in a blunt manner to keep all those feelings at bay. She was well practised.

'I'm not sure, and I don't mean unsure how I feel about you having a child, although I have to admit that's a lot, I guess I just thought . . .'

'What, Nico? What did you think?' She looked away, not wanting to see his expression of regret or disappointment. She had enough of that from Marnie.

'I thought that we had a really good connection.'

We did . . .

'I thought things were moving very quickly and in the right direction.'

They were . . .

'I can't remember the last time I'd felt so . . . optimistic about another person, like I could fall for you.'

Me too . . .

His admission softened her hardened shell and she felt the warmth in it, as her guard dropped. A little.

'I guess I thought that as we were being open about insecurities and other parts of our lives we don't normally share, it might have been the perfect opportunity for you to drop into the conversation that you have a child.'

I wish it were that easy . . . Only part of it is the existence of Edith. Far bigger is my inability to be her mother . . . How attractive would you find the thought of a future with me then?

She took a sip of the hot tea. 'I guess it's not that simple, and you're now being reactive, having had a chance to weigh up the information you have, but I wonder if your reaction would be the same had I told you earlier on, or if I'd "dropped" it into the conversation.'

He pulled a face. 'I don't see the difference.'

'The difference is you'd be amazed how much less attractive some people can find others when they think there is a small child and an ex-husband in tow.'

'You were married?' His mouth opened.

'No! I'm only saying that as an example! It's all very well casting me as the baddie, but actually I'm just very protective of my story. It's complicated.'

'I think you've made it complicated, or at least more complicated than it needed to be.'

'Oh, really? And what would Mamma Yannis make of the fact that I had a child? I can imagine that might not be what she wants for you.'

He stared at her. 'Why are you bringing her into this? How on earth would you know or not know what she wants for me? This is about you and me, not my mother!'

'You say that, but it's actually about the whole family when there are kids involved. I should know.'

'I don't know why I came really.' He put his untouched tea on the coffee table. 'This feels unnecessarily hostile, a bit too involved. You're very defensive. I didn't think it was going to be this . . . this difficult to navigate. It shouldn't be, should it?'

'No, Nico, it shouldn't be.' She put her hand on his leg. 'Please, don't go. Just . . .' She let her hair hang forward. The thought of him walking out now and not coming back left her feeling hollow inside. 'I am defensive, because every single person who knows my situation judges me.'

'Everybody judges everyone about everything! You're not unique, it's how people figure out how they feel about something. As I said, it's not so much about the fact you have a daughter, but more how we could talk about childhood biscuits, even touch on parenthood, spend great time together, hint at meeting up in LA, and you didn't trust me enough to open up. And I guess the thing I liked about you most, or one of the things, was how open you were. Or how open I thought you were.'

'I'm pretty sure if, before we'd gone Dutch on our gnocchi, I'd mentioned in passing that I had a seven-year-old daughter, you'd have felt differently.'

'Maybe, maybe not, but we'll never know, will we? Because you didn't give me the chance. And how did you see it playing out anyway? What were you going to do, hide her in a cupboard whenever I appeared?'

She removed her hand from his leg, put her tea down and crossed her arms. *Where to begin?* It was always going to be difficult, and something she had shied away from in the past, preferring to cut potential lovers loose rather than have to face it. Nico was different. She wanted to open up to him, felt it was worth the risk. Besides, he knew about Edith now; all she had to do was fill in the blanks.

'I always intended to tell you, but I also knew it was a matter of timing. And for your information, that was the . . .' She gave a small nervous cough; this admission she knew painted her in the very worst light. 'That was actually the first time she had been to my apartment.'

Nico gave a short laugh. 'Is that a joke? I don't follow.'

'It's not a joke,' she levelled. 'That was the first time I had ever brought her here and she only came because my mum, who Edith lives with, who she has *always* lived with, ended up in hospital. It was a big deal bringing her here, I was really nervous and then, erm, she spoke to Jimmy, her dad.'

'He seemed nice.'

She chose not to remind him that this was a word he felt to be insulting and mediocre, confident that Jimmy was neither of those things.

'He is. Edith spoke to him and decided she'd rather go home to his house, and just as he arrived to pick her up, you appeared on the doorstep. And that was that.'

'Why has she not been here?' He looked confused and she more than understood.

'Because I don't look after her. I never have. I don't see her that often. I'm more like that aunty who pops up on occasion and brings fabulous presents and then disappears again until Christmas.'

Her cheeks flamed at the admission, and she saw his eyes widen in response. She had told him of her quirks, her oddities, but this was by far her biggest: the fact that, unlike most other women she knew, she had given up the care of her child for freedom. And it was a freedom she loved. What she hadn't banked on was that it came with a side order of loneliness and a dressing of regret.

'I don't understand.' He held her eyeline, his expression suggesting he did indeed want to understand, and that felt like a good place to start.

'I didn't know I was pregnant for a while – quite a while, actually. I was seven months gone when I found out.'

'I thought women knew instantly.'

'In a movie maybe, or if they're experienced, or trying to get pregnant, but I didn't have any of the usual clues and I was naive really in some ways – just starting out. At least, that was how I felt, still learning so much about myself, my body . . .'

'It must have been a shock.'

'That's an understatement. I thought the best thing, the best solution for me, for the baby – for us all – was to have her adopted.' She saw him bristle.

'Really?'

'Yup, really.'

His tone, his face, his demeanour, all judging her in the way she could have predicted. It was, she had discovered, almost impossible not to. Her gut folded with nerves as she carried on. It was getting easier; the more he knew, the more she felt able to say. And she wanted him to know everything, figuring it would either give him all the information to allow him to walk away, or to fully understand if they were to stand any chance at all.

'I didn't know how it would feel being a mother, but I did know that I didn't want to be one. I knew it wasn't a life for me.'

These were almost the exact words she had used when she had told Trina of her pregnancy.

'As soon as I mentioned the word "adoption" to my parents, to my mother specifically, she leaped at the chance to have her. It was almost a given. The only option, as it was presented, was to let the baby live with them. She set fairly stringent rules – some of which I can see were well intended and have proved to be the best, like always being honest with Edith, agreeing that any lack of transparency would only lead to heartache further down the line.'

'It doesn't sound . . . easy.' His eyes crinkled in kindness, as if he understood the pain such an arrangement, such a secret, might cause.

'It's not.' She cursed her desire for tears that sprang as she spoke, as if voicing it allowed her to understand it. It wasn't easy, not at all. 'I told you already that I grew up poor, yet my mum was also insistent that I didn't pay them to raise their granddaughter, never wanting Edith to think they might have stepped in for financial gain. I've found this hard to abide by.' This was the truth, especially when her salary had risen handsomely. 'Not to offer assistance when I knew they might be struggling wasn't an option, so I kind of found ways around it.' She paid a generous sum into an account monthly with the explicit instruction that it was for whatever Edith needed or whatever they as a family might need to make their lives easier. She had no idea if her parents had drawn on it, recalling her mother's thin-mouthed acceptance of the account card that Madeleine had forced into her palm; she certainly slept a lot better knowing that it was there. 'My mum also insisted that I told Jimmy about the baby, which was difficult and odd.' She thought about that night, sitting on the bench on the towpath where he had now created the most beautiful home. 'We weren't together. Hadn't been for a while. It had been a fling, no more, and had ended months before. But as we've already established, he's a nice man.'

'That must have made everything easier.'

'Definitely. I saw him and Edith today and it's made me think . . .' She hesitated, wondering whether to voice her thoughts would draw him in or scare him off, not that it mattered either way, really; she was after all off to LA. Plus, the way he sat rather formally on the sofa, his whole demeanour changed, made her wonder about the point of him being there at all if reconciliation weren't on the agenda.

'Made you think what?'

'That I . . . I miss out. I miss out on so much of her. It makes me ask if I'm ready to be a mum, if I *can* be, in some way. More involved. Not that I really know what that looks like on a practical level, and it's hardly an option as I'm off to LA.'

'So what's stopping you figuring it out?' he asked kindly.

The thought of getting it wrong, knowing I'll never be as at ease with her as Marnie or Jimmy. Feeling like I missed my chance, knowing I'd be on catch up, having to live with a decision I made while in complete shock with everyone watching me every minute since to see if I admit my mistake or, even better, how I try to fix it . . . I'm paralysed with regret, with fear! Fear of getting it wrong!

'That's a good question.'

Nico looked at his watch. 'I have to go, Madeleine. I'm off to Munich tomorrow – a ridiculously early flight – but I wanted to see you before I left. Didn't want things to be uncomfortable for us.'

'I think that ship might have sailed. I feel uncomfortable right now, don't you?'

'Maybe, a bit.' She appreciated his honesty. 'I guess I didn't want me hightailing it up the pavement with a bottle of Tums to be the last you saw of me.'

'So is this the last I see of you? Is that what you're saying?' She hated the disappointment that formed a ball in her throat.

He shook his head. 'No, what I'm saying' – he looked right at her – 'is that I thought things were straightforward and I'm not sure they are, and so I'll take some time to process it all and you should do the same.'

'And you wonder why I didn't immediately tell you about Edi—'

'That's not what I'm saying!' he cut in. 'This isn't about her, but it's obvious to me that you don't really know what you want. You've just admitted as much. As I say, you need to figure it all out.'

'Oh, is that all I need to do?' She was aware of and embarrassed by her own flippancy; it was the crappiest of defences.

He took a deep breath that smacked of exasperation. 'We need to be on the same page, that's all. We need the honesty and open-ness that is so much more than just a hashtag. It's the foundation. To everything.' He let this hang.

'I didn't like lying to you.'

'I don't like lying to anyone,' he countered. 'And for the record, I've not felt . . . not felt this way before, the way I did – do – or did, about you. So . . .'

It was both confusing and exhilarating, his honesty. Devastating to hear, and yet her heart lifted in response to the fact that he had deep feelings for her, or at least he did. She decided there was no point chasing the topic round and around. She was already exhausted, and he was right, they needed time. Or maybe that was his way of ending things kindly.

'It's a good idea. We'll take some time, process where we are at and maybe I'll text you.' She smiled, feeling nothing but regret at the thought of their fabulous flirtation with all its glorious promise that she really didn't want to end. But right now, pulling up the drawbridge felt like the safest thing to do. Maybe he was right; she needed to figure her own head out first. No matter how painful.

'Ah, yes.' He stood. 'And I know what to do if I want to follow it up.'

'Thumbs-up.' She stood too and made the sign.

'Thumbs-up.' He nodded, leaning forward to give her the gentlest kiss on the cheek. It could have been a holding kiss, a place marker for whatever came next, but to Madeleine, it felt very much like goodbye and she wanted to sink into the floor with the finality of it.

Having watched Nico leave, she scrubbed away the day with a hot shower, before falling into bed – alarm set, night cream slathered, silk pillow beneath her cheek. She thought of Edith curled in her fairytale bed and smiled, the image of her little girl enough to dilute the sadness she felt when she thought of how things had been left with Nico.

'Sandra has a daughter, Chelsea, who is forty-eight . . . It's not funny! Chelsea has to do everything in that house!'

Her little girl was funny! The funniest.

She was still processing the incredible home that Jimmy had created, amazed that something so glorious could exist in the place that she had failed to see any beauty. It didn't feel good, the way she'd left things with him. Picking up her phone, she fired off a text.

THANK YOU FOR A LOVELY AFTERNOON.
MADS

Her phone rang almost immediately. It was Jimmy.

'I was just thinking of calling when your text came in, but wasn't sure if you'd be asleep already, didn't want to disturb you.'

'I keep laughing about Sandra.'

'Honestly, the things that kid comes out with. She's priceless.' The pride in his voice was evident.

'She is.'

'I wanted to call you, Mads, because it was unusual for us to have a heated conversation like that, and it's no bad thing, probably long overdue, but I wanted to tell you again that Edith is the best thing that's ever happened to me. She made me want to do well, to be the best version of me and to get my shit together. I have absolutely no regrets and you shouldn't either. I think we both do the best we can and I think we've *always* done the best we can.'

His words felt like a kindness she didn't deserve and her tears bloomed accordingly.

'There are things I would do differently now,' she whispered. *I am going to miss her more than I can say. I think I've always missed her . . . but I haven't let myself dwell on it because I didn't think I was allowed to feel that way . . . because I walked away . . . all or nothing . . .* How she wished she had the courage to say this out loud!

'But nothing you would have done differently at the time?'

'No.' It was that transparency thing again. 'That's the thing, isn't it? We only do what we do and choose what we choose and then we're given a lifetime to mull over those choices.'

'Because when we are making those decisions, we don't get to glimpse the consequences.'

'Because we don't get to glimpse the consequences . . .' She repeated this truth.

'You should, erm, you should come to Marnie and Doug's on Saturday. Doug's invited us all over for a cuppa to cheer Marnie up, and of course she wants to see Edith before her surgery. It'd be good if you were there, to see your parents and see Edith before you go away.'

'Yes, I'll come.'

'Edith will be pleased.' He was smiling, she could tell.

'So I guess I'll see you there.'

'Yep. Night, Mads.'

'Night.'

She lay staring at the ceiling long after the call had ended. Dr Schoenfeld's question danced in her thoughts.

Are you happy, Madeleine?

'Am I happy?' she spoke aloud. 'Am I happy?'

Placing her hand on the cool pillowslip next to her, the one where Nico had laid his head before making her that glorious breakfast.

'I don't like lying either, Nico. Not to anyone, but especially not to myself . . .'

February 16

Making her way along Piccadilly, it felt strange for Madeleine to be back at work. Stranger still that no one looked at her differently, stared, whispered about her behind cupped palms, or asked any awkward questions. No one acted as if the world had stopped spinning for a while, throwing everything they knew into confusion before righting itself again. Until she realised it was only in her world that this had occurred. For everyone else it was business as usual. She was different, felt different, changed in the most subtle of ways, but changed, nonetheless.

Her body had gone back together, but not quite. It was like having a tooth removed while your mouth and gums took a while to figure out how to close and accommodate the gap. It was like removing a mirror from a wall where it had hung for an age, and finding yourself constantly checking the blank space, surprised still not to see your reflection staring back at you. It was like having a fever dream about an exam you had already sat a long time ago, when only waking brought sweet relief and ended the panic. It was like sitting up in the middle of the bed in the middle of the night, unable to remember if she had had a baby or was about to have a baby or had imagined the whole thing, because she looked pretty much the same, felt pretty much the same, but there was no child to be seen.

It meant she felt the changes at a deeper level. There was no screaming horror of grief, no brutal pull of loss. Hers was a more general flicker of damage done without being able to pinpoint the pain.

She had carried a baby, given birth to a baby, and handed that baby over to her parents, almost unquestioningly, because it made sense! They were after all parents; they had looked after her for over two decades and had done a reasonable job. Whereas she was a mere infant herself, still trying to understand life, to carve a path, and was glad to have been able to pass the perfect little human over to Marnie and Doug, who seemed excited about the prospect – something she couldn't begin to imagine.

It was a secret.

Edith-Madeleine, who was now eighteen days old, was a secret.

This hadn't been her intention, not at all, but it was merely how it unfolded, in the way that it did when something wasn't mentioned or discussed, and the longer this remained the case, the harder it was to mention it for the first time. Besides, who would she tell? Her old flatmates Luciano, Meredith and Liesl had not been in contact since she had left and were no doubt overcooking pasta and dancing in sticky-floored nightclubs with the new girl who had taken up residence in her old room. Trina was no longer her confidante, a fact that was still sinking in, and she had nothing to say to Jimmy. The people who worked for Rebecca Swinton were not her friends, they were acquaintances for whom she had fetched and carried until her unexpected leg up on the ladder. The idea of sharing the last few weeks of her life with any of them . . . it didn't occur.

What did occur to her, slowly – again there was no jolt of reali-sation, but rather a slow seep of awareness – was that it would be lonely living life with a secret like this. It would make her guarded, cautious, wary of opening up. It meant she would live two lives. The one she presented to the public, her peers, and colleagues – that of a cool, calm career woman with her head above the clouds and her feet on the ground. And one she lived when she nipped back to the Brenton Park estate. The Brenton Park estate where her child lived, and where every visit would see her lower her stature, her voice, and her expectations, as if this was what was painfully required just to fit in.

Rebecca had invited her to lunch and here she was, standing outside The Wolseley, feeling a little otherworldly with nerves flut-tering in her stomach where her nesting baby had only recently given up residence. She was about to walk in when she heard her boss call from the pavement. Rebecca looked immaculate in her ivory silk shirt and navy cigarette pants, paired with nude heels.

'Madeleine! There you are!' She spoke as if she'd been search-ing for her.

'This looks lovely. I feel a bit nervous.' She stared up at the imposing arched windows, the pale stone and grand brass façade.

Rebecca stepped ahead and stood still as the bowler-hat-ted doorman opened the doors from the inside, then turned to face Madeleine. 'Never be nervous of entering anywhere. The moment your actions and manner suggest you shouldn't be there, you're proving that thought correct. Enter commandingly, yet calmly; hold your head high and always know it's where you belong.'

'Good afternoon, madam.' The doorman tilted his head. Rebecca responded with a slight nod.

The maître d' in his immaculately cut suit rushed forward. 'Hello again, madam.' He gave a slight bow.

Rebecca stood tall, as if she liked it. 'Hello.'

Madeleine noticed how she only glanced at his face before looking past him into the dining room, where intimate tables were set with starched white linen and silverware. The whole place carried an air of refined sophistication.

'And you're dining with us today?'

'Yes.' Rebecca looked back at him. 'Table for two, under the name Swinton – Rebecca Swinton.'

He walked to the lectern, where a bespectacled girl stood with a pen in her hand and carried an air of authority – the gatekeeper. Ignoring his colleague, he ran his finger down the computer screen and beamed up at her, as if she'd won a prize.

'Please follow me.' Again that slight bow with the incline of the head.

He paused at a table that was sat in front of the bar, almost a thoroughfare, and judging by the look on Rebecca's face, not where she wanted to sit. Not at all.

'No, thank you. Erm . . . we'll take that one.' She pointed to a table set perfectly for two in the central horseshoe of tables in the middle of the room.

'Of course, madam.' He did his best but failed to control the twitch of irritation under his left eye. 'May we get you some water for the table?' He clasped his hands at his chest, as if in prayer.

'Yes. Sparkling, thank you.'

Rebecca slipped into the chair and placed her bag on the floor, keeping her smile small and her attitude professional. Madeleine watched her every move, wanting to be comfortable in social situations, wanting to learn from her.

She studied the small, printed menu in front of her. Rebecca leaned over and whispered, 'I always know the menu of a place before I sit down. It makes me feel more comfortable. I can then practise how to pronounce things, remove the panic that sets in if someone else chooses quicker than me! I like to be prepared.'

It was a surprise to her that Rebecca had to think about her actions, and how she was perceived. It gave Madeleine confidence. If this woman who personified poise and class could do it . . .

It felt like good advice.

'I always have the salade Niçoise here. It's divine.'

Sah-lad nissswaz! Sah-lad nissswaz! Madeleine practised in her head.

'Have you always lived in London, Rebecca?' She was curious and wanted to fill in the quiet until they ordered and their food arrived.

'Good lord, no!' She tucked her glossy hair behind her ears. 'I'm from a tiny village in the sticks. My father was a drunk and my mother a victim of domestic abuse. I grew up in a falling-down cottage without running water or heat and got out the moment I was able.'

'Wowsers!' It was a surprise to say the least. 'You don't . . . I would never . . .' What did she want to say? That this was not the background she would have guessed at by *looking*? And what did that say about her if this was how she judged?

'Oh, I know.' Rebecca touched her hand to her forearm. 'No one would ever . . .' She smiled. 'But that's the trick: reinvention and only looking forward.'

And in that moment, Madeleine understood a little of why she was so drawn to Rebecca – a kindred spirit.

'I had a baby.'

She hadn't meant to say it. Hadn't meant to reveal her secret to the woman she so wanted to impress. It slipped out, as if not to share it would have felt deceitful in the face of such an exchange.

'I had a baby,' she repeated, as if this might make it real for them both.

'I know.' Rebecca held her eyeline.

'How . . . how do you know?' This was not the reaction she had expected, as she pulled the top of her blouse shut, wanting to hide. Maybe her suspicions were correct and people *were* able to tell by looking. Maybe she *was* changed.

'The day you came in late to the office, before Christmas. The day you told me your thoughts on the Old Berlin project.' Rebecca's tone and manner softened, as she leaned forward. 'You'd put leaflets, a hospital note, and a scan picture on your desk. They were just lying there. Pictures that spoke volumes about your story. And I guessed from your manner, you were in a daze. The look of shock on your face suggested that it was not necessarily something that was planned or longed for.'

'No.' Her reply was small. She had no idea! But would have sworn that she put all of the paperwork in her bag, hidden.

'You don't have to explain. You don't need to tell me about it. You don't need to tell anyone anything. It's your business, Madeleine, and yours alone.'

'I don't have her, I don't . . .' She stopped talking, unsure why she felt the need to explain, to justify. It was the first time she had heard of such a possibility, that she didn't have to explain anything. It was as freeing as it was surprising.

The waiter approached the table.

'May I take your lunch order?' He stood with his hands behind his back.

'Madeleine?' Rebecca shared a lingering look with her, a look that was encouraging and instructive.

'The salade Niçoise for me, please.' She ordered with confidence.

'Oh, good shout. Yes, for me too, please.' Rebecca nodded her approval. 'So the Berlin project,' she began. 'I guess the first question is, do you have a passport?'

Madeleine sat back in the seat and looked around at the opulence of her surroundings.

Sah-lad nissswaz! Sah-lad nissswaz!

This was it. The start of her wonderful, wonderful life.

Chapter Fourteen

PRESENT DAY

'Here she is!' her dad called out loudly as he opened the front door of the flat.

'Hi, Dad.' Madeleine kissed his cheek and handed him the fancy box of chocolates she'd picked up yesterday, before shrugging her arms from her coat, which she hung on the hook in the hallway.

'Ooh, these look lovely, thank you.' He yawned as he spoke.

'You're tired, Dad.'

'No, I'm not, I'm fine. I just like to watch her at night. Still a bit worried about her ticker.' He winked.

'Surely you don't watch her *all* night?' She hated the thought of this disturbed sleep for her dad, who was no spring chicken.

'No, don't be daft, not all night. I just sit up every hour, listen to her breathing, put my hand on her, check she's warm enough, that kind of thing. But I think I'll be less worried after her surgery.'

'I bloody hope so! Or you'll get ill. Why don't you take five now and go and have a nap?'

He smiled at her. It broke her heart that Nico and she had parted on such ambiguous terms, yet her dad's smile filled her with joy, this level of devotion. It was something to aspire to. Laughter burbled from the lounge.

'Trina's in with your mum!' He nodded towards the sound with a look of excitement, as if her friend's prior arrival was a fantastic thing – and perhaps it was for them. She, however, would have preferred some time alone with her parents before the mayhem ensued. Not that she had any right to these feelings, knowing it was Trina's coat that hung with regularity on the hook in the hallway, and she was more the guest.

It was as laughter and general chitchat bounced off the walls that she walked into the lounge, feeling instantly self-conscious. Wishing she hadn't taken time to blow dry and style her hair or ensure her make-up was on point. She wished she'd worn something more casual than her off-white jeans and camel-coloured cashmere jumper over a silk blouse. She felt formal, out of place, and ill at ease. This not unusual in recent years but no less exposing for that.

Marnie was sitting on the sofa, the only concession to her medical situation a light blanket over her knees. Her skin was pale, and she'd lost weight, her face slightly gaunt, but other than that, a lot better than she'd looked in the hospital bed. As was always the case with her mother, their previous harsh words were forgotten – or if not forgotten, then ignored, and her greeting was warm and inclusive. It was both a blessing and a curse. It made reunions like this easier but finding resolution to anything a whole lot harder.

'Hello, darling! Fancy you coming all this way! Come in! Come in!'

Madeleine kissed her mum. Her dad put the box of chocolates on the sofa cushion next to his wife.

'Hi, Trina.' She acknowledged the woman sitting in the chair in the corner by the window. She felt the lift in her spirits at the sight of her friend, as if their history and shared childhood elbowed out what had happened to them in recent years and the deceit they both wrangled with.

'All right?' Trina jumped up and stood by the fireplace, as if unsure of her place now Madeleine was home.

'You trying to make me fat?' Marnie tutted while her fingers lingered over the embossed lid of the fancy confectionery.

'Didn't know what to bring you. You look good, Mum, much better.'

'Probably because I'm having a lovely rest! And people like you bring me sweeties!' she chuckled. 'Poor old Dougie is running around, waiting on me hand, foot, and finger. He'll be glad when I'm back in hospital, I'm sure.'

'I will.' He laughed. 'Means I can get them dancing girls back again. Now, who'd like a nice cup of tea?' He clapped his hands together.

'You sit down, Dougie, I'll do it.' Trina was so clearly at home here.

Madeleine felt her guilt bristle. Misplaced, she knew, and yet to feel usurped by her best friend was no easy thing.

'I'll give you a hand.' She followed Trina into the small kitchen. As Dougie sat next to his wife, she heard the ribbon being taken off the chocolates.

Trina turned in a circle, like a child looking to hide in an empty room, clearly flustered.

'Can't remember where the mugs are!'

'In the carousel – or they used to be.' She pointed to the cupboard in the corner.

Trina opened it and, sure enough, there sat all the mismatched mugs.

Madeleine was aware of how her presence made such a change to the atmosphere; it was like the joyful air had been sucked from the room and she arrived with a toxic cloud of tension. It didn't make her feel good.

'I don't know, Mads.' Trina spoke as she filled the kettle. 'We don't see each other for an age and then twice in the same week. Anyone would think we were mates.'

'They might.' She held her nerve. Not willing to be the first to admit that she missed her friend and always had. To be rejected a second time was, she knew, more than she could handle.

Trina rubbed her face and leaned back on the sink. 'You seen that guy you like? The one you told me about?'

'Oh. No.' She felt the crush of disappointment in her chest. 'That's . . . It's not going to happen. At least I'm pretty sure it's not. I'm a bit gutted about it, actually. He's perfect.'

'Perfect, eh? Well, I'm sorry to hear it's not working out. I've been thinking a lot about our chat at the hospital. You said you wanted me to be happy.'

'I do.' She jumped in without hesitation. 'I do.'

'And yet for the longest time, our separation, whatever you want to call it, made me so unhappy.'

'You were the one who walked away, Trina. I still dream about it, you leaving the café when I told you I was pregnant, and then the one time you came here after that and it was so horrible, because everything had changed, then bumping into you in Covent Garden, when we could hardly look at each other.'

'You were with that weird bloke.' Trina pulled a face.

'Yes, Quentin the dentist. I never trusted him.'

'I'd say that was smart. He'd ironed his jeans. Never trust a bloke who irons his jeans.'

Madeleine smiled at this piece of wisdom, but wanted to keep on track. 'It was hard enough going through the pregnancy at all, but doing it without you by my side, it was . . . it was terrible. And I'm not blaming you!'

'Good.'

'I'm not.' She nodded. 'I'm blaming us. Both of us. I shouldn't have . . . God, I don't even know where to start.' That was the truth.

'We don't talk about it, do we?' Trina's voice was now low; her eyes darted towards the lounge. 'About how we broke apart.'

'No, we don't. But as you pointed out, we don't really see each other full stop, so . . .'

Trina nodded and pulled her hair tight inside its scrunchie. 'I guess I shy away from it because I know that no matter how hard it was for me to watch you go and grab a new life, one that excluded me, how hurt I was – how hurt I *am* – I always think it must have been a darn sight harder for you. I mean, you won a lot, but you lost a lot too, didn't you?'

Trina's words echoed Jimmy's in a way. Madeleine didn't want anyone to feel sorry for her. It was the worst.

'I have a lovely life.' She trotted out the justification that helped soothe her pain; pulling up that darn drawbridge, as was her default.

'Is it the life you thought you'd have? The life you wanted?' Trina was silent for a beat and stared at the back of her hands, suggesting it was a hard question to ask.

Madeleine considered her response. 'You want to know if it was *worth* it, is that what you're asking me?' It was a question she had been asking herself of late.

'If ya like.' The kettle whistled to a boil and Trina plopped teabags in the mugs.

'In some ways, yes.' *But not all.*

With her back to Madeleine, Trina spoke softly. 'I loved you so much. I loved you so, so much. You were my very best friend; I would have died for you.'

'I know.' Her reply too, no more than a whisper.

'Since primary school until the day you moved out, I felt I knew what you were thinking, could predict what would make you laugh, how to comfort you. We were sisters.'

'We were.' Madeleine liked to think of it – same hairstyles, same clothes.

'But looking back, Mads, I can see that we started to splinter long before the café.'

'Maybe.' This felt perilously close to opening up old wounds that were still weeping, and she wasn't sure in the face of so much turmoil she had the strength for it.

'Definitely!' Trina pressed. 'I remember your face when I told you I wanted to stay living at home, work in the bank, and save up. You looked at me like I was talking in a foreign language, like it made no sense to you at all.'

'It didn't. I could only think about escape, about running towards the horizon. I wanted you to come with me, wanted us both to rocket out of the postcode to dance among the stars, reaching for the high life and all that came with it. I thought we were on the same track, and suddenly we weren't.'

'You left me behind.' Trina sniffed. 'You left us all behind.'

'Not intentionally. You chose to stay, remember. And then when Edith arrived, it was like you had to pick a side and you chose her – you chose Marnie, and that's fine! It's fine' – the crack in her voice suggested it was anything but fine – 'but it's like you all put up a big high fence that was padlocked and I didn't have a key.'

Trina shook her head. 'We shouldn't have had to choose! You shouldn't have had to choose!'

'You're right! But I did! Why was it no one ever thought to reach out and help me connect with Edith, teach me what to do, instead of running me down in my absence?'

'Oh, come off it – Marnie would have jumped at the chance to help you "connect", as you put it. You never made any sign that it was what you wanted – the opposite, in fact. Every visit it was like you had one eye on the clock. And we never ran you down.'

Madeleine snorted her derision as the words landed. It was hard to hear. It was true, she had never asked for help, watching from the wings as Jimmy, Marnie – all of them – took to caring for Edith like ducks to water, and yet for Madeleine to even hold her filled her with so much dread she could barely bring herself to touch the child.

'And even before Edith, it was so much more than a case of you just being busy. I didn't fit in with your swanky new life.'

'What are you talking about?' She raised her voice. 'That's rubbish!'

'No, it's not! That time I came to meet you up west, when we went out with that bloke you lived with, Luciano or whatever his name was, and those horrible girls who ignored me. You were different. Almost overnight, you behaved different. Christ, you even spoke different! You *still* speak different!'

'I don't!' It was a harsh accusation.

'But you do!' Trina laughed. 'You absolutely do! You used to sound like me and now you most certainly do not!'

Madeleine thought of the hours and hours she inadvertently practised rounding her vowels and concentrating on getting her pronunciation right. Trying hard to shrug off the Brenton Park estate. But it was necessary! Necessary for her to sound like, look like, and become the person she wanted to be! It cut her that Trina could not see that.

'It was as if you wanted to shed your past like skin, Mads, just slither out and leave it behind. That night when we all went out, you were knocking back cocktails that cost more than my food budget for a couple of days. I felt sick. And when I said I had to chip off early, you looked . . . you looked relieved. I think that's what hurt the most.'

She was about to respond but remembered that particular night and knew that Trina was right. She had wanted so badly to fit in, to be like those fancy-pants people with spare chairs and choices. A thought that now thoroughly cloaked her with shame.

'I was relieved! But not because of who you were or how you were, but because you looked as if you wanted to be anywhere else.'

'I did!'

'Well, there we go!'

Both looked towards the door as if aware they had raised their voices. They took a moment and were quiet.

'I never stopped loving you, Trina. My sister.' It was hard to say, a reminder of how much she lost when they fell apart, but it was no less true for that.

'Nor I you, but we still have so much to figure out, Mads. And truthfully, I don't know if we can.' It seemed this was about as conciliatory as Trina could manage.

'I don't know either, but I do know, with Marnie laid up on the sofa, about to have her surgery, maybe this isn't the time or place.' She stood upright and pulled herself together, wishing her friend had reached out to hold her for a warm hug in the way she used to.

'I think it's as good a time and place as any, until the next time.' Trina lobbed the teabags into the sink and topped the teas up with milk.

'I'm leaving soon,' Madeleine reminded her.

'So you are.' Trina spoke with her back to her as if she hadn't forgotten this at all.

'I think at the heart of our – I don't even know what to call it – our "falling out" was the fact you liked Jimmy, the fact you still like Jimmy. Isn't that what this is all about? And I can't imagine how much it hurt you. How much I hurt you.'

'Well, it certainly didn't help. God, it was just the icing on the cake!' Trina sighed, turned and they locked eyes. 'I liked him all the way through school, not that I ever told him, of course, too shy when it came to it. I only mentioned it in passing to you, Mads, but *you* knew, you *knew*! That should have been enough. When you said you'd been seeing him, I was' – she placed her hand on her stomach as if this was where the hurt had balled, maybe still did – 'I was winded. I always knew I'd put my love for you before that of *any* boy. I just couldn't believe you'd done that to me, and then to discover you were having his baby!' Trina made the sound of an explosion from the back of her mouth. 'It was like getting a hard kick in the teeth from the universe.'

'I didn't plan it. I didn't plan any of it.' She felt compelled to offer some justification, no matter how small, and the words did little to ease the immense weight of guilt that dogged her.

'Oh, I know that, but the end result was just the same. You gone. And Jimmy and you are connected for the rest of your lives – for the rest of *my* life.' Trina swallowed. 'Not that I don't think Edith is the best thing ever, I do – she's magic, isn't she?'

'She is.'

Trina, she knew, had never missed a birthday or Christmas gift in Edith's life and Marnie had told her that whenever she popped in she was always happy for a quick game of Connect 4 on the rug in front of the electric fire or to let Edith brush her hair when she fancied playing hairdressers.

'And I know it's selfish of me, Mads, but it was like . . .' Trina paused, as if taking her time to get the words right. 'He was the one thing. The one thing I really, really wanted. And you took him. And . . . and it's not like you took him because you wanted him, or because you loved him or saw a future with him or anything so meaningful that I might, *might* have been able to get my head around. You took him because you could and then you ditched him, but it was spoiled for me because of you. And that was a really shitty thing to do, especially to me, who you were supposed to care about. Who you were supposed to love.'

'I did love you. I do.' She whispered from a mouth contorted with the magnitude of her friend's words that hit so hard. 'I was selfish and thoughtless and it was a shitty thing to do. I'm sorry. All I can say is that I didn't do it maliciously, didn't set out to trap him or hurt you. It wasn't important! And I had no idea of how important it would become.'

'I'm sure you think that makes it better, the fact that it wasn't important.' Trina blinked her tears. 'But it kind of proves my point and doesn't change the fact that it was important to me. It was very important to me.'

'I'm sorry. I am. I'm sorry.' To see the hurt on Trina's face was almost unbearable. Her fingers twitched with the need to hold her friend, but as they stood on either side of the kitchen – a distance of less than seven feet – it felt like a long, long way away.

'I kept waiting for you to pop up and say, "I'm back. I tried that life and I realise I just want to be at home with all the people who love me, where I have history." And we'd pick up where we left off – drinking tea on the sofa and scoffing biscuits, walking arm in arm in the park late at night, going shopping to buy a top to wear to the pub on Saturday night, we'd eat fried egg sandwiches right here in the kitchen on a Sunday morning and we'd doze in front of the telly . . . That was the life I loved – the life with you in it.'

She heard the emotion in Trina's words and felt it mirrored in her breast, knowing it was impossible to go back to that life. She was changed – *they* were changed – and she was unsure of how or even if they still fitted together.

'I'm not that person anymore.' This was the truth. The fact was she had worked hard not to be that person anymore. *But that doesn't mean I can't have a life with you, if you let me . . .* She wanted so badly to say this! Fear was the stopper that kept the words tamped down.

'Then I shall start grieving, Mads, because that means she's never coming home – that girl who was like a part of me, and that's a lot for me to get my head around. And I shall miss her, for always.'

'I miss her too, Trina, some of the time. But I do have a lovely life! And I meant what I said.' She swallowed. 'I think you should tell Jimmy how you feel.'

'Oh, you think?' Trina let her tears gather as her voice broke.

'I do. He's a great person. I don't need to tell you that.' Trina, she knew, had also borne witness to his incredible kindness and patience every time he was with his daughter. Her words came from a throat narrowed with emotion at this the hardest of conversations. 'You both deserve to be happy.'

'You deserve to be happy too.' Trina handed her a mug of tea.

'As I said, I've got stuff to figure out, but I am happy, most of the time.'

'Sure you are.' Her friend picked up the other mugs and took them to Marnie and Doug in the lounge.

Doug stood as they walked into the room. Trina handed him a mug of tea.

'Thanks, love. I'm just going to go to the, erm . . .' He pointed and walked to the bedroom, closing the door behind him.

'Sit down, girls,' Marnie instructed, and they sat. Trina sat in the chair in the corner and Madeleine on the pouffé in front of the fireplace. 'We heard every word you said in the kitchen. Think you both forgot how thin these bloody walls are.'

'Sorry, Marn, I—'

'No, I don't want sorry. I just want you both to listen.'

Trina stopped talking and they stared at Marnie.

'Seeing you both sitting there looking at me' – Marnie swallowed – 'it's like we've erased time. I can picture you both on a Sunday, sitting in here, watching telly, laughing and chatting, eating whatever you could find in the cupboards. I used to say to Dougie, "I know we wanted lots of kids, but listen to what we've got – them two, as close as can be." It was everything. It really was.'

Madeleine and Trina looked at each other, their smiles slow in forming but smiles nonetheless shared in recognition of this truth.

They heard the front door close.

'Nanny!'

'Oh, here comes trouble.' She broke off from her chat and braced for Edith, who ran into the lounge. 'Hello, my darling!'

Edith jumped on to the sofa and threw her arms around her nan. Madeleine could only look on as the two sat holding each other tight, as if their separation caused them pain.

'Hi, all!' Jimmy came in, waved, and took a seat next to her on the floor. 'The door was on the latch. How are you feeling, Marn?'

'I'm great, love,' she said as Edith released her and walked over to kiss Madeleine, before high-fiving Trina. It was strangely comforting that her little girl didn't go into raptures at the sight of her, suggesting it was normal, no big deal, just her mum hanging out on a Saturday. It felt inclusive and took the pressure down a notch.

'Where's Pop?' Edith looked again around the tiny room, as if it might have been possible to mislay the man.

'Go and give him a shout. Do you want him to help you with colouring in?'

'Yes! Yes! Yes!' Edith ran eagerly from the room. 'Pop! I'll be in my room,' she yelled. 'I'll sort the pens out!'

'That'll keep them busy.' Marnie pulled a face and lowered her voice. 'I often use the phrase "life is short". I say it to other people all the time, as if it might galvanise them to act, put the fire under them they need. But since my heart attack, I've been thinking about what it means to me. Life *is* short, and the older I get, the less of it I have left. That goes for all of us, of course, not that you three have to worry – you're all mere babies!'

Madeleine smiled. She was approaching thirty, about to head over the pond, and with plans to open her own agency; she didn't feel like a mere baby.

'You have a whole lot of life ahead of you and I think it's important you go for what you want. I used to say it to Madeleine all the time.'

'Yep, and look where that got us!' Trina tested the water with her humour.

Jimmy tittered.

'The thing is,' Marnie continued, 'none of us get to plan the life we live. We might *think* we do, but we don't, not really. Bits of it, yes, the path we choose, maybe the job we do, or the place we live, but the truth is, life carries us along in its raging rapids. It sends us challenges, it drags us under, it puts obstacles and people in our path, things we never expected to come along and they steer us in directions we might not have chosen, but so much of it is good! Because this is our one life! It has to be all good or we spend a very long time wishing things were different, and that's just a bloody waste. We don't know what's around the next bend, but we do know what we face today, and we just need to keep paddling, but also taking time to look up and see all the wonderful things that are around us.'

'The pocketsful of sunshine,' Madeleine whispered; Marnie's words struck a chord.

'That's right.' Marnie held her gaze. 'So it's about time you three figured out how to go forward. Because the clock is ticking. And one day you'll blink, look in the mirror, and you'll be wondering where the last thirty years have gone. And most importantly, there's a marvellous little girl at the heart of all this who deserves better.'

'I love you all.' Trina spoke softly. 'You're my family, right?'

Trina might not have been looking directly at her, but Madeleine knew it was another stepping stone laid down by her friend to help them cross the huge chasm, and her heart flipped with longing that it might be so.

'We are your family, darling – always.' Marnie looked close to tears.

'I need to go. Got to pick my mum up.' Trina stood.

'I'll come walk you to your car.' Jimmy stood, his manner as ever, calming.

'Oh, sure.' There was no mistaking the look of delight that made Trina's eyes shine brightly and her mouth curl into a smile.

'See you.'

'Yeah, see you, Mads.'

It was only when they'd left the room that she and Marnie let their own smiles form.

'Well.' Her mum pulled a face. 'That's a start.'

'Yep.'

'I long ago gave up the idea that you and Jimmy might make a go of things.'

'It was never going to happen, Mum. I think he's brilliant.' That was the truth. Her admiration of him after she'd told him he was the father of her child, and what she could now see was a wonderful gift; the way he had made contact with Marnie, shy at first, no doubt, no more than a kid himself trying to figure out life. His occasional visits to sit with Edith, read to her, bringing her small

317

gifts of wildflowers and items knitted by his mother. Before quite simply joining their family, forging a precious bond bound with love. It might not have been the family her parents had envisaged when her pregnancy first came to light, but she could see it was a strong family, nonetheless. And one with Edith at the heart of it. 'But we're never going to be a couple, not in that sense.'

And especially not now I understand how much I've hurt Trina; I wish I could figure out how to make amends. This she kept to herself, unwilling to admit to the feeling of contentment she had felt while ensconced in Jimmy's fairytale cottage, the way it had felt to dance with their daughter and eat good soup . . . It had woken something inside her, not wanting that life with him, not with Jimmy, but with someone? Someone like Nico? It wouldn't be the worst thing.

'I love you, Madeleine.' Marnie's words were direct, heartfelt, and moving.

'I know. I love you too. And' – she took a moment, wanting to get it right – 'and I'm thankful to you, Mum. To you and Dad. For what you did, for what you've done. You are remarkable, both of you. I can't imagine what my life or Edith's life would have been like if we didn't have you guys. I'm thankful for you both.' Her voice cracked; this wasn't easy. 'I know what you've sacrificed.'

'I gained far more than I lost.' Settling back, she stared at the ceiling and spoke softly. 'I'd do it all again. Without question. I'd take that baby girl in a heartbeat, and I'd do it *all* again. That child is—'

As if on cue Edith's raucous laughter filtered across the hallway. It warmed Madeleine.

'She's really something.' Marnie looked towards the sound. 'I think you're right. I don't think I did give you a choice, not really. But I want you to know that every decision I made, I did with the best of intentions. Because I would do anything for you, Madeleine – my only child. I would.'

'I know.' Her voice was no more than a whisper. 'I was angry – so angry, Mum. Angry with the world for what had happened to me, angry with you for not giving me the choice.'

'I saved her.' Marnie's tears were instant. 'I saved her for you. Because as much as I couldn't stand the thought of her going to another family, the only thing I hated more was the idea of you waking up one day and realising just what you'd given up. I thought, at least if she's with me, then if – *if* – that day comes, then you still have a chance. You still have a chance.'

She wanted to speak, wanted to give her thanks, to say she understood, but her own wave of emotion rendered speech impossible.

'And Trina was right. You came back different, you behaved different, you spoke different and you still speak different!'

'I guess I do.'

'You do, Madeleine, but I still love you and I know you still love all of us, even when you're distracted by the life you're building. I understand more than you think.'

'I guess that's why it hurts so much.' Madeleine wiped her eyes, embarrassed to be so emotional, unable to keep it together.

'One thing I do know, Edith-Madeleine Woods, is that you're doing your best. And as long as you're happy, then that's all I ask. And I know you must be, otherwise, what would be the point of it all?'

Madeleine looked around the walls and thought about the day she had sat in the corner and told her mum she was pregnant. The topic had been exhausting as they chased the same options around and around, bookended with more emotion than either of them was comfortable with. She hadn't slept, could barely function, weakened and obsessed by the meteor that had landed squarely in the middle of all she held dear and around which she tried to navigate. It was only now she was starting to understand that Marnie did what she did with the best of intentions, to give her a chance. Maybe she did know what was best for her . . .

'Yes, what would be the point . . .'

They heard a knock at the front door.

Madeleine jumped up. 'I've got it, Dad!' she called, not wanting him and Edith to have to cut short their colouring-in session.

Chapter Fifteen

Present Day

Jimmy stood on the walkway with his hands in his pockets. He exhaled through his bloated cheeks. 'Well, that was interesting!'

Aware of being overheard, Madeleine stepped out on to the walkway, and they both leaned out over the concrete wall, looking down on to the car park.

'Wanna talk about it?' She moved closer to him.

'Trina's the person you were talking about when you said my love interest might be closer than I thought? It was Trina, right?'

'You'd make a brilliant detective.'

They both laughed.

'She's a lovely person,' he half-whispered, and this phrase alone was enough to suggest his interest in Trina might not be romantic. No one she had ever heard who had fires of lust licking their loins or a burning desire to hold on to someone for the rest of their lives started with this phrase. She waited for the 'but'. 'But, I've never thought of her in any way other than as a friend. I've known her a long time and if I had thought any different, I'd have acted on it by now, right?' He kicked at the wall; clearly it wasn't an easy

discussion for him. 'I mean, I'm slow to take the initiative sometimes, but not that bloody slow.'

'I guess.' She could only guess at Trina's disappointment if
he had told her something similar. 'But people change. Feelings
change.'

'I suppose so. And it's not that I'm *not* into it . . . I mean, she's
beautiful and funny and Edith loves her. It's just, you know when
you haven't considered something before and it takes a while to
tune your head in?' He turned and seemed to be taking in her face
in this dull afternoon light. She felt her skin flash hot under his
scrutiny.

'I don't want to interfere,' she began.

'I think we both know that's a lie!' he laughed.

'You're right.' She took a breath, wanting to get the words
right. 'But it'd be so nice to see everyone settled and happy.'

'Well, you can rest easy, Mads, because I am both settled and
happy and busy. I guess if and when romance comes knocking,
that'll be lovely, but I'm all good.'

'You know what I mean!' she tutted.

'I actually don't.' He turned again to face her.

'I guess Marnie's words struck a chord. She's right: this life is
short and uncertain and when you find someone who wants to
love you and who you might love in return, you need to tell them
how you feel, you need to be open to the opportunity, because
who knows when the next one might come along? I said as much
to Trina.' She hoped it was good advice.

His shoulders seemed to sink and his expression was one of
deep thought.

'You really think she feels that way? Is it obvious?'

'To me, yes.' The way Trina looked at him, spoke about him . . .
'And for what it's worth, I think you'd make a lovely couple.'

'You do?' He pulled his head back on his shoulders.

'Yes! Yes, I do!'

'But wouldn't that be weird, for you, for us, because of . . . of . . . ?' He visibly reddened.

'No! We can't let it be weird. *You* can't let it be weird!' She stared at him.

His head hung forward and he stared at the ground before righting himself and standing in front her. 'It's a lot to think about, Mads. I . . . am really fond of Trina. I guess I've never thought . . .' He pushed his hair behind his ears. 'I remember I told *you* how I felt a while ago; that I thought you were remarkable and beautiful and funny and smart, and you said—' He stopped talking and faltered, as if even to remember her words were painful.

She knew *exactly* what she had said. It was her mantra, her go-to phrase to protect her heart, set expectations, and to make her stance clear. *Nothing lasts for ever. Nothing, Jimmy.*

'I know what I said.' She spared him the chore of repetition.

He nodded and looked a little relieved.

'I felt really daft for opening up to you like that. Crushed, actually,' he admitted, in the open way that he had. 'And if I'm being honest, it's made me wary, really wary of opening up to anyone. Supposing I got closer to Trina and then she binned me. I'd lose my friend, Edith would lose her friend too, and it'd be awkward if we all went over to your mum's place, and it's already difficult enough when—' He looked up as if remembering who he was speaking to. She filled in the blanks. *When you're there . . .*

She felt the sting of his words across her cheek. Nothing less than she deserved.

'If it's any consolation, Nico, I won't ever forgive myself for making you feel that way. Won't forgive myself for a lot of things.'

'Like?'

'Like . . . I should have been kinder about the drawing you gave me.'

'Oh God, the drawing! The drawing you didn't remember.' He ran his palm over his face as if this might wipe away his unease. 'I knew the moment I handed it over it was a mistake. Your face, it was like, *what*? You retreated then and I kind of knew you'd run away, and you did. I felt like such a plum.'

She shook her head and was surprised by the sadness that rose inside her. 'I did. I did remember it,' she stuttered as tears clogged her nose and throat. 'I said I didn't because I remember how hurt you looked, your face . . . and I hate that I made you feel that way.' She wiped her eyes. 'But, actually, Jimmy, it was quite an important thing for me, that picture.'

'Important, why?'

'Because . . . because . . . two things really.' She swallowed. 'First, no one had ever done anything like that for me, that grand gesture. It's the kind of thing we all think about, isn't it? Someone doing something crazy and spontaneous and brave to make their intent clear. It's flattering – lovely! The fairytale.'

'And the second thing?' He kicked against the concrete wall.

'It was the first time I thought that there might be a different life for me.'

'A life you don't want,' he reminded her.

'I'm not sure what I want right now.' She took a moment to order her thoughts, feeling as emotionally cautious as she did vulnerable, letting down her iron guard, just for a second. 'I suppose that picture was important because it was the first time anyone had shown that level of interest in me, expressed that kind of intention, and it was a big thing.'

'I see.' He stiffened a little as if still embarrassed.

'And I guess somewhere at the back of my mind, I *liked* the idea of a future like the one you drew. But one day, one day when I'm ready, when I've done everything I need to do, everything I *want* to do,' she corrected.

'When do you think that will be, Mads? When will you be ready?' He was fishing and she knew it.

'I honestly don't know.' This was her truth.

He looked past her into the middle distance. 'Do you know you just called me Nico?'

'What? Did I?' She wrinkled her nose, unaware. 'When?'

He smiled. 'Just now, when you were talking about forgiveness, about what you want.'

'Sorry, Jimmy.' She laughed, nervously. 'I . . .'

'You might want to concentrate on matchmaking for yourself, how about that?'

'You might have a point.' She wished it were that simple, confident she'd blown it with Nico. The way they'd parted didn't suggest reunion was imminent – quite the opposite, in fact, and her spirit flagged at the thought.

'You see that's the thing – someone who might have very deep, unshakeable feelings for you could wait a lifetime, sitting in the wings while you chase the next thing and the next. They might think that's too hard. They might give up, decide it's too big an ask for such an uncertain outcome.'

'Then I guess they are not the one who I'll get to sit and watch the ducks on my pond with in old age.'

'I guess not.' He reached out and tucked the loose tendril of hair that had fallen over her eye behind her ear. 'I will always think the world of you, Madeleine Woods, will always want the best for you, because you're Edith's mum. And I truly hope that when the day comes that you do know what you want, you don't look back at your life and regret not choosing a different path.'

'Why would I?'

'Because I think there comes a time in all our lives when we re-evaluate what's important. And I would hate for you to reach that point and for it to be too late, and that the thing or things you need or *want* are no longer available to you because the world has moved on.'

He reached out again and this time wiped the tear from her cheek. She hadn't realised she was crying.

'The day . . .' she began, her words coasting out on tear-laden breaths. 'The day I left the flat, handed Edith over to my mum, was the hardest of my life. It will always be the hardest of my life.'

'You could have turned back.' He met her eyeline now.

'I could, Jimmy, trouble is . . . I honestly . . . I didn't know how to have it all, how to do it all. I still don't.'

'It's not impossible. You just need to learn how. It's about making everything fit in a way that works for you.'

'I do want to speak to Nico, but I'm scared.' She sniffed, her chest heaving with the effort to contain all that bloomed inside of her. 'I want to spend more time with Edith, but I'm scared. Truth is, I've been scared since the day I woke up with a stomach ache and found out I was pregnant. And I mess up, Jimmy, I mess up all the time. I try so hard to keep it together, but be under no illusion . . .' Her tears made speaking almost impossible. 'My heart is blistered. So badly blistered it burns every single day. And when I see her now' – she rubbed her eyes, not caring that her make-up would end up on her cheek – 'it's like my arms are tied to my body, my tongue glued to the roof of my mouth, my blood runs thick in my veins and my feet are set in concrete, and I can't run to her! I can't take her in my arms and tell her all that I want to, I can't do it! And you have no idea how much I wish I could. I really wish I could! I want her to know me, I want her to really know me. I want her to know my failings, my worries, the dilemma I face every single day as I play a part and do my best, trying to be the best I can be, to reach my goals, all with my background and what I have given up snaking around my ankles, ready to trip me up. I'm a human and I'm imperfect and that's fine. She needs to know that's fine. And I want to really know her. I think . . . I think then I'd be happy. I'd be happy then, Jimmy.'

He raised his arms and she closed her eyes, ready to fall against him, to bury her head in his chest and rest awhile; all it would take was one step towards him on this concrete walkway. One tiny step . . . and to lay her head on his chest now, she knew she would forget all about paint samples, chandeliers, scratches on her fridge, meetings at work, flights to LA, Nico, the pressure to succeed, the pressure to look good, the pressure to lead, to win, to keep striving, to keep thriving, all of it. She'd forget it all, just for a while . . . It took all of her strength not to fall into him, to cast off the reality and dive entirely into the idea, to submit to the fairytale. Trina would do it, this much she knew. Trina would throw herself at this prince and make a vow. And they would no doubt live a happy life, a small, happy life . . . but she wasn't Trina.

And as Madeleine had mentioned to Dr Schoenfeld, she was wired differently.

She tried, tried again to take that step, but it wasn't Jimmy that she wanted, not in that way. Yes, he would always have a place in her heart, in her life, but Trina *loved* him, properly loved him, and she had hurt Trina by disregarding this. What Madeleine wanted was three things: to make amends, more balance between her two worlds, and openness that just might help her achieve both.

Because her life, currently, was exactly as she had described to Jimmy – as if her feet were set in concrete and she couldn't move. And it had to change. It all had to change.

Jimmy lowered his arms.

'I want you to find your place, Mads. I want you to find some-where you are content to be, where you are free to be happy, some-where that feels like home.'

'A forever home.' She quoted the words he had written almost a decade ago.

'And I told you then and I am telling you now: it doesn't need it to last for ever, just for a lifetime.'

◆ ◆ ◆

Madeleine had a flight to catch.

The last few days had passed in a blur. Organising the handover of the Stern project, making sure everything was shipshape, had taken every waking hour. Her beautiful apartment had been partially mothballed. Tan had a set of keys and was very kindly going to pop in weekly to give it the once over and remove the junk mail from the table in the front hallway, prior to the new tenants moving in. He also confessed that while the place was empty, if Ramon was annoying him, he would hide there and nap in her bed. She didn't mind, understanding the need to escape occasionally.

Rebecca had sent her a picture of Madam Marcia in her sundress with matching parasol. Her heart sank at the sight of it. Judging from the expression on Madam Marcia's face, she was none too impressed either.

Madeleine was travelling light, preferring to take a few key summer pieces and top up her wardrobe when she arrived. It was how she liked to travel, unencumbered by too much baggage.

Ha! She smiled. The analogy wasn't lost on her. Any more baggage and she'd need to pack Orna in her hand luggage, just to help her emotionally unpack!

Marnie's surgery had gone well, and she had already been discharged from the hospital. According to her dad, whom she had chatted to last night, it was business as usual, almost. Edith had an inset day today, and Jimmy was going to stay at home to look after her. The main complaint from her mum was the fact that she was using a wheelchair to get from A to B, something that didn't exactly delight her.

It was with a slightly nervous stomach that Madeleine looked up at the impressive white stucco building with its grand Palladian-inspired porch. Her last trip to see her therapist for a while. She wasn't sure how she felt about it – nervous certainly, but also a little like she'd come to the end of a course or period of study, like she'd learned something. It felt fitting to come and bid farewell to her confidante in person, to make a plan to stay in touch, and to thank her for how much she had helped Madeleine over the last couple of years, helping her figure out the jumble of thoughts that were now not quite so jumbled.

A smart-suited and -booted man was leaving as she was about to ring the buzzer – he held the door open for her and she thanked him as she walked inside. Again she trod the stairs, eschewing the lift and feeling a little wistful at the prospect of not seeing Orna every week. They had after all become firm friends and had shared so much. The consulting room door was closed. She took a deep breath, found her neutral face, and knocked.

After a brief pause, Orna opened the door.

Madeleine beamed at her, wondering how their last session would go.

'Hello! I wasn't expecting to see you.' Her therapist was obviously surprised; she looked over her shoulder and gestured behind the half-closed door, no doubt to a patient sitting on that leather sofa. Madeleine felt instantly awkward and confused; it was as if she had dropped in on the fly, which was absolutely not the done thing.

'I have a session booked!' Madeleine pulled a tortured expression, mortified by the mix-up.

'No! No, you don't, my love.' The woman pushed her glasses up on her nose, still holding the door closed, as if guarding something dangerous or forbidden. 'I have you booked in for tomorrow. I'm actually with someone right now.' She gestured with her eyes.

'And I know how much *you* appreciate an uninterrupted session.' Orna smiled, sweetly, awkwardly, as she made the point.

'The thing is I'm leaving today, after this, heading to the airport in a bit. I won't be here tomorrow!' Her embarrassment was acute.

'There's obviously been a mix-up.' Orna swallowed. 'I'm so sorry. Let me call you later.' Unbelievably, the woman went to close the door and, for some reason she couldn't explain, Madeleine put her foot in the gap. She didn't want to be dismissed like this, not for possibly the last time she might see her. It wasn't good enough.

It was strange how in that moment she understood that while it was always just her and Orna, talking freely, she was but one of a long list of patients who sank down on to that sofa and that her safe place was not hers alone. She felt her cheeks flame with embarrassment, recognising the misplaced and frankly naive sense of disloyalty and rejection that being kept outside of the room filled her with.

'No, sorry, I just—' What did she want to say? 'As I said, I'm off to LA in a few hours.'

'Yes. I understand.' Orna smiled, her movements hesitant, as she stared at Madeleine's foot in the door, her words stilted as if trying to speed things along.

'And I understand you're busy. I'll head off now, but before I go, I just want to ask you something.'

'Right.' She watched Orna look upwards and blink quickly. 'I would say email me all of this and, erm, we'll go from there.'

Madeleine nodded. 'No, I'd rather not email you, I just wanted to ask you one thing – if you could just answer this *one* question.' It felt important. It *was* important.

'Fire away!' Orna's brief smile spoke of her irritation, as she folded her arms across her chest and gave only the slightest sigh of impatience. Madeleine removed her foot from the door.

'Do you think it's possible to change your mind on something fundamental? Is it possible to want one thing aged twenty but then, as you nearly hit thirty, to look back and realise that you might have made a mistake?'

'Sure. Of course!' Orna stepped forward and held the door almost closed behind her, her voice low to maintain their established confidentiality. 'I will say this: I think you need to give yourself permission to freely give love and demonstrate love to Edith – in fact, to anyone you want to. And that doesn't necessarily mean being her full-time mother or comparing how you wish to parent with how Jimmy or Marnie do it. It's between you and Edith. I also think part of that permission is bound in a decision to stop punishing yourself.'

'I . . .' She was a little lost for words.

'We change, Madeleine, year on year, decade on decade – that's the wonderful thing about life! We are never stone. We move, we change, we grow, and if we are very, very lucky, we educate ourselves and grow in confidence, which allows us to make different decisions. That is being human!'

'Someone once told me to remember that no story is about how it starts, but always about how it finishes.'

'That sounds like good advice. Goodbye, Madeleine.'

'Bye, Orna.'

'I'll see you when you get back?'

Madeleine turned to walk down the dull staircase in the depressing hallway. 'Erm, probably not.' She smiled, hearing Edith's words in her head. 'I might just talk to my friends.'

An image of Trina filled her head, running into the café and slipping into the booth next to her.

Why are you romanticising the shiteness of it all?
And why are you shitting on the niceness of it all?

How she wished she could see her once more before she left, just the two of them. It felt like they'd made progress in Marnie's kitchen. It occurred to her then, why wait for Trina to make the move? Why not pull down her defences and reach out to the woman who was once her sister . . .

Her therapist's words resonated. It hadn't occurred to her that her inability to love and to be loved was bound in a deep-seated idea that she didn't deserve it. This was, she knew, just one strand to the complex fabric that she had woven and behind which she hid. There was one thought however, one phrase that rang out louder than all others, and it came not from Orna, but from Marnie: the simple fact that life was short.

Too short for her not to become more involved with her wonderful child and too short not to make amends with Trina. They certainly had a lot to talk about. Some topics more pressing than others. Jimmy, she decided, for too long had sat between them like a thorn. He couldn't be the reason for them not to pick up where they had left off when she got back to the UK.

She wanted more than ever to leave with a feeling of resolution, and that she had something to look forward to when she eventually came home – a network, a *family.*

Marnie was right; how *did* Edith fit into a move to the other side of the bloody world? How was she supposed to navigate that? How was Madeleine? And the answer to the most fundamental question of all came to her now.

'Yes, Mum. I will miss you. I will miss you all!' She gulped down the emotion that filled her throat as she spoke the realisation out loud. 'I will miss you all so much!'

She felt the swell of hope that she and Trina might be able to pick up where they had left off: drinking tea, scoffing biscuits, walking arm in arm in the park, shopping on a Saturday and eating fried egg sandwiches in Marnie's kitchen on a Sunday morning, because life was not black and white. It was not all or nothing. Her worlds could collide! She felt sure of it and was in fact buoyed up by the thought! Marnie had done all she could to ensure that her daughter still had a chance.

'I still have a chance,' she whispered. 'I still have a chance!' She stood in the middle of the pavement, not caring that the crowds had to navigate around her as her thoughts came thick and fast.

She reached for her phone and waited for her call to be answered, *praying* her call would be answered.

'Trina!'

'Mads! I thought you'd be up and away by now, eating a mini bag of stinky pretzels and knocking back a plastic tumbler of warm white wine.'

'I was, I will be – I mean, I should be. I've got plenty of time to make my flight,' Madeleine explained as she gripped her little bag behind her, dragging it over the pavement. 'I was going to head to the airport and work – it's as good a place to work as any – but . . .' *What did she want to say?*

There was a beat of silence. 'Is everything okay?' Trina clearly wondered at the reason for the unexpected call.

Madeleine looked up and down the busy street and knew it was a conversation she would prefer to have face to face. It was almost as if, without the pressure of work, preparing to move, and her travel plans whizzing around her head, she was able to breathe deeply for the first time in an age. Consequently breathing deeply allowed clarity of thought.

'Are you around? Have you got a minute?'

'Erm, yes, and yes. I'm on the high street, actually.'

'Shall I come and find you? We could go to The Copper Kettle?'

She heard her friend's soft laughter, probably, like her, thinking of the hours they used to waste, sitting in a booth, trying to make a cup of tea last, or maybe she too recalled the last time they had gone there, when their friendship had collapsed, and the words they exchanged on that day which still stung like a slap across her face.

'I guess so.'

'I'll see you there, just jumping in a cab!' Letting go of her suitcase, she raised her hand to hail a taxi as she spoke.

'Okay, see you there.'

As the taxi pulled up, Madeleine jumped in and placed her cabin bag on the seat next to her. Sitting back, she watched the city pass by through the window, knowing she would miss it and all the people in it she loved, until she came home.

Home...

Her phone beeped with a text from Tan. She wondered what the first emergency was. It didn't bode well that she hadn't yet left London. But it wasn't an emergency, more of an information update.

OH MY GOD! YOUR MENEGHINI LA CAMBUSA IS SCRATCHED! DO YOU KNOW ABOUT THIS?!?

Her reply was immediate.

I DO. RELAX, TAN, IT'S ONLY A FRIDGE!

His reply was equally instant.

WHERE IS MADELEINE AND WHAT HAVE YOU DONE WITH HER?

She laughed. He was right, actually, she could feel the subtle changes in her make-up. Her questions were however a little different: who is Madeleine and what does she need to do to be truly happy?

Madeleine paid the cabbie and looked through the window of The Copper Kettle. There was Trina, in the booth at the front, stirring her tea before taking a bite of a fat croissant. She observed her fondly, this woman sitting in the exact same spot where they had idled in their teens when funds allowed. People rushed by, some loaded up with evidence of shopping, others holding hands with loved ones, a few grappling with prams or pushchairs. All busy with the chores of life, the travelling to and fro, the mechanics of existence that kept all the wheels turning. Madeleine remembered what it had felt like to go about life, knowing that if she came unstuck, had something to say, or before the first flicker of loneliness could spark, Trina was there to pick her up, to hear her words and to cocoon her in a friendship that made everything feel possible. Just the sight of her right now, her best friend throughout her childhood and the only person she had wanted to reach out to when the chips were down, it was no surprise to feel the threat of tears.

She felt the bloom in her chest of something quite painful, as if the loss and desperation of their estrangement came to rest by her heart, risen to the top like a bubble. No longer was she able to keep it buried, and it hurt.

Trina looked up and smiled as Madeleine slipped into the booth.

'Look at you, slumming it back over in East London!'

She nodded and bit her bottom lip that was trembling. It was as if she'd been holding it together but the sight of her friend meant she could let it all out.

'Has something happened?' Trina lowered her head and looked into her face. 'Is it Marnie?'

'No. No, she's fine – well, as fine as can be expected. Think she's giving Dad a hard time.'

'Has your flight been cancelled? Don't tell me they've bumped you to coach?'

Shaking her head, Madeleine allowed herself a small smile.

'How many more guesses have I got?'

'That's the thing, that's kind of what I want to talk to you about. No more guessing, Trina. No more walking on eggshells around each other. I've had enough of it and the truth is, I miss you. I've always missed you.'

Trina took a deep breath. 'Sames.' The word that peppered their childhood language. They had agreed on most things; it was always sames.

Madeleine watched the tension fall from her friend's shoulders and saw the softening in her posture.

'I . . . I should've run after you on that day, Trina. When you got up and walked out, I should have run after you.' After all the years of silence, it was surprisingly easy to begin.

'I should never have walked out in the first place and left you on your own. I should have stayed here,' Trina cut in, 'or I should have turned around at the end of the road, and marched back in.'

'I should have said sorry and explained everything. I know it would have been difficult, we'd have probably rowed—'

'We'd have probably got over it,' Trina summarised.

'We probably would,' she agreed. 'Trouble is, I didn't know how to go back. Didn't know how to recover what we'd lost, Trin – didn't know how to go back to being us.'

'And I couldn't back down. It was self-preservation, like if you've ever been bitten, the next time you see the thing that bit you, you hide your hands and back out of the room – it was like that. Every time I saw you, it was like that. I dreaded seeing you and yet I'd cry for how much I missed you.' Her friend summed up her feelings in the clearest and most heartbreaking way.

'Sames,' Madeleine admitted. 'When you told me how much I'd hurt you, that Jimmy was the one thing you really wanted . . .'

'He was. He is.'

'I didn't know.' She spoke slowly, shaking her head and able, almost, to see the droplets of shame fall from her hair, hoping beyond hope that the sincerity of her words might sink in. 'I mean, I knew you'd mentioned you'd liked him, but you also said you'd marry Harry Styles . . .'

'Still would, actually.' Trina glanced at her with a hint of a smile about her mouth.

'I thought it was no big thing. That's the truth. And when I met him after not seeing him for a few years, we were both drunk and it should have been nothing more than a meaningless footnote to my twenties, something you and I might have squabbled over, but no big deal. Still thoughtless, yes, and short-sighted and hurtful and selfish of me, all of that.'

'I'm not disagreeing.' Trina pulled a face.

'And then Edith happened, and here we are. But I *promise* you, I never intentionally set out to hurt you or gave so little of a shit that I did it anyway, it wasn't like that.'

'I know, I know. Not that it made it hurt any less, but I do know.' Trina nodded. 'I remember when I met you in here on the day you found out you were pregnant, and you said you'd done a test and it was the worst minute of your life, that your whole world had imploded.'

'I don't remember what I said.'

'You said that, or something very similar, and it stuck with me and I think about it often.'

'You do?' She twisted on the seat to look at her.

'I remember thinking that you and I couldn't be any more different, and that was before I knew about Jimmy.'

'In what way were we so different?' She was curious.

'I had always thought, and I still think, that to have a baby with someone I love would be the greatest thing. To hold that stick and wait for the result, knowing it's the thing I want more than anything else.' She coughed to clear her embarrassment. 'I mean, what a moment that would be! And to hear that for you it was the worst thing.' She paused. 'I think mentally I pulled away from you even more in that moment before you gave me the punchline. Not because I was judging you but because I realised we were very different people.'

'I guess that's the thing, though, Trina, it wasn't happening with someone I loved. It wasn't even with someone I knew particularly well – it was Jimmy from school!'

'Although you lucked out, because he's great.'

'He is,' she acknowledged, noting how her friend wanted to shout his corner. 'He really is great. And I think we can be different people *and* want different things *and* still be best friends. I know we can. You were right about me never being satisfied, always looking around the next corner, never standing still, not for a single second, never stopping to enjoy the view.' She paused and looked out over the pavement, where the hustle and bustle of life continued on the other side of the window and the Brenton Park estate rose high behind them. 'That's what it's been like for me; always with my mind on what comes next, meaning I'd never arrive! I'd never be happy! I thought that was how I had to live to be successful.'

'And I told you that the small existence that you scorned was exactly what I aspired to. A life *I'd* like – a life *I'd* still love!'

'I now know it's not a small life, Trina. It was just a life I didn't understand.'

'But you do now?' It was a question that was so much bigger than the words; it was asking for a promise, a way forward.

'I think I do. Even though it might not be the life for me.' She moved closer to her friend. 'We only have this one life, Trina, this one life! I'm not going to waste a second of it.'

'Me either,' Trina whispered.

'So what do we do about Jimmy? How do we all get on? How do we pull together and make it the best it can be for Edith, for us all, without you feeling hurt or me feeling so guilty? Without it feeling easier not to show up?'

'It's simple really, Mads.' Trina drew breath. 'We forgive each other. We understand that none of us are perfect, we accept that we're family. Family who stick together through thick and thin. You, me, Marnie, Doug, Jimmy, Edith and whatever babies or part-ners or lovers get thrown into the mix as we go along.'

Madeleine pictured Nico – Nico the spectacular – and wished it had worked out differently.

'Some of us share blood,' Trina continued, 'some of us share history, but if we all share love, then we'll get through. That's enough.'

'Listen to you! That was beautiful.' She meant it.

'Mother Teresa beautiful?'

'Not quite.'

They both laughed, and a lot of the tension fled, spiralling out of the door of The Copper Kettle and up into the sky.

'Can I ask you something?' Trina sidled closer to her on the bench and Madeleine nodded, ready to answer anything. This, she believed, was how they built the bridge that would carry them into the future.

'Of course.' She braced herself.

'Them fancy heels you wore to the hospital when you visited Marn, can I borrow them?'

'You can have them, you silly cow. They kill my feet.'

'It's happened, hasn't it, Mads?' Trina asked with tears in her eyes.

'What?'

'You've come back, you've come home.' Trina took her hand, and that was how they sat for a minute or two, letting the sweet relief of reunion wash over them. 'Just like I knew you would, you've come home.'

'I think I have. And knowing that you are here for me when I get back from LA' – she squeezed her friend's fingers – 'it makes all the difference. I've got so many exciting plans! I want to share it all with you. For starters, I'm going to start my own business!'

'Well, that was never in doubt. I could make the tea!' Trina laughed.

'Or do the books?' She liked the idea very much, seeing her mate every day, keeping her close.

'I bloody love you.'

'I bloody love you.' It was the truth. 'I've already said goodbye, but I was thinking of swooping by Jimmy's and having one last hug with Edith. Plus, I need to talk to Jimmy. Do you want to come too?' Madeleine nudged her with her elbow.

'Sure.' She beamed. 'But I'd like to go home and grab some bits first. You want to come with me, or shall I see you there?'

'I'll come with you.'

'Are we paying for this' – Trina pushed the crumb-laden plate across the table – 'or are we going to do a runner?'

'One time!' She threw her head back and laughed. 'Are you ever going to let me forget it?'

'Highly unlikely.' Trina pulled out her credit card and went to settle up.

The two women walked arm in arm along the towpath. Madeleine dragged her bag behind her and Trina gripped her board game and gift of chocolate, picked up from the kitchen counter in her flat. It seemed her friend had taken her advice after all. *I believe if you want something or someone, then you have to make it happen . . . You*

should turn up at his house with an armful of board games, a box of
chocolates, a bottle of something fizzy . . . Perfect for a grey inset day,
and very appropriate when your hosts were as diverse in age as
Edith and Jimmy.

As they approached the cottage, Madeleine stopped on the towpath and closed her eyes briefly, trying to quell the feeling of urgency,
and a quickening in her pulse. Keen, if not desperate, to run up that
towpath, kick off her heels, and sink down on to that glorious sofa in
front of the log burner – not that there was time for that today. But
the thought that Edith was in that very cottage, probably dancing
or twirling, but certainly chattering to her dad, to Jimmy, the man
who had shown her a glimpse of a different life – a *happy* life! A life
that she wanted for him and Trina, and a life in which she hoped she
might play a part. Because one thing she had learned was that things
didn't have to be perfect or everlasting, they only had to be enough.

Her face broke into a smile and in her gut was a feeling a lot
like relief. Her shoulders sank and her muscles uncoiled, as if her
body called for rest.

Because Madeleine was tired. Bone tired. Tired of trying so
hard and working such long hours and exhausted by her constant
quest for perfection.

'You all right, Mads?'

She nodded. 'Bit nervous about seeing Jimmy. Not sure how to
say all I want to say, to tell him I want to see more of Edith when
I'm home, but I don't want him to worry I'm going to be muscling
in, trying to take over or anything.' She breathed out.

'Maybe don't overthink it.' Trina placed her hand on
Madeleine's arm, steadying her, reassuring her in the way she always
used to. 'Maybe just say what's in your head and let the conversation happen.'

'Yes, okay.' It was good advice.

'I'll go in and leave you two to chat. I'll try to distract the human cannonball.'

'I like it – tag team.' She smiled.

'And you think you're nervous?' Trina shivered. 'I'm hoping the guy falls hook, line, and sinker for me and I've not got my lippy on.'

'You look nice.'

'Nice?' Trina wrinkled her nose in disapproval. 'Is that the best you've got?'

'Spectacular.' She swallowed the sense of loss that rose in her throat when she thought of Nico. 'You look spectacular!'

'That's more like it.'

Staring at the green front door of the cottage, the brass acorn knocker and the letterbox cover, she felt a surge of delight at the prospect of walking through it, a beautiful oasis where she would get to enjoy time with her daughter when she came back to visit and then more often when this little island was once again her home, and just like that she knew what she wanted to say . . . *Watching Edith sleep in her fairytale room was a reminder of all that is good, a life that is enough for most people, and I want to be most people, Jimmy. I want a life that is enough. I need balance and not to be afraid of figuring things out as I go along . . . Nico would have been enough . . .* This final thought she would keep to herself.

Her decision was to go to LA for a year or so, no more, to learn everything she could from Rebecca, to squeeze every last drop of juice from the opportunity. Madeleine would also tell her of her plans to set up her own business, right here in the UK. She would seek advice from the woman who had been her mentor, who had given her a chance, her first job, and a taste of a different life. Rebecca, the woman she would forever feel indebted to; she was looking forward to face-to-face discussions over a glass of sparkling water and a decent lunch. Salade Niçoise, probably.

This new chapter in her life was about learning all she needed to be the best she could for Edith, the best daughter to Marnie and Doug and the best friend to Trina. It was about unlearning all she had worked so hard to perfect over the last few years. But primarily, it was about finding balance – it was about finding happiness!

Trina knocked on the door, standing confidently in her jeans, wellington boots and jumper, and they waited.

'Do you remember that enormous penis?' Trina whispered, nodding towards the front of the cottage.

'His name was Quentin and he was a dentist.'

They leaned into each other, laughing, just like that, just like they used to. It made her happy, so happy. *So happy.*

Jimmy opened the door and ran his hand up through his hair, a habit that had taken her, and she suspected always would, right back to him in the playground, where he did just that, part of their history.

He beamed at his guests. 'Hey, you two! Madeleine, well, this is a surprise! I thought you were . . .' He pointed towards the sky.

'I was, I am. I'll still make my flight. But I just wanted to talk to you before I went, and to give Edith one last hug.'

'Sure!' He nodded, his expression as open as ever.

Trina handed Jimmy the board game and pulled off her wellington boots before upending them on to the metal wellie rack, where they sat next to the pink ones with little unicorns on them. As if this was where they were meant to be.

Madeleine could see it then: a future where Trina came home from the bank and prepared supper or collected Edith from school, or walked up the aisle with Jimmy or had another baby, a sibling for Edith to adore, and Trina would invite Marnie over for a cup of tea and they'd talk about the weather. Trina, who would live here, make a home, and climb into bed every night to snuggle close to the person she loved and who would love her back. Trina, who would feel content, eat nice food, knowing she got to spend every average day wrapped in love.

And she wanted it for her friend, her sister. She wanted it all for the people she loved.

'I just wanted to let you know that I won't stay in LA indefinitely. I'm thinking no more than a year, and then I'm coming home. And when I come home' – she swallowed – 'I want to see more of Edith. I want to know more about her, and I guess I want her to know more about me. I know you've got things perfectly under control, and Edith is thriving! But I want to be part of it. I want more of Edith.'

'I think that sounds like a plan, and for what it's worth, I'm proud of you.' He spoke softly. 'And I know someone who will be pleased to see you.'

As if on cue, Edith bounded along the hallway and just the sight of her, hair falling over her little smiling face, her bare feet dancing on the wood, it was almost more than she could stand. The thought of how much she had missed, determined to make the most of this chance she had been given.

'Mummy!' Edith, who without explanation was in full pirate costume, complete with beard and eyepatch, jumped into her arms, and Madeleine held her close, inhaling the scent of her little girl. 'Are you going to take me to the Tower of London and Legoland?'

'Yes.' She spoke with certainty. 'When I'm back to visit at Christmas, we'll take those trips. We'll take lots of trips, if that's okay with Dad?'

'Course it is!' He smiled at her.

Edith wriggled to be free and disappeared inside the house.

'I'm not staying, Jimmy; I have to get to the airport.'

'Come on, Trina! I'm waiting for you to play the game! I haven't got all day!' Edith shouted impatiently from inside.

'I've been summoned! I'd better go.' Trina pointed inside.

'You better had.' She nodded.

'I never stopped loving you, Mads.' Trina squeezed her fingers. 'See you soon, yeah.'

'Yep, see you soon. I'll come and visit at Christmas.'

'Bring me a Barbie!' Edith yelled from the table. 'But if you can't afford it, don't worry about it!'

She held a long, lingering look with Jimmy, who smiled at her in the way that he did. 'I'll be okay, Maddie. You know that, don't you? It'll all work out how it's meant to.'

'Yes. I think I do.'

The chair in her first-class cabin was wide, comfortable and she looked forward to sleeping in it. There were far worse ways to travel. Her seat was deep inside a small walled pod, which provided both privacy and luxury. Madeleine leaned back and closed her eyes, smiling at the thought of Trina and Jimmy playing their board game with the littlest pirate. Trina, who would get to live her own fairytale.

'Sorry to disturb you, madam.'

'That's fine.' She smiled at the air steward.

'You looked so peaceful – it's just that I'm doing the rounds. Do you have everything you need?'

'I think so, yes.'

'The flight time today is eleven and a half hours, so we are on schedule to land at seven thirty local time.'

'Smashing.'

'And could I ask what your preference would be for lunch?'

The woman gave her a small, stiff card that was printed in an ornate gold script.

She smiled wryly and handed it back. 'The gnocchi for me, please.'

The plane now ascended into the sky and she looked down at the sprawl of the capital city she had always called home. The place to which she would return. Her thoughts went to Nico, spectacular Nico, who had failed to send her another thumbs-up, failed to make contact at all. It was probably for the best – better it fail now in the early stages than falling for the man even more deeply and having her heart properly smashed further down the line. She wondered whether, if she thought this often enough, it might make it easier to believe.

What she truly wanted was the chance to explain to him, to tell him truthfully about her journey, about the one choice she had made that seemed to filter into her whole life. Something that had driven her in her chosen career because she hadn't believed that she could have it all. And while other women spoke with pride about their little ones, she would have her achievements on her CV, an immaculate home, and a bank balance to reflect it, because work for her was easy, being a mother was not, and it was just how she was – this was what she had believed. This she knew was a mantra she had hidden behind, a shield of her own making, because trying to have it all had felt impossible. Until now . . .

Something Trina had said a long time ago came to her now.

I just want someone who is going to show up, someone who instinctively knows what I want and when I need it, and who just shows up!

Trying to dampen the feeling of loneliness that wrapped itself around her, she more than understood. It sounded perfect.

It was as she placed her phone face down on the tray table to her right that it beeped and a message came in.

A video no less, from . . . She squinted to read . . . Jimmy!

The moment she pressed 'Play', her heart soared. It was actually a message from Edith.

She was still wearing her pirate hat, which now sat askew on the top of her head, and there was chocolate around her mouth.

'Mummy! I know you're on your way to Lanzarote, but I wanted to tell you that the Barbie I want is vet Barbie, because I think I'm going to be a vet and look after animals. Oh, and I found Minty! We went for a walk over the school field yesterday, and I dug her up and got my sock back! But don't tell Nanny as she said dead mice are germy.'

Madeleine couldn't help the laughter that burst from her. This kid! This wonderful kid!

'Don't forget about our trips. I told Dad we can do a sleepover at your house and I can bring sweets and things for us to eat. Or we could have a picnic! Nanny takes me on picnics – we sit on the bench and have macaroni cheeeeeeeese!' She exaggerated the word, her funny, funny little thing. Edith's face was suddenly close to the camera so all Madeleine could see was the child's nostrils, as she whispered, 'And I'll remind you to get some sliced chicken! I love you and . . . Trina is rubbish at Hungry Hippos.' Edith paused and pulled the camera away, giving her the perfect view of this little girl's beautiful, beautiful face, the grey-blue eyes of her mother, grandmother and great-grandmother staring back at her. Eyes that would see the whole wide world. If they wanted to. 'And . . . that's it!'

The camera was suddenly and unceremoniously dropped, leaving Madeleine with a view of the ceiling in Jimmy's kitchen.

'Jimmy! I think your iPad might have had a bashing!' Trina's voice could be heard in the background just before the recording ended. There had been something in her tone that spoke of contentment, of happiness, as if she had found her place. Somewhere she was content to be, free to be happy, somewhere that felt like home.

Just as it should be . . . Her best friend, making the most of this one life.

'She sounds like a handful, and I mean that in the nicest way. I have two like that at home!' The steward smiled as she gathered empty glasses.

'She is a handful, but so smart, and funny! *So* funny!'

Madeleine spoke confidently, knowing she was this little girl's champion, her flag bearer, part of her support system and the one who would love her till her last breath on earth.

She shook her head, swiping at the tears that coursed down her face.

'My daughter, my daughter, Edith-Madeleine. My pocketful of sunshine.'

Epilogue

'You visiting here?' The young woman with the long white-blonde hair and deep tan behind the counter of the art supply store smiled widely.

'Yes.' He nodded and reached for his wallet.

'This your first time in LA?'

'No, no, not my first, it's a great place. Great weather!' He rolled up the sleeves on his white linen shirt.

'You find everything you need today?'

She asked a lot of questions. Or maybe it only seemed like a lot because he was in a hurry.

'Yes, yes, thank you. I did.'

'You making something?' She ran her fingers over the large white sheet of card and the black marker pens.

'I am, actually.'

'What are you making?' She popped a huge bubblegum bubble against her lower lip that made him wince.

He felt the spread of his blush and rubbed his face. 'I'm making a placard. A sign.'

'What kind of sign?'

She was incessant!

'A . . .' He couldn't think how best to describe it. 'A sign to hold up – a welcome sign, or more of a hello sign. I'm not sure.'

'Where are you going to hold it up?'

'At the airport. In the arrivals at the airport. For someone who is landing at' – he looked at his watch – 'seven thirty this evening.'

He then realised it wasn't that the woman asked a lot of questions, but rather she *only* asked questions.

'Aaaw, you going to meet someone?'

'I am, yes. Except she's not expecting me. It's a surprise. A big gesture and a big risk.' He sucked air through his teeth, his nerves spilling from him.

'She's not expecting you?'

The way she asked this question made *him* question his plan. It seemed so simple in his head. He'd write the sign, turn up, hold the sign, she'd cry and they'd go and get sushi. Simple.

'You think I *should* tell her I'm going to be there?'

'Is she the kind of person who likes surprises?'

There it was, another question. She even answered a question with a question!

'I don't know. I think she might like this one.' He smiled. 'And do you know that you've asked me a lot of questions?'

'Have I?'

She was – he found it hard to decide which – either an idiot or a genius.

He laughed.

'How would you like to pay?' She smiled sweetly.

'What are my options?' He folded his arms. Two could play at this game.

'Cash or card?'

'Card.' He handed his over; she was clearly much better at this than he.

'What are you going to write on your placard?'

'A huge thumbs-up. That's it. Just a huge thumbs-up.'

'Will she know what it means?' She handed him the slip of paper, transaction complete.

'I hope so.' He gathered his card and pens.

'What does it mean?' She folded her arms, her voice a little quieter now, curious.

He took a deep breath. 'It means that from the first time I saw her across the boardroom in the meeting at Field and Grey, she has lived in my thoughts. It means that when I had lunch with her and she sat opposite me and wolfed down her food and made me laugh, I felt myself falling for her. It means that no matter what her past holds, or how many times she thinks she has messed up, or what she may or not be capable of, I am far more interested in the future. In our future. It means that if she has one child or ten, we will find a way to make it work. It means I have never felt this way about anyone, ever, and I want to progress to a second date and take her to an island where even if you took me there blindfolded, I'd know it by the scent alone.' He closed his eyes and took a deep breath. 'The pine forests, the rosemary and thyme that's abundant, ripe mandarins, the woody-scented bark of the olive trees, eucalyptus leaves and all underpinned with the fragrant incense and oils from the church, that is like nothing else. I want to take her there and hold her tight. It means I think we have a shot. That's what it means.'

He looked at the woman who stared at him with misty eyes, clearly moved by his declaration. He could only hope that Madeleine might be similarly affected. He had also won. She had no final question and this made him smile as he grabbed his wares and prepared to head off to the airport to meet Madeleine's flight.

'You're a nice man. A really nice man. Can you close the door behind you?'

Nico turned and laughed loudly.

'Yep.'

ABOUT THE AUTHOR

Photo © 2023 Paul Smith @paulsmithpics

Amanda Prowse is a multi-million bestselling author who has published more than 30 novels and is one of the most prolific writers of contemporary fiction in the UK today.

Crowned 'the queen of family drama' by the *Daily Mail*, she writes about life's challenges – from heartbreak and loss to dysfunctional family dynamics – but also about the pockets of delight that can be found in our relationships with others, often when we need them most.

Amanda is known for her relatable characters, emotionally compelling plots, and the sense of connection that readers feel with her stories.

She is an ambassador for The Reading Agency and feels passionately about supporting other women, spending as much time as possible outdoors (preferably by the sea!) and her family.

Follow the Author on Amazon

If you enjoyed this book, follow Amanda Prowse on Amazon to be notified when the author releases a new book!

To do this, please follow these instructions:

Desktop:

1) Search for the author's name on Amazon or in the Amazon App.
2) Click on the author's name to arrive on their Amazon page.
3) Click the 'Follow' button.

Mobile and Tablet:

1) Search for the author's name on Amazon or in the Amazon App.
2) Click on one of the author's books.
3) Click on the author's name to arrive on their Amazon page.
4) Click the 'Follow' button.

Kindle eReader and Kindle App:

If you enjoyed this book on a Kindle eReader or in the Kindle App, you will find the author 'Follow' button after the last page.